The Crimson Lady

"Why do you think it is right to feel no desire, to have no need for me, and yet be willing—nay, seem eager even—to bed with me? Tell me why, Fiona."

"Nay," she gasped, her heart wrenching and her body feeling as jumpy and exposed as if she'd been strung up and left to twist naked in the wind. "I cannot—" She jerked backward again, trying to free herself away from him, but he wouldn't let go.

"Oh, God, Braedan, stop it. It just cannot be otherwise! I cannot feel want, or desire, or need. Not in that way. I feel nothing when you touch me, Braedan," she burst out in a choking cry, his silence more painful in its tenderness than a thousand biting arguments might have been. "*Nothing*. Do you understand? With you or with any man."

He remained quiet in response to her impassioned outburst, his expression somber, his eyes so gentle on her.

"Ah, lady, it is a shame," he murmured, stroking her cheek, her hair, even as he held her in a comforting embrace against him. "A sad and wasteful shame th

Other AVON ROMANCES

MARY REED McCALL

THE CRIMSON LADY

AVON BOOKS

An Imprint of HarperCollinsPublishers

This is a work of fiction. Names, characters, places, and incidents are products of the author's imagination or are used fictitiously and are not to be construed as real. Any resemblance to actual events, locales, organizations, or persons, living or dead, is entirely coincidental.

AVON BOOKS
An Imprint of HarperCollinsPublishers
10 East 53rd Street
New York, New York 10022-5299

Copyright © 2003 by Mary Reed McCall
ISBN: 0-06-009770-1
www.avonromance.com

First Avon Books paperback printing: June 2003

Avon Trademark Reg. U.S. Pat. Off. and in Other Countries, Marca Registrada, Hecho en U.S.A.
HarperCollins® is a registered trademark of HarperCollins Publishers Inc.

Printed in the U.S.A.

10 9 8 7 6 5 4 3 2 1

*For all of the teachers who nurture
and encourage creativity in their students,
especially those who inspired me
during my own years in school
from kindergarten through college,
including Mrs. Swiss, Mrs. Himes,
Mr. Foster, Mr. Seckner,
Mrs. Armstrong, Mr. Rich,
Professor Gavin, and Professor London.
From the bottom of my heart,
I thank you.*

Acknowledgments

My sincere gratitude to:

Gayle Callen, for sitting in a hotel room with me in New Orleans and brainstorming until we found the perfect moniker for my heroine . . .

David and Marion Reed, for their page-by-page critiquing and for coming up with just the right suggestions when I needed them . . .

Annelise Robey and Meg Ruley, for unfailing professional support and for sharing their immense talents with me . . .

And Lyssa Keusch, for, as always, working her special kind of magic on the raw material I give her and doing it with a smile, no matter how busy she is . . .

Thank you all.

Prologue

Chepston Hall, London
December 1281

It was the first time in two bitter months of damp, drizzle, and rain that Fiona could remember feeling warm. Or full with food and drink. Or clean from the unheard-of luxury of a bath. Soft garments caressed her skin, and her hair hung unbound in waves to her hips, already dry after having been washed and brushed out until it shone.

But despite all that, she knew deep in her bones that something was wrong here. Very wrong . . .

She was supposed to begin work this day as a scullery maid, Mama had told her. It was good, honest, labor, a position that would take her away from the hunger and cold of the streets—from the difficult life Mama herself endured as a common woman of the *stewes*, available to

1

any man who paid for the night with her. It would lead her to something better. A fresh beginning, Mama said. The answer to their prayers . . .

Fiona suppressed a shiver, clenching her fingers into the folds of the unfamiliar, silky fabric that clung to her body and slid across her thighs. It was light as gossamer, this gown she'd been given. A magical creation, worth a fortune, surely—more than Mama could make in a thousand nights of her demeaning work. So fine and delicate.

Not the dress of a scullery maid.

"Come, girl," the older woman next to her said gruffly, taking her by the elbow and leading her the remaining length of the hall, toward the carved, wooden door that loomed ahead.

They'd reached the top floor of this imposing keep, the main building of a rich, walled-in estate that stood a goodly way upriver across from the *stewes*. A man had slipped some silver coins—advance salary he'd said—into Mama's palm. Then, as she'd stood with Fiona, teary-eyed, outside the alehouse, he had hurried Fiona into a carriage and brought her the distance. But rather than leading her through the kitchen, as she'd expected, she'd been taken into the main hall, then off to a little room where the heated tub was waiting; she'd been bathed in scented water, dried, pampered, and fed all she could eat before being dressed in this crimson gown, chosen for her by the master himself, she'd been told.

It was a mistake, she was sure. A terrible, awful mistake. She'd tried to voice her protest. Hungry as she was, she'd tried to deny the food they'd put before her, fearful that she'd be made to pay for it all, once they discovered their error in treating her so well. But her worries had been ignored. And so she resolved to try again to make this stern, silent woman who was leading her along this darkened corridor listen to her, before the panic and disbelief that had risen higher in her throat with every step suffocated her altogether.

"Please, mistress, 'tis wrong, me bein' here," she whispered, more frightened than she'd ever been in all of her fifteen years. "Me mam told me—I'm to be washin' pots and scrubbin' vegetables. I don't belong abovestairs . . ."

"Hush, child," the older woman said, not unkindly. "I know well enough why you're here—and you will, too, before long, I daresay." They'd reached the massive, carved door. The woman drew up next to it, her lips pursed and her back as straight and unyielding as the wooden slab before her. Another shiver raced up Fiona's back, though this time not from cold or the sweep of silken fabric against her skin. She swallowed and twisted her fingers tighter into her gown, her gaze straining to read the meaning behind the woman's resolute expression.

"What is behind that door?" Fiona forced herself to utter, though the question seemed wispy and almost soundless, lodged as it was in the tightness of her throat.

"You're to meet with the master." The woman reached out and scratched the wood, and a muffled voice gave an answer of admittance. Reaching down to the drawstring hanging from the tiny hole, she lifted it and pushed the door so that it slowly creaked open, revealing the entrance to an enormous chamber.

Fiona hesitated. Every instinct in her screamed to turn away, to flee and never look back. Through the portal, she saw a fire burning in a grate that encompassed half of one wall; the flames writhed and twisted, reaching up, ever up, and Fiona knew suddenly that whatever was inside that chamber was as menacing as the fire-shadows playing upon the massive bed that filled the far corner. She could just glimpse a man standing there, tall and well built, dressed in a dark, hooded cape that hid his face from her view. Everything within the chamber looked lush and rich, and warmth billowed into the corridor, carrying with it the scent of roses.

Sweet, red roses . . .

Taking in a gasping breath, Fiona lurched backward, wanting to run away, back to Mama and their bitter life on the streets. To make her quell the fear that was even now shredding her heart with every tumultuous beat. But the woman gripped Fiona's elbow tighter, leaving no hope of escape.

"On wi' you now, missy," she said, nodding to the opening as she nudged Fiona across the threshold. "There's no turnin' back. The master's bought and paid for you—and he doesn't like to be kept waitin'."

Chapter 1

~~∽◯◯∽~~

Hampshire, England
April 1292

Braedan de Cantor, eldest son in a family known as noble justices to the king, stood in the middle of Thistle Lane and shook his head, sending forth a spray of icy droplets. Then he cursed aloud. Were he a betting man, he'd wager all his sodden garments that he would never be warm again. The blasted rain had soaked into his cloak, clear through to his tunic and breeches, making him feel like he'd slogged through the Thames before making the journey to this city's walls with the wind pushing at his back.

So now in addition to the countless other pains wracking his body, he was damned cold. Colder than he could remember ever having been, even when he'd lived without shelter for weeks, traversing the Continent on

his way to Saint-Jean-d'Acre to join the fight against the
Saracens. It didn't help that he'd had to keep to the
woods during every day of his travels this past week; he
hadn't even dared to make a warming fire when night
fell. Nay, it would have proclaimed him an easy mark to
the bands of outlaws that roamed the forests near every
major thoroughfare leading out of London.

Outlaws like him.

Suppressing that bitter thought, Braedan tilted his
chin up off his chest and squinted through the driving
particles of rain toward the sign that swung wildly over
the shop's entrance; the wooden plank careened in the
gusts, but he could still see the images painted onto it. A
needle and thread. It was the place, then. It had to be.
He'd traveled a miserable path to get here, led on by the
assurance of information purchased with his last two
pieces of silver at a building in the *stewes* across the river
from London. The growling in his stomach gave weight
to that truth.

It had better damn well be the place, he thought—and
Giselle de Coeur, notorious courtesan and infamous
bandit that she was, had better be nestled safely within
these walls.

Scuffing his feet against the lip of the doorway, to remove what excess mud he could, Braedan leaned his
shoulder into the solid, wet wood and pushed, feeling
the slab give easily. It was unsecured.

Did the woman not fear intruders, then?

It was possible, he supposed. If all he'd heard about
her was true, she possessed the ability to dispatch neatly
any would-be prowlers with her dagger—and that skill,
he'd been told, was rivaled only by her powers of seduction. Aye, if the blade didn't work, she might choose to

stand before her perpetrator in one of the distinctive crimson gowns she favored, a graceful concoction of silk that clung to her every luscious curve and hollow; and when she turned her head so that her dark auburn tresses shimmered in the light, to direct the full impact of her gaze on her masculine prey, the unfortunate would be brought to his knees with the swiftness of a stone sinking in water.

Or so he'd been told.

Braedan felt his lips twist into a rare smile. *Jesu*, he must be more tired than he'd realized. Giselle de Coeur wasn't a sorceress capable of disabling men with a look; she was only a woman, and a fallen one at that.

He proceeded without trouble through the darkened chamber just inside the door he'd opened—a workroom, it seemed, with tables and tools for measuring and cutting. But he'd gained entry into the shop with nary a whisper of breeze to tell of his entrance. For all her celebrated skills in the arts of dagger wielding and carnal satisfaction, the woman seemed to share a similar lack of foresight with other members of her gender concerning the dangers lurking outside her door.

Braedan couldn't help but feel a twinge of disappointment in realizing it. Perhaps she *wouldn't* be able to help him, then. Perhaps this entire journey had been for naught, and he was no better off than he'd been when he'd first managed to escape his uncle's—

"Who are you, and what are you doing in my shop?"

Stiffening, Braedan turned toward the clear voice; a woman faced him from an inner doorway nearly ten paces away, though the slender shaft of light that illuminated her from behind cast her face in shadow. Never turning her back to him, she touched the tallow candle she carried to several rush torches on the wall. After enduring the gloom and rain outside for the past few days, he squinted at the room's sudden brightness, trying to detect any sign that this was the woman he sought.

It was difficult to tell. The Crimson Lady, by his knowledge, was six-and-twenty—mayhap a year more or less—yet this woman's age was difficult to determine. Her hair was hidden beneath a wimple, the fabric circling under her chin to cover her throat and meeting the neckline of her kirtle so that not even a finger's-width of skin showed. In fact, except for her face, she was completely draped in yards of dark cloth.

It was an imperious face, to be sure, fine-boned, smooth-skinned, and young enough, perhaps, to be that of the famed courtesan. Her lips were a trifle full, lending a sensual impression, and her dark brows swooped in a graceful curve over almond-shaped eyes, but he was too far away to see whether or not those eyes bore the telltale, tawny hue he'd been told to expect. His gaze slipped lower, and his initial hopeful feeling withered. She seemed rather . . . large. Not at all the sleek temptress he'd anticipated, though with all of those layers of gown and mantle, he couldn't be quite—

"Perhaps you didn't hear me," she said more sharply, pulling his stare to her face again, even as his mind observed the cultured, modulated accent she used. "I asked what you're doing in my shop. It is well past closing time, and no hour to be about the business of buying or selling."

In the silence that followed her statement, Braedan heard the water dripping from his clothing, making soft plopping sounds as it hit the wooden floor. He pushed his sodden hair back from his brow. "I'm looking for someone," he answered at last, keeping his voice low.

"This is an embroidery shop you're in, not an alehouse," she answered, just as calmly. "If you seek someone, go there." She nodded toward the street door through which he'd entered the shop. "You can see yourself out."

Braedan might have felt a sense of admiration at her quick response if his mood wasn't as black as the weather beyond that door. "I'm afraid that is impossible. I seek a specific person. A woman named Giselle de Coeur; I was told that I would find her here."

He watched her carefully as he spoke, trying to perceive any indication that she recognized the name. She remained as motionless as before. He took a few steps toward her—close enough to see her eyes, had she been looking at him—but as he came nearer he realized that she'd averted her gaze, centering it on his chest.

"Are you she?" he asked quietly, pausing in his approach, keeping his arms loosely at his sides, and trying not to appear threatening. "Are you the Crimson Lady?"

Now she shifted, lifting her hands and slipping them into the open ends of her sleeves as she crossed her arms over her waist. "You are mistaken, sir. My name is Fiona Byrne," she intoned, her voice unreadable as before, her gaze still fixed to his chest. "I am a widow and the owner of this shop—as you would have discovered had you made inquiries in town before so rudely intruding upon my peace here."

"It is unusual for so young a woman, widow or nay, to own such an establishment, is it not?"

"And yet it is mine, purchased some three years

past," she said, still refusing to look up. Her lips pressed together, and she shifted her weight back, leaning away from him. "If you will not leave peacefully, I shall have to shout for one of my apprentices to come to my aid. It will be the worse for you, then, I assure you. You will face the town justices come morn."

Braedan resisted the urge to grimace at the irony of her threat to bring him before the justices. Whatever shred of honor he still possessed made him loath to step closer to her—made him hesitate to do what he knew he must if he was to confirm her identity. But he had no choice; other lives depended on his action. "I must find Giselle de Coeur, madam," he said at last, insistent. "If you are she, reveal yourself. If not, I ask your aid in finding her."

"I do not know of whom you speak, and I demand that you leave. Now."

"That I cannot do," he said regretfully. Without further warning he lunged toward her, gripping her arms and twisting her against him with a smoothness born of years of brutal combat and bloodshed—at the same moment that she slid a dagger from her sleeve, lifting it with almost blinding speed.

Braedan stiffened, and all motion between them ceased. But in the instant he'd grabbed for her, her head had jerked up, the heat of her stare locking with his. His breath stilled, and his gaze melted into her tawny one, soaking, it seemed, into the dark honey and butter swirl of color—a hue so remarkable that it pulled him in even as he watched rage crackle beneath, lighting her eyes with flecks of gold.

"Giselle de Coeur, I presume?" he asked in a low

voice, still not releasing her and trying to ignore the hint of sweet vanilla that wafted up to fill his senses.

"I ask again—who are you, and what do you want?"

As she spoke she fair trembled with some strong emotion. *Fury*, his mind supplied, and his relief at finally finding her—the one person who might be able to help him—flagged a little under the realization of her anger. It would be more difficult to coerce her to his will when she felt so. Her jaw looked rigid, her eyes flaming into him with almost-palpable heat. Then she shifted her arm a bit and Braedan felt the slick, cold edge of her blade bite into his neck.

He gripped her ample form tighter in response and had the satisfaction of hearing her slight gasp and seeing her eyes widen before they as quickly narrowed again upon him. Cocking his brow, he inclined his head as much as the edge of her dagger allowed. "My name is Braedan de Cantor, and I have come on a matter of life and death."

"De Cantor?" Her arm slackened a bit, and Braedan took the opportunity to twist out of their locked embrace and back away from her weapon. When she realized her mistake and made a move with it toward him, he raised his palms in a gesture of peace.

"As I am a gentleman, you have naught to fear from me. You may put away your blade without risk to yourself."

She didn't take him at his word, he noticed, but she did retreat a step or two, continuing to hold the dagger between them and fixing him with a wary stare.

He studied her. She presented an interesting figure, to be sure. Not at all what he'd expected. She smelled delicious, the delicate fragrance she wore far more tempting than the exotic, spicy scent he'd assumed she'd favor. And along with her almost-matronly looks, she sounded refined and behaved like a trueborn lady; yet he knew that could not be.

He'd learned much about her these last weeks, adding to what he'd been told by his father, God rest him, when the law was first hot on her trail a few years past; that accumulated information had been what had led him to come seeking her. She'd had numerous clashes with both the sheriff and his father when she'd been part of a group of bandits near Alton, and that had been only after earning her reputation as one of London's most sought-after courtesans. Either occupation would have precluded her from the ranks of gentility, he'd guess.

"You seemed distracted when I spoke my name," he said, hoping to draw her out. "Do you know it, then?"

"Aye," she admitted. "The de Cantors have administered the king's law near London for generations."

He nodded. "My father was the chief justice of Wulmere Forest until very recently. In truth he'd mentioned your various . . . activities to me in letters."

"Is that why you've come here, then?" she asked quietly, a flicker of something—panic, perhaps—lighting behind her eyes. Her hand went white-knuckled around the hilt of her dagger. "Those days are far behind me. I conduct honest trade now in this town and have for three years past. If you are the gentleman you claim, then do not attempt to disrupt my life because of my former deeds."

"Former misdeeds, perhaps," he murmured. But to his amazement he found himself stifling an urge to reach out and comfort her. To comfort *her*—a notorious woman and former member of one of England's most infamous bands of thieves. He shook his head and concentrated instead on the reasons he'd come here—on Elizabeth, Richard, and the task ahead in bringing his uncle to justice. "But nay, lady. I am not here to arrest you. I couldn't even if I wanted to."

"Why not? Even did you not claim connection to a family of sheriffs, common law would allow it."

Braedan paused, meeting her stare and struggling to absorb the dull, relentless ache that bloomed inside of him every time he allowed himself to think of the events that had brought him here. Of all that he'd lost . . .

"I cannot arrest you, lady," he managed to answer finally, "because I, too, have recently been named a fugitive from justice."

He watched her expression shift from surprise to doubt. But it was the truth, much as it rankled. His uncle had branded him an outlaw, with a hefty price on his head, and neither he nor anyone he knew had the power to change it. Not yet anyway. He needed proof of the man's corruption first, and that was where Giselle de Coeur—or Fiona Byrne, as she apparently called herself now—would become useful to him. Very useful indeed.

"It is rich, I'll give you that," Fiona murmured. She took a deeper breath than he'd seen since she'd discovered him in her shop and studied him, from his muddy boots, up his large warrior's form, to the dripping hair atop his head. He met her gaze unflinchingly, as she added, "And yet I never thought I'd live to see a de Cantor on the other side of the law."

Biting his tongue at the retort that rose to his lips, Braedan watched her slide her dagger back into her sleeve, though he noticed that she kept enough distance between herself and him should she decide she needed to retrieve it again.

"But if what you say is fact," she continued, "it would behoove you to do as I've asked. I have seen how the justices here do their work; they do not deal kindly with criminals or wanted men. It will go worse for you once they learn that you've broken into my shop—which is exactly what I'll tell them if you do not turn around, pretend you never laid eyes on me, and leave."

"I didn't break in. The door was open."

She choked back humorless laughter. "Even if that was true—"

"You know it is."

Now she glared. "Even if it *is*, it will not matter. I will tell the justices that you entered here against my wishes. They will believe me over you; they've known me for over three years, while you are a stranger to them."

"Do they know you're the Crimson Lady?" he countered dryly, the last of his nobler instincts cringing just a bit at her stricken expression. When she remained silent, he added, "As you've said, de Cantors are known throughout the land as keepers of justice. None will believe you if you claim me a fugitive. I will deny it, and tell them I've tracked you to this city to arrest you after three long years of searching for you—a former common woman who became a notorious outlaw, wanted for theft and the kidnapping of good citizens as they traveled the roads near London."

"You would lie, then, about your purposes?" she demanded, her face stony.

"No more than *you* would, lady," Braedan retorted. "Know this: I will do what I must to make you listen to me. I've told you already, I've come on a matter of life and death."

"Ah, I see . . . not only are you a de Cantor on the opposite side of the law, but one with tarnished morals as well. Quite a rarity," she gibed, folding her arms in front of her and leaning into the table at her back—a fine worktable, from the looks of it, with lengths of embroidered ribbon and colorful thread piled neatly at one end. "I suppose I should feel honored to meet you."

Braedan resisted the urge to cross the room and shake her into listening to him. "Enough of this," he muttered. "Will you help me, or not?"

"That depends," she answered with equally annoying coolness, "on what exactly it is that you want of me."

"I need you to teach me how to live as an outlaw. I require coin to resolve the difficult matter I spoke of, and yet in order to gain it I must first learn to navigate the underworld and mingle with other fugitives without losing my life for my pains."

"Ah—it is death you fear, then, at the hands of the evil masses you and your kind have spent your lives hunting down," she said, her expression mocking.

"Death holds no dread for me," Braedan said huskily. "I just cannot fall beneath the stroke of his blade yet."

Fiona looked at him, silent, as if measuring the truth of his answer.

"And yet training me as an outlaw will not be the limit of what I ask of you."

Again she did not respond, only lifting her brows in question.

He paused and glanced away from her as the second part of his mission here—the most important part, and the reason he'd come seeking her above all others—

gnawed at him, twisting his insides. "I need you to lead me into the deeper workings of the *stewes* across the Thames at Southwark," he finished, the words thick in his throat. "Not as a buyer, but to gather information. I must get beneath the surface in a way that one like me could never hope to do on my own. I need your knowledge of those places in order to find the right people to question about a woman—"

"Nay," she broke in, her face ashen. "Teaching you how to thieve is one thing; going back to the *stewes* is another entirely. I won't do it."

"You must. A life is at stake."

"Aye—mine!" she retorted. "I've come too far, and I will not risk losing everything to go back there again."

"But you *will* lose all you've worked to build if you do not go back," Braedan countered harshly. "I have no choice in this. I must find my foster sister. She was brought to one of those hellish places; it is all I know of her whereabouts. I must remove her from that disgrace, but I have no coin to do it, not to mention the fact that I cannot very well walk in freely and announce myself as I look for her. Not now, as a fugitive—which is what the man who betrayed both me and Elizabeth knew when he declared me an outlaw."

"Appeal to the king, then," Fiona answered, her desperation almost palpable. "Your family has lived only to please the crown for generations. Surely he would not deny you in favor of a stranger's charge against you?"

"It is not so simple as that."

"Why not?"

"Because the one who charged me is *not* a stranger— he is my uncle through marriage, an appointed justice and man of law in his own right."

Braedan pushed back his hair from his forehead again, weary, and drained—feeling every muscle in his body strung tight enough to snap from his bones. "Christ's Blood, woman, don't you see? As unsavory as I find all this, I cannot falter. I require what you alone can give me if I am to be successful. If you will not aid me freely, then I must force you to it. And I will do whatever is necessary, do not mistake me."

"Then you are a bastard," Fiona whispered in a raw voice.

"I've been called by many names in my life, lady, but bastard is not one of them," Braedan said, struggling to rein in his temper. "It is precisely because I am *not* that I must do this. The last time I saw Elizabeth, she was a child of eight, waving farewell to me at the start of my journeys. That was nearly ten years ago. When I returned home two months past, it was to find most of my family dead or missing; my father and a brother had succumbed to the fever, my mother was secluded behind the walls of an abbey, and my fifteen-year-old brother, Richard, was being kept under lock and key at my uncle's estate, his ward by decree of the king.

"I was assumed dead in battle, thanks to my long absence without message. When I was finally able to meet with Richard, it was clear that he was living miserably under our uncle's influence, yet he managed to whisper to me of what had happened to Elizabeth."

Braedan paused, his gaze sweeping over Fiona, taking in her milky pallor, the emotions that seemed to be at war in her eyes. "My foster sister was sold into ignominy, lady—into the kind of shameful life that I believe you know too well; I must find her and free her from it."

The silence stretched between them, Fiona's body taut with whatever emotion she was forcing herself to contain. "You might almost sound like an honorable man, Braedan de Cantor," she answered at last, her words echoing hollowly. "And I might almost be fooled into believing you, were you not dangling my life before me as the stick with which to beat me to your will."

Another pang of remorse shot through Braedan, but he smothered it. "I am not heartless, lady. I realize that this may be difficult for you—"

"You know nothing about it."

"I know that I wish you no harm. In truth, I am prepared to do what I can to help you, once this is over." He took a step toward her, realizing with a sense of shock that he was himself gripped tight in the clutches of desperation now. "I vow that I will protect your secret in this town and ensure your continued prosperity here once you return. If it is possible I will even try to secure a pardon from the king for all of your past crimes, but I must have your help first. Only after Elizabeth is found and released can I pursue my own case and seek vengeance against my uncle. I will not risk arrest and a long imprisonment awaiting a grand assize while she suffers further. Her freedom must come first."

"So you say," Fiona answered at last, her tone, her posture, everything about her sending frigid waves of anger and distrust billowing out toward him. "And now pray tell, Lord Tyrant, is there anything more that I should hear before I make my decision? Any other part to this story that is supposed to help me to forget I'm being threatened with the loss of all that I have if I do not comply with your demands?"

"Nay," Braedan answered, refusing to be baited. "It

is simple. Teach me to survive as an outlaw—help me to save Elizabeth—and I promise to do everything in my power to ensure your safety and security when it is over."

"Somehow, I am not overwhelmed with confidence," she muttered, crumpling her gown with fisted hands.

"And yet it is the truth," Braedan responded quietly. "You need not—"

"Mistress Byrne? Are ye all right, mistress?"

The voice that rang through the chamber cracked on the question, and Braedan swung his gaze to its owner, standing, now, in the doorway—a youth of about six-and-ten, he'd guess. Fiona looked at the lanky boy as well, her mouth tightening into that severe line that made Braedan want to kiss it to lush softness again. The jolt of that realization shot through him and rendered him speechless long enough so that the lad, brandishing a broom handle, took a threatening step toward him.

"Stuart," Fiona chided gently, "what are you doing? It is too late to be about. All is well; go back to bed, now."

The youth didn't answer her; instead, he advanced a few more paces toward Braedan, who held his ground, unable to quite smother his grim look of disbelief as he faced down this clearly loyal protector of London's most tarnished woman; the boy must be daft. Tired as Braedan was, it was still painfully obvious that he could disable the lad with little more than a look if need be.

"It is all right, Stuart," Fiona said again in a low voice, stepping closer and raising her hand as if to soothe an agitated child. "Everything is fine. But we must keep quiet or we'll wake your mam; then she'll be cross, and perhaps there'll be no sweet buns come morn."

"No sweet buns?" Stuart croaked, stopping short with a stricken expression. "Oh, I'll keep quiet, mistress—I promise!" he called, wincing, apparently, when he realized how loudly he'd made the vow. Lowering his voice to an exaggerated whisper, he added, "I won't wake Mam. Mmmmm, mmmmm, mmmm, I won't," he repeated, clamping his lips tight and shaking his head emphatically.

Braedan narrowed his gaze, taking a closer look at Stuart. The boy turned his head to glower back at him, and Braedan suddenly understood why Fiona was behaving as she did. Stuart was a simpleton—by accident or birth it was impossible to tell—but it was clear that he possessed the mind of a little child.

Stuart continued to stare at Braedan before noticing, apparently, his sodden, travel-worn condition. "Why, yer all wet!" he blurted, seeming to forget his stick weapon; he let it swing to the side so that one end clattered down to the wooden floor. "And yer drippin' on Mistress Byrne's fine oak boards! She don't like that—no, not one bit, she don't."

"It's all right, Stuart. I can wipe it up later," Fiona said gently. "Now why don't you—"

"Who are you—and what are you doin' in here talkin' to Mistress Byrne so late in the eve?" Stuart demanded, keeping his scowl fixed firmly on Braedan.

"That is a very good question, Stuart, and one that I'd be happy to answer," Braedan murmured, glancing at Fiona. "You see, I am a knight, only recently returned from the wars abroad—the son of a king's justice, who in turn was the son of an appointed sheriff—and I am here because I'm afraid that I have to—"

"Because he has had some unsettling news to tell me,

Stuart," Fiona broke in, taking a few steps closer and tightening the triangle that had formed between them. She avoided Braedan's gaze, focusing only on the young man as she added, "It seems that a relation of mine has fallen ill. That is why this knight has come here so late, to tell me so."

"A relation—fallen sick?" Stuart asked, frowning.

"Aye," she answered calmly, the lie slipping from her tongue with a skill born of years' practice, Braedan couldn't help but think.

"Because of it I may need to take a little journey," she continued. "To see this . . . relation and make sure she's all right."

Stuart's face crumpled as the import of her words sank in. "You're going on a *trip*? Without me and Mam?" He shook his head, the motion reminding Braedan of a bear cub trying to escape a persistent, stinging bee.

She cast a dark look at Braedan. "I'm afraid I must. But it will only be for a short time."

"Wh-when will you go?" Stuart's voice cracked again.

"Tomorrow mor—"

"Tonight," Braedan interrupted firmly. "We will be leaving tonight, just as soon as your mistress can gather her things for the journey."

She shot him another glare, before gentling her expression for Stuart again. "Aye, perhaps tonight would be better," she murmured, though Braedan saw the tension in her face and jaw as she spoke. "I think it would be best if you woke your mam after all, Stuart. I'll need to leave the shop in her care while I'm away."

Stuart nodded slowly, the broom, forgotten now, clattering to the floor as he clenched the fingers of one hand against the other. Turning stiffly, he mumbled to himself and shuffled from the chamber to complete the task assigned him.

Fiona moved crisply away from the portal once he'd left, stalking past Braedan without sparing him a glance; she stopped near a table behind him, rummaging in a drawer until she found a ledger she'd apparently been seeking. Withdrawing it, she slapped it onto the table and split it open, poring over what was written on the pages as if he no longer existed to her.

He stood in silence for a moment, watching her. He was grateful that she'd finally agreed to his plan, yet he still felt a vague sense of unease at the method he'd used to obtain her cooperation. Coercion, even of a woman of such obviously questionable morals as the Crimson Lady, wasn't his way. Her back remained stiff in her position bent over the papers, and again he was struck by the seeming *sturdiness* of her. No slender-waisted nymph, this lady. Nay, she looked as solid and substantial as the most well fed peasant lass he'd met on any of his journeys.

She had a striking face and eyes, it was true. And who knew what carnal tricks she'd learned after years of trade in the *stewes*. That had to be what accounted for her popularity as a courtesan, he decided. It could be little else. Men hadn't sought her out for her figure, he'd wager. *Or her light demeanor.* Nay, she seemed far more intelligent and resolute than many of the vacuous beauties whose charms he'd sampled in the past.

Even Julia . . .

The painful bent of his thoughts was interrupted by the sound of Fiona slamming the ledger shut. She spun to face him, her expression still cool and calm. All except for her eyes; they glowed with the same golden flames of rage.

"Your intrusion here is more than inconvenient," she said, her words precise and delivered like arrow shots. "It will take me some time to go over the accounts with Stuart's mam, as well as discuss what must be done in my absence. And I need to prepare some clothing for the journey and afterward if we are to make efforts to rejoin those with whom I worked before."

"I'll wait."

Her mouth twisted. She looked as if she might say something more, but then turned away from him deliberately and walked to the door, taking the two torches from their holders as she went, so that the chamber was left flickering in shadow behind her. Yet just before she disappeared through the portal, she called over her shoulder, "I will take what time I need to prepare, Braedan de Cantor. Know that I will not be rushed, by you or anyone else."

"Somehow I don't doubt that," he murmured in response, but she'd already left.

The sweet fragrance of vanilla lingered after her, and he found himself shaking his head, trying to dispel the strange effect that it—and the woman wearing it—had on him. The Crimson Lady was an enigma to him, far more than he'd anticipated, and that would make the quest they were about to undertake much more difficult than he'd planned. Were it not for Elizabeth, he'd have forgone all of this and simply found his way to the king, throwing himself at his sovereign's mercy, even if it meant suffering a long imprisonment until the whole mess with his uncle could be sorted out. But that wasn't a consideration now. Not with Elizabeth's honor hanging in the balance.

Braedan breathed in deeply and leaned back against the counter, sparing another glance at the darkened and quiet corridor beyond the portal. It was as still as a grave.

He might as well get as comfortable as his bruised and aching body would allow him, he decided. He sensed that the Crimson Lady was going to make this wait and all that came after as drawn-out and painful for him as possible, for as much as he was the seeming captor and she the hostage in this sordid affair, he had no doubt that she would try to take control of the situation if she could; she wanted to make him pay for what he was forcing her to do, he knew—and that process was beginning tonight.

Right here and now it had begun, as he cooled his heels in this darkened chamber, at her mercy until she deemed herself good and ready to grace him with her presence again. He shook his head once more and sighed, tipping his chin up to stretch his stiff neck, and closing his eyes as he did. Aye, she was going to do this her way.

And so, blast it all to heaven, he would wait.

Chapter 2

The steady rhythm of their horses' hooves might have lulled Fiona to sleep had she not been jolted to full awareness time and again by the animosity pricking at her. For what must have been the twentieth time in the past two hours, she turned her head to glare at the bedraggled example of manhood riding next to her. He seemed oblivious to her stare, hunched over as he was, his hood drawn up over his brow and looking as if, even riding, he might fall asleep astride his mount.

A mount supplied with *her* coin, she fumed.

Gritting her teeth, she tried to make herself dwell instead on the chill beauty of morn stretching damp and luminous fingers out all around them. Whether or not Braedan had promised to return the money once he'd earned enough to do so had mattered little. It was adding insult to injury, as far as she was concerned, to make her furnish their transportation, and she liked it

25

about as much as she relished the nighttime trek he'd ordered them to take.

But it hadn't gone as he'd planned, at least; she could take comfort in that. They'd left her shop and traveled only a few hours before the rain had forced them to find shelter off the main road. Any latent fear of being accosted by bandits had dissipated long before that in the face of the foul weather unleashing itself all around them. The terse words they'd exchanged while making the decision to stop had been their only conversation since she'd first succumbed to his bullying tactics.

In the end they'd rested for a few hours, wrapped in cloaks and tucked under the branches of a huge tree—completely separated from each other by their steeds and the small cart containing her trunk and a few provisions—until the worst of the rain had passed and he'd insisted that they push on.

Now he was paying for his ridiculous tenacity, she thought, allowing herself a flare of satisfaction. Though it had been years since she'd had to go a whole night with so little rest, she still appeared to be in far better shape than Braedan; he looked ready to topple at any moment, and if she wasn't mistaken, those muffled growls of complaint weren't coming from his mouth, but rather from the depths of his clearly empty stomach.

But then he coughed, and Fiona swung her gaze to him again, her smugness faltering a bit. Frowning, she studied him more closely. That hadn't sounded good. Nay, not good at all.

She was readying to say something to him when the cough resounded again from deep in his chest, harsh and wracking. She narrowed her eyes, peering at what she could see of his face beneath his hood. He looked flushed. Could he have taken ill?

It was possible—and if he had, then perhaps she'd be finding herself free of him sooner than she'd thought.

The renegade idea wound through her mind, and her tattered conscience struggled to suppress the hope that filled her. If he fell ill, she might be able to sneak away without worry, leaving him to whatever the fates intended. She could flee back to her sewing shop and pack up, moving to a new city much farther to the north, perhaps, where she could take on another name and begin again—

"We need to stop soon for food and to dry out. An inn that will do sits not far from here."

The clarity of his words yanked her from her baleful reverie, and she looked over at him again, finding herself caught, suddenly, in the calm, cool scope of his gaze. It was directed right at her, and though his face still looked flushed, there was nothing cloudy about his eyes. They were blue and piercing, seeming to see inside her secret soul to the dark thoughts that had been lurking there. To her surprise, she felt her own cheeks heat under his perusal.

"I am not hungry."

Her peevish answer came from somewhere unbidden. It was a lie, of course; her stomach, too, had begun growling not long after they'd taken to the road again from their brief respite.

"That matters not. You must eat, as must I." He turned his face forward again, relieving her of that penetrating gaze of his. "We will stop."

An answering burst of resentment swept through her.

How dare he order her about as if she were his chattel? Panic churned below the surface with that thought, bringing back with it too many painful memories. Remembered years of powerlessness and despair; she pushed the old terror down, determined not to give breath and life to it again. Not now. Not ever, if she could help it.

To mask her sudden weakening, she let her stare bore into him once more, snapping, "Just how do you intend to purchase victuals and time before a drying fire? Have you thought of that—thought of anything beyond your addle-minded scheme to track me down and force me to your bidding?"

"Aye," he replied calmly. "We will use your funds to buy some meat and drink, just as we did when we acquired the horses. I will replace what you spend—and then some—once I've managed to procure my own supply of coin."

"And if I refuse to allow you further use of my money?" she countered, unable to contain the spite in her tone.

He turned his head to look at her again, the motion weary, though his expression glowed intense. "We have already discussed this, woman. Do not test me further. If you will not cooperate, then so be it; I will bind you and drag you back to Hampshire to face prosecution for your past crimes. Then I will needs find another to assist me—one who is certain to be less skilled and far less knowledgeable in the arts of thieving and whoring, the two pursuits most necessary for me to understand if I am to free Elizabeth. It is not what I would choose, but it is what will happen if you continue this obstinacy."

Cheeks still burning, Fiona stifled a gasp and snapped

her gaze forward again, struck dumb as the sick sensation she'd almost forgotten bloomed in her belly. Anger had helped to mask it before this, but now it reared up, dark and relentless. It was accompanied by that old voice inside of her, the one filled with self-loathing, whispering of her sinfulness, her worthlessness. Braedan de Cantor had just named it outright, and there was no more escaping it; he had sought her out above all others because she was a notorious whore and thief, the most tainted woman he could find—a paragon of wicked skill that surpassed every boundary.

Aye, she was that; she couldn't deny it. She'd stolen from many as part of a group of bandits well-known for their criminal success. And long before that, her innocence had been purchased for the price of a few coins, after which she'd been trained in all manner of unholy acts at the whim of her master. The fact that he had never allowed another to bed her in all the years he'd owned her—that he himself had orchestrated the elaborate ruse they'd used to gull the many men who'd ended up believing they'd bedded her—had no bearing, she knew. This powerful mercenary knight, born to a family who lived only to uphold the law, would never believe it. And it would make no difference if he did, for whether by one man or many, she was still ruined, her virginity stolen, her body and soul corrupted.

And yet in these past years, she'd almost managed to pretend it wasn't so. Wrapping one arm around her waist, Fiona squeezed her fingers into a fist against the bulky padding beneath her bliaud and cloak as her mount jounced down the rutted and muddy road—clinging to the disguise she'd worn for nearly three years to help her believe the lie she'd created for herself. And it had worked until this vengeful warrior had come bursting into her life, dragging her sordid past into the light of day again and making her remember everything, making her despise herself all over again . . .

"Bear in mind," Braedan broke into her thoughts, his voice raspy from his recent bout of coughing, "that I ask the temporary use of your coin not for myself but for my foster sister's sake—a woman who needs the help you can best provide her by assisting me. Think on it that way, if it is easier to swallow."

She remained silent, the confused emotions inside of her swirling in a queasy jumble. The plight of Braedan's foster sister did tug at some deeply buried part of her, but it didn't make what he was doing to her any easier, she thought. Nothing made it easier.

What in God's name was she thinking, letting this man lead her willingly along on a journey back to a hell she'd sworn to have forsaken forever? Eyes stinging, Fiona lifted her face to feel the caressing warmth of the morning sun, her desperate gaze taking in their surroundings. Her heart thundered an uneven beat. They were nearing Alton. The bend in the road ahead was familiar, as were the groupings of trees, with their rain-dampened branches gnarled and crooked low to the ground, the moss hanging from them in tattered swaths.

In another few minutes they'd reach Whitbow Crossing. Once over that, they'd approach the inn and go inside . . . then money would change hands, questions would be asked, and information would need to be gained to find the hiding place most lately favored by Will and his company, so that she and Braedan might attempt to rejoin them. And though Braedan didn't know it, when that time came, the life she'd savored as a plain and hardworking, honest embroidress named Fiona Byrne would end abruptly.

She shuddered. Aye, it would end just as swiftly as if Braedan de Cantor had lifted his blade and laid a vicious stroke to sever her head from her neck.

Braedan took another swallow of the bitter brew that the serving wench had placed in front of him, trying to ease the burning in his throat. It had gotten worse in the hour that they'd been here, even though the warmth inside the rough-hewn walls of this establishment had dried him, and his belly was pleasantly full from the mutton stew on which he'd supped. It was almost too warm where he sat, he thought, rubbing his hand across his brow; he'd chosen a shadowy corner of the main chamber, away from the majority of the patrons and far from the heat of the blaze behind the grate, yet still the atmosphere oppressed.

The sounds of conversation, swinging from muffled to raucous, continued on around him, accompanied by the clanking of cups on the tables and the giggling squeals of the women when one of the more drunken patrons reached out to sample their rounder parts.

Braedan shut his eyes; they felt like hot coals in their sockets, and he was more than a bit wobbly. Shoving the cup away, he grimaced. Perhaps he'd better forgo any more ale himself.

Letting out an exasperated sigh, he turned to look once more at the door that led to the sleeping chambers above the inn. Where was Fiona, damn it? She'd been up there nigh on the entire hour since their arrival. Having had his share of experience with women and their need to stroke their vanities with excessive grooming, he'd prepared himself for her to take some time before descending again to sup, but this was getting ridiculous.

The people in the inn would be the only witnesses to any fussing over her appearance. Whom did she hope to impress? Not him, surely. They were there to gather information, eat, and rest for a bit, nothing more. She'd assured him that they'd learn the whereabouts of her former band of thieves here—it was close enough to their old haunts in the forest that someone at the inn would know—as long as no men of law were hanging about, she'd added, instructing him to scrutinize every patron to ensure that no justices or sheriffs were present.

He'd done as she'd asked, but damn if it would do them any good. Grimacing, he decided to neglect his former decision to cease drinking by tossing back the remainder of his tepid ale. They'd get nowhere with her out of sight, arranging her wimple or donning another of those singularly unattractive black kirtles she seemed devoted to wearing. By God, nothing would happen as long as she cloistered herself up there.

Unless she wasn't abovestairs after all.

Blast it, he hadn't even considered that. What if she'd decided to do something foolish and attempt to flee from him and his demands on her? Gathering all of his waning strength, Braedan pushed himself to his feet, preparing to go and find out if his suspicions were true. But he swayed a bit as he stood, knocking his cup to the floor.

God's bones, it must be a potent brew. The thought wiggled through his brain like a heat-slicked worm, elusive and boggling, leaving him feeling even more confused than before. Rubbing his hand across his brow again, he shook his head and squinted. A dark shape filled the doorway. Fiona, at last?

The whisper of vanilla cooled his senses as she swept toward him, keeping in the shadows along the wall so as not to attract attention. She stopped in front of him and his newly brimming cup of ale. It had been replaced by a buxom wench with flaxen hair, who'd been glancing at him from across the room with a half smile every time she caught his gaze. The woman had sidled back toward the other patrons with Fiona's entrance, he noticed, apparently pouting over the fact that the return of his female traveling companion would make it unlikely for him to respond to any additional interest she might show him.

Dismissing the woman and her carnal disappointments from his mind, he redirected his attention to Fiona, subduing the relief he felt at her return by eyeing the long, hooded cape she wore.

"Why the devil are you wearing that inside? We're not going anywhere soon."

She didn't answer, instead reaching for his cup and lifting it to drink.

He sat down again, adding wryly, "I take it you're thirsty."

She only kept drinking, pulling the cup away for a moment to breathe before tipping her head back again and draining the last of it. She set the vessel down when she was done, delicately wiping her mouth with her fingers.

He scowled at her, beginning to become annoyed at the way she continued to ignore him. "Enjoy that, did you?"

She looked askance at him this time, her face still shadowed in the folds of her hood. "I haven't tasted public ale in a long while, but it is as awful as I remembered."

He didn't possess the strength to ask why, then, she'd

gulped it down like it was elixir. He closed his eyes for a moment, determined to work through this fog that seemed to be settling over his brain. She still hadn't answered his first question about her cloak, he realized, and he wanted an explanation. Her severe, matronly gowns and wimples had been bad enough, but this garb could attract unwanted notice that might hamper their objective in being here.

Grimacing again against the damnable scratchiness in his throat, he said, "It is passing strange to see a woman so shrouded within doors; I ask you once more, why are you dressed so?"

"You'll see in a moment," came her cryptic reply, though he saw that she glanced furtively from beneath the cowl to allow herself full view of the inn chamber. "Have you noted any men of law about? Any justices or constables among those here?"

"Nay," Braedan answered. He looked up at her from his seated position, feeling more irritated with each passing second, whether from her secrecy or his own unsettling shakiness he wasn't sure. He only knew that he wasn't in the mood for games. "Your requirements have been met, Fiona, so let us get on with learning the whereabouts of your former thieving partners."

"Your eagerness to take up a criminal's life inspires me, my lord," she answered quietly, refusing to meet his gaze again, as she continued to look carefully around the room. "And yet perhaps it will not be so when reality settles in—which will be in the next few moments, unless you agree to reverse this foolish path you've set us on and release me from my part in your plans."

A surge of denial rose in him, urged on by Elizabeth's

need. He shook his head in refusal, though the movement made his skull ache even worse than before.

She paused, the silence tight, before she said, "As you wish, Braedan de Cantor. But know you that from this moment on, there will be no turning back."

"So be it," he rasped.

"Aye, so be it," she echoed.

She remained still for a moment, then, taking a deep breath, she closed her eyes, and he saw in profile how her lips moved as if in some sort of silent prayer before she reached up to the fastening of her cape. He watched her, amazed, as she eased the hood back from her face, letting it fall onto her back; when she shrugged her shoulders the entire cloak followed after, sliding to the floor with a muffled swish.

The image that greeted him then hammered through his fever-beleaguered brain in a molten tide, maddening and tantalizing. Standing in front of him was a temptress—a woman completely different from the one he'd met in the embroidery shop. Her voice was the same, but by the Rood, this lady was as unlike the matronly shopkeeper as the glorious sun was to a blackened stone. It was a mortal shame that she was a fallen woman, he thought, struggling with his sense of shock, for in other circumstances he'd have been hard-pressed not to try to win her for himself.

She wore no wimple now. Nay, her hair shone in the rushlight, pulled back from her brow by a delicate circlet to fall unfettered in glossy waves to her waist. Its dark cinnamon hue took essence from the crimson gown she wore—an elegant confection that looked as if it had been crafted just for her. It was dazzling . . . long-sleeved but scooped low on her shoulders, clinging to the curve of her breasts and the slender length of her sides, down to where a golden girdle encircled her hips. From there the fabric fell in loose pleats, flowing to a long train that she'd apparently been holding up, concealed, beneath her cape.

In short, she was stunning. There was no other way to describe her, and no way to deny the effect her beauty had on him.

The inn began to fall silent as the patrons noticed her standing there. Braedan knew he gaped as well, yet he couldn't seem to stop himself; if he hadn't already been sitting, he'd have slumped to the nearest bench he could find, so overwhelming was his reaction to the vision standing before him.

When he could find his voice, he croaked, "By all the saints, Fiona, I—"

"It is Giselle," she broke in quietly, turning her head a little to look at him. "Giselle de Coeur." Her eyes glittered at her utterance of that name, and the coils of desire that had been winding through his feverish body were suddenly tempered by the conflicting emotions he saw churning in the depths of her gaze.

"Fiona is gone," she continued. "Destroyed by your command."

An aching pit opened in his belly as she looked away again and began to walk slowly toward the center of the chamber. She was perfection, Braedan thought absently, the idea floating into his consciousness. The embodiment of pure, emotionless beauty, at once both scorching and icy.

He swallowed hard, his throat hurting from more, now, than just the raw sting of fever. He had done this to her. Aye, he had. For whatever secrets this woman had to hide, whatever pain was buried beneath the disguise she'd used to conceal herself, it was clear that he was forcing her to bring it all into the light again. But it couldn't be helped. There was no other way for him to accomplish what needed to be done. She was the absolute fulfillment of all he'd hoped to find when he'd conceived his plan for rescuing Elizabeth. Aye, she was the one. For a little more than two weeks ago, he'd come in search of the Crimson Lady—the most desirable courtesan and notorious thief in all of England . . .

And it seemed that today, he'd finally found her.

Chapter 3

F iona held herself stiffly as she moved toward the center of the chamber, the despised, crimson-hued gown swishing as she walked. It was difficult, so very, very difficult to take this up again. She felt awkward, the flow of her steps, the understated, swaying motion she commanded of her body off-balance somehow. And for a moment panic swelled.

She couldn't have forgotten in only three years, her mind screamed silently—it was impossible. It had been one of the first lessons Draven had forced upon her, making her practice the way she walked over and over, until it seemed part of her very blood and bones. The movement . . . the teasing yet subtle tension of steps as she crossed a room, calculated to drive a man wild with longing before he ever felt the brush of her cool fingers against his flesh . . . she'd somehow lost the rhythm of that skill, and the awareness of it frightened her to the point of sickness.

What if she couldn't do this any longer? What if she'd forgotten all that she'd been made to master—ways of moving, talking, touching . . . yea, even breathing—that comprised her embodiment of the Crimson Lady? Apprehension tore her with needle-sharp claws. The store of decadent knowledge she'd once possessed seemed to have deserted her, leaving behind nothing more than the sinful memory of all the acts she'd been made to commit, the sensual performances she'd been commanded to deliver. Those images were graven, she knew, bloody and deep into her soul, but oh God the actual knowing seemed to have—

There.

The sensation swept over her body, and suddenly everything fell into place as it should, the seductive rhythm regained, as if never lost at all. Like an outgoing tide, her sense of alarm receded, her mind clearing enough so that she finally heard it—the whispers rising all around her, people breathing her name, forming it, savoring it with their tongues before releasing it in wafts of moist, hushed air, like something both tainted and beguiling.

The Crimson Lady . . . 'tis the Crimson Lady, I tell you . . . Nay, it can't be. She's long gone—surely . . .

'Tis her, I say! Look at her. The very same woman, it is . . . Giselle de Coeur . . . The Crimson Lady . . .

Bringing herself to a halt in the center of the chamber, Fiona stood regal and silent. An answering quiet settled uneasily over the room, and she let her gaze drift to meet the glances of those around her, paying attention to the men in particular, noting the various expressions of surprise, disapproval, suspicion, or interest on their faces. But most of all she saw hunger . . . hot, unabashed lust.

The certainty of it washed over her, leaving her feeling both shamed and oddly reckless. It had been a long time, and she couldn't stop the flare of satisfaction in the very male reactions she was inspiring in this room, even from the virtuous Braedan de Cantor, who'd almost toppled off his bench when she'd revealed her true form.

Aye, when all was said and done, the immoral woman she'd done her best to bury these past years was worthy, perhaps, of good people's disdain—but none could deny that she was gifted. Remarkably, wickedly gifted where men were concerned. It was a poor recompense for all the pain and self-loathing that was already beginning to churn in her breast again, but it was all she had, and so she reveled in it. In truth, Draven had unwittingly given her a measure of power when he'd forced her to perfect the art of bringing men to their knees, and she planned to wield it to her advantage.

Right now that meant using it to gain the information that Braedan had demanded of her.

"Does anyone here know the whereabouts of Will Singleton and his men?" she called out, modulating her voice to resonate in the husky tones of the Crimson Lady.

A faint grumbling began in the farther reaches of the chamber, but no one answered her outright. Fiona decided to wait before saying anything more, to let her appearance sink in; three years was a long time, and she wanted to let those who might remember her recall that, though they were undoubtedly still loyal to Will, they owed her at least a share of allegiance for all of the filched wealth she'd convinced him to share with the people of Alton during the time she'd worked with him and his men.

From the side of her gaze, she saw someone dart out the door to the kitchens, most likely to fetch John Tanner, the blustery owner of the inn. It was just as well. Tanner would remember and vouch for her—he'd been one of the prime beneficiaries of their plunder, his reward for providing a safe haven and alibi whenever one of the blasted king's men had gotten too close.

Aye let him come in, she thought. It would speed things up immeasurably.

"Why don't they answer?" a voice rasped in her ear.

Fiona resisted the urge to turn and glare at Braedan, instead muttering over her shoulder, "They just need some time to be sure they're doing right in telling me. Now go and sit down. I'll take care of everything if you'll but leave it alone."

More grumblings had begun as soon as Braedan stood and moved next to her, and Fiona saw renewed suspicion tightening the faces around her, heard the hissed comments concerning the possible identity of the stranger—for though he was a de Cantor, by his own admission he'd been gone from Alton for even longer than she, and surely none would remember him.

"Who is that with you, Giselle?" someone finally called out from the back of the room.

"Hold off there," called another, more commanding voice. "How do we know she's really Giselle de Coeur? Might be a trap, set by the new sheriff to capture Will and the boys."

More mumblings of agreement and dissent arose, and then the second man who'd spoken separated from the crowd, walking toward her, as he added, "I say we don't tell her nothin'—not until we get us some proof that she is who she says. The Crimson Lady I heard of didn't travel with *any* man, 'ceptin' Will Singleton, and I don't think this is her. If 'twas, she'd know where he is all by herself."

Fiona directed her gaze to the dissenter, letting it move with unmistakable judgment over his entire frame, from head to toe, until she was rewarded with the flush that spread across his face. He wasn't young, but he wasn't old either. He might very well have been in or around Alton when she worked with Will; if he'd heard of her, he might also remember what she was known for—and just exactly how she'd made herself useful to Will and the boys in their roadside snares to steal from wealthy and corrupt noblemen.

"I *am* the Crimson Lady, sir," Fiona said at last, "and I must seek out Will because I am only now returning to Alton after three years' absence."

Many of her old instincts were returning she noticed, now that she'd overcome that first, most difficult hurdle; almost without thought, she called up a supremely innocent expression and leaned just a bit toward the man, murmuring in a husky plea, as if for his ears alone, "Surely you can understand my need for help in finding him after all this time. Won't you aid me? Please . . . ?" she breathed as an afterthought, staring directly into his startled brown eyes.

Her actions had the very effect she'd hoped; her accuser flushed an even deeper shade than before and looked away, his Adam's apple bobbing. He backed away a step, crushing his cap in his hands and doing everything he could not to meet her gaze again, and she couldn't help thinking that he looked like a drowning man afraid of going under one last time.

"Aye, I might be able to—I mean, I can help, I think," he stuttered, backing off another step. "That is, we—we might be able to lead you to Will again. We could take you to the place where—"

"But you still have no proof, man," a drunken and more malevolent voice called from a table to the left of Fiona. She turned and saw its owner, a burly mountain of a man with a thick beard and leonine hair, lurch to his feet, flanked swiftly by two of his friends as all three crossed the short distance to where she and Braedan stood.

A tingle of warning slid up her spine. This man looked dangerous. She'd never seen him before, of that she was certain; she'd have remembered someone of his size and appearance—and she didn't like the look of him now, especially not the way his lips curved on his face. It was the sort of leering expression she hadn't seen since Draven had made a sport of parading her before his friends at one of his frequent feasts, like a sweetmeat to be tasted.

"I be a traveler from London," he said thickly as he looked her over, "not from this shire, and yet I've heard my share about the famed Crimson Lady." He glanced around the inn now, spreading his arms and showing off a line of thick, strong teeth, as he confessed, "I'd always planned to sample Giselle de Coeur's charms myself, knowin' as I do the lord who'd eased her on the path to . . . disrepute, shall we say. But I never got around to makin' the arrangements before she disappeared. And while she were in London, Lord Draven, the bastard, kept her to himself most of the time."

"Draven . . . ?"

The raspy growl of the name came from Braedan, and now Fiona did twist around to look at him, frowning at the black expression clouding his feverish eyes.

"Did you say Draven?" he demanded of the burly intruder.

"Aye, what of it?" the man slurred in response, clenching his fists and scowling threateningly at Braedan. "I may not be a high-and-mighty, but I know his lordship as well as any. I be a smithy by trade, and he places some curious orders with me, he does, for shackles and the like. I always fill 'em, just as he asks, and he rewards me with a chance at the women he knows. His name be Kendrick de Lacy, Viscount Draven, though in the *stewes* he's better known by the name he fashioned for himself—the Whoremaster of London," the smithy crowed, "which is just what he is, by spittle and piss!"

"Christ, it can't be," Braedan muttered, grimacing and rubbing his head, trying to make it stop spinning. He swayed a little before he managed to say, "Lady, I have to tell you something. It doesn't seem possible, but—"

"Back away, man—I weren't finished with 'er yet," the wild-haired giant suddenly groused, stepping between Braedan and Fiona, and directing his avid gaze back on her.

Reaching out to steady himself against the table, Braedan tried to regain his position, but his legs felt like jelly, his mind awash with seemingly a thousand disjointed thoughts and images. He clutched again at the burning ache that was his head, locking his knees to keep from tipping over. There was something he needed to tell her. Something important. About Draven . . .

"I never had a chance at the Crimson Lady," the smithy continued, speaking loudly enough for the benefit of the entire gathering, "but I still know a way to tell any who wants if this be her—aye, that I do, and I learned it from the master himself. Proof positive. Left her a little token of his esteem, he did, and it should be right here—"

As he spoke his meaty fist darted out with surprising speed, his fingers latching into the scooped neckline of Fiona's gown. In his fever-induced confusion, Braedan didn't react at first. The vague thought that it was probably useless anyway to jump to the defense of a woman as tarnished as the Crimson Lady flitted through his mind, but then his natural instincts surged to the fore and he staggered into action, drawing his sword from its sheath with a hissing sound to level it at the foul-breathed ogre who was using her so roughly.

"Unhand her. Now," Braedan muttered, squinting to keep himself and his blade steady, and hoping that the resulting expression on his face looked more menacing than woozy.

He must have done well enough, he thought, hearing the gasping sounds of awe echoing around him, even as the brutish smithy's face blanched a grayish white. But after glancing up, he realized that the gasps were only in response to the sight of his sword—a mercenary knight's fine-tooled weapon, likely worth more than a year's wages of any man in this chamber . . . and that the pale, gaping look on the smithy's face was only in reaction to the blood that was coming from the gash Fiona's dagger had sliced into the flesh of his palm.

"The bitch cut me!" the smithy echoed in disbelief, stock-still as he stared at the flow. Before Braedan's eyes, he seemed to pale further, stumbling back toward his comrades before lurching forward again, as if he would fall on Fiona. At that, Braedan blindly threw himself in his path, intent on taking the brunt of his weight.

But there was no impact. There was simply . . . nothing. Braedan blinked and shook his head, wavering on his feet where he'd come to a stop. As the black spots swirled across his vision, he realized that the giant had toppled sideways instead of forward, knocked off-balance by several from the crowd who had leapt up to intervene. Fiona had stepped back a few paces, and now Braedan managed to twist around to look at her. But the motion deprived him of any little balance he still had, and he careened dangerously.

The slow stream of images that played out then were like a dream—but it was no imaginary stone slab that rose up and slammed into him. Nay, it was hard and cold, packing a solid wall of pain into his lungs, every hint of breath removed. As if from a great distance he heard his sword clattering to the stone floor, saw through the shrieking blur of torment in his chest and head the mob of people milling about, some attempting now to restrain the smithy or scuffling with his friends, while another enormous man came waddling from the kitchens, shouting commands in an effort to lessen the uproar.

Braedan's gaze managed to find Fiona; though she still clutched the bloodied dagger, no one had approached her. Before he could think further on it, his burning lungs took over, forcing him to draw in his first, agonizing breath since crashing to the floor. His eyes squeezed shut, his face contorting with the pain of it, and when he opened them again he saw that Fiona had come to kneel beside him. She frowned and gripped his shoulder, calling his name. But he couldn't hear her. Her mouth moved, but it was empty of sound thanks to the buzzing and his own raspy, shallow breathing filling his ears.

God help him but the blackness was winning, and he knew he had to tell her something important before it overwhelmed him entirely. He had to make her stay. He couldn't let her escape after he fell senseless; not when he needed her help so badly.

He had to make her stay for Elizabeth . . .

"Lady, you must listen to me," he tried to say, though the words refused to push past the scorching needles that raked his throat. Ignoring the torture of it, he made himself swallow again.

"Don't try to speak," she cautioned.

"Nay," he said hoarsely, grasping her hand in a death grip as he struggled to lift the lead weight of his head off the floor. "You must listen, lady—the one who has Elizabeth . . . it is Kendrick de Lacy . . . Lord Draven."

"*Draven?*" Fiona said, frowning more deeply than before. "The fever has muddled your mind; Draven is the man who bought *me* those many years ago. He has nothing to do with your foster sister." He saw the lines of disbelief etched into her face as she looked away from him toward the stairway. "I'll have you brought above stairs. You will feel better after you rest."

Braedan shook his head, desperate to make her understand before his senses slid completely from his grasp. "He will bring her to shame," he muttered, digging his fingers into Fiona's sleeve so tightly he could feel the delicate fabric shredding beneath his nails. He pulled her closer—close enough to hear his impassioned whisper even as the darkness rose up, trying to drag him down into the oblivion he craved.

"You can't leave . . . promise you won't leave . . . I need your help to stop him, now more than ever—"

"What are you talking about?" she murmured, her stricken look belying the composure of her question.

"I need to tell you, lady . . . you must listen—I know he has Elizabeth, because Draven is my . . ."

Braedan's voice trailed off, his mouth refusing to form the words anymore, as Fiona suddenly started to shatter and dissolve before him, fading into the whirling, black storm that finally began to close over his head. But just before it pulled him under, he managed to add in a mumbling whisper, ". . . he is my uncle."

Chapter 4

⟨a decorative flourish⟩

Fiona wanted to curl into a corner and sleep for a week, so deep was her weariness. She tossed the water-soaked cloth back into the bowl before sinking down next to the hearth again. Sighing, she leaned back onto the warm stones, wavering a little in her battle with exhaustion, though she knew that by resting at all she risked unleashing the demons that had begun returning to haunt her. They'd become stronger these past few days, slithering out whenever she wasn't completely vigilant against them. She pinched the bridge of her nose, lifting her head to watch Braedan and trying to keep his condition and not her own fatigue at the center of her thoughts.

He slept quietly now, though his peaceful state had been hard-won; it had taken most of the past three days to bring him to this point, and then only thanks to her near-constant attention with the cooling rags and doses of herbed wine she'd managed to make him swallow. He'd been senseless through most of it, either deathly still or thrashing with fever, his body's heat searing through the garments she'd eventually stripped from him in order to cool him.

It was that action that had finally produced success— and some unexpected information as well. She'd discovered that he'd been beaten and confined recently, the raw, festering rope marks on his wrists and mottled bruises over the rest of his tautly muscled body giving evidence of a less than pleasant captivity. But it was the other partially healed injuries she'd found—the painstakingly carved gashes on his torso and arms—that had sent a chill of foreboding through her. She'd treated the cuts with her herb poultices, but the very sight of them had sent her demons into a wild frenzy again. It had taken all of her will not to flee the chamber, the inn, and Alton altogether, leaving Braedan to whatever Fate intended for him.

But in the end, she'd stayed, knowing she was powerless to reverse this path she'd been set upon, determined to see it through, now, no matter what. For those cuts had convinced her as nothing had before that this brooding mercenary knight had spoken the truth to her about his purposes and his foster sister's plight. The gashes had clearly been made with a sharp instrument of some sort, their placement chosen with an eye for producing the utmost discomfort in the victim.

Just the kind of wounds Draven would relish inflicting.

The hollow feeling that had settled in Fiona's stomach swelled, and she held her breath against it. She'd done everything in her power to keep Kendrick de Lacy, Lord

Draven, from invading her thoughts again, but the disturbing torrent of memories kept streaming back. She had tried to escape him. Tried to tell herself that when she ran far away, changed her appearance, and resumed her old name, she would finally be free of his honeyed touches, his seductive charms—his brutal obsession with her and the fear it sent spilling through her veins.

But he was still there, like the gilded snake of Scripture, tempting, beckoning, and all the more deadly for his wicked beauty.

Braedan's breath caught as he slept, his body stiffening and his head thrashing on the bolster for a moment, bringing Fiona to her feet again so that she might check on him. She pulled her stool closer to his pallet, leaning over and brushing her fingers over his brow. He was still cool.

Adjusting the blanket around him, she quickly inspected the bandaged wounds on his arms and chest, satisfied to see that they looked clean; he'd have scars, but nothing worse than the other marks his powerful body already bore from unknown battles of the past. She wasn't so certain that Braedan would appreciate her knowing what she'd learned about him in the course of tending him, but there'd been no help for it. Tipping a fresh cup of the cooled, herbed wine to his mouth, Fiona forced a few sips past his lips, watching his throat move as he swallowed. After a little while his breathing calmed once more.

It was likely naught but a bad dream that had disturbed him, then.

Returning to her position at the hearth, Fiona resumed watching him, unmoving; the gray, predawn light in the chamber cloaked him in peaceful silence, his dreams banished for the moment. But she couldn't help wondering what images those nightmares had held, connected as they undoubtedly were to Draven.

Reaching up, she brushed her hand over her own scar, the one carved above her breast in the jagged shape of a heart, closing her eyes against the remembered pain and humiliation of that night. It had been an evil act, dark and sadistic. Draven's patience with the women he selected and personally trained was legendary in the *stewes*, but that night his restraint had finally snapped, shifting to vicious retaliation. He had tied her down, then—he who had always prided himself on never needing to use force to bring any woman he wished under his complete control.

Aye, Draven was a man who'd savored his slow, deliberate seductions. Aided by his near-perfect face and form, he had always relished the game, turning the full power of his wicked charm on his chosen female prey until she lay panting and limp in his arms. Yet young as she'd been, Fiona had resisted for what she'd later learned was far longer than any other woman he'd known, unwittingly whetting his appetite for her. She had become his obsession, her introduction into carnal pleasures his only vocation.

And she'd succumbed, eventually. Given in to all that he commanded of her—even participation in the outrageous pretense that had ensured no other man but he would actually bed her. He had informed her of his decision to keep her for himself when her training was nearly complete, though she'd known that it was his perverse fascination with her and not some nobler instinct that goaded him into the proclamation. But when the time came that she should have been sent to one of his lodgings in the *stewes*, he had stayed true to his word and kept her back, installing her instead in chambers of his main residence at Chepston Hall. Then he'd applied his considerable intellect to coming up with a solution that would reconcile his uncharacteristic desire for her with his need to secure the profit he would lose by refusing to sell her to other men.

His plan had been shocking, yet brilliant as well . . . and she had hated him for it. Hated him for the degradation he inflicted by his own use of her, heaped with the vulgarity of the lie that was the Crimson Lady—hated him with a coldness that went bone deep, even as she continued to betray herself by pretending to respond to his undeniable skill and silken touches. But she'd never relinquished her heart. Nay, nor her soul either. And it was that withholding that had finally thwarted his obsessive desires and brought her, after several years in his keeping, to the night of unforgivable humiliation and pain at his hands.

Dragging in an uneven breath, Fiona forced her eyes open again and pushed away the bitter memories. None knew the secret of her past except for herself, Draven, and Will. Undoubtedly no one would accept the truth of her limited experience, discounting it, rather, as a fantastical tale, even were she foolish enough to try to defend herself with it. It was far easier for those who saw the Crimson Lady to believe her a fallen woman of the worst sort—and she'd never argued the point, for in spirit she knew they were right. She was well and fully ruined in every way that truly mattered, forever dead to gentle emotions or the ability to feel love. It was Draven's legacy to her, branded into her soul as surely as the perverse heart had been carved onto her chest.

Blinking, Fiona lifted her gaze to Braedan, sleeping peacefully on the pallet—a seeming paragon of virtue, willing to risk his life for the sake of a foster sister's honor. But what kind of man was he, really? Compared to Draven, he appeared tantamount to a saint, but she wasn't sure she truly believed the purity of his motivation in coercing her. Based on her knowledge of men and their workings, it was near impossible to accept that he would be willing to imperil himself in such a way for the simple sake of another's honor or safety. There might well be other forces that drove him in his quest, forces she hadn't been able to discern yet.

Still, that he sprang from a family known for justice and honor couldn't be denied; she'd almost fallen over in shock when, sick as he was, he'd drawn his sword in defense of her in the common room belowstairs. Never could she remember any man having put himself in harm's way for her sake. As a street waif she'd been beneath most men's notice, and then later, after her transformation into the Crimson Lady, she'd been worth even less in society's estimation.

Aye, Braedan de Cantor had surprised her with his action on her behalf. But she couldn't forget that he was also the same man who had burst into her life brandishing threats and bearing a damning connection to the one person she despised most in the world.

He'd assured her that it was an association by marriage and not by blood, and she believed it, now more than ever, for while both men were tall and well built, there were undeniable differences between them. By her figuring, Draven was nearly ten years older, his coloring and bearing darkly exotic, the beauty of his face rivaled only by the perfection of his elegant form. Braedan, however, possessed a warrior's body, powerfully muscular, and he was of fairer complexion, square-jawed and resolute, with wavy hair of rich walnut hue and startling blue eyes that seemed to pierce her defenses. Neither man made her feel the least bit comfortable, but she had to admit that even with the panicked anger Braedan had inspired in her from the start, she'd somehow sensed that she would be safe in his company.

With Draven, that had never been a consideration.

Breathing deep and exhaling on a sigh, Fiona forced herself to unclench the twisted ball of her fingers, clasped in a death grip atop her upraised knees. She flexed her hands, wincing at the tingling stiffness, while her thoughts spun round the unavoidable truth. Sooner or later she would once again need to face the man who had stolen her innocence and corrupted her beyond redemption. If she complied with Braedan's coercion, it was a foregone conclusion. She'd avoided it as long as she could—had *intended* to avoid it for the rest of her days, preferring padded, matronly obscurity to the chance of attracting Draven's notice again—but now it seemed inescapable.

The situation was going to become even more complicated, she knew, once they rejoined Will and his men in the forest. She was going to have to convince Braedan to keep quiet about their true purposes; if Will learned of their plan, he would be furious, entirely opposed to the risk she'd be undertaking by returning to the *stewes*. The fact that she'd be helping to rescue an innocent woman from the same evil web that had ensnared her eleven years ago wouldn't matter. He wouldn't understand, either, the muted call for vengeance that she was just beginning to recognize in herself—the reckless need to thwart Draven and make him pay in some way for what he'd done, now that the chance had fallen so clearly into her lap.

But her decision had been made. In those first, dark hours after Braedan was brought, feverish and incoherent, to her chamber, she'd resolved to stop fighting it—to cease looking for a means of escape. She was going to help him, whether or not he was the honest man he claimed to be. Draven's involvement had changed everything.

Fiona tilted her head back, her eyes fluttering shut at last under the force of her exhaustion. But just before she drifted off into dreams writhing with painful shadows, Braedan's image filled her mind, his gaze full of sincerity, his voice echoing with that husky, persistent entreaty that had somehow captured her attention from the first, even when she didn't know the truth of his plight or his suffering at Draven's hands.

Aye, it was a fine predicament Braedan de Cantor had mired them in, she mused, frowning as she slid deeper into restless slumber.

A mess that would require all of her skill if she was to free them of it with bodies and souls intact.

Braedan struggled to open the lead weight of his eyelids, wincing at the ache that gripped his head in the blinding light. With a groan he flung his forearm over his face, only to stiffen when he felt a thick bandage brushing his cheek. He frowned, blinking and lifting his arm again as he tried to focus on the white padding wrapped round his wrist; another pad was bound with linen strips up near his shoulder. *Blood of saints, what was this . . . ?*

Biting back another groan, he pushed himself to a

half-sitting position and squinted down at his torso, looking at the numerous dressings covering the cuts his uncle had ordered dealt to him during his days of captivity and torture at Chepston Hall. But how had they been tended to without his knowing? He scowled. What had happened to his shirt and his—

Suddenly, memory slid back into place and he sat up straighter, ignoring the thousand jabbing pains that lanced through his body with the movement. The Crimson Lady. Ah, yes. He'd found her . . . brought her back to Alton with him . . . they'd been in the common room of the inn, where she'd revealed herself and asked for information about her thieving partners. And then . . .

"You're awake, I see."

Bringing his hand to his eyes, Braedan rubbed, trying to clear the blurriness enough to see Fiona where she stood in the doorway. She swept into the chamber without another word, carrying a tray on which balanced a pitcher, a dark-crusted loaf of bread, and a bowl of something warm enough to send curls of steam twisting above it.

"How long have I been here?" he said, wincing at the gravelly, unused quality of his voice.

"Nearly four days."

She stopped near the bed and set the tray on the little table next to it before turning back to him and bending to examine the wounds on his chest and arms in a matter-of-fact way. Of a sudden Braedan was acutely aware that he was sitting half-clothed in the presence of a woman he hardly knew; he shifted in embarrassment, and then as abruptly stiffened. *Christ's Blood.* It wasn't just his tunic and shirt that had been removed. *All* of his garments were gone. Every bit of clothing.

Fiona didn't seem to notice his discomfiture, continuing to inspect his bandages and feeling his brow until he squirmed again, pulling away from her touch to tuck the bedcovers more firmly around his hips. She straightened and backed up a step at his show of modesty, surprise and perhaps a bit of annoyance showing in her expression. But then she just shook her head and made a clicking noise, moving instead to the task of readying the food she'd brought in for him.

Relieved to have proved the victor in this minor clash of wills, at least, Braedan leaned back on the bolster, not entirely feigning his fatigue, all the while trying to pretend it didn't matter to him that Fiona had seen him naked . . . that she'd likely been the one who'd stripped his clothing from him. It *shouldn't* have bothered him, he knew; she was a courtesan, after all—a woman of vast experience who had surely seen hundreds, if not thousands, of men completely undressed.

But not you, a voice inside of him chided—not until now, anyway, when he hadn't even been awake to say aye or nay against it.

"You must be hungry," Fiona murmured. "If you'll sit up a bit more, I'll help you with this pottage."

"Nay."

His response was too quick and far too vehement, he knew, but he covered his awkwardness by adding in a mumble, "I'll eat later. Just leave it here, and I'll get to it eventually."

"Nonsense," she answered, plunking herself down onto the stool at his bedside.

Cursing himself for the heat he felt spreading up his neck, Braedan decided that he had better reassert his masculine independence without delay. He shifted his gaze to her, intending to use the force of his glare to intimidate her into obeying his request. To his dismay, he saw thinly veiled amusement lighting her eyes and quirking her sensuous lips.

She raised her brow. "Stew should be eaten warm, you know. Besides, you need to rebuild your strength and quickly if we are to meet with Will as I've arranged for tomorrow noon."

"You found him?" Braedan sat up straight again in his surprise, wincing both at his own sudden movement and the spoonful she thrust at his mouth.

"Aye. I was able to send word to him, and he responded in kind," she answered, making him take the bite. "It will be an hour's journey to reach him."

Instinctively chewing and swallowing the richly seasoned pottage, Braedan glowered and yanked the bowl none too gently from her with a grumbled comment about being well capable of feeding himself.

That half smile flirted over her lips again, but she leaned back to watch him, seeming content as long as he continued to eat on his own. They settled into a companionable silence, the only sounds that of his spoon scraping the bowl and the birds chirping in the breezes outside the shutter. After a bit, she murmured something about tasks to accomplish and got up again to begin tidying the chamber, putting some odd-looking pots and bundles of dried herbs back into a leather purse and humming a bit as she poured water into a basin to wipe down a mortar and pestle.

Between bites Braedan watched her, noting that she seemed calmer—even more comfortable, somehow, in his presence—than he'd seen since that night he'd found her. He couldn't help wondering what had brought

about that change in her demeanor. Was she biding her
time, confident in some plot she'd hatched against him
to escape? Logic denied it. The fact that he was resting
here and not being held under guard gave him reason to
believe that she hadn't called in the law on him. Nay,
he'd wager his sword that she'd even tended to him in
his illness herself, using in the process some of those
herbs that she was stowing away now. Vaguely, he remembered the sensation of swallowing some bitter liquid in the midst of his fever; it was she who was
responsible, he was sure of it.

*And that meant he owed her a debt of gratitude, not
only for sheltering him but for helping to heal him as well.*

The thought caught him for a moment, the idea of it
as discomfiting as his current lack of clothing. He'd always believed women of her ilk to be self-absorbed creatures, dedicated to their own concerns above all else.
The enigma of her increased with every hour he spent at
her side, and he wasn't so sure that he liked the way she
kept unbalancing his neatly ordered perceptions.

Setting his empty bowl down, Braedan turned his full
attention back to her. She was in the process of sweeping
out the hearth now, and he noticed that she wore a kirtle
of a far plainer weave and design than the crimson garment she'd donned for her first appearance at the inn.
But like that magnificent gown, this one was also fitted
to her shape in a way that her former dark and matronly
garments never had.

It was clear that whether she wore sackcloth or silk,
the true Fiona was an exceptional beauty, with a contrast of angelic face and tempting curves that would call
any man still capable of breathing to sin. In fact the sight

of her now, bending and twisting as she went about her tasks, not to mention the alluring, delicate scent of her that wafted through the air as she moved by, set his pulse to racing and released an unexpected flood of heat through his body, sweeping in a direct path to his groin and hardening him uncomfortably.

Damn.

It wasn't like him to be so affected by a woman. Not he, the blistering sword arm of the king, used to battling for his sovereign's right in all manner of foreign climes, surrounded by countless exotic females who offered themselves freely for his taking. Shamed, he shifted in an attempt to prevent Fiona from seeing the painfully hard evidence of his lustful reaction to her, forcing himself to look away toward the window shutter. He tried to concentrate on discerning the time of day by the amount of light outside—anything to keep his mind from the heated thoughts her nearness inspired.

He'd almost brought himself under control when she apparently finished what she was doing and sat on the stool next to him. The tantalizing whisper of her scent gripped him again, and he swallowed hard, knowing that he couldn't avoid looking at her forever. He decided that a conversation about a necessary but uncomfortable topic might do much toward helping him suppress his disruptive imaginings.

"What have you done with my clothing?"

He willed his gaze to be steady on her as he asked the question, pleased that he managed to make his voice obey in kind.

"They are down below, in the kitchen chambers." That hint of humor colored her tone again as she continued, "I thought it best to have them cleaned while you were unable to make use of them."

"Aye, well I have use of them now." Braedan resisted the urge to look away from her again, despising the renewed warmth in his face. "*Right* now as a matter of fact."

"I'll fetch them in a moment." She sat forward a bit and fiddled with something beneath the edge of the fitted smock sleeve at her wrist. "We need to discuss a few particulars about tomorrow first."

"Is it that important, that we cannot converse about it after I'm fully clothed?"

"If you value your continued safety and the eventual deliverance of your foster sister, aye."

He debated arguing further, then thought better of it. If she deemed this so important, so be it; he'd just have to overlook his less than dignified state of dress. Without saying anything he nodded his agreement.

She'd stopped playing with her sleeve, he noticed, and now she met his gaze squarely, her expression serious; he tried not to allow himself to dwell on the way the tawny hue of her eyes seemed lit with beautiful, dancing flecks of light. Clearing his throat, he murmured, "Go on, then."

"The first matter we must needs discuss concerns my name. Those who know me through my past activities think of me only as Giselle de Coeur."

"Even the outlaws?"

"Aye. Except for my childhood and the years that I lived in Hampshire, it has been my identity."

"But why did you not return to your true name as soon as you left Draven?"

"It is complicated," she answered, glancing away.

Her expression was tight and her eyes troubled. "Perhaps I still dressed in crimson and answered to that name even after leaving Draven because it had been so long since I had known anything else—it was a part of me I could not separate at first. The woman known as Giselle de Coeur also helped the outlaw group in their robberies. I only worked with them for a year, but they were able to use my notoriety to entice male travelers into stopping at the roadside. By the time word spread about the traps being laid on thoroughfares near Alton, baited with the Crimson Lady, I had already left for Hampshire."

"I see."

"I hope so. Because you must remember that calling me Fiona in front of anyone else could be dangerous and expose us to suspicion the likes of which you saw in the common room when we first arrived."

He nodded. "In future I will make the correction—though it will be a bit peculiar, knowing myself to be the only person aware of your true name."

She paused. "Actually you're not the only one. There is one other."

"Who?"

"Will Singleton," she admitted, "though he, too, calls me Giselle for the same reasons that you must." She flushed a bit then, and Braedan got the distinct feeling that there was a good deal more to her connection to this leader of her former band of thieves than she was letting on.

"And my uncle?" he asked, refusing to betray the stab of animosity that had shot through him at the thought of Will's apparent intimacy with her. "You spent a good deal of time with him. Does he not know as well?"

"He didn't care to learn it. He chose the name Giselle de Coeur for me on my first day with him. It is why I decided to resume my old identity as Fiona Byrne when I set up shop as an embroidress, to keep him from finding me so easily."

"And yet I found you simply enough."

"You were willing to go to some trouble, a long journey, and much coin. For sake of his pride, I knew that Draven would never venture that far or spend so much to find me. It would be beneath him. It was the same when I lived as an outlaw; I knew he wouldn't come looking for me, though I was working the thoroughfares but a few hours from London. However, that might change if we actually go back into the *stewes*—"

She broke off, glancing down and biting at her bottom lip; Braedan caught a glimpse of her face and was taken aback by what he saw there, a look telling him that this woman who had lived her life on the fringes of some of the most violent segments of society was for some reason feeling hesitant . . . or perhaps even fearful. She seemed stricken, and lost, and—

Christ she looked like she needed nothing more than to curl against his chest and be told that he would keep her safe from all the wickedness in the world.

The realization pounded through him; when she met his gaze after a long moment, her eyes were filled with the shadows of her need, twisting and blending in a disruptive swirl. But before he could react she spoke again, her words only adding to his dismay.

"Draven's attempts to take me back were unsuccessful, in part because he would not allow himself to appear weak among his cohorts by instigating an open search for me. But since I will likely be traveling back into his area of the *stewes* to gain information about your foster sister, it is only fair to tell you that if he realizes I have returned, he will almost certainly go to great lengths to . . . reacquire me."

"Why?" Braedan fairly growled, shaken by the urge that had filled him, the fierce desire to protect her from anything that might cause her hurt. With ruthless force he squashed the emotion, reminding himself that he wasn't worthy to safeguard anyone—and that she was naught but a common woman and a thief . . . a tool in his quest for justice, nothing more. His voice was flat, his choice of words cruel, he knew, when he added, "My uncle has more wealth than a desert prince and cannot possibly covet the amount of coin your notable talents would provide, should you resume servicing men under his direction."

She flinched almost imperceptibly. But, thank the saints, the vulnerable look in her eyes slipped away, leaving in its wake raw pain, followed swiftly by something mocking and cold. After a long pause she answered, "You're quite correct. It is not the coin that would prompt him, although he has always relished his wealth and sought to increase it, I can assure you. It is a far more personal reason, pertaining, as I have said, to his pride."

"He has more than enough of that to spare, I'll grant you," Braedan groused, struggling to tamp down the last embers of the burning sensation in his gut. "What would be his reason, then, pray tell?"

"I escaped Lord Draven under cover of darkness those years ago," Fiona answered quietly, "and your uncle is not a man used to losing his possessions against his will."

She had managed to shutter her feelings from him by then, favoring a cool expression of composure that was eerily reminiscent of the look she'd worn when she'd revealed herself to everyone as the Crimson Lady. But as she'd spoken, he noticed that she'd pulled from her sleeve whatever it was she'd been toying with on and off during their conversation; Braedan only just kept himself from jerking back on the pallet when he saw that it was the dagger she'd used against him in her shop, then later on the burly man belowstairs. She kept rolling the blade along her fingers, the palm's-length edge curving wickedly and glinting in the streaks of sun from the window as she moved it.

She noticed his reaction after a moment and gave a bitter laugh, flipping the dagger up and sliding it with effortless perfection back into the leather case he could just see now, strapped beneath her smock sleeve. "My apologies. I rarely unsheathe this without a purpose, but occasionally, when I am alone and cursed with some memory of Draven, it happens."

"It is of no matter," he mumbled, "it was just unexpected."

She gave that cold smile again. "That was one of the reasons Draven commanded my mastery of the skill—for its ability to shock those for whom he ordered me to display it. It amused him, you see." Nodding, she indicated the dressings across his chest and arms, her words biting at him this time as she said pointedly, "Though I suppose I needn't tell you about your uncle's perverse entertainments. It seems that you've experienced some of his talent in that area yourself, recently."

"These weren't delivered by his hand." Braedan glanced down at his bandaged wounds, clenching his jaw at the painful memory of their infliction. "He set one of his lackwit men to the task, though he remained in the chamber as witness."

"How long were you in his control?"

Braedan was caught for a moment by the dispassionate tone of her voice, as if it was a foregone conclusion that Draven kept whomever he wished in his control, for however long he liked.

"A little more than a fortnight," he answered after a pause. "I was kept in the lowermost chamber at Chepston—not the most pleasant of places to take a sojourn—as I'm sure you know, if you ever had the misfortune to see it," he added, hoping to shift the conversation away from himself and back to her again.

"Only once," she breathed, her face stiff and her eyes unmistakably haunted behind their glittering hardness. "It was enough."

Before he could question her further on it or anything else, she stood, the movement so quick that she had to catch the tray to keep it from toppling off the table with the cup of wine and loaf of bread. After steadying it, she grasped his empty pottage bowl and spoon, murmuring something about needing to retrieve his clothing as she turned away, walking halfway to the door before he could muster the presence of mind to summon her back.

"Wait!"

She stilled with her fingers on the latchstring.

"I need to ask you something, lady," he said, his voice gruff.

"What is it?" she murmured, still not facing him.

"When I fell ill, you could have fled and been rid of my claims on you—yet you stayed and helped to heal me with your powders and herbs. I want to know why."

She twisted a bit, back toward him—just enough to glance over her shoulder at him. The haunted look was there, still, in the depths of her eyes, though it warred now with a steely resolve that might have knocked him back onto his bolster was he not already resting against it.

"I have my reasons, Braedan de Cantor," she said softly, "though I will not be sharing them with you or anyone else. Just know this: You are not alone in wanting your measure of justice against Draven. Our path in seeking that end may not be the one I had intended for myself, and yet here it is—and here I am, ready to take up my part in it. It is all you need to know."

Speechless, Braedan watched her swing back toward the door, lifting the latchstring and pushing the panel open.

"I will be back with your clothing in a short time," she murmured before she walked out the door. When the wooden slab cracked shut behind her, he realized that her evasive answer had only succeeded in leaving him feeling more stunned and unsettled than ever.

He leaned his head back against the wall, closing his eyes and releasing a sigh of pent-up frustration. His conscience gnawed at him; he'd lashed out at her in an effort to keep her at arm's length where she would be less of a danger to his balance and his unruly emotions. The memory of the way he'd talked to her stung him, even though he knew there had been no other choice. She'd gotten too close with her softness, her gentle need—and the feral intensity of his response to her had been too great. It was unexpected, the way she'd made him feel, and so he'd deliberately hurt her, forcing her retreat. It had worked perfectly; she had left him as soon as it was feasible, a clear indication that he'd achieved his goal.

Sighing again, Braedan threw his bandaged arm over his eyes and sank farther into the stuffed ticking of the pallet, one thought nagging relentlessly at the back of his mind . . . forcing him to question why, then, he felt more out of control than ever where the maddening and all too enticing Crimson Lady was concerned.

Chapter 5

◡◡◡

It was an unusually hot sun for springtime, Fiona thought as her mount followed the narrow path deeper into Wulmere Forest. The warmth beat down through branches gently furred with the lace of newly unfurled leaves, creating a patchwork of gold and green all around. She heard the soft clumping sound of Braedan's steed just behind her, picking his way over mossy ground and winter-thawed bracken, and she closed her eyes, trying to relax. The rocking, easy sway of her mare lulled her; breathing deep of the scented new growth and moist dirt, she felt the sun soak into her hair and cloak to chase the chill of morn away.

After a little while she opened her eyes again with a sigh, reluctant to face reality. She'd needed that moment of blissful reverie to steel herself for what was to come this day—both in the next few moments, then later on, once they reached Will's encampment. It would be soon, if Will's missive held true. Another quarter hour's travel should bring them very near the spot he'd chosen as their meeting place.

And that meant she could postpone no longer, even though what she was about to tell Braedan irked her in the mere thinking of it, no less the actual doing—especially after the way he'd spoken to her yestermorn. The sudden, dark slant of his mood then had taken her by surprise, his cutting remarks about her value for Draven in the *stewes* seeming designed purposefully to wound. And she had been hurt; she couldn't pretend otherwise. She'd spent years trying to distance herself from the shameful feelings she'd endured as the Crimson Lady, but it was clear that Braedan de Cantor wasn't going to allow her to forget that that was all she was in his eyes. An infamous thief and whore.

But one he needed desperately if he was to find his beloved Elizabeth.

Mollifying herself with that thought, Fiona pursed her lips and prepared to give Braedan his final instructions. He wasn't going to like what she had to say any more than she did, but he would have to accept it if he wanted his search for his foster sister to go forward without delay.

A small clearing opened ahead. Reining in her mare as they entered the glen, Fiona twisted in her saddle, and murmured, "We must stop. There is one thing else I need to tell you if we are to ensure that you'll be accepted by Will and his men."

Braedan raised his brow, not commenting, though he halted his steed near hers. At her nodded gesture, they dismounted and left their horses to graze while they walked to a spot a little ways off, out of the direct slant of sun. She stopped and turned to face him, feeling a little shock as she did. He had been either ill or astride a horse for so much of their time together that she was startled anew by his height and powerful build. He stood patiently with his arms crossed over his chest; in general, she'd noticed that he carried himself like a man used to being in charge, and she found that it annoyed her beyond measure.

But then he spoke, and her irritation pitched infinitely higher.

"So, what is it, then? What did you neglect to tell me that is so necessary to being welcomed by your criminal friends?"

Gritting her teeth, Fiona reminded herself to maintain composure, not for his sake, but for her own. He'd not be able to gloat later over any loss of control on her part. "I did not *neglect* to tell you—I simply hadn't settled on a feasible solution to this dilemma until recently."

"Very well then," he said, sounding exasperated. "Get on with telling me so that we may proceed. Too much time has been wasted on my illness already."

"By the saints, but your manners could use some polish," Fiona couldn't stop herself from snapping. "If you hope to survive the next few weeks, you should make an effort to sweeten your tongue. And have a care, too, in how you choose to describe Will and his men. They do not consider themselves criminals; most came to the outlaw's life through means as unjust as your own seem to be, and you would be wise to remember it."

Dead silence greeted her. When Braedan at last deigned to speak, it was with a tight jaw and scowling expression. "As you wish."

For a moment Fiona thought that he might accept her

rebuke without further comment. But then he straightened before bending into an elaborate bow, adding, "And now I beg of you, my lady, to proceed with my instruction. I humbly await the knowledge that you have offered to share with me, your lowly and quite unworthy servant."

"You overdo your niceties now, sir," she muttered, fixing him with a glare, "but I suppose it is better than your other boorish behavior."

"I am relieved that you think so," he rejoined, and she saw that his blue eyes glimmered with unmistakable humor.

Of a sudden her own lips quirked with the realization of how ridiculous their squabbling was, and though she made an effort not to break her stern gaze on him, in the end she had to look away to avoid smiling. He was incorrigible, she thought, biting the inside of her cheek—an overbearing oaf one moment, then worse than a mischievous boy the next.

"Are you going to tell me, then, what it is you deem necessary for me to know before meeting with Will?"

Braedan's question pulled her attention back to him, and any remaining cheerfulness vanished. She swallowed, readying herself for what was to come. "Aye, I'll tell you. It concerns a pretense we must enact in order for him to accept my traveling back here with you. Will, of all people, knows how much I wished to leave Alton and our thieving for a life of honest trade. It is imperative that I have good reason for returning to the outlaws' fold again."

"And what will that be?"

"My recent marriage to you."

"Your *what*?"

Braedan's reaction was no worse than she'd expected. He was staring at her now as if she'd sprouted serpents for hair and a forked tongue besides. *And why wouldn't he?* a harsh voice whispered from deep inside. *You aren't the kind of woman a man like Braedan de Cantor would ever consider as a wife. Not in a thousand lifetimes. A union with you would only shame him and blacken his family's name.*

Despising the heat that filled her cheeks at that undeniable truth, Fiona tipped her chin up and gazed at him with her best affectation of haughty poise. "Of course it will not be a marriage in reality, but rather an act we must play."

"Whether in play or in earnest, it is profane to mock a sacrament so."

"If it was in *earnest*, it would be no mockery," she couldn't help retorting, biting back the hurt that swelled in her. "And yet since a true marriage between us is unthinkable, a sham it must be. Either that, or you risk Will's suspicion and hence his rejection of our request to rejoin his men and share in their plunder. And then you will have no means of acquiring the coin you need to undertake your search for Elizabeth."

Braedan was mute for the second time that day, only now she sensed that his silence stemmed from discomfort rather than anger—and she realized, suddenly, that she far preferred the anger.

"It is the only solution I can conceive for appeasing Will's certain wariness about my return," she muttered, desperate to remain impassive in the face of his rejection. "If you know of another that will work, pray offer it up and save us both from the prospect of having to enact a feigned union."

She glanced away, the backs of her eyes burning. Why Braedan's contempt should affect her so was mystifying; she'd weathered far worse disparagement in the past without pause, yet this rebuff hurt in a way that went deeper than she'd thought possible. It was foolish, she knew—even childish—to maintain sensitivities that were more suited to an innocent maid, but she couldn't stop herself from feeling wounded nonetheless.

"Could we not simply pretend to be lovers rather than a wedded pair?" Braedan asked at last, frowning as he jabbed his hand through his hair.

"Nay," she answered, jaw tight. "Will would know it is a falsehood."

"And how could he possibly discern the difference between that deceit and the lie of a marriage between us?"

"Because he knows me as well as anyone can—and he is well aware that I would never take a lover. Ever."

"By the Rood, woman, you sold yourself nightly in the *stewes*," Braedan scoffed, disbelief apparent in every tense inch of his muscular frame. "And as for Will Singleton—the man seems to know more about you than God Himself. Were you not *his* lover during the time you thieved with him?" Without giving her a chance to answer, he swung away, running both hands through his hair again in exasperation. "God's holy blood, your logic escapes me, and I cannot—"

His remaining words were cut off by a sudden shout and crashing sound in the wood around them, the clamor followed almost immediately by the blur of four male forms hurtling into the clearing directly toward him with their weapons drawn. Stunned, Fiona pulled out her dagger and scrambled for a stick to use as well in defense, watching as Braedan stiffened and twisted around to face them, managing only at the last moment to clear his sword from its sheath as the two closest assailants set on him with howling battle cries.

The clang of blade on blade filled the clearing, punctuated by an occasional growling shout or grunt. Fighting furiously, Braedan disabled one of the first two men with a slice to the leg and the other with a blow to the head, even as the remaining two intruders slipped past him in an attempt to attack from behind. The chaotic struggle continued, with Braedan dodging and lunging, slashing and swinging—handling his blade with such skill that even Fiona, who had seen more than her share of vicious swordplay both in the *stewes* and during her years of banditry, was left breathless watching him.

Braedan welcomed the surge of dark battle instinct rising up in him, relishing the way it masked his still-diminished strength, helping him to maintain complete focus on his prey; he heard nothing but the pounding of his blood, saw nothing but the nameless enemies at the end of his sword, weighing their skills in an effort to defeat them more efficiently. In minutes the third man was down; a moment later the fourth found himself flat on his back with the point of Braedan's blade pressed to his throat.

Concentrating on pulling back and letting his awareness expand again to include the rest of the clearing—the other bandits who lay senseless or wounded, as well as Fiona—Braedan held very still, but after a rush of that magnitude, it was difficult to make his mind obey. His breath rasped harsh in his throat, and he shook his head, blinking the sweat from his eyes.

"Do you yield?" he growled softly to his attacker.

"Aye," the man grunted, as he struggled to get from beneath the deadly blade.

It was a futile effort; Braedan kept the point fixed, intending to question him first before granting him freedom. But when a renewed crackling and swish of branches erupted from the clearing's edge, he had no choice other than to straighten and face the new danger, allowing his captive to slip away.

"Well done, de Cantor," the stranger who stepped from the forest called out. "You handled yourself far better than Giselle's message led me to believe you would."

Fiona made a soft sound of reproach, dropping the stick she held and looking askance at the man. "Saints, Will, what were you thinking to arrange such a welcome?"

He shrugged. "I needed to know what he was capable of, and your message gave me no information on the matter."

"And why would I discuss Braedan's fighting skills in my message? I was only trying to find out where you were and arrange a meeting." She shook her head, her expression stern as she slid her dagger back into its sheath beneath her sleeve. "You could have learned what you wished had you but waited to see us. Just look at his sword," she said, nodding briefly toward Braedan, who'd brought the tip of his blade to rest against the ground as he watched their bickering with cool interest. "No man owns a sword as fine as that," she continued, not seeming to notice his wry expression as her gaze slipped back to Will, "without knowing how to use it."

"Possession and mastery are two very different things," Will argued, also seeming to ignore the fact that

Braedan was standing right in front of him. "Havin' the coin to purchase it, I can see, but where would a de Cantor have learned to use—"

"My ability with a sword is directly related to my wish to survive," Braedan broke in, forcing them to look at him and acknowledge his presence there. "I was a knight for my lord the king," he added in a flat voice, keeping his gaze steady on them, "and such skills were necessary in our battles against the Saracens."

A charged silence settled over the clearing. Fiona seemed as though she might say something to him then, but she was distracted from it by Will, who chose that moment to cross the remaining distance between them and take her hand, smiling as he said, "Ah, well, enough of that for now. Come, love, and let me see you. It has been three years too long since last I looked on you."

Braedan jammed his sword back into its sheath, then, watched them as they embraced and exchanged murmured words; oddly enough witnessing their reunion sent an answering twist of something unpleasant in his belly. It was of no matter, really, he told himself. Fiona's obvious pleasure at seeing her former lover had nothing to do with his sudden desire to throttle the man where he stood. It was simply the result of his annoyance at the ruse that had been played, compounded by frustration at how drained he felt after his illness. That was all.

In truth, for a moment he'd been forced to entertain the possibility of defeat at the hands of his four attackers—the kind of unfavorable outcome he'd managed to avoid for most of the past decade by endlessly honing his sword skills. Aye, Will Singleton should be thanking his stars for his unusual lack of stamina, Braedan decided, for that was all that was keeping the knave safe from the beating he so richly deserved for instigating this ridiculous test.

He sized up the object of his antagonism, noting that Will had moved away from Fiona now and was taking stock of him as well. The outlaw leader stood for a moment, his arms crossed and his weight cocked back on one leg. His flame-colored hair glowed in the sun like a fiery halo, setting off the half grin he flashed at Braedan.

Braedan scowled in return.

"Ah, let it go, man," Will said, uncrossing his arms to lift one hand and rub the back of his neck. "It was nothing personal, just a bit of a trial, is all. I confess I didn't hold out much hope for a lad whose family fed him from infancy on the flaccid teat of the king's justice. But I'm not too proud to admit that I was perhaps too quick in my judgment. We might find some use for an arm like yours after all."

"How reassuring. I'm relieved to have proved myself to your satisfaction."

"You did well enough."

Though he wore the same half smile, the aura of challenge and distrust emanating from Will was almost palpable; Braedan returned the frosty look, raising his brow to meet the man's hostile gaze.

"I do, however, have one question that needs answerin' before I'll be free to lead you back to our settlement and introduce you to the others," Will said.

"And what might that be?"

"Just this," he continued quietly, his voice all the more menacing for its facade of calm. "Because more than anything, I want to know how in hell you managed to get my sister to come back to Alton with you."

Chapter 6

❦❦❦

"**Y**our *sister*?" Braedan swung his gaze to Fiona, but she looked no less exasperated and off-balance than he felt.

"Pardon us for a moment's talk in private, would you, Will?" Fiona murmured, as she swept past him to take Braedan's arm and lead him, bewildered enough so that he didn't fight her on it, to a spot out of Will's hearing.

"Just keep calm," she said, holding up her hand in an attempt to stop him, he supposed, from bellowing the slew of questions that were raging through his mind at that moment.

"You're Will Singleton's *sister*?" he finally choked out.

"Aye, though we do not share the same father."

"Then why in God's name did you lead me to believe he was your lover?"

"I never led you to believe anything," Fiona said

coolly. "You decided what you wished about the nature of my relationship with him all on your own."

That set Braedan back on his heels for a moment. Even through the ever-increasing annoyances this day was presenting, he couldn't really deny that truth. Fiona had never made comment on anything about Will, other than that he was her thieving partner and that he knew her better than anyone. He'd supplied the assumption about the whys of it all.

But she'd never disabused him of his erroneous beliefs either.

"You could have corrected me when I spoke of him being your lover a few moments ago."

"I never had the chance."

"Christ, woman." Braedan shook his head and released his breath in a rush, glancing over to Will, who kept looking over at them suspiciously even as he checked on his wounded men. Meeting Fiona's gaze again, Braedan tried to reconcile all that he'd learned just now with what he'd thought. As usual, she seemed to have a knack for disrupting his ordered views of the world—and his perceptions of her in particular.

"All right, then, let me be sure that I am clear on all of this," he murmured. "Will Singleton is actually your brother. We must play a wedded pair in order for him to believe your reasons for being here, but we cannot tell him about our plans to search for Elizabeth. Once we undertake that search and return to London, my uncle will most likely try to bring you back into his control." He clenched his jaw, not happy about how thickly this all was piling up on him. "Is there anything else that I should know before we get on with this, then?"

"Nay." Her face was smooth—more beautiful than

ever in this lush, sun-kissed glade, and when she lifted her gaze to him, he felt a twist in his heart at the sincerity he saw there. "I am truly sorry for the surprises and deceptions, Braedan, but there is no help for them. Above all you must keep silent about our plans for returning to the *stewes*. Will is very protective of me and would call a halt to everything if he found out it was our intent."

"I have difficulty believing in the protectiveness of a brother who allows his sister to thieve with him," he rejoined tightly, "not to mention what he was doing . . . or not doing, as it may be, during the years you were under Draven's control."

A beat of silence passed, and Braedan felt the tension winding through her. Her expression hardened, and it sent a welcome fist of pain into his belly, banishing, for the moment, the confusion of the more tender feelings that had been gripping him.

"You don't know the truth of the matter," she said finally. "Until you do, it would be best for you simply to accept what I say without constant argument."

"Is that so?" he challenged. His tolerance this day had already been far overreached, and he found himself unwilling to back down, even though he knew it was foolish to pursue this destructive path further. "And tell me, just how long was it that you plied your skills for Draven? Two years—perhaps three?"

Fiona met his gaze head-on, and he was almost relieved to see the glittering wall of anger beneath the surface of those beautiful eyes, pushing him away. "I was with Draven for almost seven years."

"I see. Quite long enough, then, for someone to have

intervened—aye, even a brother perhaps," Braedan clipped, "if he had been so inclined."

"I'll say again—you know nothing of this. In fact it was only because of Will that I—"

"Because of Will that you what, love?" her brother said, coming up beside them. Braedan favored the man with a scowl, as angry at himself for having failed to notice his approach as he was with Will's supremely aggravating presence.

Looking flustered, Fiona turned to her brother, somehow pulling an affectionate smile from the depths of the animosity she'd been directing at Braedan. "I was just telling Braedan it was because of you that I encouraged him to consider the area near Alton as the place to settle."

"*You* were the one who prompted this return?"

"I was," she lied, though as with each falsehood Braedan had heard her utter before, the words fell so trippingly, he'd have believed her to his last breath had he not known better.

"But since certain members of his family still reside nearby," she continued, "he was hesitant to come back and take up the thieving life he has been forced to embark upon since being named an outlaw."

"Aye—and *that* is a story I look forward to hearin' later, you can wager," Will said with a grunt. "A de Cantor on the other side of the law . . . God's blood, I never thought I'd see the day."

The familiar tightness clenched in Braedan's gut at the words, but before he could answer, Fiona broke in again. "Be that as it may, I managed to convince Braedan to take up this locale by reminding him that knowing one's territory well is far easier than having to learn the lay of new lands. I also promised he'd receive a warm welcome from you"—she gave her brother a slightly wounded look—"though I have to say that you're making me seem less than trustworthy in that respect thus far. In truth, you've been less than pleasant, Will."

"Not without reason," her brother answered, touching her cheek before letting his hand drop to his side and shifting his unyielding stare to Braedan. "I still haven't gotten an answer to my earlier question about why the two of you are travelin' together. Your situation is one thing, de Cantor, but my sister givin' up the trade she worked so hard to establish in Hampshire is quite another." He glanced to Fiona again. "No mention was made in your message, love, and I'll know the full of it before I'll be cozyin' up to anyone or bringin' either of you a step out of this glen."

"There is no great mystery to it, man," Braedan grated, determined to erase that superior look from Will's face, even if it meant sinking up to his neck in the lie Fiona had concocted for them. "Your sister came to Alton with me because it is customary for a wife to follow her husband."

"*What?*" Will choked out, his attention snapping to Braedan again.

Braedan felt a flare of satisfaction at Will's shocked response, but he tried not to let it show. Fiona's brother wore the same gaping look he imagined he'd sported himself moments ago when he'd learned that they were siblings, and he relished it. Settling more fully into enacting his ruse with Fiona, he reached out and swung his arm over her shoulders to tug her gently to him. She fit well against him, he noticed, realizing too late that his action was igniting a slow-burning, pleasurable reaction to her warmth and her closeness.

"Aye, your sister and I are married. We've been a happy pair for . . . oh, it has been a goodly time, hasn't it, dearest?" he murmured as he looked at Fiona.

"I—I, yes—a goodly time," she stuttered. She held herself stiff against him, offering up a feeble attempt at the kind of expression a contented wife might wear.

Another flare of something dangerous swelled in Braedan, and he stoked the embers of it, deciding that if he was going to have to play the role of loving husband, Fiona needed to warm to her part in a more credible way as well. Rubbing his hand up and down her shoulder, he tipped his chin down and pressed a kiss to the silken top of her head before drawing her more fully against him.

It was Will's turn to scowl at them now. "I—I had no idea," he mumbled, his expression shifting from that dark, unsettled look to one of great perplexity. He looked at Fiona. "In truth I am stunned, lass . . . I never thought that you would marry . . . I mean after all that happened and everything that you—"

"Yes, well, people do change, Will," she broke in breathlessly, her voice sounding high and strained. She ended her comment with a forced little laugh, finally pulling herself completely out of Braedan's embrace on the pretext of brushing a leaf from Will's coppery hair, murmuring, "I hope that you'll be happy for us."

"Aye, brother," Braedan said blandly, reaching for Fiona's hand and tugging her back against him. "We pray you'll be happy for us—and that you'll welcome us into your family of outlaws."

Fiona continued to try to extricate herself from his

embrace, but Braedan held her close. Once she sensed the futility of it, she began to shift and fiddle with her skirt and her hair, her hands in a state of constant movement. It was clear as the sunrise that she yearned to distance herself from the unfamiliar intimacy of his touch, and though it surprised him that a woman of her experience would balk at such closeness, he wasn't about to let her escape so easily.

When Will remained silent, Braedan went on, "I have no doubt that your sister will recall the practices you perfected those years ago for lightening travelers' purses—and in truth I know some of what may prove useful toward such endeavors . . . but I am a de Cantor, after all," he added, his tone echoing with the faintest note of sarcasm, "bred to uphold justice and right, and I will most surely need the kind of aid and instruction only you can provide if I am to master the skills necessary to be of service to your company of men."

"And women," Fiona muttered, clearly still contending with her desire to yank free of his embrace.

At her interjection, Braedan lifted one of her hands to his lips and murmured, "Aye, my darling—and women," before pressing a tender kiss to the delicate skin of her wrist. Her involuntary gasp disappeared under the words he uttered next.

"So what say you, then, Singleton? For your lovely sister's sake, will you accept me or not?"

Will was still staring at them with a look that was half-stupefied shock and half-scowling anger. With apparent effort he brought himself under some sort of control, enough at least to mutter, "I suppose the answer must needs be yes, de Cantor, if 'tis true that my sister has chosen you as her own."

"Aye, it is—in fact it was your sister herself who de-cided that we should become man and wife," Braedan said wickedly, cupping Fiona's cheek with his palm and pulling her head to him so that she had to either rest against his shoulder or risk ruining their deception by jerking away from him.

She chose to comply with their ruse.

Will spent one last moment looking from Braedan's face to Fiona's and back again before murmuring, "All right, then. I suppose I must welcome you to the family, man." He held out his hand to Braedan, who was forced to release Fiona at last in order to grip it and acknowl-edge the acceptance. Right afterward, Will stepped up to kiss her cheek, murmuring his wish for her happy future before he turned away, still clearly troubled, to gather his men and prepare to lead them all from the clearing to the outlaw's encampment.

Braedan glanced at Fiona, who'd remained unmoving since Will's utterance of congratulations on their false marriage. The high color in her cheeks remained and her hands were laced tightly in front of her, but when she fi-nally swung her head to meet his gaze, he found that he could no longer read her feelings in her expression; she had once again managed to close herself off from him in that way of hers that so astounded him.

"I think it best that I go and ready our mounts," she said, not waiting for his answer before she turned to walk back to where they'd left the horses feeding on the grasses at the clearing's edge.

He watched her go, his own emotions unnerving him. The ease with which he'd uttered the sweet nothings— the surprisingly natural way Fiona had felt pressed against him—had been nothing less than astonishing to

him. He had been affected, and powerfully so. It had to
be his long-suppressed desires surging to the fore, he decided. There could be no other answer for it—though he
wasn't at all sure that he liked being tempted into weakness again that way, any better than he liked having to
admit to it. And she was a courtesan, he reminded himself. A woman who had bedded hundreds of men. She
wasn't the kind of woman he should yearn for, no matter
how alluring he found her to be.

Aye, it seemed that his playing at being Fiona's husband was going to be dangerous in more ways than one.
For it would require a special care, not only in keeping
Will in the dark about the truth of their relationship, as
was needed if they were to fulfill their plans in seeking
Elizabeth, but also in ways he'd never considered before.
There might well be something else to all of this, something potent enough to test his innermost moral strength
and his vows against illicit temptation . . .

Something, God help him, that he sensed could push
him to the breaking point—and perhaps beyond.

Chapter 7

⟡

Will led them the remaining distance to the outlaws' settlement in less than an hour's time. The man who'd been wounded during the feigned attack on Braedan rode close behind him, with Fiona and Braedan following. The remaining men, only slightly injured, had been sent to retrieve Fiona's trunks and herb pots from the inn, a boon for which she was immensely grateful. She only hoped they would hurry in their return—and that Will had chosen a spot for his latest settlement near a stream, as had always been his habit in the past—for she couldn't wait to bathe and exchange the dusty, sticky bliaud she was wearing for one of the fresh gowns in her trunk.

She deliberately avoided looking at Braedan as they plodded along behind Will, not trusting herself to meet his gaze yet. She remembered how difficult it had been to keep her feelings hidden to him back in the glen, before she'd excused herself to get their horses; she'd been completely unprepared for the sensations he had sent coursing through her when he'd jumped so heartily into acting out their pretended marriage. But worse still than the feigned physical closeness had been the gently murmured phrases and affectionate glances. He'd led her astray with those unexpected endearments, and she had yet to completely regain her sense of calm and control.

Of course, it didn't seem that she'd have much to fret about in that area again anytime soon; Braedan appeared to be in a black mood now, with his shoulders tight and his face rigid. He'd looked so since they'd rode from the glen, and though she had no idea what had sent him into such a dark temper, she was nonetheless grateful, as it likely meant he'd be keeping those sweet words of his to himself for now.

Her thoughts were curtailed in the next moment as their group emerged from the thick, cool protection of the primeval forest into a less densely wooded area. A half score enormous oaks of the kind Will favored for his people's shelter ringed the clearing; they served his purpose well, with hollowed trunks wider than two horses standing tail to nose. They were perfect for keeping everyone concealed by nature in a way that would have been impossible had they actually constructed a village of huts. Much of the other foliage had been trimmed back to make a pleasant encampment for his band of outlaws, though the whole effect was still one that allowed for successful hiding from the law.

As they rode fully into the area, Fiona saw that a few cook fires were scattered about, burnt to coals that were then piled beneath steaming pots, while a larger fire at the center of the area glowed under a rudimentary spit, roasting a large, sizzling piece of venison that had been undoubtedly poached from the king's own stock of deer in this forest.

Surprise tingled up her neck; it was a change from years past, to be sure, and a dangerous one at that. Everyone knew the penalty for poaching the king's meat was at least the loss of a hand, and at worst, death. That someone had risked it now was a sign that all was not well with Will's band of outlaws—at least not as well as it had been when she left them three years earlier.

Pulling her horse to a halt behind Will, she dismounted, taking measure of some of those who rose from the fires or emerged from the tree shelters to greet them. Someone came up to help the wounded man into one of the tree shelters, and a few others who recognized her called out greetings. But the rest hung back, uncharacteristically reticent from her recollections of the rollicking welcome that had always greeted their leader's return. They were a motley assortment of men and women, many of whom were strangers to her, and these new faces especially turned toward her and Braedan, studying them with unabashed interest.

Will took one blond-haired woman's arm and led her over to where Fiona stood with Braedan. "I have a few surprises of my own to tell you about, sister," he murmured, "and this is one of them. Joan Prentice is my intended. She joined us shortly after you left, taking up your old role in our arrangement—though with your return, it will be a boon to be able to divide the duties and perhaps send out two groups at once, on different roadways."

Fiona met Joan's gaze, and Joan smiled, her expression tentative as she looked from Fiona to Braedan and back again.

"Will has told me much about you," Joan said, her voice soft as she glanced at Braedan before fixing her eyes on Fiona again. "He wondered why you'd be travelin' with a king's man—and I did, too. But since you're here, he must be satisfied with your reasonin' on it."

"We've discussed it," Fiona answered, still struggling to conceal her surprise at Will's news.

"She is married to him if you can believe it," Will admitted with a laugh, his words loud enough for everyone in the little settlement to hear him; the onlookers' murmurs were punctuated with the sound of him thumping Braedan hard on the back. Fiona glanced over at Braedan, wondering how he would take this ribbing on top of the insult of having to pretend their union, but other than grimacing in response to Will's blows, he didn't react in any way.

"My sister, wed to a de Cantor," Will continued under his breath, shaking his head and flashing that mocking half smile again. As he spoke, he ambled away from them toward one of the cook pots, bending to lift the ladle from it and blowing on the contents before taking a taste. Then, making a grunting sound of approval, he straightened and tossed the ladle back in, spreading his arms to call out, "Ah, well, Christ knows stranger things have happened, eh? I propose a feast to celebrate my sister's return to the fold, with a husband at her side! Bring on the food!"

A cheer rose from the company, men and women alike joining in the happy din. At the call for victuals, a number of bedraggled-looking children tumbled out of the tree shelters and found places around one of the fires.

There were eleven of them, all seeming under the age of ten. *Six more babes since she'd left, then.* The entire outlaw group was a good deal increased, and from their pinched faces, and the grasping, thin hands reaching for the bread trenchers being passed round to share, they weren't always getting enough food.

Another change from years past.

But her troubling thoughts wavered to more immediate concerns, as Braedan sat next to her on the mossy pad she'd chosen by the nearest fire. Without a word he handed her the dry trencher she realized they were to share; as a married couple, it was only right, and yet the strange familiarity of it caught her by surprise. Pursing her lips, she scooped some of the stewed vegetables into the curved, hard bread, berating herself for her lack of foresight concerning this and many other aspects of her life that were going to have to change for the time being. Peculiar as it all felt, she knew she had no one to blame but herself for coming up with the idea.

Silently, she handed the trencher back to him, by her action inviting him to sup first while she cut their portion from the roasted venison that was making its way around the fires. She was surprised to see that he disregarded her offer, choosing instead to wait until she'd sliced off a few small hunks of the sizzling meat. It was another bewildering courtesy, she thought, daring a glance at him as he sat—especially considering that he still looked as brooding as a storm cloud about to rain. She decided it would be best not to attempt a conversation, settling instead into a rhythm of eating with him, taking a bite of the vegetables and venison, and then blowing on her fingers to cool them.

A pouch of ale made the rounds of each fire as well; conversation swelled and ebbed around them, punctuated by laughter and the occasional cough. Will and Joan were sitting at another fire, and those with Fiona and Braedan seemed reluctant to talk, even sitting a bit removed from them. Fiona tried to make eye contact with one of the children sharing their fire—a young girl of no more than four or five, whose eyes sparkled in the firelight. The girl ducked her head shyly, leaning into the shoulder of a woman who must have been her mother, from the similar hue of her sandy blond hair.

Fiona smiled at the child. "What's your name, lass?"

"Rosalind," she lisped, before tucking her head again behind her mother's arm. After a moment, she apparently worked up enough courage to peep out with half her face, adding in a whisper, "Is it true that you're the Crimson Lady, mistress? The one who makes men fall in love with naught but a look at you out of your smock?"

Rosalind's mother hissed a scolding, and Fiona felt Braedan stiffen beside her. Her own heart seemed to skip a beat, and the bottom dropped out of her stomach. It had been a long time since she'd had to face such a question from a child—so long that she'd almost forgotten the emptiness that always filled her when it happened. The lump that formed in her throat now prevented her from answering at first, and her eyes stung, making the firelight suddenly waver behind the glaze of tears.

"Some have called me the Crimson Lady, it's true, Rosalind," she managed, forcing herself to blink them away. Swallowing against the thick feeling in her throat, she tried to muster a smile, wanting to set the girl and her mother at ease. "Here in the forest with Will, and people like you and your mum, I've always been known just as Giselle."

"But you don't look crimson—you look light blue."

That brought another smile, this one less forced than the last, even though the truth behind the subject was another painful memory for her. "Aye, I am wearing light blue today, Rosalind. As it happens, I rarely wear crimson anymore if I can help it."

"Why not?"

Fiona could feel the weight of Braedan's attention on her, waiting to hear her answer, along with that of the little girl's mother and everyone else seated around their fire. She tried to focus on the little girl's gaze and think of a way she might make sense of it for her, without getting into the darker aspects.

"Perhaps I could best answer that with a question of my own, Rosalind. How would you like having naught but black bread every day, in the morn, for dinner and then for supper, too, for a whole year—nothing but black bread?"

Rosalind wrinkled her face. "That was all we *did* have this past winter, lady, every day. Naught but foul black bread."

"Hush, child. You should be grateful for having it at all," her mother chided.

Fiona's heart lurched; she hadn't considered that her analogy might be so apt for the girl. Patting Rosalind's hand, she continued, "It is not easy to like, is it?" When the girl shook her head, Fiona finished, "That is how it is for me with the color crimson. I wore it so much that I got tired of it and do not like to wear it at all now, unless I have to."

"Crimson gowns or not, lady, are you going to be helpin' us in the way the others told me about? The way you used to before you left?" Rosalind's mother asked, her expression so hopeful it was heartbreaking.

Fiona paused again, looking around at the ragged lot of Will's people, at a loss for how to respond, knowing as she did the truth of the matter. Much of what she might gain from her renewed activities here would likely be demanded by Braedan to fund his search for his foster sister. But before she could muster a sound, Braedan answered for her, his silky voice slicing her with more precision than if it had been her own blade on her flesh.

"Aye, my dear wife will be getting back into the fray soon, I daresay." He swung his head to look at her then, his expression bland, but his eyes glittering hard and unyielding. "And though I have never seen her in action myself, I am told she is quite gifted in the chase for gold. I recall hearing of her exploits in years past. It seems the preferred method was to set an elaborate trap, for which she serves as the injured bait. Isn't that right, darling? In order for your partners to make the steal, you pretend to be a damsel in distress at roadside . . . a pretense, enacted to perfection?"

"Aye, it was something like that," she mumbled, pulling her gaze away as the barbs of his words sank deep.

"Clever," Braedan said with a soft and achingly empty sound of feigned approval. "Very clever."

It was about all she could bear of his veiled comments, she realized, and she lurched to standing, calming the startled looks of those around them by forcing a serene look, and murmuring, "I'm afraid I'm suddenly feeling a bit tired. The trip here was long, and the dust of the road clings. I think I'll go find whatever water is nearby to bathe before settling in to sleep."

Some of the others reacted with surprise at her intention, likely because they knew that, however hot the weather had been lately, the water would be chilly nonetheless this time of year. Besides, in their minds bathing of any kind was, as always, dangerous to one's health. But she pretended not to hear their murmurings, having long ago chosen the sensation of being clean over any fears she might have once harbored about catching a dread disease from immersing herself in water. Braedan said nothing, and she was just as glad, for she'd have argued openly with him if he'd tried to stop her, feigned marriage or no.

Will, of course, knew the quirks to her nature better than anyone; he simply smiled and pointed to the north end of the clearing, saying, "The stream we use for drinkin' water is just over the rise there. It feeds into a pond that is deep enough for bathin', if you wish."

She nodded her thanks and turned to go, but he stopped her when he added, "But perhaps you'd better wait. Your trunk hasn't arrived yet, for you to change your gown afterward."

Curses. She'd forgotten about that, and yet she knew that she had to get away from Braedan, and as quickly as possible. "I suppose I'll just make do with changing garments later, then," she said, as she took a few steps in the direction of the pond.

"Wait a minute, now. There may be something I can do," Will interjected, forestalling her flight from the clearing yet again. "Joan has a chest of some fine new bliauds, gowns, and the like in our dwelling. A noblewoman's garments taken during our last robbery. We'd planned to use them in future thefts, but you're welcome to take one for yourself. Joan will show you where they are, won't you, lovey?"

Joan looked startled at the suggestion, but she said nothing. With a nod of consent, she stood and gestured for Fiona to follow her to one of the hollowed-out trees.

They ducked inside, the dimness dispelled by the sputtering tallow candle Joan lit with a twig she'd brought from the fire. Quickly, the woman moved a few steps to the trunk, which, though not overly large, seemed massive in this small space filled with bedding and provisions. After a moment of jiggling the clasp, she threw open the lid, then straightened and turned back toward the entrance.

"You'll find a goodly selection, I think, lady," Joan murmured, looking almost shy as she flushed, then ducked out into the clearing again.

Fiona's bemusement lasted but a moment; she'd never dreamed that her lively brother would choose such a timid future mate. Shaking her head, she bent to the task of choosing her garments, directing her thoughts to the pleasure of the bath that would soon be hers.

Soon, she was ready, with a plain but finely made linen smock thrown over her arm, along with a simple green bliaud that looked as though it would fit her well enough with the matching belt pulled tight. It would have to do until her own gowns arrived.

Taking, as an afterthought, a plain square of worsted to use for drying, she left the tree shelter and headed toward the short path that Will had pointed out, leading to the pond. As she made her way through the encampment, she noticed that Braedan was still seated at the fireside where she'd left him, motionless and not speaking to anyone around him. She tried not to think about him or the disquieting effect he had on her, instead looking forward, gritting her teeth, and trudging ahead.

Soon enough she found the place; it was an idyllic spot, surrounded by fragrant pines and waving ferns. She stood at the water's edge for a moment, soaking up the waning rays of the sun and breathing deep, schooling her mind to the necessary blankness she'd perfected when she'd been under Draven's power. It had always helped to calm her, this emptying of her thoughts, helped to give her a sense of control over her own being, no matter what was happening to her body or what she might be made to do.

It had been the only way she'd managed to survive those years.

This ability continued to serve her well now, and, with another deep breath, she pushed away all the lingering hurts and worries that had been assailing her, listening to naught but the sounds of nature all around her. Her breathing mingled with the soft birdcalls and gentle sound of the breeze flirting with leafy branches; her skin felt it pass by, barely perceptible, like a lover's caress. Opening her eyes, she looked around her, the peace of the setting illuminated by fingers of sun winking through the trees. She was ready.

She set her bundle of garments and worsted cloth on a mossy patch nearby and quickly unraveled the side laces of her sleeveless overdress, kicking off her slippers as she lifted the garment over her head. Her belted, long-sleeved smock followed it soon after, along with the sheathed dagger she kept strapped above her wrist. Finally, she reached up and removed the circlet from her brow, pulling the single, thick plait of her hair over her shoulder to unwind the bit of fabric securing its end. As she ran her fingers through to loosen the braid, the unbound fall of hair swept across her naked back and buttocks, leaving in its wake a pleasurable little trail of gooseflesh. But she didn't linger over the sensation, instead gulping a deep breath and taking a few running steps before diving headfirst into the pond.

In the next instant she burst to the surface, water sluicing over her face and into her mouth as she gasped and uttered a little laughing shriek. It was cold. Even colder than she'd expected. But it was so good to feel its clean sensation on her skin. Smiling, she stretched her arm above her and then to the side, her body following in a graceful arc as she moved her legs back and forth beneath the water.

She spent a few minutes swishing her arms and legs and twirling herself around, lamenting the fact that her pots of scented soap were all still in her delayed trunk. She'd have to remind herself to show one of the women—perhaps even Joan, if she could keep her from running off, she thought with a smile—how to make the soft concoction. It would be good for them to have on hand anyway. Her own supply was beginning to wane, and some of the people back at camp looked and smelled as if they could use a good scrubbing.

After floating on her back for a little while, she thought that perhaps she'd better consider getting out soon. She readied herself for it, starting to squeeze out her hair, when she realized she wasn't alone. Stiffening, she swiveled her head to stare at the intruder standing on the bank of the pond. Her gaze locked with Braedan's, and she startled at the heat simmering in his eyes; he shifted them for an instant to her pile of clothing, assessing her state of undress with a slight lift of his brow.

"What are you doing here?" Fiona asked, careful to keep her face as smooth and expressionless as it was before he came.

"I'm watching you."

"That is quite obvious." She kept her jaw tight to help conceal the fact that she was beginning to shiver, though she was loath to get out of the water with him standing there, staring at her. "Why?"

"A husband is expected to protect his wife in such situations. It is my duty to watch you bathe—as well as my right," he added, his eyes still dark with that dangerous, smoldering combination of anger and wanting.

Fiona steadied her gaze on him, wondering what kind of game he was playing, since he had no audience to impress with the sham of their marriage. Beneath the surface of the water, she crossed her arms over her chest. "I need no such protection, having fended for myself quite capably for these many years, as well you know."

"Perhaps I was thinking of bathing myself, then, and was just checking to see what shade of blue your lips had turned before I committed myself to the act."

Fiona shrugged in a way that she hoped seemed nonchalant, not believing for one second that he would even consider the possibility. "In truth I find it refreshing. A bit cold, but not overly so. To a warrior of your experience and prowess, it will likely seem as tepid as bathwater."

"Likely."

"What are you doing?" she asked in alarm, her eyes widening as he began to peel off his tunic, then his shirt, pulling them over his head. It was only then that she saw the small, folded pile of garments that he must have brought with him, resting on the ground nearby.

"I'm coming in."

"But you can't!"

"I can, and I will. I've decided that a swim, cold as it might be, would be most invigorating."

"Well, I'm getting out."

"As you wish," he said, standing for a moment with his hands on his hips, his hair tousled boyishly, and his very adult male body by now naked before her.

Before she could muster a word against it, he flashed her a devilish look, took a few steps, and dived with a splash into the water. In less than a second he broke to the surface with a shout, following it with a stream of curses.

"Christ in heaven, woman, this isn't just cold—it might as well be thick with ice!" He swiped his eyes to clear the water from them. She was still crouching below the pond's surface, but Braedan stood up now, tipping his head back and lifting both arms to push back his wet hair from his face. The water came to just below his taut belly, his sudden movement making little waves lap teasingly at the dark hairs that formed a dusky path from his navel to some lower part concealed beneath the surface.

Fiona frowned at the sight he presented, affected in some way she couldn't quite name. In her days as the Crimson Lady, she'd seen many men, some of them very strong and attractive men, without their clothing. Even Draven, as much as she'd despised him, had possessed a body that many would have called perfection.

But Braedan was different, somehow. Standing here before her, with steam rising from him at the collision of his body's heat with the frigid water, he looked like some primal force of nature, dangerous, imposing, and utterly masculine. His chest and arms rippled with muscle, his skin scattered over with battle scars and the partially healed cuts she'd dressed for him back at the inn. And then, when he lowered his face to meet her gaze again . . .

She felt as if something had sucked every bit of air from her. That smoky glint in his eyes had intensified, if it was possible. The devastating expression was fixed solely on her, making her instincts rise and sweeping a shiver up her spine that had nothing to do with the temperature of the pond. She felt herself moving backward a step, unsettled by him in a way she'd never felt before. In a way that was almost pleasant.

It couldn't be tolerated.

"If you're through bullying your way into my private bathing time, I would appreciate you turning around so that I can get out of the water now to dress."

"Turn around?" he echoed quietly. "If I didn't know better, my dear *Giselle*, I'd think you were suffering from some sort of regrettable memory lapse—a condition that seems to make you keep overlooking one important detail. We are supposed to be a married pair. Such connection implies a certain intimacy . . . and the husband you have made of me sees no need to turn around while you leave the water. Go ahead, *wife*, and do as you'd planned. I wish to watch you dress."

Another achy feeling shot through her, this one not nearly so pleasurable as the first. *God, didn't he know what he was doing to her with this mocking of their feigned marriage?* Some unfettered part deep inside screamed out in the agony of it, mourning anew all that she'd long-ago given up hope of having for her own. All she'd been made to forsake. Braedan was dangling her long-ago dreams of husband and home before her like a perverse child in the act of dismembering a new plaything. He was bleeding her drop by drop, as ruthlessly as a torturer who relishes prolonging his victim's suffering.

As mercilessly as Draven had toyed with her before he tried to make her his own, body and soul.

Something stony clicked back into place then, blocking out the pain and burying without pity the miserably few tender parts that remained. Damn Braedan de Cantor. If he wanted to revel in the fantasy that was the Crimson Lady, then she would let him—but it would be on *her* terms, by God, not his.

Without uttering a word, Fiona released her hands from her shoulders, letting her arms float down to her sides. Then she straightened her legs, rising up and facing him with her back tall so that the water trickled over her bare breasts and slid down the flat of her stomach. She left only one tendril of hair in front of her, using it to cover the scar Draven had left.

Keeping her head high, she ignored the blatant hunger that filled Braedan's expression, the deepening flare of desire she saw in his eyes as she slowly made her way up and onto the bank again. She gave him a good view of her rounded curves and delicately shadowed parts as she bent to take up the square of worsted she'd left folded near her borrowed clothes, moving with an unhurried grace that she knew, even as she hated herself for the instinctive wisdom, was the perfect choice for the man standing so boldly in the water behind her.

Though she didn't face him, she felt the burning weight of his gaze on her the whole time she dried herself, felt his stare as hot on her flesh as if he was running his hands over every inch of her body. But it was a heat that skimmed the surface, just as always before with every man who'd ever lusted for her, never delving deeper to the true woman beneath. Squeezing her eyes shut against that truth, she lifted up the clean linen shift to pull it over her head, as if the fabric might warm the chill invading her body from both the pond's water and Braedan's merciless treatment of her.

But before she could also don the long-sleeved overgown she'd brought, he was behind her as well, rising onto the bank with a trickling splash to retrieve the cloth of worsted she'd discarded. From the side of her gaze she saw him wrap it around his waist—though why he would bother to cover himself now eluded her. It was all too clear what he intended to happen between them next; she'd seen that look on too many men's faces to mistake it. The only difference here rested in the fact that, during her years with Draven, his elaborate plan with its sedating herbs and strange unguents had protected her from actually bedding any of the countless men who thought they'd purchased her favors for the night.

With Braedan no such safeguard would exist.

She swiveled to face him, uncertain about how they would progress to the physical joining he sought, knowing only that it would happen, and that she would let it. She was tired, so very tired of it all, sick unto death of the insinuations, the glances, the words that cut like shards of glass into flesh that had somehow lost its brittle, protective covering in the years since she'd abandoned her life as the Crimson Lady. Reckless anger flooded her, a feeling that drove her to tempt and entice Braedan in spite of herself.

It was almost laughable, remembering how she'd wondered for a few brief moments if he might be different, if he might be the one man out of ten thousand who would see beneath the mask. But he wasn't; she knew that now. Because it always came down to this. This lusting, and the never-ending hurt that came from being viewed as naught but an object for someone else's pleasure.

Braedan had gone still and silent before her, she noticed, his expression conflicted, his chest rising and falling swiftly with the force of whatever was happening inside him. It was as if he warred against something, and his struggles were all that kept him from reaching out at this very moment and dragging her to the grass beneath him.

She faced him, challenging him with her eyes even as she kept her overall expression cool, calm, and just a touch vulnerable—the perfect facade of the elegantly seductive Crimson Lady. They stood close enough that she could have touched him had she reached out her arm at full length. But it wasn't she who made that overture first. Wordlessly, Braedan lifted his hand and gently brushed the backs of his fingers down the bared expanse of her arm, from shoulder to wrist. The warmth of his touch against her chilled flesh almost made her shiver.

Almost, but not quite. The Crimson Lady had been trained well; the only reaction she would ever betray would be by choice, not accident.

"You are beautiful," Braedan murmured.

"It is a beauty made for your pleasure alone," she answered, forcing herself to repeat the odious words she'd said thousands of times before. To speak in the low, modulated tones she'd perfected so long ago. Her eyes burned with the hatefulness of what she was doing, but she continued on with her performance as her finely pitched instincts told her it must be played, glancing up at him through her lashes in the semblance of shyness she knew would increase the heat of his fantasy tenfold.

Aye, she was good at what she did. Acting the part came with such wicked ease that it should have frightened her, were it not so very necessary to maintaining her composure right now, and she felt both sickened and grateful for the gift of detachment that came with plying her notorious skills.

"I want you. Badly," he said, his quiet voice an admission of guilt that was echoed by the shadows in his eyes.

"I know," she whispered.

She stood unmoving before him, feeling herself curl away deep inside where she would be safe, unconsciously emptying her mind in that way that had become a means of survival for all of those years . . . preparing herself for the inevitable step that would come next . . . the completion he would demand from her. He would impose a physical joining with her body, just as Draven had done, whether or not her mind and heart agreed to it.

She had had no power to refuse back then, owned as she was by the man who had purchased her innocence— and she had no will to deny Braedan now. The fact that it was she herself who had led him to the brink with this illicit enticement only made that more certain, and so now she would make the decision to finally step over and off the edge of the cliff that had been looming before her. She would commit this act and make herself a whore in truth, bringing her outward self at last to a place that would match the dark inner reality Draven had forged in her all of those years ago.

That would match the perceptions the rest of the world already held of the seductive temptress that was Giselle de Coeur.

"But you do not want *me*, lady."

The simplicity of Braedan's statement and the raw emotion behind it jerked her from her center, forcing her out of that floating place of nothingness to which she'd retreated. What did he mean? She frowned, shocked and unbalanced by the direction he'd suddenly taken.

"*Want* you?" she repeated dully.

"Aye. You have no feeling for me in that way. No desire, no need for my touch upon your skin, my hands upon your body, as I have for you."

He spoke in a husky murmur, his words surprising, revealing an insight that couldn't be real. His assessment was as brutally honest as if he'd seen a glimpse of the truth, even though she'd painted her mask on so flawlessly, so cleverly. It was impossible . . . a figment of her imagination. It had to be, and she was angry with herself for even entertaining the notion. To accept it would be intolerable and far more dangerous than clinging to the dark reality she'd lived with for nearly eleven years, the certainty of men and their ways, of their voracious wanting and thoughtless taking.

"I am well versed in every imaginable act of love, Braedan," she said carefully, struggling not let her inner turmoil show. "Anything you desire, just speak it and it shall be done, to a level of fulfillment you never dreamed possible. That is all that matters."

"It is not all that matters to *me*."

"It is the way of things," she answered, exasperated. "You cannot change it."

"Tell me why, then," he demanded in a husky growl, gripping her shoulders and forcing her to look at him. "Why is that all you want? Why do you think it is right to feel no desire, to have no need for me, and yet be willing—nay seem eager even—to bed with me?"

Her composure was slipping; she could feel it sliding further from her grasp, and she lashed out blindly, fearful, adrift on waves that would crush her like tinder against the rocks if she didn't find a way to maintain her control. But he was relentless, his touch like velvet steel, imprisoning her with warmth and strength, and squeezing her heart even as he released her arm to cup her chin in the tender insistence of his palm.

"Tell me why, Fiona. If I can command anything I wish of you, then I demand you answer that question for me."

It was the hoarse utterance of her name that finally pushed her past saving, and she scrambled to clutch at the oddly dissolving fragments of her protection—the pragmatic, reserved persona she'd hid behind as the Crimson Lady—only to feel it trickle through her fingers. A raw, aching cry ripped from her throat, so low and anguished that at first she didn't recognize it as coming from herself. But the safety of her rage was still there, battling for precedence, gripping her as she struggled to free herself from the painful pleasure of his touch, the impossibility of his words.

"Nay," she gasped, her heart wrenching and her body feeling as jumpy and exposed as if she'd been strung up and left to twist naked in the wind. "I cannot—" Her throat tightened, cutting off the rest of her words under a flood of hurt and pain so overwhelming that she couldn't go on. She jerked backward again, trying to free herself from him, but he wouldn't let go.

"You must tell me, lady," he murmured, pulling her to face him, to look into his eyes again. "Tell me why."

"Oh God, Braedan, stop it. It just cannot be otherwise! I cannot feel want, or desire, or need. Not in that way. I can drive men to lust, perform every carnal skill to perfection—and to my shame, my body sometimes responds by instinct to the acts that have been performed upon me—but inside I am dead. It is cold and empty and—"

She broke off again, blinking, her voice cracking with the strain, frantic and panicking at the warm shades of understanding sweeping across his face as he looked at her. Anger reared its head anew, clawing forth in a last, desperate attempt to erase that look of awareness from his face.

"I feel nothing when you touch me, Braedan," she burst out in a choking cry, his silence more painful in its tenderness than a thousand biting arguments might have been. "*Nothing*. Do you understand? With you or with any man."

He remained quiet in response to her impassioned outburst, his expression somber, his eyes so gentle on her. She held herself stiff against the onslaught of bitter emotion, afraid that if she even breathed too deeply she might crack. But then he touched her again, reaching out to stroke her cheek and slip his hand beneath the damp weight of her hair at her neck to tug her to his chest, and suddenly the last bit of her resolve shattered, crumbling into a thousand pieces as a guttural sob broke forth along with the hot liquid that seeped from between her tightly squeezed eyelids.

"Ah, lady, it is a shame," he murmured, stroking her cheek, her hair, even as he held her in a comforting embrace against him. "A sad and wasteful shame that it is so."

She fought to stifle her crying, her nails biting into the flesh of her palms as she held back against the urge to let go in his arms. It was so hard to be strong. She kept her eyes closed, simply breathing in and out, soaking in the scent of Braedan's skin, the solid warmth of his chest beneath her cheek, hearing the firm and steady beat of his heart. His powerful hands cradled her to him like a precious creature to be cared for and loved.

"Do you want to talk of it?" he asked gently. "I will try to listen without judgment if I can."

Another sweep of something indescribable surged through her—gratitude, perhaps? Or maybe even tenderness. It had been so long since she'd felt anything like it that she wasn't sure of its origin. But fast behind it came the darker flow of memory and anguish and impotent pain. To talk of those years with Draven, of all that had happened, all that had led her to what she was right here and now, so damaged and detached that she knew not the truth of her own feelings . . . it was a step she knew she could not take without being crushed by it, with or without Braedan to help her. Not now. Perhaps not ever.

Wordlessly, she shook her head, opening her eyes at last and pulling away from him enough to dash her fin-

gers across her cheeks. He still held one of her hands, his
thumb moving back and forth along her palm as he continued to look down at her with that warm expression
full in his eyes. Her chest felt heavy, her world shaken by
the unexpected gift of his understanding.

She cleared her throat, glancing away before meeting
his gaze again, a frown creasing the tiny area between
her brows as she fought to keep from crying anew. Then
she simply shook her head again, knowing not what to
say, how to explain.

"I understand," he murmured gruffly. "It will come
in time, I think, and when it does, I will listen. Until
then, know you that you have nothing more to fear
from me in our arrangement together. I vow that I will
not pursue anything between us again without your
consent."

At her nod, he squeezed her hand, holding her gaze
for an instant more. When he finally released her and
stepped back, neither of them moved farther, and she
couldn't help but wonder if he didn't feel as she did
right now, off-balance and changed in some powerful
way.

After a bit he glanced down, seeming to become
aware again that he was wearing naught but a simple
cloth round his waist. His mouth quirked up on one
side, and he shook his head. "Perhaps it would be best if
I dressed now."

While he gathered his discarded clothing on the bank
of the pond and donned the fresh garments he'd brought
with him, she twisted away to pull on her borrowed
gown as well, tying the belt firmly round her hips. Soon
they were both fully clothed, and he turned to her, the bit
of worsted slung over his arm. She felt strangely hesitant

before him, she who had faced countless men in far more intimate settings, with the prospect of far more intimate acts ahead of her than the ruse of marriage they would need continue to play once they returned to the encampment.

"We should go," he said at last. "Your brother will wonder what has become of us if we tarry longer."

He was right, of course, yet in some odd way she wanted to hold on to this moment for just a little longer. She could never speak such a thing to him, though, and in truth, she wasn't sure she would, even were she able to find the words for it. It was all too new, these feelings and the understanding they seemed to have reached here together. Too fresh. She needed time to mull over what had happened.

They started down the path back to the settlement, a profound silence surrounding them, the weight of it not so much awkward as full with their spent emotions. By the time they arrived, her eyes felt heavier than she could ever remember, her head so tired from all that she'd experienced today that she thought she might fall asleep the moment she rested it, even if it was on a hard stump or moss-covered bit of rock. But she needn't have worried about the shelter they would have for the night. Will and Joan had moved their own belongings farther back into one of the hollowed trees, giving up some of their precious space for Braedan and Fiona to spread out blankets near the shelter's entrance and make a bed for themselves.

With a sigh, Fiona stretched out, a fuzzy warmth surrounding her as Braedan shifted into place behind her and pulled another blanket over the top of them. It felt natural, somehow, not frightening or painful, as had always been her experience before when she'd been compelled to lie next to a man. It was pleasant, even . . .

Encompassed in the peacefulness of the clear night and the security of Braedan's arms, Fiona sighed, and closed her eyes—and for one of the few times in her life, drifted off into easy, dreamless sleep.

Rest did not come so freely to Braedan. He could hear Will's muffled snores and Joan's occasional coughing behind them as he lay very still, soaking up the feel of Fiona stretched out so close to him. He listened to her soft, even breathing and took in the faint scent of vanilla that clung to the dampened mass of her hair near his cheek, watching how the dying fire's embers cast her face in a flickering, rosy glow. All seemed calm and peaceful.

But still sleep eluded him.

So much had happened, it fair boggled his mind to think on it. What he'd learned today about Fiona—about himself—made the prospect of easy rest impossible. Those moments beside the pond with her had stunned him, disrupting his certainties and rattling his preconceived notions of the woman she was. He'd gone to find her there with something dark and dangerous at work inside of him, something that had driven him to seek her out in private; he hadn't been able to stop himself. She'd gotten inside his defenses, somehow, tempting him, teasing him with her lush beauty, the idea of what she was and what she'd been to other men before him luring him like a forbidden fruit, waiting to be tasted.

And then to have to endure the tantalizing illusion of acting as her husband, the one man all the world would think privy to the pleasures of her body . . .

Braedan rolled onto his back, slowly, so as not to disturb her, throwing a forearm across his eyes. It had been too much, pushing him toward a resolution that he'd decided could be found only in the slick heat of her most intimate embrace. He'd intended to bed her on the pond's bank, to take her savagely and completely . . . to lose himself in her softness and thereby banish the desire for her that seemed to seethe inside him. He'd gone to the spot where she bathed with that purpose, even though in doing so he would be forsaking the vows he'd made after the excess he'd indulged in as a crusading knight. But it had been the only cure he could conceive of for drowning his maddening want for her.

It hadn't gone that far, thank God. He'd still been man enough to recognize the emptiness in her eyes and pull back before it was too late. She would have let him take her, he knew that, but their joining would have been nothing more than a chore for her to finish, a job to be done—and he'd realized, suddenly, that it wouldn't have been enough. He wanted more from her, a deeper completion that he was only beginning to recognize.

Aye, in those moments next to the water's edge he'd come to an astounding realization about Fiona. Crimson Lady or nay, he'd been forced to accept that she was a woman first. A woman with thoughts, feelings, and a past that had helped to forge her soul in ways that were unknown to him. Something inside him had twisted to awareness in that instant, allowing him to see the truth, the reality of what the world must feel like from where she stood, and he'd been rocked to his core with the knowledge.

Shame filled him at the memory of all the nameless

women he'd bedded during his foreign travels, all of the favors he'd enjoyed without any real thought, the same as every man at whose side he'd battled for the king. But, unlike some of those knights, he'd never taken a woman against her will—was sickened at the very idea of rape. However, it seemed to him now that what he'd done with those women was almost as terrible; until today, he'd always contented himself with the belief that the act of bedding a female who freely sold her body for profit was no more a sin or crime against her than buying a tapestry from the one who'd woven it, or purchasing a cask of beer from the brewer who'd made it.

Now he sensed it was not so simple as that.

He knew only that when he'd looked into Fiona's eyes and saw the vast emptiness there, it was as if he'd plunged headfirst again into the icy embrace of the pond. It had slammed a fist of agony into his gut, and he'd suddenly wanted more than anything to take that darkness away and fill it with something light and good. His body had continued to burn with desire for her. It burned even now. But he had resisted its demand, realizing that he couldn't go through with his intention to bed her, any more than he could have grabbed her, thrown her to the ground, and forced himself on her had she been a virgin maid and pure.

Rolling back toward Fiona, Braedan reached over to brush a tendril of hair from her brow, studying the calm beauty of her features as she slept. She was an enigma to him, complicated and compelling, the quiet dignity beneath the surface of her calling out to him in a way no mere carnal temptation could. That she was also a creature of lush sensuality couldn't be denied; the throb of his erection, as he lay here next to her, confirmed the truth of her physical allure without a doubt—and yet he knew that his attraction to her stemmed from so much more. . . .

With a breathy sigh, Fiona shifted in sleep, turning to face him as well. Her arm lifted to stroke along his side, coming to rest, finally, draped with drowsy weight at his waist. He held his breath, stiffening. A wordless murmur escaped her lips as she snuggled closer, tucking her head under his chin so that the soft and sleep-relaxed contours of her mouth brushed against his throat, exposed at the opening of his shirt. The moist warmth of her exhalations caressed him, and he knew the tender agony of her body's sweet curves pressed so perfectly against his.

His groin ached with renewed throbbing, the hardness there almost unbearable. But he was loath to disturb her rest by moving away. It was that alone, he told himself, which barred him from shifting from her, and not his own desire to continue holding her close. With a quiet groan of surrender, Braedan lifted his arm to embrace her in kind, cupping her head with his hand, his fingers absently stroking back the silken hair that fell onto her cheek. When he brushed a kiss across her brow, it was to savor the warm sweetness of her skin against his lips. The confusion that had been muddling his mind and twisting in his heart eased for a moment as they lay entwined together, joined with a kind of innocent intimacy he'd never known or hoped for before with any woman. Nay, not even with Julia . . .

His heart twisted at the thought of his former betrothed, a lady of unsurpassed virtue. He still kept her

miniature with his small pack of belongings, taking it
out only rarely, when he thought he could bear the sting
of looking on it and reminding himself of all he'd lost.
She had been the perfect bride for him, he who was the
heir to the de Cantor legacy—the kind of woman he'd
yearned all his life to call his own. But their betrothal
had been dissolved after his return home and the clash
with Draven that had followed, her family appalled by
the sordid events, enough so that they'd petitioned the
king to break the long-arranged union.

He hadn't blamed them, really. Didn't blame them
now. What else were they to do? He no longer deserved
such a lady as Julia; he'd have been the first to say it. Not
he, an outlaw and soon-to-be-thief, a man damaged,
perhaps past repair. And yet he couldn't stop himself
from hoping that he might still salvage something, once
Elizabeth was rescued, Richard brought to safety, and
the charges that had named him an outlaw settled. Aye,
perhaps . . .

Resolving to push aside such painful thoughts for the
moment, Braedan sighed and tried to settle into the
lulling rhythms of breathing that would lead to sleep.
But before he drifted off, he stroked his fingers once
more along the exquisite silk of skin at Fiona's temple.
Trailing them gently down her cheek, he let his hand
come to rest at the back of her neck, captivated by this
unusual creature—this fallen woman—who had turned
his world around in such unexpected ways.

He gazed at her in silence, uncertain about where all
of this would lead them, but knowing only that his instincts told him to have a care with her. To remember
that inside the sought-after beauty's tempting form beat
a woman's tender heart.

"Aye, slumber in peace, my Crimson Lady; dream of happy things," he murmured softly, his breath brushing her cheek in the darkness, "and know that I will be here with you still when dawn breaks again."

Chapter 8

***I**t was a fine day for a robbery,* Fiona thought. She breathed deeply of the morning air, relieved that the clear night had given way to a cool, rosy dawn, with the promise of sun later. Such mild weather would entice the kind of nobles and overfed churchmen on whom they usually preyed to set out on a jaunt to London. By necessity, some would take the main road that wound around Wulmere Forest, and when they did, she, Will, and the boys would be waiting for them.

"Are you ready, lass?" Will called to her from where he stood next to her mount, adjusting the broken saddle that would serve as part of the ruse they hoped to arrange that day to make their plan a success.

"As ready as I can be, with three years' break from the skill." Fiona forced a smile for him, trying to quell the sudden clenching feeling in her middle as she stuffed a dry loaf of bread and some cheese into a sack. Braedan remained silent where he stood next to her, likely as anxious as she about participating in the day's coming events. She'd awoken this morning nestled in his arms, surprised at how comfortable she felt there; warmth filled her even now, remembering his gentleness to her last night. But he'd betrayed no acknowledgment of it in his conversations thus far today. In fact, he was all but avoiding her gaze now as he donned a long, dark cloak of the sort they were all wearing.

Too soon, it seemed, it was time to start out. As she walked over to Braedan's mount, Fiona eyed the others who would be participating in the affair today: Will led the way, followed by old Grady, a burly tinker-turned-bandit she remembered from years past, and reliable Rufus Dinkins, her brother's most trusted right-hand man. She, Braedan, and a newer outlaw about thirteen years old, a lad named Nate, would round out the group.

Palms damp, she allowed Braedan to help her up onto his steed in front of him, her long absence from all of this making her jittery. The purposefully broken saddle on her own mount made riding with Braedan necessary, though the arrangement was complicated by the long train on the gown she wore, chosen from Will's stash of confiscated, rich garments. It was a noblewoman's finely made bliaud of deep green, and she'd stitched it last night so that now it fit her perfectly, presenting an enticing yet still noble appearance; the gown, combined with the brown silk mantle and golden circlet Will had added, would go far to create the illusion of gentility they intended for their ruse.

"How long, do you think, until we reach the spot where we will perpetrate our crimes?" Braedan murmured into her ear, interrupting her thoughts.

His powerful arm gripped her tight to him as he urged his mount to a canter to keep up with Grady's steed, but the pleasant sensation of his embrace was drowned under a flare of annoyance at his words. "You must stop considering what we do a crime, Braedan," Fiona chided, twisting to look at him. "There is much that compels us to it, including the need to fend off starvation for the children we left back there. If you hesitate at a crucial moment because of misplaced sensibilities, then the plunder we seek will be lost, and the potential for someone to be injured or killed increased."

"It is difficult to think of robbing unsuspecting travelers in any other way," he answered tightly. "Nearly impossible, actually, considering that I spent my life prior to these past months doing what I could in my own way to prevent similar activities."

"How wonderful for you, considering that you lived so many years of your virtuous and noble life far from here, away from the corruption of the—"

"I never said I was virtuous *or* noble," Braedan broke in, his tone even darker than before. "I said only that I tried to uphold the law."

"Aye, well England's law is as flawed and corrupt as the powerful men who created it," she retorted, her frustration glossing over his rebuttal. "It can drive many to take desperate measures if they hope to survive the other side of it. After what happened to you upon your return to England, I would think that you, of all people, would appreciate the truth of that."

Braedan remained silent then, and Fiona pursed her lips, finding it difficult to stanch the swell of resentment that rose in her at his seeming refusal to understand the complexity of their position.

"What you've said is the truth as you see it, Fiona," Braedan said at last, speaking carefully after his silence, "but you must understand that it is different for me. I have never fought for a purpose that I did not believe to be just and right; now that I am faced with committing an act that is neither, I cannot deny that it will be difficult to do so—to maim or possibly kill someone—for the sake of a few coins."

Fiona's irritation waned at the quiet struggle she heard in his voice. She twisted to look at him again, her softer instincts rising up. "Try to remember that what we do *will* ultimately be noble in cause, Braedan, undertaken in order to help you find Elizabeth. There is a good chance that you will never need use your blade against anyone; those we intercept usually cooperate, once they see it is easier to do so than to fight."

She squeezed his hand where it was wrapped around her waist, savoring the feeling of his chest pressed against her back. But his troubled look remained, and a muscle in his jaw twitched.

"It will be all right. Truly, it will," she murmured in a last attempt to reassure him, and at that he shifted his gaze to hers for one brief moment. She saw a flare of something in the depths of his eyes, then—a kind of gratitude for what she was trying to do for him, she thought—before he jerked his head in a nod and pressed her closer. With a sigh, she looked down the road; both of them remained silent for the rest of the journey, lost in their own thoughts of what the next hours might bring.

When they arrived at the spot where the robbery would be staged, it was late morning, and the sun shone hot, soaking into Braedan's back like the blast from a smithy's furnace. He felt edgy and longed to remove the cloak Will had given him as part of their disguise, but he resisted the urge, resolving to see the day through without mistake. If luck held, their take would be substantial. And though what they were about to do went against every instinct in him, he knew that the more swiftly he could amass the coin he needed, the sooner he could pursue his plan to free Elizabeth and help his brother Richard.

Keeping that idea at the front of his thoughts, he dismounted his steed and helped Fiona to the ground, following Will's lead in securing their mounts in a concealing, leafy grove just out of sight of the road. Nate darted off to scout for approaching travelers of means, keeping to the trees as he went; if he spotted anything interesting, he was to run back to the group and set their entrapment plan into motion.

Braedan watched him go, his gut tightening in a way that was similar to what he'd felt before every battle in the Holy Land, only with the added heaviness of knowing he was about to do something unlike anything he'd ever done before. Something ignoble. But he was enough of a pragmatist to know there was no help for it. He took the position Will indicated a few feet away, crouching into the bushes just off the roadside across from Rufus. Fiona and Grady, meanwhile, positioned themselves near her disabled mount, adjusting the saddle so that it was hanging from what looked to be a nearly severed girth. She lifted a handful of sweet grass to the horse's nose after a bit, all of them waiting for Nate's return.

It was only a few minutes later when the lad came bounding through the brush, his face flushed and his chest heaving. "There's a covered carriage comin' with escort," he called, grinning. "It looks to belong to an earl at the very least, all silks and gold—a prize ripe for the takin'!"

"We approach lone riders or pairs only," Will said in a low voice. "We cannot attempt a guarded coach with only four of us to take it."

"Five, countin' me," Nate grumbled. " 'Twould be a fine, fat purse, I tell you—mayhap the only we'd need this day!" He looked down at the ground, clearly disappointed, kicking at the dirt as his shoulders sagged.

Will paused for a long while, his face a studied scowl. At last he shook his head, cursing under his breath. "Ah, lad, you could talk a knight out of his spurs, I think. Exactly how many men are guardin' it?"

"Only two on horseback," Nate said, perking up and straightening as he added, "The nobleman 'imself is seated inside the coach. I swear—'twill be an easy take if this one is as good with a sword as you say!" he added, jerking his head toward Braedan.

Braedan frowned. "I can handle myself well enough, and yet I have never tested my ability in this way. Do not rely on me in deciding whether or not it will be a success."

Tightening his lips, Will seemed to consider the possibilities. After a moment more of thought, he glanced to Braedan and then back to his sister. "We still outnumber them. Let's do it."

He made a hand signal to Fiona and Rufus that sent the older man back into hiding, while Fiona met Braedan's gaze and nodded encouragingly before seating herself on the thick grasses at the roadside. Nate skidded over to a position next to her, looking as if he was checking over the mount's legs for breaks, while Grady took a knee near "his lady," seeming to offer sympathy and a drink from the waterskin at his side.

Fiona took his hand and stood with the graceful elegance of a queen just as the small coach came into view round the bend in the road; the sight of her was arresting even to Braedan, who knew the truth of their ploy. Her auburn hair was loose and waved down her back, reflecting the sun's fiery hue, her creamy skin flushed and set off to perfection by the deep green gown that clung to her curves in subtle invitation. As a finishing touch, she'd called up a vulnerable expression that was perfect for the stranded lady she was playing.

He didn't think she could look any more alluring if she tried. But then the conveyance pulled to a stop near her, and she sighed deeply, the action lifting her breasts taut against their thin covering of silk—and Braedan felt his mouth go bone dry.

He swallowed, forcing himself to look away and study the carriage and the men who guarded it. But even as he assessed their strength and sized up their weapons, he couldn't get the image of Fiona's beauty from his mind. Hell, he knew without a doubt that if he'd been the one they were targeting, he would have stopped, not only to offer his assistance, but to drink his fill of her with his gaze as well.

"Are you hurt, lady?" one of the guardsmen called down to her from his steed. "Need you some aid?"

"Aye, thank you kind, sir," she replied, glancing up at him and taking a limping step nearer. "I fear that I have twisted my ankle in falling from my mare."

Her voice carried a tremulous quality that made Braedan's heart flop in his chest. By the saints but she was talented at this. More so than he'd have guessed, even having witnessed her in action as the Crimson Lady at the inn near Alton. He could only imagine what the poor wretches on horseback must be feeling as they looked on her pleading beauty, unaware that they were serving as pawns in the plot that was unfolding against them.

"Why are we stopped, Riggs?" a querulous voice bellowed from the coach's interior. "We must resume at once. These roads are not fit for travelers who value their safety. Move on!"

"It is a gentlewoman, my lord," the guard answered. "She has been injured in a fall from her mount and cannot ride for a broken saddle."

"A gentlewoman, you say?"

The voice inside of the coach changed subtly in quality, a kind of suspicion edging it where none had been before. Of a sudden, the silken flap was pushed aside, and Braedan saw a man's round, shaven head lean out. It was clearly a churchman, and his numerous chins jiggled when he moved. He grunted a few times as he lifted his heft from the interior so that the top of his body emerged from the conveyance like a snail pushing out of a shell.

Suddenly his eyes widened at the sight of Fiona, a flush darkening his already-ruddy skin. A stream of curses spilled like drops of spittle from his lips, and he jerked back into the covered carriage, shouting, "By the devil's hide, it's a trap! Ride on man—go! We've been—"

"Right you are, my lord," Will called out, leaping from his position in the brush as he drew his sword, followed in kind by Rufus, Grady, then Braedan, who decided that it would be best to follow suit. The surprised guards had no time to react; Braedan lunged and pulled the guard closest to him from his steed. He got his blade

beneath the man's chin before the guard could unsheathe his weapon. Rufus and Grady took the second
guard, while Fiona stepped back so that Nate could
grab hold of the coach horses; Will moved past the
guard Braedan controlled and flung open the door to
pin the overfed occupant to his seat with the point of his
blade.

"It is simply not safe to travel these roads," Will murmured in mocking singsong, shaking his head. "Especially if you're foolish enough to carry a purse fat with
coins for purchase of goods—or perhaps sweetmeats,"
he added, poking at the churchman's bulky middle with
his sword. "Now hand over what you have my lord, and
you can be on your way, none the worse for it."

"This is sacrilege, accosting one of God's own servants," the man sputtered, scowling to the point of
apoplexy, so dark was his face. "I am a pardoner of the
Holy Church, recently come from Rome, and I will not
comply with this outrage! Sacrilege, I tell you—it is sacrilege!"

Braedan felt the tension curling thick through the air.
He kept his arm locked in position, with the blade beneath the guard's chin, warning him with his gaze and
willing the man not to move a muscle, lest he be forced
to take further action.

When Will finally spoke again, it was in a voice that
had gone flat and cold. "What is sacrilege, man, is for
one of God's own to practice self-indulgence while thousands of his countrymen starve. Now give me your
purse, so that I may share your wealth with some of
those less well fed than yourself."

The pardoner seemed taken aback, his beringed fingers, gripping the edge of the coach's window opening

until the puffy flesh turned white. Suddenly, his expression shifted from one of outrage to something much more benign.

"You are wise for your years," he said, shaking his head and setting his jowls to wiggling again. "We must all needs try to share what largesse God has placed in our way. I have recently come from Rome, as I said, and I have in my possession several pardons, signed by the Pope himself. I would be glad to give you one of those in lieu of my purse; they can be used to cleanse away any sin you wish—even your crimes as a thief if you so desire." He glanced around at the others as if gauging their support of him, before turning his gaze back on Will.

"Who said such was my goal?" Will asked, raising his brow. "Were I made new-clean as the driven snow through one of your holy writs, it would be but a matter of weeks before the sheriff had me up on false charges again." He shook his head. "Nay, churchman, your pardons do not interest me."

The pardoner looked furious at being thwarted in his offer, but Braedan noticed that he managed to keep his voice even when he spoke again. "Perhaps, then, you'd better like to receive a holy blessing and protection from one of the sacred relics I carry with me as well." He fumbled on the seat next to him, glancing down for just a moment before he raised a scrap of faded blue cloth to the window. "Take this, for instance," he went on, making a show of crossing himself and kissing the fabric. "It is a piece of the Virgin Mother's veil, God bless her miraculous soul, come to me through marvelous means while I sojourned in Rome. But a touch of this veil, and all ill fortune will flee from you, never to return. I will allow you to touch it without paying the usual fee for the privilege, if you will but let us pass unhindered."

He nodded again and held the cloth out to Will, apparently encouraged by his lack of argument to the offer. But Braedan had had just about enough. Twisting his mouth in derision, he jerked his head toward the pardoner and said, "What you have there is nothing more than a bit of *bedsheet*, man, and yet you would try to pass it off as a relic of the Holy Mother?"

"It *is* a relic—from the Holy Land itself!"

"Liar," Braedan growled, tempted to take his blade from the guard and put it where it might truly do some good, against the corrupt cleric's throat. "If it were, it would not be in the hands of a traveling pardoner such as you, I can assure you that."

Will shook his head again. "It seems you are more foul than I first realized. Give over your purse now, for I warn you my good humor is fast fading, and I do not know how much longer I can keep my arm restrained against you." Will punctuated his words by dragging the point of his blade from the pardoner's thick waist up to the center of his chest, his eyes as steely as his sword, as they skewered him to his seat with their menacing expression.

The pardoner blanched pasty, a squeak slipping from his throat. "I—I—there is no need to get excited. No need, no need," he gasped, his chins again wobbling furiously as he shook his head. "I will give you my purse, though you should know that I had intended to bring it to the abbey just beyond London's gate for dispersal to the poor."

Braedan scoffed at the pardoner's clearly deceitful claim, uttered atop his other bald-faced lies, but he said nothing further as Will lifted the man's jingling purse and tossed it to Fiona. She stood by patiently as they finished the task of relieving the pardoner of his gem-encrusted rings and a fur-lined shawl he had spread over the false relics in his coach. It was a woman's garment, Braedan was sure of it by its cut and size.

He frowned as Will folded it and added it to the sack where Fiona had placed the purse, wondering just what use a man of the Church, supposedly on his way to offer alms for the poor on an exceedingly warm day, would have for such a garment. But he had little time to ponder the question as they disarmed the guards and took anything else of value they could find on or within the pardoner's coach.

Soon they were finished. With a slap to the lead horse's flank and a warning nod to the remounted guards, along with a murmured recommendation that they not stop for anything or anyone else until they reached Londontown, they released their captives and watched them career down the road, dust billowing behind them. Then, jerking his head, Will led the way back into the shelter of the forest.

And as the group made their way deeper into the misty cool of the wood, Braedan felt a bittersweet twisting in his belly. It was done, then. Back at the roadside, it had been both easier and more challenging than he'd anticipated. In truth, he couldn't say that he regretted his part in lightening the obviously corrupt pardoner's purse, and yet . . .

He rode stoically behind the others, Fiona cradled against him, the strange feeling still roiling in his gut. For he realized that no matter what, now, he couldn't go back. This day he had crossed a threshold that, in all of his life, from boyhood to manhood and on to his years as a warrior knight for King Edward, he'd never dreamed he would willingly take.

For today, he had finally become an outlaw in deed as well as in name.

Chapter 9

It had been a profitable fortnight since they'd joined Will's group, Fiona thought as she made her way up the empty path from washing clothes with the other women. So much so that it would be but another few weeks before Braedan would have enough coin to make the trip to London to gain clues on Elizabeth's whereabouts. But even the dark imminence of that journey back to the *stewes* couldn't quell the pleasant sensation that thoughts of Braedan set off inside Fiona.

She nibbled her lower lip as she walked, hugging the folded garments she carried tight against her. She couldn't remember ever having felt so before about any man. Watching his efforts to contribute to the group, to fit in with the very people he'd been raised to condemn— feeling his gentle patience with her and the unspoken understanding he showed in his everyday actions—all of it strummed at her heartstrings in a way that was most confusing. She didn't know how to react or what to believe, having never known anyone like Braedan before. In truth, he had caught her off guard with his caring ways, and though she worried about the dangers fraught in allowing herself such tender emotions, she couldn't seem to stop thinking about him.

Wrapped in the warmth of her musings, she entered the settlement clearing, keeping to the outer edges as she made her way back to their tree shelter. Will had called a day of rest from their roadside excursions, freeing the time for everyone to undertake chores, rest, or even have a bit of fun—a suggestion that many of the children had taken to immediately; even now they cavorted around the clearing in a game of hoodman blind, having tired, apparently, of their earlier sport of hot cockles.

Fiona paused for a moment, smiling at their antics and listening to their hooting jests, wondering absently if it was possible that she'd ever felt so carefree as a child. She couldn't remember any such moments, even in those early years before Will had left in order to make his own way in the world. She could only recall the sameness of each day—the desperation and the hunger that never ceased . . . that and the weary, lost look on her mother's face when she'd come home every morn to their decrepit rooms above the alley from her work in the *stewes*. It had been a life Fiona had been eager to escape, though she'd never suspected that, when the chance finally came, it would be to a hell of a different kind. One a thousand times worse.

Shaking her head against her uncharacteristic, brooding thoughts, she again picked up her pace toward the tree shelter. It was already past midmorn; the dew had dried, and with the washing done, she planned to scour the forest for some of the herbs and flowers she needed to replenish her pots, which had been depleted during her treatment of Braedan's illness.

Ducking inside their dwelling, she put the folded garments in her trunk and took up one of the baskets left perched near the doorway, leaving again quickly so that she might begin her gathering before the sun rose too high. But something made her pause once more before she left the settlement, her attention drawn by some activity going on at the far side of the clearing.

Squinting, she raised her hand to shade her eyes, her heart beating more rapidly when she recognized Braedan's tall, powerful form in the midst of a group of older lads and several of the men. He was shirtless, his muscular torso and arms flexing under a faint sheen of sweat as he led them through what appeared to be a sword exercise. All the others held either sticks or weapons that had been confiscated during robberies, and many a brow was furrowed in concentration as the men struggled to follow Braedan's lead. He was magnificent to watch, his motions fluid, his blade flashing in the light as he lifted it high above his head, then twisted to the right. He paused in that position, looking over his shoulder to explain something to those behind him before bringing the blade down to slice at an unseen opponent.

That pleasant fluttering in Fiona's belly erupted anew, watching him move so. He was like a stunning, sleek predator, at once enticing and dangerous. It was clear that he commanded superior battle skills; the way he wielded his blade, both when she'd seen him use it during the feigned ambush and on the roadside gave weight to that truth.

Yet to know him as she did was to appreciate his

physical prowess even more, for though he possessed the ability to deal a killing strike at will, she'd come to realize that he never failed to maintain complete self-discipline. He was a combination of strength tempered by consummate control, and the remembered sensation of those powerful hands slipping beneath her hair to gently knead the muscles of her neck, or gliding with a feather-light stroke along her cheek, sent a tingle of longing through her that blended with the confusing warmth from her earlier thoughts of him.

She nurtured the sweetness of these unexpected feelings, wondering, with a start of surprise, if this might be what true desire felt like. In the past she'd known the bite of stark physical want under Draven's sinful tutelage, but this was very different. It was sensual, yes, but it was more as well. It went deeper somehow, spiraling into a kind of yearning she'd never experienced before. The realization of it left her aching, breathless, and more than a little flustered—so much so that she at first didn't notice that Braedan had ended his lesson and was approaching her with long, firm strides.

He'd apparently decided to cool himself after the sword exercises by dousing himself with water, and now, as he walked closer, he raked his fingers through his wet hair. By the time he reached her, her breathlessness had increased, though whether from the devastating effects of the smile he directed at her or something else entirely, it was impossible for her to tell.

He'd already redonned his shirt, and he was straightening the sleeves as he nodded toward the basket in her arms. "You're hard at work, it seems. But it is a smallish vessel for carrying the washing, is it not?"

"Aye, it would be, were that its purpose. But since it is

actually a basket for gathering herbs to replenish my pots, I think I am safe in its size."

"Ah, I see," he said, his blue eyes glimmering with humor. "You're off to hunt for more bitter remedies with which to plague me."

"It was either dose you with them or leave you to suffer," she quipped in return, cursing the heat that their playful banter sent spilling into her cheeks. But the tone of her answer coaxed a deeper grin from him, and she swallowed, struggling to manage the unfamiliar, riotous feelings he was provoking in her. "I should hope that you approve my choice to treat you."

"Indeed." Braedan met her gaze, his eyes brewing with something even more tantalizing than humor now. "And I am grateful for your care of me. So much so that I would like to offer my services in collecting more of the damnable things. I am finished with the work I had planned for the day. Would you care for me to join you in your forest quest?"

His suggestion caught her by surprise, and she paused, long enough that he added with mock seriousness, "You know these woods can be quite dangerous to wander about in alone. You might need my aid to fend off who knows what—wild boars or wolves—mayhap even a pack of dogs. The forest abounds with all kinds of ravenous creatures—"

"The only ravenous creature I'm likely to see this day is *you*, Braedan de Cantor, and well you know it," Fiona said, a smile tugging at her lips.

"I wouldn't be so certain. Gathering flowers can be a perilous venture."

Fiona laughed aloud this time. "You are impossible. But I would enjoy the company."

"Then I am at your service, my lady, prepared to defend you to the death," Braedan answered, giving her a courtly bow.

Still smiling, she swung the basket at him, so that he was forced to grab at it with an exaggerated grunt of surprise. "Here, take this and I'll get another to use for the plants. You can fill it with some bread, and perhaps a few of the winter apples Will has stored with the other foodstuffs. It will be past noon, and you'll no doubt be hungry before we're finished gathering what I need."

She'd looked away as she considered what else to bring on their venture, but when Braedan didn't respond, she looked back to him and felt a rush of warmth fill her. His teasing had given way to something much more serious, she realized, his expression revealing what seemed an almost-painful desire as his gaze fixed on her.

"In truth I am hungry *now*, lady," he murmured at last, his words caressing her like the stroke of his hands over her sensitized flesh. "Though with a kind of appetite that may never be sated. In the meantime, I shall have to content myself with gathering our meal."

Fiona stood rooted to the spot, her pulse racing and her senses afire; she looked at him helplessly, not knowing how to cope with what she felt. But in the next moment he took pity on her, releasing her from the pleasurable torment of his gaze by tipping his head in another little bow. He murmured something about meeting her at the path in a few moments. Then he turned and sauntered off to complete his task, swinging the basket in time to a tune he whistled as he went—and leaving Fiona scrambling to hold on to whatever remained of her completely disheveled wits.

* * *

By the time they were deep into the forest on their search for clumps of dog violet and betony, Braedan was cursing himself for his brilliant ideas. What in hell had he been thinking when he'd offered to come along? Being in such close proximity to Fiona, watching her move and bend among the greenery looking for the perfect tuft of flowers . . . catching the delicate scent of her hair, warmed by the sun that reached through the dense, lush-branched trees—all of it was torture, pure and simple, and he wasn't sure how much more he was going to be able to take.

He was a damned fool. That was the only way to explain it. He'd put himself into this position, knowing full well how it would make him feel. Day after day he spent his time in tantalizing nearness to her, acting for all intents and purposes like the husband he was supposed to be.

And then at night . . .

Biting back a groan, Braedan tried to concentrate on finding a patch of the violets she'd described to him, rather than looking at the sweet curve of her backside as she bent over to examine another plant. But the thought of how that bit of her felt pressed against him as she slept, cradled in his arms each night, nearly undid him, and he cursed himself again.

He'd had the perfect opportunity to avoid the temptation of being near her; Will's call for a day of rest had surprised him, but he had seized on it gladly, feeling a sense of bittersweet relief in knowing he could distract himself from his constant thoughts of Fiona with other things. His offer to show the other men one of the sword exercises he'd practiced during his years in foreign climes had stemmed in part from his need to burn away some of

what had been smoldering inside of him because of
Fiona. But it hadn't worked. Not really. It had taken the
edge off, aye, but the respite had been only temporary.

*How could it be otherwise, you idiot, when right after
the exercise was finished, you made a direct line to her
side again?*

Braedan winced at the mocking voice in his head,
knowing that he couldn't deny the truth of it. And now
here he was, suffering again with the painful pleasure of
being right next to her. *Alone* with her. It was a torture of
the self-inflicted kind that made it that much the worse
to bear.

"Oh, look at this, Braedan," Fiona called from her
bent position, not seeming aware of the agitation she
caused him in that pose. "There's a fine growth here already, thanks to the break in the trees."

When he didn't come closer, she turned her head to
him, and he was stunned anew at her beauty. Her cheeks
were flushed with pleasure at her find, and her auburn
hair shone lustrous in the shaft of sun. He tried to clear
his throat, his movements stiff and his legs feeling weak
from the force of his attraction as he made himself take
the few steps that would bring him nearer to her and the
plants she wanted him to see.

She'd already sunk to her knees next to one of the
leafy stalks she'd found with its budded flowers, and now
she reached absently for the basket he carried for her. Her
hand brushed his in the process, the warmth of her skin
somehow erotic in the cool of this grove, and he stilled,
desperate to do anything, say anything to divert his attention from the throbbing heat her nearness inspired.

He flipped open the basket's lid for her, watching in
complete distraction as she paused, murmured a little

prayer, and made the sign of the cross over one of the almost-knee-high stems before breaking it off near to the ground. That action startled him from his misery for a moment, and he frowned, asking, "Why did you do that?"

She lifted the stalk to examine it in the light, her concentration and the studious expression it called to her face enticing in a wholly unexpected way. "It is customary to do so when collecting this herb. Physics call it vervain, which is its proper name, I suppose, but most common folk call it herb of grace or herb of the cross, since it is believed to be the plant used to stanch Christ's wounds at the crucifixion."

Braedan clenched his jaw, closing his eyes for a moment as he tried to control the raging demands that were coming ever more powerfully from his lower anatomy. He focused his thoughts with an effort, finally managing to ask in a strangled voice, "How does it work?"

"Hmmm?" she murmured, intent on securing the plant in the basket. He repeated the question as she broke off another stalk, and she glanced at him with a bemused expression. "Oh. It is thanks to a certain property of the fresh leaves; a poultice of them, mashed, is pressed onto wounds. It causes the flesh to tighten, helping to slow the flow of blood."

Braedan made a noise in his throat, muttering, "I could have used such knowledge after some of our battles for the king." He was still trying to do all he could to avoid looking at Fiona, and so in an attempt both to subdue his attraction to her and satisfy his curiosity in the matter, he asked, "How is it that you came by such detailed learning, lady? Your life in the *stewes* surely wouldn't have called for such skills, yet you seem better

trained than most of the healers I've had the misfortune
of meeting in my travels."

Even without looking right at her, Braedan could tell
that she stiffened at the question. He glanced at her then
and was startled by her pained expression, but in the
next instant she'd masked the reaction with renewed
motion. Making the sign of the cross and plucking another stalk to place it in the basket, she answered lightly,
"Did you not know that your uncle was well versed in
such matters? He once knew an alchemist, since executed by the crown. It was that man who taught Draven
all he knows—and Draven who decided to instruct me
with bits of the skill."

"Why would he have wanted to do that?"

"For the same reason he taught me the use of a dagger, or how to speak and carry myself like a lady—
because it amused him."

Braedan frowned. "The man who taught my uncle
about the use of herbs—you say he was executed by the
crown?"

The bitter smile came back full force. "Aye. His
alchemy was not dedicated to healing alone, you see. He
dabbled in the darker arts as well, and when he was
caught, he was burned for it. But not before he imparted
much of his unholy wisdom to Draven."

"I had no idea . . ."

Fiona nodded, the shadows haunting her eyes.
"Draven proved quite a gifted scholar of the skills." In
the next moment she seemed to pull herself from that
place with an effort to look over at him again, her face
pale but composed. "And yet, I cannot say it was all bad,
for I learned a great deal of what has proved helpful, for
myself and others. My knowledge of this plant, for in-

stance," she said, making the gesture again with her hand and breaking off another stalk. "It has other uses besides the treatment of wounds. When the leaves and the pods just below these flower buds are dried, brewed with honeyed water, and sipped, it is a fine method of reducing fever. Without it, I would not have been able to help you as I did during your illness at Alton."

She glanced sideways at him, then, a shade of the more playful look returning to her gaze. "In fact, it is likely the herb you remember from your time of sickness. It has a bit of a bitter taste, and I dosed you with it often those four days, trying to ease your fever."

"Likely it is the one, then," he said, frowning as if he was remembering that uncomfortable time rather than thinking about the new information he'd just learned concerning Draven.

As he spoke, Fiona nodded and twisted away from him again, leaning forward and stretching to reach the last remaining stalk from the clump of vervain that had been growing there. Braedan made the mistake of looking at her at that moment, his guard down and his mind distracted as it was with the thoughts of his uncle. Too late he realized his error, but by then the tantalizing, carnal image that the sight of her bent over before him was already stamped into his brain, spinning like warmed honey through his blood. A renewed tide of hot desire followed close after, slamming into him with a force that nearly took his breath away.

Barely biting back a groan, he lurched to his feet, desperate to put some sanity-saving distance between them. "What else do you need to gather, then, lady?" he nearly choked. "We have some betony and now this herb. Are the violets truly necessary, or can we go back?"

Her gentle laughter washed over him as she, too, stood and brushed her hands off on her skirt. "If I didn't know better, Braedan de Cantor, I'd say you were trying to escape the remainder of our task here."

"It is not the task I am trying to avoid."

"What, then?"

She turned to face him, and he realized, suddenly, just how close they were standing to each other—so close that her delicate fragrance filled his senses. He could almost feel the brush of her body against his, and the realization made his skin burn at every point where her delicious contours would mold to him, were she but a few inches nearer. The desire he fought against pitched infinitely higher. God in heaven, but this was impossible. It was a lost cause, and he could feel himself being pulled along on the incredible tide of it, helpless any longer to resist.

He cursed under his breath, finally exhaling in a sigh of defeat. "Ah, Fiona, there is no work that would be too challenging, no battle I would not willingly undertake in the cause of right. But today . . ." Slowly, he reached out to cradle the curve of her jaw, his yearning growing more fierce with each passing heartbeat. ". . . today I am finding myself quite unequal to the task of not pulling you into my arms as I've been longing to do all morning. It is *that* which makes me eager to leave this place, nothing more."

She was silent in response to his passionate declaration. But though she'd gone very still before him, the look in her eyes gave him hope that his words were not entirely unwelcome; he brushed his thumb over her cheek where he cupped it, the satiny warmth of her skin intoxicating.

"I know that because of the circumstances of your

past, the thought of such things leaves you cold," Braedan added after a moment, keeping up the rhythmic stroking with his thumb, "and yet I have felt"—he paused, wanting badly to get this right—"I have hoped that I am not wrong in sensing something different in you of late toward me."

After a long silence she swallowed, her gaze searching his. "It is true that I do feel something . . . different when I am with you, Braedan," she answered at last, "but I do not know what it is or even how to explain it."

"In this life I have discovered that there are some things which defy explanation, lady," he murmured, as he slid his other hand up to join the first in cradling her face with the gentlest touch he could summon, "like the way I cannot seem to stop feeling when I am near you, or the overwhelming urge I have to kiss you right now."

"Why do you not, then?" she whispered, keeping her gaze locked to his, her pulse beating wildly under his fingers.

"Because I promised you once that I would gain your consent in such things first. So I ask you now, Fiona, will you allow me to kiss you?" He gazed deep into the tawny depths of her eyes, yearning to see something there, a spark of passion, perhaps, that would let him know he was not alone in these feelings that had consumed him. That she *did* feel something when she was with him . . .

Then the unexpected happened; her eyes closed, briefly, but when she opened them again, a glistening of tears moistened their depths. Braedan stiffened with surprise. Tears were not what he had hoped for. Nay, it was not at all the emotion he'd wished to inspire in her. Not sadness . . .

He frowned. "Lady, why do you cry?"

She gave him a tremulous smile, lifting her hands to rest atop his and tilting her head to press her cheek more fully into his palm. "I am not crying, Braedan, truly. It is just that you are the first to ever—" She broke off in a hitched sigh, bringing his hands down with her own, keeping her fingers twined with his. "It is just that until now kissing, touching—anything of the kind was always simply done to me without question or care. My feelings never came into the matter."

"That is likely why you have never been able to feel pleasure in such things, then."

"Perhaps." She glanced down for an instant, her teeth worrying her bottom lip, before lifting her face to his again. "And yet I think that I would feel pleasure in it now, Braedan . . . in kissing you . . ."

"I was hoping you would say that," he answered, his voice husky, "for I think that I would feel great pleasure in it, too."

Releasing one of her hands, he touched her chin again, using his fingertips to tilt her face gently up to him as he bent his head to brush his lips over hers, leaving for an instant and then coming back to taste again. A thrill of rapture shot through him. She was pure ambrosia, her mouth responsive and so tempting he could not help but go back for more. The taste of her intoxicated him, pushing him into some mindless place. He used the tip of his tongue to lightly stroke the tender curve of her lips before dipping into the honeyed recess, and she moaned softly, opening to him, her tongue moving cautiously, delicately in time with his, sweet and slow.

Braedan's heart thundered in his chest as Fiona leaned closer to him, the press of her body driving him to near insanity. He slid his hands down her back, stopping at her waist, and it was all he could do not to pull her closer, not to drag her deliciously up against his entire length. But he held back, thankful for this small gift of intimacy from her. It was a start, after all, as incongruous as it was for him to find a woman of her experience owning such tender sensibilities.

Fiona felt swept away by the sensations engulfing her. Moaning again, she let her hands drift up to Braedan's shoulders, gripping him when she feared her legs would buckle beneath her. She kissed him back, reveling in the taste of him, in the sweetly seductive stroke of his mouth across hers. It was beautiful and humbling all at once. She'd never known a man's kiss could feel like this. It was like floating at sea, her body carried on rolling waves. Her pulse raced, her breath shallow under Braedan's heated ministrations, and so she closed her eyes, trying to regain some sense of balance.

It was hopeless. She was lost in him, drowning in sensation, and she never wanted it to end. "Braedan," she whispered against his lips when she could bear to tilt her mouth away from his just a bit, "It is wonderful, but—"

"It's all right," he murmured, kissing a path from the corner of her mouth, along her jaw, to nuzzle the tender spot just beneath her ear. He moved up a bit then to the shell of it, his breath warm and moist, sending a delicious tingle through her. "We'll go slowly. Just allow yourself to feel the pleasure of it, lady." Her neck felt as limp, her head tipping back instinctively as his mouth claimed access to the now-exposed length of her throat.

"Ah, Fiona," Braedan said softly, "your skin is like silk—"

"Mistress Giselle!" a faint voice called frantically from somewhere far behind them in the forest, and

Fiona was jerked out of the sweet cloud of sensation she'd been floating upon in Braedan's embrace. Gasping, she whispered, "Did you hear that?"

"Aye." He'd pulled back, though he still held her waist with his strong hands. Now he stepped away completely, looking around them as if trying to ascertain from which direction the cry had come.

Fiona felt a shuddering begin in her stomach. Something was wrong; no one from the settlement would come looking for her deep in the wood like this unless it was something serious.

"Mistress!" The high-pitched voice rang out again, a bit nearer to them this time, accompanied by the dim sounds of crackling undergrowth, and Fiona called back, hoping the person would hear her. In the next moments her efforts were rewarded; one of the younger lads who had been playing at hoodman blind a few hours ago came crashing into the glen.

"Stephen Fisk, you frightened us near to death. What is the matter?" Fiona asked, moving quickly to him. She took his arm and helped him to sit, glancing over at Braedan, who approached as well, looking as worried as she felt.

"Mistress, 'tis bad—very bad," Stephen stuttered between gasping breaths. "Nate's been hurt. Poachin' he was, even though yer brother forbid it after what happened to Thomas. He's been shot through."

"Christ," Braedan muttered.

"How bad is it?" Fiona asked, gripping Stephen's hand. "Where was he hurt?"

"His leg, with a bolt from a crossbow. One of the king's foresters caught him huntin' and tried to take him in to the sheriff, but Nate got free. They shot him when he ran away." Stephen took a few more gasping breaths and continued, "He made it back to camp, but the bolt stuck in his leg, and there be a stream of blood comin' from him, steady-like."

Stephen's face was twisted in his attempt not to cry, though he couldn't stop his eyes from tearing. "I—I saw him, mistress, and he—he looks like a ghost, he does. Some of them back at the settlement was whisperin' that such is what he'll be if'n we can't stop the bleeding soon. 'Tis why they sent me for you. They said you know more than any of us of such things." Stephen turned his wide brown gaze on her, the hopeful expression in his eyes making her insides lurch with compassion. "Can ye do it, mistress? Can ye save Nate?"

"I don't know, Stephen," Fiona said grimly, swiftly taking up the herbs while Braedan picked up the basket of food they'd never had a chance to eat. "But I will do my best, you can be assured of that."

"Come, lad," Braedan murmured to Stephen, leading the way from the glen. And so without another word, the three of them set off for the settlement again and the gravely injured boy who awaited them there.

Chapter 10

Fiona tightened the poultice-soaked bandage around Nate's thigh, wincing at the pain she knew he was going to feel when he woke up. Thankfully, he'd fallen senseless several minutes ago right after the worst of the treatment they'd been forced to give him in order to keep him from bleeding to death.

She clenched her jaw as she worked on him, remembering the stoicism in his face as they'd cauterized the wound. She'd had Braedan do it with the flat of a sword, heated red-hot, asking Will and Grady to help hold the boy still through the excruciating process. He'd been brave; she'd seen grown men undergoing similar treatments thrash and scream from the pain of it, but Nate had remained rigid and silent. When it was done, Braedan had reached down and brushed his hair back from his pale brow, his own face tight, murmuring words of praise for his show of courage. Then the men had moved off to talk about the situation, and she'd been left to apply the herbs and poultices that would hopefully help him to heal. Only time would tell if it had been too much for his body to take. Fiona prayed with all of her heart that he would be strong enough to recover from the wound and blood loss, though, if he survived, she knew his leg would be badly scarred from the ordeal.

Using the back of her soiled hand to push a strand of hair from her eyes, Fiona sighed and sat back on her heels. She'd done all she could for him; there was nothing left but to look at the bindings every hour and keep checking him for the fever that would inevitably set in. After giving instructions to one of the women who would be sitting first vigil with Nate, Fiona pushed up to standing and approached the men, where they were embroiled in deep discussion.

"Why the devil was he out there alone to begin with?" Grady was arguing. "Damn fool boy, gettin' into what he shouldn't have."

"He shouldn't have been alone, that's true," Will muttered, "but he was only tryin' to do good."

"How so—by gettin' himself maimed?"

"Lads his age rarely think of the danger to themselves," Braedan interjected, his face still grim. "I saw enough of them die on the field at Saint-Jean-d'Acre with the shock of it on their faces to attest to that."

That sobering thought silenced everyone for a moment, though Grady piped up again, "Well he should have thought about it this time. Will told us all to stay clear of poachin' until further notice."

"You can't blame the lad, Grady—he's been hungry like the rest of us, and in his own mind he was tryin' to help," Rufus argued. " 'Tis only since Giselle and de Cantor came that we've taken enough roadside to warrant a trip into the village for supplies. A group is to be sent to the village tomorrow, isn't it, Will?"

"Aye," her brother said somberly. "We've enough coin now to ensure that everyone's trencher is filled." He cursed under his breath and looked away. " 'Tis my fault this happened. I should have told him about the trip for supplies. If he'd known, mayhap he wouldn't have—"

"Christ almighty, Will, he knew better even so," Grady said, swiping his beefy hand across his eyes to clear the telltale signs of how much he really cared for the lad. "He saw Thomas after the sheriff got him. The old man's got nothin' but a stump where his hand used to be. And now Nate . . . blasted hell, if the lad dies because of this . . ." Grady's voice trailed off into a choking sound, and he looked away.

Fiona felt anguish grip at her heart again. She'd recently learned just how close Grady and Nate were—like a father and son, Rosalind's mother had told her. Neither one had anyone else, either sickness or the law having taken off whatever family they'd once had, so they'd taken to each other and made a new family of just the two of them. She stepped forward and put her hand on Grady's shoulder, and he swung his head to look at her, his eyes streaked red.

"We'll do everything we can, Grady, I promise you."

"Thank you, mistress," he said gruffly, clearing his throat again. "You are truly an angel of mercy, as good of heart as that devil of a sheriff is black of soul."

Fiona frowned. "He must be a monster to sanction cutting off old men's hands and shooting at boys. It is worse, even, than I remember it from three years ago, though the sheriff then was bad enough. Who is this new man, and how long has he been in power over these lands?"

Everyone stiffened at her question, Will and Braedan looking at her with almost-identical expressions of dismay; it sent a chill through her, though she forced herself not to react. Not yet, at least until she had an answer. After an awkward pause, her brother finally cursed under his breath, and spoke. "I thought it was common knowledge, lass, or I would have told you myself."

"Told me what?"

"I thought you knew as well," Braedan said quietly, meeting her gaze again. "It's Draven, lady. He is the sheriff. He was named to the post not quite a year before my father's death."

"Aye, Draven is a bastard all right," Grady muttered, looking over at Nate's still form resting under blankets near the fire. "May he roast in hell for eternity."

Fiona couldn't answer at first for the squeezing, sick sensation that was rising up into her throat. *Draven* was sheriff? Nay, not him, of all people. He was corruption incarnate, the one man she knew for certain would pervert true justice at every opportunity for the simple pleasure of it.

"It can't be . . ." she murmured at last.

"I'm afraid it is," Will said, his face somber, "though I'm sorry you had to learn of it this way. He still lives like a king at that estate of his, givin' dictates to the forest justices and the rest of his men to keep our lives a misery. Every outlaw band from here to London feels the bite of his brand of justice. I'd like to have a chance at him, to show him what I think of his ways, but he's yet to make an appearance around here." He shook his head. "More's the pity, but I don't think there's any danger that he'll be leavin' his seat of luxury to seek us out anytime soon."

"Aye, no danger," Fiona whispered, looking away.

Braedan stepped up next to her. "Perhaps you should rest now. You may be needed in the night to tend to Nate. Come." He nodded to the others and led her toward their quarters; she went without resistance, her entire body feeling as insubstantial as a waft of smoke from the fire. The idea of Draven in a position of that much authority—of that much power over the lives of innocent people—made her skin crawl with a kind of foreboding worse than any she'd experienced since the first day she'd been brought to his lavish estate at a tender fifteen.

Once they'd reached the darkened seclusion of their shelter, Braedan guided her to sit on the trunk near their pallet. When she was settled, he leaned back against the wall, his arms folded over his chest, his face telling her far more openly than words ever could how much he regretted having to share such disturbing information with her.

"I am still having difficulty believing it," she said at last, shaking her head.

"I thought you knew, Fiona, or I would have made certain to tell you long ago," he answered quietly. "It must be a shock to learn of it so."

A bitter smile twisted her lips. "After hearing about Tom and seeing Nate, I cannot say that I'm surprised to discover it is Draven behind it."

"My father hated him for the cruelty he showed with acts like that, you know. He wrote as much in his private papers, and even sent a letter of complaint to King Edward, under his authority as Chief Forest Justice, detailing his concerns, but the sickness took him before the matter could be addressed. Richard told me that Draven gained the sovereign's ear shortly afterward and soothed any remaining concerns with his usual brand of lies."

Fiona nodded, still struggling with the nausea that gripped her. "I remember some of the dealings we had with your father those years ago; he was a thorn in our side much of the time, it is true, but he would overlook the law, on occasion, if it was clear that it was hunger and not greed that had been behind the breaking of it. He seemed a fair-minded man, overall." She looked up at Braedan, then, startled by the understanding that suddenly struck her. "You are much like him, I think, though I did not realize how much at first."

"Nay, lady." Braedan pushed away from the wall then, his eyes dark. "My father was a good man who strove to make life better for others. I cannot claim the same. It is beyond me, it seems, to protect even those most vulnerable in my care." He made a scoffing sound. "I am naught but a pretender compared to what he was."

As he'd spoken, he'd moved to his bundle of possessions, taking the little leather purse from inside it to begin counting their share of the plunder they'd been collecting since joining Will's band of outlaws. She bit the inside of her cheek as she watched him, resisting the urge to tell him just how good a man she'd found him to be—to tell him about the kindness she felt radiating from him, even when he did nothing more important than brush back the hair from the brow of a wounded boy. But he wouldn't accept her praise, she knew. Especially not in the frame of mind he was in just then.

"How much more do you think you will need to warrant our trip into London and a search of the *stewes*?" she asked quietly, after he'd finished tallying the coins and tying the purse strings tight again before replacing it in his sack. He was sitting back on his heels, having taken something from a folded piece of cloth to tuck it between his tunic and shirt.

"Another take like the first with the pardoner should be enough, I think, or several smaller to equal it. Either way, I dare not wait much longer, and will make do with whatever we manage to accumulate in the next few days. I want to leave for London by next week at latest."

Even though she was surprised, Fiona started to reach out to him, something inside of her wanting desperately to comfort him, but at the last moment she kept her hands fisted on her lap. "Will has said that a group will ride tomorrow to set up a take on a different stretch of road," she said. "I will tell him we wish to be a part of it, rather than among those traveling to purchase supplies. Perhaps we will gain enough from a few hour's work there that we can set out the day after to begin your search in the *stewes*."

Braedan nodded, his mouth still tight, his blue eyes somber with the conflicting emotions at war in him. Glancing away, he said, "Try to rest now, Fiona. I will return by nightfall."

"Where are you going?"

"Nowhere—anywhere . . . I just—" He broke off and sighed, jabbing his hand through his hair as he swung toward the door and called out over his shoulder, "I'm going to check on our mounts. My steed needs to be given full rein to run now and again, or he becomes restless."

Fiona watched mutely as the cloth that covered the

tree shelter's door swished back into place behind Braedan, leaving her alone with her thoughts, her fears, and the strange emptiness she was beginning to feel, like an ache inside her, whenever he wasn't near.

Moonlight spread cool and luminous across the clearing by the time Braedan approached the outlaw settlement again. His self-directed ire had dulled a bit in the intervening hours, though it had never entirely disappeared. While he knew logically that there was no help for his delay in seeking Elizabeth, his heart continued to protest in relentless complaint—so much so that he'd had to ignore it forcibly in order to pursue any rational plan for helping his foster sister.

During that dark time when he'd first learned of Elizabeth's plight from Richard, he had reacted in the way that came most naturally to him, storming into Draven's private quarters at Chepston and confronting him. Yet attacking Draven had achieved nothing more than the satisfaction of landing a few well-placed punches. Soon the scuffle had turned deadly, and though his uncle was known for his impressive sword skills, Braedan had been better, ultimately pinning him at the end of his blade. But before he could gain information concerning Elizabeth's whereabouts, Draven's men had converged on him; there had been too many, and in the end they had overpowered him and confined him in the rooms below the main keep.

The torture had commenced then, with Draven directing the entire process—his way of making Braedan pay for his assault and besting of him. If nothing else, Braedan had learned, and painfully so, just how important Draven's pride was to him. His uncle had toyed with him for a certain measure, and then he'd used his power as sheriff to level false charges of treason against him, arranging in a written message to the king for the trial to take place at Chepston Hall. Within days, a jury of his hand-chosen men was in place, guaranteed to bring in a verdict of guilt and subsequent execution.

Braedan had known then that he had to escape; it was either that or allow Draven to take his head, and with it any hope for Elizabeth's rescue and Richard's future safety. It had been difficult. He'd been weakened by the torture and a lack of food and water. But his survival instincts had been stronger than the pain, and he'd fought himself free of the lower chambers and Chepston Hall, leaving behind the mangled corpses of four of Draven's men and a slew of frightened kitchen servants. His search for Fiona had been undertaken the week after, once he'd attempted to navigate the *stewes* on his own for information about Elizabeth, with nothing to show for his efforts but suspicious glances and slammed doors.

Now here he was, within a few days of having enough coin to undertake a more effective search, and yet he was allowing the debilitating guilt to eat away at him again. It weighed on him, making him feel unsettled and vaguely annoyed. So much that had happened in the past few months had thrown him off-balance—his return from Saint-Jean-d'Acre to a family nearly destroyed by illness and evil, his arrest, torture, escape, and branding as an outlaw, the public dissolution of his betrothal to Julia . . .

And then, of course, meeting Fiona . . .

He paused for a moment just inside the clearing, his gaze searching for any glimpse of movement. There was none. The entire settlement seemed at rest. Perhaps his counterfeit bride was sleeping, then, or tending to Nate in the little shelter that had been constructed apart from the main settlement for treating those who were ill or injured.

He scowled, clenching his fist over the miniature of his former betrothed, the tiny, gilt-framed painting of Julia that he'd taken from his belongings earlier that day. He'd been aware of its weight and mocking presence at his side all evening—had brought it along with him for that purpose, to remind himself of what it was he wanted in his life when all this insanity was over.

Of the kind of woman he would need to reestablish his honorable existence and place in society once Elizabeth was saved, Richard secured, and Draven dealt with.

But it hadn't helped, because no matter how many times he looked at the exquisite portrait, or tried to recall the impeccable qualities of the woman it represented, his mind kept drifting to another face. To an image of a woman with tawny eyes and auburn hair, whose demeanor revealed a capacity for passion layered beneath with a quiet sense of dignity and honor.

To Fiona.

He'd realized today that he didn't really want Julia, or even any woman like her. He wanted *Fiona*. He wanted her in every way a man could want a woman, in a way that went beyond physical desire, enticing as she was. He'd tried to fool himself into believing it was simple lust for long enough. It was more than that; he knew it now. He yearned to taste something deeper with her, a giving of soul that a mere joining of bodies could not hope to imitate.

And it had made him damn angry to realize it.

He'd tried to argue himself out of it, wanted more than anything to resist what he was feeling, but he couldn't. After escaping Chepston Hall, he'd initiated his plan to track down the Crimson Lady and coerce her to help him with his eyes wide open, knowing full well that she was a notorious courtesan and thief; he'd been prepared to use her for what he needed, then let her go to resume her sordid activities at will. But his assumptions had been proved false. Again and again, she'd turned his world upside down, rattling his beliefs of what she would be with the humbling reality of who she was.

He'd come to appreciate things about her that he'd never thought possible, to recognize attributes that he'd never dreamed a woman of her history could possess. But they were there. Shadowed past or not, Fiona was a giving, caring woman, full of tender feelings, hopes, and fears, and he wanted her more with every breath he drew. Running off and riding the wind on his steed hadn't changed that fact one bit.

It was quite a dilemma . . . one that he had no idea for resolving, except in the fantasy of his own thoughts—for how could he reconcile what he wanted with who he was—the kind of man he'd been his entire life and hoped to be again? Deep down, he didn't believe himself an outlaw any more than Fiona was the noblewoman she sometimes played. He was the son of a crown justice, doing all that he could to regain his status of respect—the inheritor to a way of life that was in direct opposition to the one from which she came. And yet . . . and yet . . .

Making a sound of disgust and shoving the miniature

into the fold of his cape, Braedan shook his head, setting out to find the object of his tortured thoughts. It was too much to worry about right now. He didn't need to make those kinds of decisions yet; first he had to do what had brought him to Fiona in the first place and rescue Elizabeth. Helping his brother and bringing Draven to justice would come next. The rest would have to work itself out in its own time, for good or for ill.

Pushing aside the flap to their tree shelter, he ducked in and let his eyes adjust to the moonless interior. The mounded forms at the back of the hollow showed that Will and Joan were already at rest, but the pallet he and Fiona shared was empty. She was with Nate, then. He should have expected as much, knowing her as he did; she'd not be sleeping easy and far from the lad's side until he was past the worst with his wounds.

Tossing his cloak onto their pallet, Braedan left their abode again and headed for the shelter where the ill and infirm were housed at the settlement's edge. A fire glowed just in front of the roughly constructed lean-to, and as he approached he could tell that though a few flames flickered on the surface, it had burnt down mostly to coals. The light from the fire was brighter than the moon's glow, however, and he saw that Nate was stretched out on a pallet of blankets within the shelter, while a woman sat hunched before the low-burning blaze. *Fiona*.

He held back for a moment, suppressing the surge of gladness that went through him at the sight of her. She was beautiful, even wrapped in a coarse-spun blanket against the night air. As Braedan watched, she got up from her position at the fire to check Nate's bandage, feeling his brow and adjusting the coverlet over his still form before returning to her vigil at fireside. The boy seemed to be asleep, though his face was flushed and his breathing shallow. He wasn't in the clear yet, it seemed, his body still fighting the wound.

Braedan's mouth tightened at the memory of Nate's suffering, and he resumed his approach; Fiona turned upon hearing him, making a motion for quiet. He completed the distance in silence and sat down next to her near some overturned logs round the fire, noticing that several others, including old Grady, were spread out asleep on pallets all around. When he'd gotten himself settled, he asked quietly of her, "How fares the lad, then?"

"As well as can be expected." She took a twig she'd been spinning in her fingers and tossed it into the coals before glancing over at Nate again.

"He looks feverish."

"He is, still. It began a few hours before sundown, but it seems to have lessened a bit this past hour. And his pain has faded enough with the herbs I gave him that he no longer moans in his sleep."

Braedan nodded, relief mingling with the strange satisfaction he felt at being near to her again. He'd missed her. *Even for those few hours,* he realized. The idea of it baffled him. He'd never felt so about anyone before, most especially not a woman. But it was there now, undeniable, the gnawing ache that had crept in when he was gone somehow soothed by her nearness.

As if she'd read his thoughts, she glanced over at him, hesitating before she murmured, "I—I am glad that you're back, Braedan. I was beginning to worry, wondering what might have kept you so long."

Warmth slid through him at that, but he looked away, not wanting her to see the power her words had over him. Clearing his throat, he answered, "I told you I would return, lady; you needn't have feared—and I am here now as always, at your service."

"That is not what I meant, Braedan." The enigmatic quality of her voice pulled his gaze to her again. "It is not because of what you can do for me that I am glad you've returned. I just wanted you to know that I—" She stopped, picking another twig from the pile of branches stacked nearby and fiddling with it as if considering whether or not she would complete her thoughts aloud. At last she added more quietly, "I suppose it is just that I feel more at peace when you're here, and I wanted you to know. I do not understand why that is, and it is likely illogical to feel so, but—"

"I do not find it illogical, lady," Braedan answered, his voice low. She met his gaze again then, a fleeting look, and even in the fire's dying light he could see the faint blush spread over her cheeks. With a self-conscious smile, she ducked her head and looked away again, but he wasn't ready to abandon their conversation yet. "You've been awake overlong. Why don't you stretch out on one of the pallets for a bit? I'll take the remainder of the watch for you."

"Nay, I cannot." She shook her head, looking at Nate again. "You wouldn't know what to do if he becomes feverish again."

It was a good argument, Braedan conceded, but it wasn't going to achieve the sleep he knew she needed. Without saying more, he slid behind her, tugging her back against his chest.

She protested at first, but after a while she eased into his embrace with a grateful sigh; the rightness of it settled over him, and he cradled her close with his hands linked around her waist. Peaceful quiet fell around them, and his breathing slowed, the moment overtaking his senses. It was wonderful, holding her like this. It astonished him, the way that something so simple could be so satisfying. Moving in slowly, to more fully enjoy the sensation of her in his arms, Braedan brushed a kiss over the delicate skin of her temple, stilling afterward to stare into the flickering coals with her.

"This is much better, don't you think?" he murmured in her ear.

"Aye, much." She sighed again, and he could feel her relaxing in his arms, her fingers stroking the backs of his hands in an intoxicating pattern.

"Rest now. I don't want you taking ill yourself from too little sleep," he added, closing his eyes at the wonderful sensations she was causing with her touch.

"It is of no matter, really. I have stayed awake until dawn many times before."

Braedan couldn't stop his instinctive stiffening at her answer, his mind latching on to thoughts of her past and the reasons she might have had for going without sleep in the years before he knew her. Her fingers stilled in response to his reaction. But in the next instant he realized that he didn't care if her work as the Crimson Lady was what she meant; it was part of long ago, something she couldn't change. Perhaps she didn't want it changed—it mattered little to him. He saw her for what she was to him, and that was enough for now. Tugging her back more firmly against him, he said, "You should close your eyes while you have a chance, then. I will wake you if Nate seems worse."

"Nay, I will sit here with you, but I do not think I should close my—"

"Sleep, Fiona," he said more firmly, kissing her cheek

and shifting to make her lean back more comfortably into him. "I will wake you if you're needed, I promise."

After a moment more, she pulled his arms closer around her, nodding and snuggling into his embrace. She'd hardly exhaled again, managing to mumble a sleepy "Thank you," before she was asleep.

Smiling, Braedan held still and soaked in the moment, reveling in the feelings coursing through him, the pleasure it gave him to do something for her for once—he who from their first hour together had by necessity done nothing but take. It was a welcome change, assuaging some of the guilt he'd been experiencing ever since he'd walked into her shop and coerced her into helping him. But it was something more, too. Even with their divergent paths in life—she the courtesan and he the son of a crown justice—it was right somehow, he realized. Having her in his arms like this was another small gift to savor.

Settling back against the log behind him, Braedan breathed in the faint, sweet fragrance of Fiona's hair blended with night air and the drifting smoke from the fire, relishing the warm weight of her against him. . . .

And quieting, with the simple act of holding her, some of the bitterness that had long been churning in his soul.

Chapter 11

Fiona eyed the handful of coins and the single silver ring that Will was adding to the sack of their day's take thus far. It had been a less than successful morning, the marks they'd been forced to choose being lone riders or pairs only, but a few coaches or litters having passed by, and those too well guarded for Will to order a confrontation. The weather hadn't helped either. An early-summer shower threatened to unleash from the skies at any moment, the darkening clouds and stirring winds only adding to the feelings of frustration among the group, who at the moment were standing nearly a hundred feet off the road in a pocket of leafy, concealing trees.

"I say we split up—half of us to Yardley Cross, over the hill, and the others to stay here," Tom Thatcher groused. "At least we might be able to collect double the pittance we've been gettin' so far here today."

"We're already thin in numbers with Grady and Nate back at the settlement," Will answered, tossing the sack of plunder to Rufus. "We shouldn't divide further. Besides, Tucker Tilton's gang takes the area near Yardley Cross; we can't afford to set him off against us again by steppin' into his boundaries."

"Then at least let us take a coach or two, Will!" the man argued.

"Nay—not unless the odds are right."

"With Tom, me, and Jepthas we've got a total of six men and Giselle here now," Henry Fisk offered. "That's more than you had when you took the pardoner's purse two weeks ago."

"Aye, but there were only two guards and the coachman then—and even so we were lucky it worked as well as it did."

"But we can do it, Will!" Tom said. "Let's just take a rich coach or two and be done with it for the day, before the rain turns the road to mud and stops the travelers from comin' by."

Will remained silent, his weight on one leg and his fist against his hip, looking around the group. Fiona knew the risks her brother was considering—and knew also how much he had hoped for a few profitable takes that day to continue their luck of the previous week, how much he wished to provide some security for his band of outlaws, who had suffered too long under the gnawing bite of hunger this past winter. His gaze settled on Braedan, who was standing next to her with his arms folded across his chest. She glanced at the man who had been occupying her thoughts so completely as well, sensing his answering disappointment in this day, and knowing before he spoke what his answer would be to the question Will asked him next.

"Well, what's your opinion on this de Cantor? Are you for trying to take another coach?"

Braedan nodded. "If it is meet with the rest of you, I'm for it."

"Then we'll scout the next to come through. The road branches off not far before us, though, so we will need two men as runners to spot from either direction. It should be a coach that looks to be rich but not overly guarded."

"I'll go!" all five men said nearly simultaneously, and Will's mouth quirked on one side as he shook his head.

"I suppose I should be grateful for the enthusiasm, but we have to divide the tasks. Jepthas and Tom can go, and the rest of us will stay here to set up the ruse. Without Nate, we cannot enact the stranded noblewoman, and yet a coach will not stop to aid a simple peasant," Will said, indicating the plain attire they'd had Fiona wear for the morning's work thus far. "Giselle will have to change into the fustian kirtle and circlet we brought and ready herself to play the part of a noblewoman beset by outlaws—" he grinned fully this time, his blue eyes sparkling, "—my favorite of our ploys, I confess."

Braedan frowned, glancing at her. "I never said I was willing to put her in harm's way. This sounds more dangerous than other parts she's played."

"Oh, don't worry, man, it is only a pretense," Will broke in, drawing Braedan's attention again. "She won't be hurt. She might be your wife, but she's my sister as well, remember? This ploy just tweaks my humor, is all. We get to enact that which we already are, and in doing so, we catch a purse from the kind of person who usually overlooks the rape, robbery, or attack of women who cannot claim noble blood and title. Call it playin' to my fine sense of justice if you will," her brother added, winking at Braedan.

Braedan continued to frown, turning to her and asking quietly, "Are you comfortable with this, lady? I wish to hear your thoughts on it before I'll agree to take part."

"It is fine, Braedan," Fiona answered, flushing as she caught her brother's eye-rolling bemusement. "Quite safe, really. I've done it many times before." She glanced up at him, then, the swell of strange feeling inside her at his concern making her cheeks feel even warmer. "If you'd feel better about it, you can play the man who has me in his grip. That way you'll know I am safe."

"I'm not sure I could make an attack on you look convincing."

"Aye, it would more likely seem a lover's embrace, if all this mooning is any indication," Will drawled, sauntering forward. "You'd better let me take that part, sister." He swiveled his head to Braedan. "You can trust me to keep her safe in it, can't you, de Cantor? I know what to do to make it look real without harmin' a hair on her precious head."

Braedan still didn't look happy about it, but at last he gave a jerking nod, and they all dispersed to get ready for their respective parts. Soon Fiona was ready, having changed, in the privacy of the wood, into the dark blue kirtle Will had brought with them, belting it with a gold braid. All that remained was the circlet, and so she unbound her plaited hair and started to slide it in place.

"Here, let me help."

Braedan's low voice caressed her even as his hands

deftly adjusted the mass of her tresses around the circlet to help secure it.

"Thank you," she murmured, still feeling the tingling pleasure from his touch even when he'd finished assisting her. She turned to face him, then, her breath catching at the look in his eyes. She glanced down, her senses rising to meet the heat smoldering in his gaze.

"You look beautiful, Fiona," he said, never breaking his stare.

"It is but borrowed finery—all a part of the role that I play," she answered lightly, trying to distance herself from the turbulent emotions his nearness was causing her. She smiled and began to move past him to make her way to their roadside position.

He took her arm, gently tugging her to a halt and making her look at him. She swallowed and felt her mouth go dry. He held her mesmerized, and she knew she'd have been still before him whether or not his touch on her arm restrained her.

"It is no role, this beauty of yours, lady," he said, his voice husky. "It comes from deep within you, something you cannot disguise or change. In truth you seemed as attractive in your peasant garments as now. Even when you hid yourself under the bulky pads and widow's weeds when I first met you, I could see the light that shone from inside. It was why I continued to pursue an answer from you, even though by outward appearances you couldn't have been the temptress I sought."

"So you consider me a temptress, then?" she asked, looking away, trying to mask the inexplicable hurt prompting that question.

"Nay." He lifted his hand to cup her jaw tenderly, bringing her back to meet his gaze. His blue eyes were so serious, so calm that she knew without a doubt that what he was saying was nothing less than the truth to him. "You're not at all what I first thought you would be—not what I'd led myself to expect in the Crimson Lady. Whatever your past, whatever you've had to do up until now, you are not she, Fiona. And yet you do tempt me. Like no other woman I've ever known, you tempt me."

She felt speechless for the feelings sweeping through her at his declaration. She'd never known the like of him before either. Braedan de Cantor seemed as different from other men as the moon was from the stars, and she was still struggling to accept that truth, to be able to acknowledge it in her heart, where the danger of letting go and believing was so great. More than anything she wanted to be able to say it, to make her words match her feelings, but it was still too frightening, and she still felt too vulnerable to give voice to her deepest thoughts.

He tilted his head down to brush a kiss across her lips. When he pulled back, a slight frown marred his brow. "We haven't much time left before we'll need to be ready for Will's call. You must promise me to be careful, Fiona. The whole idea of this ruse sits badly with me."

"I will be fine. Will and I have enacted this dozens of times. Besides, I am not the one who will be wielding a sword and demanding payment. It is you who needs be careful."

"Only if you promise the same."

"Aye," she nodded. "I promise."

"It's settled then." He leaned in for one last kiss just as Will strode toward them, calling in a loud whisper that they were ready to go. Tom had run back a moment ago with news of a coach approaching on the path from London, and he, Jepthas, and Rufus had already taken their positions, hidden in the overgrown, leafy cover along the roadside near Fiona's mount. All that remained was positioning Braedan, placing Fiona so that those in the coach could get good view of the "attack" Will would perpetrate on her, and arranging Henry at the roadside as if he'd been knocked senseless so as to be unable to aid his lady.

They achieved their poses just before the coach came into sight. Quickly, Will pulled Fiona's arm as if he were dragging her away from her mount, then twisted her around in his grip so that her hands were behind her, slamming her back against his chest so forcefully that it knocked the wind from her. As he lifted his dagger to her throat, thumb beneath the edge to prevent her from being cut, she hissed in her breath. "Saints, Will, go a little easier, will you? I'd rather not be bruised when we're done."

"Sorry, love," he murmured, before growling more loudly, for the benefit of the approaching coach, "I'll be takin' what jewels I like, milady—and samplin' anythin' else that strikes me fancy, too!"

With that cue, Fiona let go a shriek, crying out for help as she began to struggle in his arms. From the corner of her gaze, she saw the coach slow a bit; it was a plain but large and finely made vehicle, a covered carriage of darkened wood, polished until it gleamed. Two coachmen rode in front, and there were two other riders at the back. A shock of surprise shot through her at the sight of them. Tom had risked much in calling a mark on this one; there were too many men—almost an even number to the outlaws, and that if only one person was concealed behind the heavy draperies that kept the interior of the coach from sight.

She felt Will's arm tighten with what she knew had to be the same concern she was feeling, but she continued to struggle, enacting their ruse even as she caught the faint movement of the draperies on one side. Two loud thumps resounded from inside the coach, and of a sudden the drivers pulled up to a stop a few feet away from them. Not a word was spoken. But in the next instant the foreboding she'd experienced bloomed into pure terror as the doors at the back of the coach burst open and four more armed men hurtled out, wearing the colors of the king's soldiers, to join the coachmen and the two at the back in charging at her and Will with their blades drawn.

And then chaos erupted.

Fiona's mind whirled with the shock of what was happening as Braedan and the rest of their group leapt from hiding to help fend off the unexpected attack. Will was forced to push her aside in order to meet the slashing thrust of one of the unknown men, but in her surprise she was slow to reach for her own dagger, and in what seemed less than a heartbeat a soldier was upon her, gripping her wrists and twisting her hands up and behind her; he secured her in a position that was ironically much the same as the one Will had feigned with her only moments ago—only this time the blade that was held to her throat bit all too sharply into her skin.

With that cold metal pressed to her and her arms yanked painfully up her back, she was dragged a little away from the fighting, closer to the carriage itself, and though she fought and twisted as hard as she could, she achieved nothing but the burning pain of her wrenched shoulders and the sting of the dagger's edge at her neck. Soon the man had hauled her around behind the coach, so that she was blocked from sight of Braedan and the others.

"Cease now, woman," the soldier growled low in her ear, giving her a brutal shake as he uttered the directive. "It will go worse for you if you fight." Fiona felt her breath coming hard and fast, but she continued to struggle against his gauntlet-covered hands and steely grip, unwilling to give up.

With a sound of exasperation, the man jerked the blade up, digging it beneath her jaw, and she froze, unable to stop herself then from obeying him in the face of the brutal death that had suddenly become her only other option. She stood there, completely still, her neck arched at a painful angle by the blade that was forcing her almost up on her toes, unable to see anything but the unyielding wooden panels of the coach. In a few moments the noise of fighting and the clashing of swords began to lessen around them, fading into groans and some rustling sounds.

A bolt of fear shot through Fiona. Unable to turn her head, she moved her eyes instead, gazing around wildly, trying to see something, *anything*—but it was useless. Her captor seemed patient in his stillness, holding her rigidly as if he was waiting for something more to come. Then suddenly, the area went completely silent. There was nothing—no sound of any voice she recognized, and her heart sank, swirling with the fear she refused to allow herself to feel when she thought of what might have happened on the other side of that coach. She prayed to God that Will, Braedan, and the others were all right, and that the hush didn't mean that they were dead.

The fact that she herself hadn't been killed yet likely meant one thing, she knew; nausea churned in her belly as she steeled herself for what was sure to come, unable to stop from wondering if her captor was waiting for the others to join him before they would take her in a mob, or if they planned to force themselves on her, one at a time, in relative privacy.

She was readying herself to make one last attempt for freedom, when a string of curses suddenly echoed through the silence. She stopped breathing to listen, and the curse came again, followed by the same voice calling out her name. Her heart leapt. It was Braedan.

"Christ, Will, where is she?"

She couldn't hear much more but a muffled response from someone that sounded like her brother, but she couldn't be sure. Unless she could get the soldier holding her to move back toward them, she'd not be able to see anything. She shifted her weight sideways, suddenly, throwing him off-balance—not enough to allow her escape, but sufficient to make him take a step or two nearer to where she'd been when the attack began. Her movement caught Braedan's notice, and as she was jerked to attention again by the blade and growled command from her captor, Braedan's startled gaze met hers for an instant.

He made a move as if he would come toward her, but he was held back from the action by necessity of keeping at bay the two men he faced down with his sword. "Are you hurt?" he called across the short distance between them, no longer looking at her, thanks to the standoff. She tried to reply, but her answer was choked back as the man holding her pressed the dagger more firmly against her throat.

Will stood, chest heaving and his face sheened with sweat, near Braedan, and though he held his weapon up in a defensive pose, blood darkened his sleeve from an apparent gash near his shoulder. But he kept the soldier opposite him occupied, forcing him to keep complete attention on their upraised blades. Four of the original eight attackers lay motionless in various positions on the ground—whether wounded or dead, she couldn't tell—but another still stood, having pinned Rufus on his back near the edge of the trees. Tom lay still and very pale, sprawled in a thickening pool of blood a few paces from Henry, who also wasn't moving, though he didn't seem to have any wounds that she could see. Jepthas was nowhere to be seen.

Tension blanketed the area, so thick that she felt she might suffocate; no sound marred the silence but the breeze in the branches overhead, a few rumbles of thunder, and the occasional muttered curse that came from one of the men in their positions of combat impasse. It was an uneasy standoff, with no means of resolution that she could see.

Then a movement and the shifting of curtains from inside the coach pulled everyone's attention in that direction and worsened everything, if it were possible, a thousandfold.

The distraction sparked the scuffling between the men again, only this time her brother's still heavily bleeding wound made the outcome less favorable. After a few fierce clashes with his opponent, Will began to stumble—whether from loss of blood or another strike, Fiona couldn't tell—but it meant that Braedan had to shift his attention to cover him, and in that moment, the standoff was over. The two soldiers converged and managed to disarm Braedan, throwing his weapon aside and binding his hands tightly in front of him before doing the same for the injured Will, lashing the two of them together with a piece of rope. Finally, they helped their third comrade to drag Rufus over to be tied to them as well—and then the soldiers stepped back, swords leveled at their captives, waiting. For what, Fiona wasn't entirely sure . . .

Until the door at the side of the coach creaked open, and a hooded, cloaked figure stepped out.

Fiona's back tightened, stabs of shock racing up her spine in the instant before the man straightened to full height and reached his gloved hands up to ease his hood back. The images flashed into her mind then with stunning, brutal force. He was tall and well built, garbed in black, from his fine leather boots to the cape draping from his shoulders, all except for a sashed tunic of deep sapphire. Even the waves of his shoulder-length hair were black, as were his eyes—a fathomless obsidian, she knew, before he ever turned his exquisitely handsome face to lock his gaze with hers. When he did, it was as if time stood still and she'd been sucked into some sickening, airless void, pulled into the depths of a quagmire from which she knew she'd never escape.

Draven.

Sweet God, it was Draven standing before her, staring at her. And as she struggled to control the trembling that began deep inside at that realization, his lips slowly curved into a smile. He made no effort to order his man to stand down and release her, rather seeming, by his expression, to enjoy the precarious position she was in, taking his time in pulling off his gloves, one finger at a time, as he approached her.

"Ah, Giselle; it has been too long . . ." His words trailed off, the tone he used as deep and velvety smooth as always. He stopped when he was very close to her, his familiar, faintly spicy scent hitting her like a fist to the belly. "Have you no greeting for me, then?" he asked with a hint of mockery, clearly aware that she couldn't speak a word with the dagger pressed against her throat. She wouldn't have anyway. It was all she could do to keep the impassive facade she'd been struggling to maintain since the moment he'd stepped from the carriage; she'd not give him the satisfaction of hearing her voice shaking atop it all.

With a motion of his hand, he ordered the soldier to release her. The man seemed grateful to comply and quickly stepped back a few paces. With the regained freedom, Fiona let her arms fall to her sides, surreptitiously pressing her fingers against her thighs and then letting up on the pressure, trying to banish the numbness his grip had caused.

Draven watched her in silence, his expression inscrutable. She met his gaze, reminding herself to be strong, to show no emotion. She could do this. If she could just get some of the feeling back in her hands, she might be able to reach for the blade tucked under her sleeve. At the very least it would be useful for defending herself against Draven or his remaining men, and at most it might turn the tides, providing some time so that Braedan and the others could somehow escape. A burning tingle already raced through her palms and up her arms. Aye, it was working . . .

"Give me your dagger, Giselle."

Surprise caught her for an instant. The command in Draven's voice was unmistakable, but she wasn't about to surrender her only chance at freedom. Before she could utter a denial he made a move toward her, and she jerked the weapon instinctively into her hand, the action swift and fluid.

Draven was faster. He intercepted the dagger before she had the hilt of it fully clasped in her palm. With a simple flick of his fingers, the blade sank into the ground at their feet, at the same time that he caught her wrist in a punishing grip.

"It was I who taught you that move, sweet. 'Tis foolish of you to attempt its use on me now." His glance swept over her, assessing her, leaving a chill in its wake. "I see that what I had feared has indeed come to pass; you've become quite disobedient in your absence."

Never releasing her gaze or her wrist, he leaned in closer and still closer, not touching her anywhere else and yet somehow leaving her feeling as if he was taking possession of her again completely, just as he had years ago. She held very still, determined to show no fear, no reaction at all. But then slowly, he reached out with his other hand and threaded his elegant fingers into her hair, his touch warm and insistent as he cupped her head with his palm.

Tingles of shock jabbed through her. *Oh, God, he was going to kiss her*. He would press his lips to hers, his touch intimate, questing . . . invading her in that way he knew so well. He was a master of the art, and the memory of the way his kisses had shattered her so many times before terrified her now. She held her breath, the panic spreading.

But at the very last moment before his mouth would have slanted across hers, he turned his head, his breath fanning her cheek warmly, his lips brushing her ear as he murmured for her hearing alone, "My defiant, naughty Giselle. You know I cannot kiss you until you are properly dressed. As I've told you many times before, only one hue is suitable for you, and it alone should comprise your wardrobe. You belong in crimson—nothing else."

Her stomach clenched, and she couldn't stop herself from arching away from him. He pulled back just enough to look into her eyes, that perfect smile of his chilling her to the bone. Her throat ached with the rasping breaths she took, her body frozen with anguished memories, unable to strike out at him as her mind and heart longed to do.

"Yes, we have a good deal of catching up to do, you and I," he continued quietly. His gaze held her captive, his finger sliding along her cheek, down to the stinging cut his soldier had left on her throat, his gentle touch stroking away the thin line of blood. "It is clear that you need reminding of certain truths about yourself and me, and I confess that I've been anticipating the process of helping you remember for a very long time."

"Leave her alone, Draven."

Braedan's voice rang across the area between them. Her nemesis stiffened, his handsome face tightening almost imperceptibly. But he didn't turn around. Not yet.

"And why would I do that, *nephew*?" Draven asked softly, never taking his stare from Fiona's face. "She's mine."

"Not anymore."

The iciness that swept through Draven's eyes in response to that comment nearly made Fiona gasp, but she maintained her composure. His gaze bored into her, his expression implacable and yet at the same time somehow pained, as he murmured, "How disappointing . . ."

Swiveling to face Braedan, he said more loudly, ". . . but whether or not you've managed to sample Giselle's charms, de Cantor, you should make no mistake about the fact that she *is* mine. She always will be. We were just speaking of reminders to that effect, moments ago." He swung back toward her again, both his expression and his tone ripe with mockery. "Weren't we, darling?"

"We were discussing nothing," Fiona managed to say through the tightness in her throat.

"If I thought you'd abide by any laws at all," Braedan ground out, "or that you would comport yourself as the nobleman you're supposed to be, I'd throw down my challenge right now and force you to prove your claim on the field."

"How thrilling. So valiant of you," Draven mocked before stifling a yawn. "Your fervor was entertaining for the first week, nephew, but I am afraid that you've become quite a bore now. Almost as bad as that vacuous young woman who started all of this between us. Thank heaven none of us share a blood connection, or I might believe I have cause for worry."

"You're not fit to speak of Elizabeth." Braedan took a threatening step toward Draven, yanking Will and Rufus with him, much to the chagrin of their guards. "And you will pay for what you've done to her. Make no mistake on it."

"Pray let us not be quite so dramatic, shall we?" Draven carefully pulled his gloves back on again, and Fiona shivered, remembering too well how he used that elegant affectation—along with several more—to divert others' attention from his impressive physical strength and fighting abilities. "No one had made an offer for her yet, even with the ridiculous dowry your sire had set aside for the purpose. In truth, I did nothing but aid her on her chosen path—a fact that your brother conveniently omitted from the tale he told you of her leaving."

"You're a liar."

"And you, it seems, have become a thief, in addition to your many other sins," Draven answered dryly, nodding to his man to stand guard over her again as he approached Braedan with slow, sauntering steps. "I wonder what the virtuous Julia would think to learn of it, eh?" he added, and Fiona startled at the look of pain that crossed Braedan's face before he was able to mask the expression.

"I confess, having witnessed your overdone sense of honor myself," Draven continued, "I didn't give much credence to the information I'd received of your alliance with this ragtag lot." His gaze swept over Will and the others. "But it appears now that my sources were correct. How unfortunate for you, that you've been stupid enough to cross my path again with your head still attached to your neck. I think I shall take great enjoyment in witnessing it struck off."

"You need me secured in your custody for that, *uncle*. Something that proved quite beyond your grasp the last time you attempted it, if you recall." Braedan nodded toward the bodies of four of Draven's soldiers, sprawled on the roadside. "But if you're so eager to keep sacrificing your men in the effort, pray continue. It gives me the practice I need, though it is costly on your part; I think the count I've dispatched for you stands at eight now, doesn't it?"

Draven flushed, not answering at first, though Fiona could tell the statement rankled. "You're in no position to be making threats, de Cantor," he said. "And never fear; containing you won't pose a difficulty this time. I've arranged everything to ensure you're unlikely to move from whatever cell you're put in, once I'm through with you."

Thunder rumbled overhead again, louder than before. It was followed by a flash and another boom, setting off a swish of cooler breeze through the stifling air. Then a light rain began to fall. Draven squinted up into the droplets, cursing under his breath. "Come, we haven't much time before it will be a deluge," he muttered to his men, then nodded in the direction of their captives. "Get them secured behind the coach." Looking back through the thickening shower toward Fiona, he started forward, barking a command to her guard to confine her inside the conveyance for the ride back to his estate.

But when he was halfway there, a flurry of movement broke out behind him. With a shout of warning to Will and Rufus, Braedan lunged forward, pulling them with him, connected as they were by the ropes. Together, they knocked the two closest guards off their feet, but the third jumped out of the way and then came at them, followed by Draven, who was heading back toward them to help his guards in the fray.

Seeing a moment of opportunity in the confusion, Fiona darted forward, focused on reaching her weapon, which was still buried up to the hilt in the ground. But the soldier in charge of her grabbed at her, and she slipped on the rain-slicked grasses at the roadside. In the motion, he caught her wrist, wrenching her backward and drawing a cry from her as she instinctively clutched at her arm to try to stem the pain that shot all the way up into her shoulder.

Draven whirled back to her at the sound, calling an order over his shoulder to his other men to contain their rebelling captives before his expression fixed on her guard with deadly intent. "I warned you before not to harm her," he muttered, stalking toward the soldier, "a command that you've now disregarded twice!"

Braedan sucked in his breath as he saw Draven walking away from their scuffling, knowing that this kind of chance wouldn't come again. He forced himself to push his worry over Fiona to the back of his mind for now, needing to concentrate on what he was doing so that he could help her in a more effective way. The two fallen guards had already gotten to their feet and were reaching for their swords, while the third was swinging at them with his blade. Everything seemed muddled and chaotic. The rain fell thickly, serving as a sort of buffer while he, Will, and Rufus sidestepped and dodged the blows of the guards.

Squinting in the rain, Braedan pulled the group nearer to where the soldiers had tossed their swords in a pile; as they careened around in their connected struggle, he managed to slip his toe beneath the hilt of one weapon, flipping it up in the air to catch it with his bound hands. Then, tipping the blade skyward, he released his grip and let its weight slide the edge against the wet rope at his wrists, cutting through it as if it were no more than string. Released at last from both his bonds and the tether to Will and Rufus, he grasped the hilt again and swung around, just catching the stroke of one guard's blade against his arm in the process. Swallowing a grunt of pain, he retaliated, disabling the man with a sharp blow to the head.

He managed to hold off the other two guards until Rufus and Will could retrieve their swords and cut loose their own bonds as well. Though Will looked more pale and haggard than before, Braedan knew he had no choice but to leave him and Rufus to handle their captors so that he could go to Fiona's aid. Draven had already pushed her into the coach and was securing the door as Braedan approached with a feral growl, hurtling at him with sword upraised. His uncle must have sensed the attack, for he spun around, unsheathing his own weapon as he did to meet the deathblow Braedan had aimed at him.

Heat and battle instinct surged through Braedan as he fought the man who had caused him and his family so much misery. The sudden rain shower was beginning to ebb, but the air still felt heavy with moisture; the fertile scents of wet greenery and dirt filled Braedan's senses as he breathed heavily with the exertion of the fight, his wounded arm aching each time he clashed his sword with Draven's.

Their skill was almost evenly matched, but where Draven had trained in castle yards and tournament lists to master his impressive technique, Braedan had been tested in deadly battles abroad—and even wounded as he was, it was giving him the advantage. Using a move that had saved his neck more than once on the field at Saint-Jean-d'Acre, Braedan came at Draven straight on, lowering his blade at the last moment to catch it under his uncle's upraised hilt. With a spinning twist, he hooked it and sent the sword spinning from Draven's grip, leaving him vulnerable to an assault.

Draven looked startled for an instant when he realized that Braedan's blade was pressed to his throat; he froze, palms up in surprise. But in the next breath his usual expression of calm control settled over his face again. Braedan longed to drive his blade deep into his bastard uncle's throat—to end it all right there and then—but something about Draven's expression held him back. He glanced first toward Will and Rufus, who, thanks to Will's weak condition, had been subdued once more by their guards, then he looked at his coach, where Fiona was framed in the window, still confined there by the soldier Draven had chastised earlier, his sword leveled at the door.

"It seems we are at an *impasse*, nephew," Draven murmured, his sensuous mouth twisting. "You have me at the point of your blade, but I have your friends and sweet Giselle at the point of mine . . . figuratively of course."

"It will be a moot point if you're dead," Braedan muttered, putting more pressure on his blade, enough to draw blood and a flare of animosity from Draven's midnight gaze.

"I would consider your choices very carefully Braedan," Draven intoned in a low, even voice. "With or without my direct command, my men will slaughter their captives—all of them—if you take similar action against me. So while you may succeed in killing me, you will needs bear the guilt of knowing you sent three others to their deaths in the moments before my men converge on you and send you to your maker." He shifted his gaze to Braedan's wounded arm. "You may be very skilled with that weapon of yours, nephew, but my men are well trained also; you'll stand no chance of surviving their combined attack. It will be three on one. Think on it."

Braedan stiffened, aching to drive the point of his blade home, but his common sense battled against the move. While he was more than willing to risk his own life for the pleasure of removing his corrupt relative from the face of the earth, it was another thing altogether to sacrifice Fiona, Will, and Rufus in the process. He narrowed his eyes on his uncle, his jaw tightening over what his own better judgment was going to lead him to propose next.

"It seems that we will need to reach some sort of agreement."

"Oh?" His uncle sounded cautious, though a glimmer of triumph shone in his eyes.

"Aye—your life for the others. Order Giselle's release and command your men to stand down from their captives. When it is done, you and your soldiers will be allowed to board your coach unharmed."

Draven made a scoffing sound. "A delightful plan, de Cantor, but for one thing."

"What's that?"

"There will be nothing to stop you from killing me once Giselle and your cohorts have been released."

"You have my word that I will abide by our agreement, if one is made."

"The word of an *outlaw*?" Draven mocked.

"I am less of a criminal than you are, Draven, and you know it. Decide."

Draven went still, looking supremely annoyed at having been placed in the position, and Braedan felt a surge of satisfaction in witnessing his discomfort. But the feeling faded a bit when his uncle spoke again. Draven's jaw looked tight, his elegant, dark brows pulling together in a scowl as he muttered, "It seems I have little choice; I will have to accept your offer."

Braedan's disappointment swelled, part of him still yearning to feel free in making a corpse of the man. But the agreement was struck, and he couldn't go back on his promise now, not if he wanted to live with himself afterward.

"Order your guard to release Giselle from the coach, then. Once she's free, he can see to those of yours who have fallen and load inside any who are not dead, the others over the backs of the two mounts behind, with the help of one of those over there," Braedan ordered, glancing at the soldiers guarding Will and Rufus. "After that is done, the last of the three can drive the coach while the others go inside with the wounded. You will be led over last and secured inside with them, at which time you'll be allowed to turn around and make your way back to London."

A charged silence settled over the area, Draven's expression as black as the thunderclouds that were passing overhead.

"You honestly expect me to trust that once your men are released and all of my men are unavailable to me, you will nonetheless escort me, unharmed, into my coach and allow me to *leave*?" he asked in final, quiet resistance, his eyes glittering with anger.

"You know the de Cantor name, Draven. Long before you married my mother's sister," Braedan answered tightly, his own enmity simmering just below the surface, "you knew my father, God rest him, and cannot deny that he was a man of his word. I am his son and will uphold what I have said. Do not question it again."

The muscle in Draven's jaw twitched. Never taking his stare from Braedan's face, he barked a command to his men to commence what had been discussed. Soon, Fiona stood out of danger's way at the edge of the forest near Will, looking pale and drawn, but nonetheless safe, while Draven's men were secured in the coach or on the backs of their mounts.

Braedan walked Draven to the conveyance door, keeping the edge of his blade always at his uncle's throat. Once he'd secured him inside, he jammed a stick Rufus had handed him through the door pulls as an extra measure of protection to prevent those inside from leaving the coach until they reached their destination. Then he stepped back, nodding to the scowling guard who'd been forced into the role of coachman. Draven was sitting next to the window, and he pushed the drapery aside just before the vehicle lurched into motion.

His uncle's gaze found Fiona, and a half smile curved his lips, sending a warning stab through Braedan an instant before Draven called out to her in a lilting voice, "Never fear, Giselle. Soon we will meet again . . . and then I shall have you back where you belong." He blew her a kiss and mouthed something else to her in silence, grinning as the coach rumbled away and out of sight down the roadway.

Braedan turned to look at Fiona. She had gone even paler than before, if that was possible, her eyes wide and her hands fisted in her skirts. With a strangled sound of distress, she suddenly spun on her heel and ran into the woods, ignoring Braedan's shout to wait. The noise of her flight soon faded into a silence disrupted only by the dripping of the trees and the breeze through the branches.

Cursing under his breath, Braedan sheathed his sword and looked at Will, who was wincing under Rufus's ministrations as he bound his shoulder. Through gritted teeth, Will said, "Go on and follow her, man; Henry and Tom are dead, God rest them. So is Jepthas, lying in that ditch over there," he added, jerking his head toward the edge of the copse where the men had first crouched right before the attack. "But my sister will be needin' some added care after meetin' up with that bastard again. Go to her. We'll take care of what's left here."

Nodding, Braedan took off into the woods after Fiona, concentrating on keeping to the trail she'd left in the wet forest . . .

And hoping that, once he found her, he might find a way to chase away the demons that Draven had released to torment her again.

Chapter 12

Fiona ran blindly, her throat choking with panic. Tears slid, burning, down her cheeks, and her stomach twisted as she stumbled through the wet bracken, pushing rain-soaked branches aside and welcoming their cool sting against her skin. She needed to flee, to run away—to where she didn't know. She only knew that she had to get away from Draven. Far, far away . . .

After what seemed a very long time she was forced to slow, her body rebelling against the pace she'd set. It was no use. She jerked to a stop in the cool damp of a little clearing, bent over and gasping, her heart finally acknowledging what she'd wanted to deny so badly. She'd known it all along, but seeing Draven again out here, where she'd never thought it would be a possibility, had driven the point home with agonizing clarity. She couldn't escape him.

You're mine.

Those words he'd silently mouthed to her just before he left still pounded through her mind, terrorizing her as he'd known they would. No matter how far she ran or how long she was gone, he would always be there . . . the one man who would never relinquish his claim to her in his twisted sense of mastery and ownership. The enormity of it overwhelmed her, and she fell to her knees, retching. But her stomach was empty, and it offered forth naught but dry, painful heaves. When it was done, she wrapped her arms around herself, the throbbing pain of her wrenched wrist nothing compared to the horror snaking through her. She remained bent over, rocking, a soft, keening cry coming from deep within, and the salt of her tears on her lips.

"Fiona . . . ah, lady, do not weep . . ."

Braedan's utterance, spoken low and in a voice full of tenderness, snapped her from her haze of sickness and fear; she stumbled to her feet, feeling disconnected and shaky, and turned to face him where he stood at the edge of the glade, having difficulty believing that he was there at all.

"Why did you follow me?" she managed to whisper.

"I needed to know you were all right." He gazed at her, his expression so concerned that it made her long to throw herself in his arms. But she couldn't do that, not now, not ever. The encounter with Draven had reminded her all too clearly that she wasn't fit for a man like Braedan de Cantor. Not she, who'd been branded in every sense of the word by Draven's ruthless possession.

She tried to breathe in deeply, but the air could barely squeeze through the constriction of her throat; the effort only made it ache more than before. Her nails bit into her palms, and she held herself as rigidly as she could, afraid to move, to blink, even, everything feeling off-balance and raw. It was as if Draven had reached in and curled his fingers in a brutal grip round her heart, claiming her once more with his words, his eyes, his touch. Her skin crawled with the memory of his hands on her, his breath on her skin. She felt like she'd never be clean again, and she didn't know if she could ever make Braedan understand that.

"I should go back to help with the others now," she said as she lurched forward, her voice husky with the effort it took to talk. "It was selfish of me to run off like that when the wounded might need tending."

"Nay," Braedan said lowly, holding his hand out to her silently and stopping her still. His eyes looked pained, and foreboding settled over her like a shroud. "Rufus was binding Will's shoulder when I left, and both will be well in time. But the others . . . the others are dead, Fiona."

"*All* of them?" Fiona barely whispered, feeling the shock of what he'd said rock through her.

"Aye, lady. I am sorry for it, but it is so. Your brother and Rufus will see their bodies safely back to the settlement, and so there is no reason that we cannot stay here as long as you need. I want to help you, Fiona."

"There is nothing you can do, Braedan," she said hoarsely, clenching her fist over her middle and trying to force back the tide of pain. ". . . nothing you can do for me."

"I don't believe that, and neither should you. I know that seeing Draven again upset you, but he is—"

"Upset me?" she broke in, choking out a bitter laugh. "Nay, for the past three years the thought of what just happened back there has *defined* me. I have lived my life during all that time doing my best to avoid him entirely, dressing in disguise, using another name, moving away from everyone and everything I knew. And for what? Here I am today with three men needlessly dead because of me, and with no better prospect for my future than was true the night I escaped him. It is even worse, perhaps, in that his twisted obsession with me has only been whetted by my absence."

"He cannot control you if you don't let him."

She swallowed another dark laugh, the urge suddenly rising up in her to give release to the tears she was trying her best not to shed in front of Braedan. She looked over at him, standing there so strong and resolute, within a few paces of her and yet allowing her to keep whatever distance pleased her—always the gentle warrior concerned with her comfort, her feelings. Hurt welled up again, the irony of it all thick in her chest. Oh, if only he knew. But he couldn't. Not unless she told him all of it, and that would mean exposing herself to the possibility of more pain.

"You don't understand, Braedan," she said haltingly, glancing up at him, her eyes feeling swollen and her insides empty and aching. "It is more than you could possibly realize."

"Tell me, then."

"I cannot. It is too complicated." She squeezed her eyes shut, knowing she couldn't bear the look of denial, the disgust she was afraid she would see in his eyes if she told him the whole truth of her history with Draven.

"Weeks ago, I said that I would listen without judgment if you spoke of your past," he said, as if he'd read her thoughts. "I am still willing to listen, Fiona. Right now, if only you'll trust me with it, so that I can understand."

She opened her eyes, then, though she didn't allow herself to meet his gaze or the tenderness she knew would be there. Braedan de Cantor was a powerful man, a man capable of great violence if need be; she'd seen that with her own eyes today. And yet he was always so tender with her—with her, the celebrated courtesan, who had known many things from many men, but never such consideration and care. Oh, God, if she could only unburden her heart and soul of all the hurt and the vile memories. But she was too frightened of what he might think of her when it was done . . .

"*Trust* me, Fiona."

That quietly spoken plea battered down the last of her defense more effectively than a hundred commands could have done, and with a long, hitched breath, she lifted her gaze to his. "It is so ugly, Braedan." She hesitated, troubled by the swell of it all inside her. Her jaw felt stiff, and her eyes burned as she continued, "Back there, when Draven touched me, when he laid claim to me again, it was like he had never let go . . . like all of that time I'd been gone and struggling to make myself free hadn't mattered. He was in control, and I—I couldn't even speak to deny him. I was weak and afraid, and I hated myself for it, almost as much as I hated him."

"You were shocked to see him. You cannot blame yourself for that."

"I should have been stronger, but he knew . . . oh, Braedan, he knows me so well. Heaven help me, but he made me what I am, and I will never be able to escape it!"

"And what exactly *are* you that is so terrible, Fiona?"

Braedan demanded, stalking over, close to her then, forcing her to look at him. "What in your mind is so awful that you must condemn yourself to a lifetime of confinement, in your heart or in truth, with Draven as your keeper?"

"Don't you see?" she cried, the pain rising up to overwhelm her, "I am his possession, something to use or discard as he sees fit; that is all."

He shook his head in denial, but she continued, driven by the horrible memories filling her that erased all else but the anguish left behind. Swallowing, she met his gaze, swiping at her eyes as she said, "You have to understand how it was . . . Draven created me. He molded me into the temptation he'd envisioned from the moment he'd laid eyes on me, purchasing me outright from my mother for that purpose when I was fifteen—a wretched, starving girl like hundreds of others who live on the streets of London."

"Your mother *sold* you to him?" Braedan murmured in disbelief. "My God . . ."

Fiona shook her head, not wanting to relive the betrayal that memory called up in her; over the years its power had become more muted, but it could still burn if she was careless. In her mind she knew that her mother had been trying to open the way to a better life for her when she gave her over, but her heart did not recognize the distinction and likely never would.

"Draven was a master of many things, not the least of which was persuasion," she continued. "He had seen me at the market fair that autumn and had begun to ask questions about me. Before long, one of his men followed my mother to the *stewes*, where she rented a chamber in a broken-down hovel for her work. With the lure of a few gold coins and some talk of betterment for me, she was eventually convinced to give me over. It was the beginning of winter, and I was grateful for the warmth and shelter my new position would provide. I thought I was to begin work as a scullery girl, you see," she whispered, looking at Braedan, unblinking.

Even though she was doing her best to stem the tide, the old feelings of shock and powerlessness were coming back to grip her. "Once Draven had me secured at Chepston, he ordered that I be bathed, fed, and garbed in costly robes, and then I was taken to his chamber, where he slowly and surely set about taking my innocence."

Braedan cursed under his breath then, his face troubled and his eyes showing, as always, the swirl of emotions in their depths. She shook her head and pulled away from his sympathy, unable to bear such tenderness while she was so locked into the memories of that dark time.

"It was clear that Draven enjoyed the act of seducing me," she continued woodenly. "I was young and still untouched; I suppose that surprised him, considering the conditions of my life up until then, but as such I presented him a challenge. I unwittingly made it worse by resisting him until he could think of nothing but taming me. He did so, eventually, breaking my will to his and training me to master the performance of many carnal acts. He interspersed those lessons with instruction on behaving and speaking like a true lady, saying it provided an interesting contrast to the extravagance of my skills in the bedchamber."

Fiona stopped for a moment, her throat aching in her effort not to let loose the remembered panic and despair that battered at her from within. She swallowed.

"Draven was obsessed with me, though in my ignorance of such things I could not give a name to what was happening. I only knew that it left me feeling confused and lost. With every breath I took I hated him more for it, and I told him so, over and over. But it didn't matter. He would only smile and then take me to his chamber again, destroying me a little more with each act. Before long I came to realize that nothing mattered but Draven's needs . . . his plans for me."

She pulled back, her gaze searching Braedan's almost wildly. "Do you see now?" she whispered, "Draven brought me under his power, then he made certain I could never, ever be free of him, no matter what I did or how far I managed to go from him. I cannot escape him because he is *inside* of me, lurking there always, like a serpent waiting to strike. I thought I could separate myself from him. I tried to live my life free and independent of his influence on me, but I cannot. Seeing him again today, hearing his threats reminded me how foolish I have been to believe I could."

Braedan was silent after she'd finished, the look on his face so pained that it shamed her more, almost, than the telling of her past had. She squirmed under his gaze, waiting for the rejection she knew must be imminent. "You understand, then," she said, her voice nearly cracking with the strain, "You accept that I cannot be the woman you think I am, no matter how I try to convince the world or myself otherwise. With or without the scarlet gowns, at the core I am naught but Draven's creation—Giselle de Coeur, the Crimson Lady. It is all I am and all I ever can be."

"Nay, Fiona," Braedan answered after his long silence, his expression intense upon her. "You are much,

much more to everyone—more to *me*. And I understand one thing all too well: My uncle is a bastard for what he did to you. You own no blame in it and should cut him from your heart and mind like the pestilence that he is."

His response took her by surprise, so much so that she actually ceased breathing for a moment. It couldn't be. He was talking as if he couldn't yet see her weakness or the lasting power Draven had over her. Desperate to make him recognize the truth of what she'd spoken, she uttered a little cry and yanked at the neckline of her kirtle, exposing the area just above her breast . . . the ugly, heart-shaped scar Draven had carved into her before she'd escaped him four years ago.

"Look, Braedan. Here is proof of what I am saying. It is your uncle's mark upon me, branding me forever as his. He did this to me himself, cutting into me the image of the heart he claimed I didn't possess—the one thing I refused to give him."

The kindness that had filled Braedan's eyes darkened at the sight of the scar. He stroked his fingertip gently over it before lifting his hand to her cheek; but when it seemed as if he would speak again, she pressed her fingers gently to his lips, trying to silence him, knowing that no matter what he said, it couldn't change anything or take away the horrible feeling inside her.

But he wouldn't be stilled. Taking hold of her hand, he kissed her fingers before pulling them away to speak very deliberately. "Draven does not own you, Fiona. He is but *one* man, not a god or a demon, even, for all the evil in his soul. He deserves no more importance in your life or your memory than any of the other animals pretending to be men that you were forced to bed during your years as the Crimson Lady."

Her brows came together in bewilderment for an instant before the unwitting falsehood of his argument washed over her. A rusty laugh broke from her at this final insult—at this last truth that she'd been doing her best to avoid telling him. She closed her eyes, sucking in her breath. Her mouth twisted with the effort it was taking to hold back her emotions, but though she'd sworn she wouldn't cry, tears seeped from between her lashes nonetheless, to roll down her cheeks. "Ah, Braedan, there is no way you could know . . . but as much as I wish to, I cannot make happen what you're saying," she said huskily. "Of all things, that is utterly impossible for me to do."

"Why?"

"Because it is not based in truth. It is the one part of my life with Draven that I have not told you about, the part that seals my fate to his, binding me to him in ways that no one but he, my brother, and now perhaps you, will ever understand."

"Go on," he said quietly, reaching out to stroke a rain-dampened tendril away from her brow.

She stilled, soaking in his touch, trying to impress the sweetness of it into her memory, not knowing if she'd ever feel the likes of it again once he had heard the full extent of her wickedness and participation in Draven's scheme to keep her as his own. At last exhaling on a sigh of resignation, she murmured, "The truth is that I have never actually bedded anyone *but* Draven. The countless men you spoke of—those who purchased the favors of the Crimson Lady—none of them ever completed the act of joining with me."

Braedan reacted as if he'd been struck a blow that nearly knocked him from his feet. He jerked back from her, and her heart twisted in misery. Here it was, then. The rejection she'd been expecting all along . . .

"What are you saying?" He frowned, the blatant denial in his expression raking her soul. "Such a thing is not possible. You are the Crimson Lady, are you not? There has never been any question concerning the grounds for your notoriety . . . it was the reason I chose you as the one who might best be able to help me find Elizabeth. Unless you're telling me that all of England has somehow been gloriously duped, you cannot be speaking true."

"I am, as impossible as that sounds," she answered bitterly, "because Draven never allowed any other to have me in that way but him."

"How, then—?" Braedan challenged, sounding almost angry. "The entire country cannot be daft! I heard numerous accounts of your skills from knights and high-ranking nobles alike who had known the pleasures of your bed before leaving for Saint-Jean-d'Acre— firsthand, *detailed* accounts. Are you saying every one of those men was lying about what they'd experienced with you?"

"Not to their knowledge, nay. But in truth, none of it happened as they thought."

Fiona swallowed, trying desperately not to be sick again, not to sink to the ground in a boneless heap for the agony this was causing her. It was a horrible, perverse thing, made worse, somehow, by having to share the details of it with Braedan. The breeze gusted, sweeping through the glade at that moment and loosing a sprinkle of raindrops from the leaves above them. It soothed her somehow, and she breathed deep, committing herself to finishing and letting the pieces fall where they would.

"It was Draven's idea and his wicked knowledge that

allowed us to commit our ruse against all of those men," she said, finally, as much to fill the painful, incredulous silence Braedan had fallen into as to attempt to convince him of the truth, "but I went along with his scheme, much to my shame."

She clenched her fingers in front of herself, pressing them into the damp, crushed folds of her kirtle. "After I'd been at his estate for nearly two months, he decided to keep me for himself. It was as much a surprise to him as to me, I think. He told me he had never before felt so about any woman he'd purchased to train for one of his bawd houses, and I believed him."

"Had he fallen in love with you, then?" Braedan asked hoarsely.

"Nay." Fiona nearly strangled on the word, restraining herself from saying what first came to mind concerning her thoughts of Draven and love. Instead, she settled for bare fact. "He wanted to own me completely, but he still was not willing to forgo the sizable amount of coin he'd lose by keeping me out of the *stewes*."

"I don't understand, then. If he would not allow you to bed the men who'd purchased your favors, how did you earn the coin he sought, not to mention your reputation?"

"Draven bought the services of someone who could help him to create a grand illusion, but who would also be compelled to remain quiet about it." Fiona glanced at Braedan, unable to resist watching his response to what she was about to say next, though she knew it would hurt terribly to see it. "Do you remember the alchemist I spoke of when we were gathering plants in the forest— the one who was executed for his crimes in the dark arts?"

"Aye."

"It was he who gave Draven the formula of herbs that allowed us to perpetrate our deceit. Knowledge of the mixture had been passed down for centuries amongst certain secret groups. It was a foul concoction that caused the men who took it—either as an unguent rubbed into the skin or swallowed in wine—to fall into a sort of spell, marked by wild imaginings that took color and form from whatever they were doing before the potion took hold." She looked away, trying to keep her emotions in control.

"Draven set me up in a chamber and instructed me on how to begin each seduction, which for the customer included either drinking some wine laced with the herbs, or if that was refused, a massage with the specially prepared salve. Draven would watch from a hidden compartment to make certain that all went as planned. Once the man had fallen into the expected stupor, Draven would bring me out and send in one of the women he had set aside especially for the purpose, someone to actually finish what I'd begun. All had been specially chosen by him for their auburn hair and slender height, and each always entered the chamber wearing a crimson gown . . ."

She glanced down to her tightly clasped fingers. "The men we tricked in that way awoke the next morn with pounding heads, but also with vivid and usually detailed memories of the night they believed they'd spent with the Crimson Lady. And so Draven got what he wanted, collecting a prodigious amount of coin for my notorious services, while still maintaining complete possession of me for his use and pleasure."

"Christ Almighty . . ." Braedan breathed, as the entire import of her claim began to sink in.

Fiona felt herself withering under the aversion he clearly felt toward what she'd described. His disgust was no more than she deserved. She knew that, and yet she hated every second of it.

"It was lawless and evil, I know," she continued, ruthlessly attempting to crush her own weakness. "The kind of crime for which people are burnt in village squares and castle greens every year. We were fortunate that we were never caught in the act of committing it. No one ever knew, except for God Himself, of course," she added softly, locked in the painful swell of memory, "and He punished me for my sin by rendering me barren, so that I could never bring an innocent life into the evil world I had helped Draven create."

Braedan remained silent for a moment, clearly stunned by all she'd told him. When he looked at her again, his expression was troubled. "Did the ruse never fail, then, that the authorities were not called? Were the herbs so potent that no errors were ever made?"

"There were a few mishaps," she admitted, frowning with the memory of those times. "It was why Draven remained in secret observation, to handle any problems as they arose. Usually, however, all went smoothly. Exactly as he'd planned."

Braedan fell quiet again, too shocked, no doubt, to speak more on the subject. It was done, then. Tremors began in her stomach as of old, and she stiffened against their onslaught. The vividness of her memories had brought back the unwelcome sensations, and she found that no matter how she tried she couldn't suppress them.

Closing her eyes, she turned away, leaving Braedan to his thoughts and the condemnations of her that she knew he was too much of a gentleman to voice. Wrapping her arms around her middle, she tried to stop the trembling; she realized that the earlier rains had saturated her borrowed finery, and she picked at the sodden material at her elbow, miserable and afraid of what was churning inside her.

Heaviness filled her. She'd known it was inevitable that Braedan would eventually learn the truth of what she was . . . that he would come to recognize the damaged and immoral woman inside her . . . but for a short time she'd indulged herself in the pleasure of his refusal to see it. It had felt so good to bask in the light and warmth of someone's esteem—of *his* esteem—for a little while, and it hurt so much, knowing she was losing it now.

Reaching deep, she willed her icy facade back into place, covering the agony she was feeling with the pretense of calm that Draven had forced her to perfect so long ago. She needed to regain her composure so that when she turned back around to face Braedan, he wouldn't know how much his newfound loathing of her hurt.

"We should go find the others now," she managed to say, her voice husky with suppressed emotion. "You have heard all there is to know about me. Nothing more need be said."

Utter silence greeted her, and she squeezed her eyes shut, swallowing the pain of it. He didn't even think her worthy of a response, then. She shouldn't have been surprised. It was no more than she'd contended with hundreds of times as the Crimson Lady, but, somehow, the fact that it was Braedan dealing her the blow wounded her more than she'd known it could. Releasing her breath slowly, she let her hands fall to her sides, stiffening her back to at last turn around and leave the glade with as much dignity as she could still manage to muster. Yet before she could move past him he stopped her with his low-voiced request.

"Wait, Fiona."

She went still, not trusting herself to meet his gaze. "Why?" she asked quietly. "We have finished here. I am calmer now; you have accomplished what you intended, and I thank you for it, but there is nothing else to say."

"Nay, Fiona. Stay," Braedan murmured, stepping closer to her. He took her hand, his touch sending pleasurable warmth spilling through her. She stared at the broad, strong expanse of his chest, struggling against the urge to lift her gaze to his—afraid of what she might see there. "I do not wish to discuss my past further, Braedan. I have told you all, and I feel shamed enough by it without being made to relive it all again. I cannot—I will not—do that, for you or anyone else."

"Discussion is not part of what I had in mind, lady."

As he spoke he moved past her, circling around behind her so that she could no longer see him, even had she possessed the courage to meet his gaze. But she could feel him, and his warmth against her back, his breath wafting over the sensitive skin of her neck, sent sensuous shivers down her spine.

"What you have told me is horrible indeed," he continued, his voice caressing her, "but more than anything it shows me that tenderness and care have too long been absent from your life."

Fiona closed her eyes again, staggered by the impossibility of what he seemed to be saying. Perhaps he wasn't rejecting her, then; he didn't want to push her away. Oh, she wanted to believe that he had heard the entire, vile truth and could still care for her in spite of it, but she hadn't dared to hope.

The time had come to find out once and for all.

Heat stung her eyes as she turned to face him. "Do you truly believe that, Braedan?"

"Aye."

Her breath caught. "If it is so, then I am glad for it. But it still does not explain what more you want of me here."

He didn't answer for a moment, his blue eyes intense—both troubled and full of warmth as he stared at her from under knitted brows. "I want you to let me hold you, Fiona," he said at last, gruffly. "To let me give you what I know you need but will not take from me." He held her gaze with the heat of his own, the intensity flowing from him in a molten tide, sweeping her away with sudden understanding. With the same longing that even now filled his eyes . . .

She felt poised at the edge of some momentous decision, knowing what she wanted but was too afraid to accept, come to a place she never thought she'd be after Draven and all that she'd been through with him. Braedan's face swam before her, tears welling as she worked up the courage to voice what was deepest in her heart.

"I—I am so afraid, Braedan," she whispered, her voice ragged with all that was at work inside of her. "I do not know what I will be able to feel—*if* I will be able to feel. Draven has been the only one for so long."

"He does not have to be anymore," he said firmly, squeezing her hand in gentle encouragement, though the resolute look in his eyes made her heart pound. "Just speak the word, Fiona, and I will do all that I can to wipe your heart and mind clean of his foul presence." He lifted his hand to the tender spot just below her chin, cupping her there with his palm, his fingers stroking gently, and she swallowed a moan of surrender.

"I have never felt so about anyone else, Braedan . . . never known what you make me feel."

"Nor have I, except with you," he answered, that fierce, yet passionate gaze still trained on her face. "Ah, lady, let me wash away the memories of what he did to you so that you may start anew, free of the burden you have carried for so long."

As he spoke, the breeze cast another sprinkling shower of drops down onto them, and Fiona's hands found his dampened sleeves beneath his cloak, her fingers clenching into them convulsively. She wanted to let go. She wanted to believe that it could happen . . . to feel the completion of this sweet aching inside of her.

"I wish I could," she whispered, at last, her pulse racing and her limbs heavy. "God in heaven, I do, but I know not, even, how to begin. He was always in control of me and of what we did together. Always—"

"Command me, then, lady," Braedan broke in hoarsely. "Tell me what to do. It will be as you wish, or not at all, I swear that to you, until you feel safe and whole again."

Fiona gazed at him, overwhelmed with the emotions sweeping through her. She remained silent for a long while, weighing what he'd said. She yearned to believe that Braedan could help her, that he *wanted* to help her, and that her newfound feelings for him could banish Draven's taint from her forever. She wanted to laugh, cry, and shout all at once, but in the end she settled for a whisper that resounded through her soul.

"Kiss me then, Braedan." She brought her fingertips to her lips, shyness battling with her growing sense of power as she did so. "I want you to kiss me here . . ."

A blaze erupted in his eyes, and with a tender expression he murmured, "As you command, my lady," before leaning in to brush his mouth over hers, savoring her. She kissed him back, tentatively at first, then with a slow building of her passion, the rain mingling with the taste of him, salty and wonderful on her lips.

When he pulled back, she was startled for a moment, until she realized that he was only awaiting her next command. He stood there, unmoving, watching her, his cape thrown back and his muscular arms and torso revealed in sheer relief by the sodden folds of his shirt. Glints of sunlight streaked through the still seeping clouds, illuminating the diamondlike drops misting over them. She soaked in the sight of him, his hair brushed back wetly, the angled, handsome lines of his face stark with unrestrained passion.

"Here," she whispered, never breaking her gaze with his as she loosed the laces of her bodice to bare her shoulder. "I'd like you to kiss me here now."

"It will be my pleasure," he answered, the look in his eyes nearly undoing her, even before she felt his lips against the smooth, damp expanse of her skin. The light rain sprinkling around them felt cool, the heat of his mouth providing a seductive contrast that left her breathless. And when he used the tip of his tongue to make delicate swirls as he kissed along her shoulder and the tender flesh leading to the column of her throat, Fiona couldn't stop from moaning aloud, feeling as if her knees might buckle from the incredible sweep of moist-hot desire that spilled through her in response.

"What next, lady?" he murmured against her, his lips moving over her as he spoke. "Tell me what you wish of me. I long only to please you . . . to see your bidding done."

She lifted her face to the gently falling shower, closing her eyes and feeling the beauty of being with Braedan like this. What was happening here was good and pure, sprung from the exact opposite of the deliberate possession she'd experienced with the man who'd purchased her innocence. And she wanted more, she realized. She wanted to feel Braedan with every part of her, to absorb him into her.

He was still kissing her neck, moving slowly up to just beneath her ear; it was challenging to focus her mind enough to voice her next request of him. Her head tilted to the side, her hair damp from the storm, its weight heavy on a neck suddenly gone boneless under the thick and swirling desire coursing through her. She gripped his shoulders tightly as he kissed her, needing that anchor to remain standing, and now she used his strength to pull herself straight again, her palms finding his face, bringing his mouth away from her to gaze into the passion-heated depths of his eyes.

She sucked in her breath at the yearning she saw there, wanting to meet it with action of her own. *But not yet,* she told herself. *There* was *still time*. She would go slowly, wait for just the right moment. Until then, Braedan was waiting for another directive from her.

"I want to begin anew," she told him, her voice low and husky. "To be washed clean here with you in this green-and-gold forest. I want to stand in the rain with you, Braedan, with absolutely nothing between us but the truth of our feelings."

Braedan's expression hadn't changed from the intensity he'd shown from the moment she'd pulled away. Only a renewed burst of desire in his eyes, followed by a flickering shadow, revealed the instant of surprise he felt. "Are you sure, Fiona? It is what you truly want?"

"Aye," she whispered, bold in the knowledge of exactly what she was asking of him.

"Then it will be as you command, lady," he answered, his voice caressing her much as his lips had moments earlier. "With a most eager heart, I do your bidding."

He continued to look at her—only at her—as he untied the laces to his cloak and swung it off of himself, spreading it like a blanket next to them on the rain-dampened mosses of the forest floor. Her pulse raced at the look in his eyes as he continued, untying and then pulling his tunic and shirt off over his head, baring his chest. She paused at the sight of the gash on his arm, already crusting over with dried blood, but he shook his head to assuage her worry, moving on to the laces of his breeches, loosening them enough to reveal the flat, muscled planes of his lower abdomen before he ceased the action and reached down to remove his boots.

She couldn't help that her gaze drifted to the teasing shadows beneath the unlaced breeches, until he slid them off at last and added them to the pile of his clothing; then he straightened, naked and beautiful, his powerful arms hanging loosely at his sides. He paused, not seeming the least bit uncomfortable standing so before her; his chest heaved, and the rain slicking over his skin made him look even more the sleek predator than when she'd first seen him unclothed near the pond weeks ago. In truth, he was magnificent. Her heart raced as she watched him blink the wetness from his eyes, lifting his hands to rake the hair back from his face again, all the while staring at her with a heat that made her feel as if she was aflame even in the cool damp of this woodland.

"Shall I help you with your clothing, Fiona?" His voice echoed low, but he smiled as he raised his hands to the sun-laced shower, letting the drops splash onto his palms. "I would have you know the pleasure of this, too."

"Aye," she managed to say through the dryness in her throat, astounded at the depth of need she felt to be near him, to be with him, in ways she'd thought taken from her forever by Draven's cruelty. With her answer, Braedan stepped silently closer, his movement causing a brush of air against her that was somehow more erotic than the most intimate caress she'd ever experienced. The feather-light weight of his touch came soon after, sending rippling paths of awareness from each point of contact his hands made with her skin as he helped her to disrobe.

Soon she was as naked as he, consumed with unexpected shyness, until he threaded his fingers through hers and lifted her hands with his own, raising their arms to the cloud-swirled sky. She tipped her head back along with him, reveling in the sensation as the rain washed over her. Standing so with Braedan brought with it a feeling of freedom—of rightness—unlike anything Fiona had ever known, and she couldn't help but laugh aloud with the joy of it.

He, too, must have felt something of the same, for she heard his chuckle reverberating with her own. After a moment, the weight of his arms tugged her hands down, though he still kept his fingers laced with hers. He pulled her slowly and gently closer to him then, pressing her full-length against him, and the feel of his naked, wet body, so hot and insistent against hers, drew a gasp of surprised pleasure from her.

Loosing one of her hands, he lifted his palm to her cheek, gazing at her with laughter still dancing in his eyes but mixed now with the unmistakable intensity of passion. "Ah, Fiona Byrne," he murmured, his gaze caressing her, "do you know how beautiful you are to me? I never knew such depth of soul could exist in a woman until I found you."

She felt herself flushing and tried to look away, but he wouldn't let her, holding her still. "Nay, Fiona, you must hear this." He looked at her for another breathless minute, adding at last in a halting, husky tone that sent another surge of honeyed warmth spiraling through her, "You are everything I never knew I was missing in my life. I don't deserve the gift of you now, but I'll take it, by God, and be grateful for every moment I have with you."

Her throat closed with tears, but she fought them back, a smile blooming through the heady emotions. "It is you who are the gift, Braedan," she whispered, reaching up to stroke the rain from his face and letting her fingers glide back into the thick wetness of his hair. "I don't think I will ever be able to thank you enough for all you have done for me."

She lifted her face and kissed him then—kissed him freely and openly, the first time she could ever remember initiating such an act without either instruction or coercion. It was wonderful, so she kept kissing him, tasting him and reveling in the unbelievable sweetness of his response, her senses drinking him in like the ground soaking up the rain.

His scent was masculine and fresh, unmasked by any artfully concocted fragrance; he surrounded her, filling her with yearning. She slid her palms up his arms, feeling the hard muscles beneath the slick coating of rain. Still kissing him, she kneaded the tautness of his shoulders, relishing the guttural groan that came from him as she let her touch stroke down his back to his hips and buttocks.

"God, Fiona, I want you," he murmured against her mouth, his hands traveling their own heated trail across her back. His fingers stroked over her in a mesmerizing rhythm, drawing a moan from deep inside her even as his lips moved to her throat again. Her head tipped back, her body afire with the need to feel the part of him that was jutting so hot and hard against her belly buried deep inside her, to share with him something that for the first time in her life would be an act of loving passion rather than finely orchestrated lust.

She writhed against him, the friction of their wet bodies tantalizing and the pooling, silken heat between her legs burgeoning into an ache of unbearable need. The pleasure only intensified as her nipples rasped across his chest, the fullness of her breasts cushioned against his hard contours; his muscles shifted and flexed as he moved his arms, stroking his hands from the top of her back down to cup her buttocks before traveling in a sensual path upward once more.

She moaned again, finally managing to voice in a gasping whisper, "Ah, Braedan . . . are you still willing to be ruled by me?"

"Aye, lady, command me to your bidding," he answered hoarsely.

She felt the sting of grateful tears welling again, silent tears that spilled down her cheeks this time to mix with the rain. She went still, and her voice choked with emotion as she made one last request of this beautiful man who was so carefully and selflessly pulling her from the depths of her emptiness. "Then make love to me, Braedan, here and now . . . Oh, please—banish him forever with the power of your touch upon me."

Braedan pulled back to look at her, his hands coming up to cradle her face in the strength of his palms. His own eyes glistened with unspent feeling, and he said huskily, "Aye, Fiona. If it is in my ability, it will be done. You deserve no less than all that I can give you."

A tremulous smile worked through her tears, and she nodded, the tenderness and understanding he was showing nearly undoing her. Using exquisite care, Braedan slid his hands once more down the length of her back, stopping at the curve of her buttocks. In the same, smooth motion he lifted her almost effortlessly, her thighs spreading around him as he raised her to just above his waist, pausing there for one, heart-pounding moment as he stared straight into her eyes. She met his gaze, feeling her lips trembling and her eyes stinging again at the expression of giving—of love—on his face.

"Keep looking at me, Fiona," he murmured. "Do not close your eyes. Know that it is me and no one else here with you like this. Only me . . ."

Her breath caught, and the world seemed to slow as he began to lower her tenderly, steadily onto the hard length of his erection. She felt herself sliding over him, inch by glorious inch, and her fingers clenched into his shoulders, her nails digging into his skin as tremors of pleasure took hold and began to build from that point of delicious fullness.

She kept her gaze locked with Braedan's, seeing his restraint and the toll it took on him, feeling his remarkable consideration for her; she wanted to cry out with the love she felt for him, but she schooled herself to silence, simply absorbing the sensations spreading through her. When she was completely impaled on the magnificent length of him, he paused, his breath coming shallow.

"Are you all right, lady? Shall I go on?"

His words came out in a half growl, half groan, and she could feel the muscles in his arms twitching against her with the effort it took him to remain still. But she didn't want him to, the creamy fullness at the juncture of her thighs demanding the same completion he so clearly yearned to know.

"Oh, don't stop," she managed to gasp, her hands tangling in the thick, damp waves of hair at the back of his neck. "Please don't stop . . ." As she spoke she squirmed against him, desperate for him to continue, and he groaned again, this time deep and full-voiced, throwing his head back as he clenched her buttocks tighter and began to move her, sliding her up and down on his jutting heat until she thought she would scream from the pleasure of it.

"My God, Fiona, you feel incredible," he said through gritted teeth, his face a study of passion. "Like heaven in my arms . . ."

She did cry out then, the wordless, throaty sound coming from somewhere inside of her not governed by logic and sense. It was pure feeling, and she felt herself going over the edge to the splintering beauty of orgasm. As the shudders of fulfillment began to take over her body, her head tipped forward, exquisite sensations rocking through her with power enough to send a sweep of black spots before her vision.

She gasped and sobbed out her bliss against the salty warmth of Braedan's shoulder, taking all he could give and giving it back to him, stroke for stroke. It was what she'd been seeking all along, the healing force of Braedan's love driving out the darkness and dissolving its power over her, bringing her to a place of peace, calm, and perfect love that she never dreamed she'd deserve, no less claim as her own.

Braedan's climax followed soon after, his thrusts deepening with her writhing and the clenching of her slickly heated sheath around him. Groaning her name, he jerked his hips once more, and she felt the flood of his seed spreading hot and deep through her—a gift that for all of her experience with Draven, for all her sinful training as the Crimson Lady, she'd been denied ever knowing before except as a completion of lust . . .

Her last remaining innocence given over willingly, completely to the one man who with the awesome power of his love had finally broken the barriers that had imprisoned her heart for nearly half a lifetime.

Chapter 13

Braedan's knees buckled in the aftermath of their climax, but dimly, Fiona was aware that he'd managed to lower her to the softness of his cape before collapsing over her, holding his weight up by locking his elbows. They held still like that with chests heaving, his face tilted down as if he was trying to gather his senses again after their explosive release. Their legs were still tangled together from the position they'd taken as they made love, and now Fiona tried to ease away, thinking to make him more comfortable. But he reached out one hand to stop her, his eyes closed as he sought to catch his breath.

"Nay, love," he murmured. "Stay near to me."

Her heart contracted at the sweetness of hearing that endearment from his lips, and she drew in her breath. She couldn't speak for the lump in her throat, so she simply swallowed and concentrated on trying to stem the cursedly familiar tightness there. If she didn't cease having this reaction with Braedan at every turn, he would begin to think that all she could do was cry. Clearing her throat, she willed the raspy feeling to recede, determined to speak normally as soon as she could gather her wits to explain what she was feeling for him.

But before she could give voice to anything, the breeze picked up again, chilly now that the rain had passed, and an involuntary shiver swept over her; Braedan cursed under his breath, sliding into place beside her and tossing their clothing over them to use as a blanket, before finally tucking the edges of his cloak around them for added warmth. Then with a sigh of contentment he tugged her closer to him, cradling her against his shoulder as he closed his eyes again. After a few moments spent absorbing the pleasure of nestling so beside him, Fiona shifted to look up at his face, studying every line and shadow, feeling her heart sing at his fierce, almost primal beauty.

He must have felt the weight of her stare on him, for he opened his eyes. Lifting his arm from her waist, he brushed his fingers along a damp tendril on her cheek, pushing it back. "What is it, Fiona? Are you regretting what happened between us?"

She bit back a laugh, thinking that might be an insensitive reaction for her to give him so soon after their lovemaking. "Nay, Braedan, I am not sorry about it," she admitted. "It was wonderful."

"What, then?"

"There is nothing wrong. Truly there isn't," she said, wanting to convince him while still fighting her own confusing display of teary emotion. Swiping her hand over her eyes, she tried to banish the damning signs, but for every tear she wiped away, another followed, until she was both laughing and groaning at the futility of her attempt. Finally giving him a watery grin, she said, "I know it's difficult to believe, but I am simply so happy that I can't seem to avoid crying about it."

Braedan laughed with her then, relief filling him as he hugged her close. Thank God. For a moment there, he'd thought that he'd failed her—that her demons had risen up to claim her again. "You are an amazing and complicated woman," he murmured, pressing a kiss to the top of her head and holding her close against him. "But as for your penchant, lately, for crying," he added looking down at her with a devilish grin, "I think you should go ahead and indulge all you want. It isn't like we aren't already soaked to the skin anyway."

She gave him a good-natured shove at that, laughing and wiping at her eyes again. But rather than settling back against him as he'd hoped, she began to squirm and shift, seeming as uncomfortable as if they were lying on a bed of nails.

"What is the matter now?" he asked, still chuckling.

"It just feels as if something is beneath me, digging into my side." She eased herself up onto one elbow, her face a picture of consternation.

He rolled back a bit while she groped for the offending object, stiffening when she pulled it from beneath her and raised it to the light. It was a bit of oval-shaped metal attached to a linked chain. *The miniature of Julia.* It must have slipped out of the fold in his cloak, damn it to everlasting hell. A stream of colorful curses followed that thought in Braedan's mind, but he gave it no voice, simply reaching out in an effort to take the portrait from Fiona's grip. She wouldn't relinquish it right away, though, peering at it as it swung and twirled on the end of the chain.

"Why, it's a tiny painting," she murmured incredulously, sitting up with the chain still wound in her fingers. His shirt happened to be the garment he'd first thrown atop her in his haste to warm her, and she clutched it to her breasts now, he noted, not quite succeeding in covering up her voluptuous curves.

"She looks like a noblewoman," Fiona said in a soft voice, seeming to calculate not only the expense of the art itself but also the costliness of the garments worn by the subject.

"She was—I mean she *is*," he corrected himself, having to work even harder this time to stem the new string of curses that rose to his lips. "She comes from a family of minor nobility, long respected for their good works."

"How do you know her?"

"Her sire shared a bond of friendship with my father."

Fiona looked from the miniature to Braedan and back again, an O of understanding rounding her pinkened, well-kissed mouth. Her brows came together in a most endearing way as she perused the fine, patrician features and glossy tresses he knew were portrayed so well in the tiny painting. "I can see why you've been so worried about her," she murmured, bringing her stare back to him in utter innocence. "If this likeness is apt, it's clear that Elizabeth would have attracted Draven's notice."

This time Braedan did groan aloud, following it up with one of the milder curses he'd been entertaining in his mind.

"That isn't a portrait of Elizabeth," he admitted at last, his mouth tightening. He sat up next to Fiona, finally retrieving the blasted miniature from her hand and jamming it under his side of the cape. He didn't speak further, half-hoping that she would choose to leave well enough alone.

It was an exercise in wishful thinking.

"If it isn't your foster sister, then who is she?" Fiona's frown had intensified, except now that expression was directed right at him.

"Her name is Julia Whitlowe."

"Julia . . . ?" Fiona breathed, and Braedan did his best not to grimace at the stricken expression that swept over her face.

"I heard Draven mention that name to you," Fiona said, her expression still vulnerable. "Who is she to you that you would carry her portrait?" Her question was couched in an almost-nonchalant tone, he noticed, but he could see the wounded shadows hiding in her eyes.

An odd twisting began around Braedan's heart, but he knew he couldn't avoid the truth in this. It was bound to come out between them sooner or later . . . he just wished it had been much later. "Julia was my betrothed," he said grimly at last. "Our union was agreed upon before I went to fight abroad."

"Oh . . ." Fiona's voice sounded high and far away. "I am sorry. I didn't realize . . ."

"It's of no matter. Her family broke the contract between us once I was named an outlaw to the crown." Startled, he paused, realizing that for the first time since the day he'd lost Julia, that knowledge no longer had the power to wound him. He reached for Fiona's hand, wanting to reassure her of his very real and compelling feelings for her; but she wouldn't let him take it, tucking it instead into the folds of shirt she was using as a blanket.

"It must have been devastating for you," she said quietly. She shifted her gaze to him again, somber and calm. "And you must love her very much to still carry her likeness close to your heart."

"Nay—I mean, aye, I did care for her, and I was upset at the time that our union was dissolved, but it isn't what you're thinking," he argued. Though she didn't move a muscle, he felt her pulling away from him, and panic began to wind its way into his heart; struggling for the words to make her understand, he continued helplessly, "By the Rood, Fiona, she was going to be my wife. In truth I had prepared for most of my adult years to marry her, but it seems like a lifetime ago now, and I—"

"There is no need to explain, Braedan," she said, shaking her head, that expressionless mask he'd come to hate slipping over her delicate features again. "I understand. And do not fear. You will not face any further expectations on my part now that this has happened between us; I have always known my place in such things." She gave him what he supposed was to be a cheering smile, but he saw that it didn't reach her eyes. Then she scooted back a little, apparently looking to retrieve her clothing from the jumble of garments both over and surrounding them.

"Fiona, I think we should talk about this more. I—"

"Nay, it is fine. Truly," she broke in, hurriedly pulling on first her *chainsil* chemise, then the blue kirtle again. Her skin was alabaster perfection but for the heated spots on her cheeks. "We can speak of it again another time, if you like," she murmured, "but right now I really think we should get back."

He sat still for an instant longer. She didn't understand, dammit. But it appeared that helping her to do so would just have to wait. "All right," he said at last, jaw tight, "I will comply with your wishes, as long as you agree to discuss this later." At her nod, he pushed himself up to stand, quickly beginning to don his damp clothes alongside her.

But as he pulled on his boots and fastened his cape, which smelled faintly of crushed grasses and sweet vanilla, he couldn't stop from feeling as if he'd lost something of great importance just now—something above and beyond what he feared he'd lost to Fiona weeks ago . . .

The entirety of his careworn, battered heart.

They entered the outlaw settlement again near dusk, having stopped on their way to see if Will, Rufus, or the fallen men were anywhere to be found. The spot where they'd left them had been deserted, with nothing to mark the day's events other than the trampled bracken and churned-up mud of the road. Braedan had remained silent, for the most part, on the short remainder of the journey, wanting to respect Fiona's wishes concerning the further discussion of Julia, and yet feeling as though what had been left unsaid hung between them like a weight.

Once they arrived, any chance of further talk vanished; the settlement was abuzz with activity, some unexpected visitors having arrived in their absence. Fiona jerked to a halt, and, even without looking, Braedan felt the way she tightened up at the sight of the newcomers who sat around the fires in the clearing, drinking, talking loudly, and gesturing. His own hackles rose from pure instinct, something about the half dozen or so men setting off a warning jangle inside of him.

Someone spotted them, it seemed, for the conversation ebbed, then fell silent. Naught but the sound of mourning rose at a distance from the clearing, where the bodies of Henry, Tom, and Jepthas were being prepared for burial. Fiona stood quietly beside him, looking at the strangers. But before Braedan could ask her anything about who they were and what they might be doing at the encampment, she pursed her lips, and an odd expression—whether annoyance or anger, he couldn't tell—sharpened her delicate features. She stalked forward again, in a direct line to Will, who sat, with his shoulder bandaged, looking pale but none the worse for wear, next to the largest and most central fire.

Braedan followed behind. At Fiona's approach, the man who was sitting next to Will stood up. He was compact and muscular, with dark blond hair that hung to his shoulders. Green eyes gazed out at them from beneath golden brows, and a smile flirted over lips that looked as if they were used to sneering. And when he spoke, Braedan's sense of antipathy edged several notches higher.

"Greetings, lady . . . it is good to see you again." The words were murmured like a caress, the man's oddly cultured tone and inflection startling Braedan. He frowned at him from across the slight distance, noting his fine, stylish clothing. What kind of man, he wondered, would be educated enough to speak in a manner worthy of Edward's own court, yet still seem completely at ease out here in an outlaw's settlement?

"Clinton," Fiona answered, giving the stranger a curt nod. Her attention shifted to her brother, her glance indicating his bandaged shoulder. "Does it pain you much, Will? I can prepare a poultice if you'd like."

"Ah, sister, I'm glad to see your husband has finally

brought you home," he said, his words a bit slurred, likely from whatever he was imbibing.

Braedan noticed how Clinton stiffened at the mention of the word *husband*, his gaze slashing into Braedan before shifting to Fiona again. Obviously unmindful of the tension, Will raised his pouch of drink to them to continue, "But I am happy to say that this fine sack has taken care of the worst of my aches, so, though your offer is appreciated, sister, I'll not be needin' any of your herbs right now." He gave a bitter laugh. "Clinton and his men arrived an hour past, and I was just relayin' the details of what's happened. 'Tis only meet that they know to watch for Draven in their own work, now that he seems to have taken to the road for sport, the bastard."

Will swallowed convulsively and tipped the pouch to drink deep again, the firelight glittering on his reddened eyes. Braedan's jaw clenched in sympathy, knowing all too well himself the pain of losing men and recognizing what Will was trying to hide now with his bravado. But he was forced to leave off those thoughts as Clinton spoke again.

"Care you to sit down, Giselle?" Clinton gestured to a place beside him, still ignoring Braedan, and glaring at his outlaw friend, who was already sitting in that spot until he shifted over with a grunt. "We were just beginning to discuss our plans for handling Draven's latest action. Perhaps it would interest you."

"I think I'll remain standing, thank you," Fiona answered evenly. "I'll be going to help the other women with the burial preparations shortly."

Braedan watched her face, for the first time feeling a swell of satisfaction in her ability to maintain a facade of complete composure—as long as it was directed toward this brute and not him. He decided that perhaps it was time to step forward and force Clinton, whoever he was, to acknowledge him. He took a position next to Fiona, resting his hand on the small of her back; after the awkwardness over Julia, he wasn't sure how she would react, but she didn't flinch from the contact. If anything, she seemed to lean into him as if it was the most natural thing in the world for her to do.

Braedan's surprise only deepened when she pulled him closer to the circle at the fire to say in a warm, bold voice, "Braedan, this is Clinton Folville and some of his men. He and his brothers lead another band of outlaws that work the area just north of us."

Braedan hid his negative reaction to the man beneath a nod and some murmured greetings. Clinton gave him a wary acknowledgment, while the others grunted their response, at which point Fiona moved up onto her toes and pressed a kiss to Braedan's cheek, nearly stilling his heart, before whispering something about going, now, to help the women at the other side of camp. Then she was gone, slipping into the darkness outside the fire's circle of light. He watched her go, amazed as always at her ability to surprise him. He only realized he was still wearing the bemused look her kiss had inspired when he saw Clinton scowling at him as if he'd like to bring a crushing slide of rocks down on his head.

Never one to back down from a challenge, Braedan decided to sit at the spot previously cleared for Fiona.

"I was wonderin' when you'd get back with my sister," Will said, still seemingly unaware of Clinton's antagonism as he offered Braedan the sack to take a drink. "You were gone a goodly time."

Braedan relished the brew sliding down his throat for

a moment, taking a couple of good swallows before he swiped his hand across his mouth and returned the sack to Will. "She was more than a bit upset. It took a good deal of talking before she was ready to leave."

"Oh, aye, de Cantor," Will joked, giving him a knowing grin. "I'll wager 'twas all talkin' you were doin'. You'll have to be more original than that if you want to explain your time away with her."

Braedan raised his brow and smiled, but he didn't get a chance to answer thanks to Clinton, who had choked on his drink and started coughing. After the fit passed, he fixed another black scowl on Braedan, and spat, "You're a de Cantor?" Without waiting for an answer, he swung his golden head toward Will. "What by all the yawning fires of hell is a goddamned *de Cantor* doing married to your sister?"

" 'Tis a fine turn, is it not?" Will laughed, raising the sack to Braedan in salute. "I admit I never thought I'd see the day, Clinton, but I'm tellin' you, a better sword arm you'll never find than Braedan's here—or a heart so willin' to fight on the side o' right." He sobered a bit, his focus veering off both men toward the place where the bodies were being tended, as he added, "I'd even go so far as to say if 'tweren't for him, I'd likely be among those men over there grown cold and stiff as the dirt in which they'll be lyin' come morn."

"You didn't do so badly yourself, man," Braedan offered gruffly.

"Aye, well, even with your wound you managed to best Draven, which is more than I can claim," Will said, taking another swig from his ale. "I confess, learnin' that you're his nephew, even if 'tis by marriage, came as a bit of a shock, but—"

"He's Draven's *nephew* as well?" Clinton broke in with a growl. "Christ Almighty, Will, what kind of viper have you let in here?"

"The kind who spent years fighting Saracens and learning the best ways to separate men's souls from their bodies," Braedan said lightly, though with an unmistakable edge to his voice. "I'll be glad to introduce you personally to one of those methods right now, Folville, if you think you'd like to offer me another insult. I've had just about enough of them from you this night."

"Is that right?" Clinton growled. "Then perhaps we should just—"

"Ah, hell," Will roared, lurching to his feet and waving his sack of ale. "Isn't it enough that three of my best men were took off today? Should we add to the number by havin' a duel over the same bastard who's responsible for it?" Without waiting for anyone to answer, Will rounded on Clinton. "And as for you, old friend, I know who my sister's husband is and what he is, and he's a damned good man. 'Tis all you need to know, besides the fact that their marriage means you can't have another chance at her—which is what is *really* at the bottom of all this twaddle, if you want to know the God's honest truth."

Clinton mumbled something under his breath and looked away. Will shook his head in the tense silence and sat down again, muttering to himself, before settling in, and saying, "In case you're wonderin', I saw it with my own eyes today just how de Cantor feels about Draven, whether the man be his uncle or nay, and I need no further proof of his loyalty to us. But you clearly do—so if you wouldn't mind tellin' him, Braedan . . ."

"It is quite simple," Braedan said, obliging Will's request. "I despise Draven, and if given the chance, I will bring him to justice for what he's done."

Clinton glared at him, as if measuring the truth of his words, and Braedan returned the stare, his brow cocked in silent challenge. Finally, Clinton looked away, muttering his acquiescence, and the other members of the Folville gang jerked their heads to show their solidarity with their leader's decision.

" 'Tis settled, then," Will said, tossing aside the empty sack and reaching for a new one. "Blood o' saints, I was beginnin' to wonder if 'twas possible."

"Ah, Will, stop your bellyachin' and have another drink!" old Grady called out from his spot at a nearby fire. A few more grumbles and a shouted jest echoed through the clearing, dissipating some of the tension, and Braedan found himself smiling despite his ill temper. Someone tossed him a full pouch of ale, and he unwound the neck, tipping it to drink, before passing it on to Clinton, who took it with his first indication of acceptance yet this night.

It was a start, anyway. But he wasn't about to spend the entire night sitting, drinking, and exchanging pleasantries with Clinton or anyone else. Draven's setup on the road today made clear that he was more of a danger than Braedan had previously anticipated; in truth, he'd hoped to have the advantage of surprise and anonymity over Draven when he'd conceived his plan of using Fiona's old contacts and knowledge to help him find Elizabeth.

Now it was obvious that such a thing wouldn't be possible, and he certainly couldn't allow Fiona to face the danger of entering the *stewes* again in their search, either. Not after what he'd seen with Draven today. He wouldn't. And that meant he needed a new plan for dealing with his cursed uncle; if he was lucky, it might very well include some of the disgruntled and vengeful outlaws sitting all around him.

Now was the time to broach the topic, if ever there was one, he decided. Though the hum of jesting and conversations continued, Braedan stood, waiting until it fell quiet and everyone's eyes were trained on him. Then he let his stare sweep round the clearing, meeting the gaze of young and old before he called out, "All right, then. What say you we get down to discussing some important matters? Namely, what can be done about stopping my bastard uncle—for I'd say it's well past time he faced his reckoning."

Chapter 14

Fiona lay alone in the silence of their tree shelter a few hours later. She could hear the men still talking where they sat around the fires at the center of the clearing, Braedan's deep tones and occasional low chuckle weaving naturally among the rest, yet somehow distinguishable to her ear above the others.

She sighed and rolled to her side, looking at the cloth partition Will had hung for them inside the shelter on their second night at the settlement. It was to give them some privacy as a wedded pair, he'd said. Yet here she was on the first night that she might actually have felt as close as a wife to Braedan and she was alone. She longed to have him near her, even if just to feel the comforting warmth of his body lying close to hers, but it looked as though it might well be a goodly time until he came seeking his rest, thanks to their lingering talk at the fires about Draven.

She'd finished helping with the burial preparations not quite an hour ago, retiring with the other women and feeling, as she left, a depth of sadness that surprised her, considering that she had barely known the three men who had died in the roadside conflict that day. But the fact that she remembered too many similar times from her own life, nights of grief and mornings of burial both during her years in the *stewes* and then later in Hampshire, had made it impossible not to feel empathy for the women who were suffering the loss of their loved ones now.

She rolled to her other side, facing the door flap, where she could see the low-burning glow of the fire under the bottom edge, though the conversations continued to elude her. Sighing, she tucked her arm under her head, the need to be near Braedan filling her anew. More than anything, she wanted to be alone with him, she realized, not having to keep a strong front for Will or Clinton or anyone else. After this afternoon and the sweetness of what she'd shared with Braedan, she didn't think she could maintain the falseness of her cool facade successfully for any length of time. Her feelings were still too tender and her heart too vulnerable.

Aye, she couldn't deny that she'd been hurt when she'd found the miniature Braedan had carried with him. The thought of his tenderness toward another had stung her to the quick, part of it stemming from the knowledge that Julia Whitlowe was the kind of woman she herself could never be: a respected and proper lady. The kind of woman Braedan had loved.

But she'd realized other things in the hours since then, understandings that had helped to lessen the sting a bit. It would be unfair of her to hold the past against him, any more than he had with her. She'd lived a life most men would have scoffed at rather than believe, yet Braedan had accepted her with open arms.

And though she might not be a lady of Julia's pristine virtue and nobility, Fiona was no fool, either. She and Braedan had shared something special this afternoon—a gift that had freed her from Draven's evil hold on her— and she wasn't about to discount the power of that. Braedan might not ever be able to feel the same about her as he had Julia, but he cared for her enough to give of himself so that she might be healed and whole. It was enough for now, and she planned to enjoy every moment with him granted to her—and to ensure that he enjoyed it, too, if she had any say in it, she thought with a smile.

As if on the wings of her thoughts, the leather flap at the door was pushed to the side and Braedan himself ducked in.

He stood for a moment in the gloom, letting his eyes adjust to the light. It was quiet in here, compared to all the talk and boasting that had gone on round the fires. But it was winding down now, and none too soon, he decided, tormented as he'd been by his need to find Fiona and pull her into his arms.

He shouldn't be indulging in such thoughts, such yearnings, he knew; what he had experienced with Fiona had been wonderful, more special than anything he'd known before, and yet a part of him ached with the knowledge that what they shared was only for a time and no more. It couldn't last, not with their vastly different histories and the uncertainty of their futures.

Closing his eyes for a moment, Braedan breathed deep, resolving not to think more on it now. There were more pressing concerns to be faced, like whether or not her seeming easiness with him and the enigmatic kiss she'd pressed to his cheek had been sincere or for the benefit of those sitting round the fires.

He was about to find out.

"Fiona," he called softly, lest he wake her from sleep.

"Aye, Braedan?" she answered, and his heart thudded at how wide-awake she sounded. He'd seen her enter the shelter nearly an hour ago, and yet she wasn't sleeping. Perhaps, then, she'd been waiting for him and wanting him, too. . . .

He knelt beside her, his eyes adjusted enough now to make out her features and the soft expression she gave him. His heart leapt anew, and he smiled, drawing a matching look from her. Reaching out, he pushed the edge of the hanging partition back a little, peering into the shadows at the rear of the shelter and the empty pallet there.

"Where is Joan? I thought the preparations finished and all the women abed by now."

"Aye, it is all done. But Joan decided to stay with Ella this night to give her comfort. The loss of Jepthas sits especially hard with her, as they were new-married only last year," Fiona explained. He saw her glance toward the door flap of the shelter, clearly noting the quiet that had settled over the clearing. "And what of Will? Why hasn't he come to bed?"

"He fell asleep by the fire, exhausted, likely, as much from drink as from the nagging of his wound," Braedan answered, stretching out beside her. "But Clinton and the others are sleeping there as well, and it is a warm night. He will be fine," Braedan assured her, adding wryly, "though I cannot say how his head will feel come morn."

He felt her nod from where she lay, having rolled onto her back when he'd stretched out beside her; they lay silent, staring up into the dark recesses of the hollowed-out trunk. Quiet settled all around, everything still but for the sound of the night breeze and the occasional call of an owl heard faintly from the wood.

Braedan remained still, though it was one of the most difficult things he had ever done, wanting to hold Fiona as he did. But she'd offered no indication of wanting the same, and he *had* resolved to let her take the lead in such matters, he thought, cursing himself for his brilliant ideas. Loving her this afternoon hadn't banished his need for her, as he'd naively thought it would all those weeks ago at the pond. Nay, it had only increased his desire; she was like a fire in his blood, so much so that he doubted he would ever be able to quench the flames. But her comfort mattered more to him than his own need to touch her, to taste her . . . to feel her warm, naked skin pressed against him.

He shifted in torment at the images that shot through his mind then, his groin hardening and his fists clenching to keep from rolling over and reaching out to her. He wouldn't be a selfish brute like Draven or any of the men who had thought to take their pleasure with her. Her needs would come first with him, and he was loath to disturb her peace if such was all she sought from him now. Swallowing a groan, he closed his eyes, resolving to think of other things. Of anything other than what he wanted to do with Fiona right now.

"It seems we are going to be alone here this night, Braedan."

The husky, suggestive undertone in Fiona's voice broke through his tortured thoughts, unhinging the last of his restraint and jerking him to total awareness. He snapped his head sideways to look at her, half-believing he'd imagined her speaking in his near delirium of want, but she was already facing him, running the smooth length of her palm over his chest. Her hand found the opening in his shirt to brush across the skin beneath, and he nearly jumped from the pleasure of her touch, his body rising to an even more unbearable level of readiness, as if he was a green boy again and she the first woman he had ever known.

It was almost shameful, in truth—but when Fiona leaned forward to press her mouth to his, he forgot about anything but the taste of her, the sweetly seductive feel of her. The gentle weight of her breasts pressed into his chest, and he reveled in the silky fall of her hair spilling over him in a perfumed curtain. Pulling his senses together enough to react at last, Braedan reached up, touching one hand to her face as she kissed him, the other reaching up to stroke along her back, drawing a shudder of pleasure from her.

"I was waiting for you to come to bed," she whispered into the dark, pulling back enough that he could see the playful light in her eyes, set off by the sweet curve of her lips. She smiled deeper, then, her teeth worrying her lower lip as she gazed at him. "You took a very long time to get here."

"Aye, well, there was much to discuss tonight," he answered, smiling, too, as he added, "Though if I'd known you were waiting for me like this, I'd have hurried things along a bit more."

"I am glad to hear it," she murmured, before pressing her lips to his again. She continued to kiss him, moving to the very corner of his mouth, using her tongue there

to tease him gently. His body throbbed in response, and
he shifted, intending to roll to his side and take her in his
arms. But she stilled him with her hand to his chest,
shaking her head so that her hair feathered over his skin
with the movement and sent shivers of longing sweeping
through him.

"Nay, Braedan," she said, with a hesitant smile. "If it
is meet with you, then this night I would like to do something . . . different. To share with you all of myself, in
the many ways that I know . . ."

"Ah, Fiona, I—" Braedan couldn't finish he was so
taken by surprise, so he swallowed at the tightness in his
throat and reached up to stroke his fingers through the
hair at her temple, tucking it behind her ear. After a moment he managed to continue hoarsely, "You do not
need to do this, lady. It was no hardship for me to make
love to you the first time, nor would it be again, a thousand more times if you were willing."

"It is true that I am hoping what happens will lead to
such again as well, eventually," she said softly. "But first
I wish to make love to *you*." Her words and her expression grew more confident—bold, even—as she spoke.
"Let me love you, Braedan, as I yearn to do."

His head fell back on their makeshift bolster, then, his
breath escaping in a rush as she followed her words with
the magic of her touch, her fingers deftly opening his
shirt and pushing it aside before loosening his breeches
and *braies*; she eased them down from his hips, her
hands flitting over him, setting him on fire with each
gentle brush of her skin against his, until he was naked
before her. He lay there, watching her, seeing the open-
ness and beauty of her face as she paused only long
enough to remove her own clothing, pulling up over her

head first her bliaud, then her shift. Moonlight spilled into the tiny chamber from the slits at the edges of the door flap, bathing the smoothness of her skin and the rosy tips of her breasts in pearly light, alternating with spans of teasing shadow.

But in the next instant all rational thought vanished as she leaned over him, her face tilted down and the silken sweep of her hair caressing him, to press gentle, tender kisses across his chest, her hands stroking and her mouth traveling in a leisurely trail to his shoulders, his arms, down to his sides and to the flat of his abdomen. She paused there, her mouth stilling, the moist, warm puffs of her breath tantalizing that steel-hard part of him that lay just beyond her lips, while her hands continued to sweep gently over the sensitive flesh at his hips and the tops of his thighs.

He hung, suspended in pure, sensual torture, waiting, tensing, until with one smooth and perfect movement, she took pity on him and stroked her hand up the aching hardness of his shaft to take him into her mouth. His world exploded into a blinding whirl of unbelievable sensation, and he groaned aloud, his back arching up at the red-hot pleasure of it. She caressed him in ways he'd never imagined, no less experienced before. Her hands moved gently, tenderly, cupping and kneading, the path of her touches followed by the wet heat of her mouth.

After a few moments she shifted away a bit from that point of ultimate sensation, and the world started to come back into focus; dimly, he was aware that his chest was heaving with his gasping breaths, and that she was murmuring soft endearments as she stroked her hands over his entire body, her lips brushing feather-light kisses again over his chest and arms, down his legs and up again, all while she kept touching him, sweeping ever closer to the hotly jutting part of him once more . . .

Abruptly gripping her hand, Braedan stopped her progress and pulled her up to rest on his chest, bringing her face into direct line with his. He searched her with his gaze, unable to stop from staring with heated fascination at her lips, which looked rosy and wetly plump from their recent ministrations on him. His breath still rasped, his mind awhirl with the sensations flowing through him; he tilted his head back for a moment, took a deep breath, then tipped his face up to her again to murmur huskily, "I think that perhaps it would be best if you waited for a little while before doing that again, Fiona. I do not know how much more of such sweet torture I can bear right now."

"But we have only just begun," she said, smiling gently down at him. "There is so much more I want to share with you . . ."

"Aye, well, we can space it out a bit, can't we?" he groaned, laughing with her then, before reaching up to twirl a silken auburn curl around his finger. Tugging gently, he guided her face down to his, taking her lips tenderly, sweetly, wanting to give her even a glimpse, if he could, of all of the feeling that was inside him.

Her weight atop him felt delicious, and though he ached with the need to bury himself inside her, he held back from initiating that next step, kissing her instead. When she finally lifted her head to look down at him, he was struck anew at her unusual beauty . . . her delicate features, that luscious mouth . . . and those eyes. They looked soft in this muted light, but it was the expression in them that took his breath away. The feeling

in those tawny depths made something rise in him that
he hadn't known he'd ever find in his life—something
he'd never considered a true possibility for him until
this very moment.

His hand was shaking as he lifted it to her face, cupping her cheek, and their breath rose and fell in tandem
as he spoke. "You are a miracle to me, Fiona . . . a precious, unexpected miracle, and I want nothing more
right now than to make love to you, in the way a man is
meant to love a woman."

He stroked her cheek again with his fingers, letting
his hand slip into her hair to brush over her ear and
down to the side of her throat, shifting his hips to ease
her body astride him. She moved into that position
with effortless grace, perching herself just above the
aching part of him she had loved with her mouth just
moments past; he could feel the creamy warmth of her
against his abdomen, and he reveled in it, groaning
with her at the sensation that resulted when she shifted
a little more to let the swollen wetness of her sex brush
against him.

Leaning forward, Fiona lifted her hips, kissing him
tenderly as she murmured, "Ah, Braedan, you feel so
wonderful . . ." She rocked back just a little, allowing
the tip of his erection to slip into her silky heat. He
sucked in his breath, his stomach tightening and his fingers threading with hers; she pressed her weight down
on their joined hands to lift her hips again, teasing, sliding just a fraction more onto him with each tender
stroke.

"I want to feel every bit of you filling me . . . loving
me . . ." she gasped quietly as she began to rock back

onto him, her body sinuous and graceful. He watched her move on him, lost in the abandon of her feeling, moaning his name and tipping her head back to expose the long, smooth column of her throat and the glorious curve of her breasts; the ends of her hair brushed his thighs in an erotic caress as she rocked onto him a little more deeply . . . a little more . . . and then a little more . . .

Stars blinded Braedan's vision at the sweep of incredible pleasure when she finally impaled herself fully on him, and a sound that was half growl and half groan erupted from his throat in time with her gasping cry. Murmuring her name, he gripped her hips and rose into her, meeting her downward thrusts with powerful strokes of his own, carrying her together with him into that wonderful and ancient cadence of passion.

After a few moments her fingers tightened on his, their hands locked in a kind of intimate embrace of their own as she began to tense; her movements slowed just a little, her strokes against him coming shorter and her breaths reduced to shallow gasps as the incredible feeling between them swelled to an overwhelming tide. . . .

Suddenly, she cried out his name; shudders of fulfillment wracked her body, rippling with rhythmic strokes over him and driving him off the edge into his own magnificent completion. He sat up with the force of his orgasm, losing himself in the sweet-hot rapture of her embrace and spilling into her with a power that sent numbing tingles down his legs.

When it was over she fell against him, gasping and spent, and he held her cradled to his chest, as overwhelmed as she seemed to be by the rush of feeling.

"Hush now, Fiona," he murmured, still holding her close and stroking her hair as he rocked her slowly, tenderly. "I am here. I won't let you go."

After a few moments, when they had both quieted a little, he guided her down to the soft pallet again, stretching out behind her and pulling her back into him so that they were nestled together along the complete length of their bodies.

"Braedan . . ." Fiona exhaled his name on a sigh, and he brushed her hair from her face, seeing her flushed complexion along with her smile, so tremulous and beautiful, illuminating her expression of utter contentment. "Oh, God, I never knew it was possible to feel so . . . so . . ."

"Happy?" he offered, in a husky murmur.

"Aye, happy," she echoed, nodding and nuzzling closer to him. "And content, and so . . . at ease, I suppose—with myself, with you. With us." She twisted her head up to look at him, then, and he pressed a kiss to the tip of her nose. "I have never felt so complete in all of my life, Braedan de Cantor. I want you to know that."

"Nor have I, Fiona," he said softly, pulling her more snugly against him and brushing his lips over the delicate curve of her cheek before resting his head on his arm. "Nor have I."

Fiona lay in the stillness of early morning, that darkest moment of the night just before dawn would light the new day, listening to the steady, even sound of Braedan's breathing. He'd fallen asleep at last, and, though she'd dozed, she hadn't been able to follow him into actual slumber. Her body felt pleasantly drained, the tender place at the juncture of her thighs aching sweetly from their frequent lovemaking this night. But that wasn't what had kept her from her rest. Nay, it was just that so much had happened and been discussed between them tonight—most of it wonderful, some that had given her pause—but her mind was too full with it all at the moment to sleep.

She traced her fingertip along the strong, graceful contour of Braedan's hand where it rested on her, his arm having been flung over her when he'd turned in sleep. The memory of those beautiful hands stroking her face, her hair . . . strumming her body to a fever pitch again and again sent a pleasurable shiver through her. She knew, somehow, that she would never tire of looking at Braedan, of touching him and loving him.

The realization of it swept through her like a gentle tide, lapping at the edges of her senses, as natural as if that feeling for him had been there all along. She blinked away the stinging heat that welled then, knowing that it couldn't last forever and yet wanting it more than anything she'd ever known. She turned her head to gaze at him in the darkness, committing every line and shadow to memory . . . the shape of his jaw, his sensuous mouth and deep-set eyes, admitting to herself openly for the first time just how deeply she cared for him. When she'd given herself to him so completely she didn't know, and yet it was there, as real as the heart beating within her—the one Draven had claimed she didn't possess.

But it had only been waiting for Braedan to awaken it.

Draven still had some power remaining in him, though, she thought, shifting a little on the pallet; so long as he was free to impose his brand of justice on the people of the shires he governed, none of them was truly safe. Braedan, Will, and the others knew it, too—which was why they'd devised a plan, Braedan had told her just before settling into slumber. They were going to organize an attack on Draven's estate at Chepston, taking him captive and holding him, not for ransom, as was usually the case with outlaws in possession of a nobleman, but for a hearing from the king's representative.

Pray God that it would work, and that the man sent by the sovereign would be impartial, unlike the beholden men with whom Draven chose to people his juries.

Before any of that happened, Braedan had told her, he planned to ferret out the information he needed concerning Elizabeth's whereabouts. Then they would be able to bring her back home, perhaps not completely unscathed, but at least to a place where she could be given the kind of care that would help her to heal from the trauma she was sure to have endured. And if they managed to stop Draven, then Braedan's brother, Richard, could be freed as well and returned to the comfort of the home he'd known before Draven had arranged to have himself appointed the lad's guardian.

The Folvilles were considering joining with Will and his men when the time came, and they'd discussed the possibility that the Coterel gang could be enticed to participate as well, based upon the severity of punishments Draven had imposed upon them in the past. It was a bold plan and a dangerous one, but it stood the best chance of success in stopping Draven's evil for good. Preparations were to begin on the morrow, with the Folvilles' departure; anyone wishing to take part was to meet just outside of London in a week's time, with Draven's capture and the demand for hearing to take place before the fortnight had passed.

Fiona sighed and snuggled more deeply into the crook of Braedan's arm, deciding that perhaps she'd better try to get some sleep. Only another hour or so remained until daybreak, and she knew that with such plans under way, it would be a busy morning. It couldn't come soon enough, she thought, lack of sleep or nay; Draven's dark reign had to end—yet she couldn't help feeling a kind of dread that went beyond the danger of what they were about to attempt . . . a trepidation that had far more to do with her intimate knowledge of Draven than anything else.

For she couldn't help wondering just what else Draven had planned in his certain plot to seek his revenge on Braedan and reclaim her as his own. She knew how much he liked to be in control; his studied ambush at the roadside had made that perfectly clear. He rarely allowed himself to be taken by surprise. After the violence that had taken place yesterday, he would surely be expecting some kind of retaliation attempt from Braedan and Will. Suppressing a shudder, she squeezed her eyes shut and tried to think of other things. But the shadows remained, throbbing in the back of her thoughts as dark and relentless as Draven himself.

He had warned her of his intent toward her just before he'd driven off in his coach, and as much as she wanted to believe that her newly formed bond with Braedan might somehow protect her from Draven's possession again, she found that she couldn't completely stifle her apprehension. Because she of all people knew too well that he never failed to get exactly what he wanted, no matter how difficult it was or how long it took to achieve.

And the terrifying truth of it was that Kendrick de Lacy, Lord Draven wanted *her*—back in his life, in his bed, in his control . . . and she feared he'd stop at nothing and for no one to get her.

Chapter 15

❝I am not staying behind when you go to London, Braedan, and that's all there is to it."

Braedan looked at Fiona where they sat near the morning fire, breaking their fast, noting the stubborn line of her mouth, the heat in her eyes, and the way she held her jaw at a mutinous angle. It wasn't good. Nay, not at all. Several of the women stared as they moved past, and Will whistled through his teeth, shaking his head and clearly struggling not to grimace at the pounding ache that must have commenced from the motion. Clinton just ripped off another hunk of bread and popped it in his mouth, grinning.

After he'd chewed and swallowed, he said, "Your sister's still as malleable as ever I see, Will old man." He shook his head, too, now, casting a look of masculine sympathy in Braedan's direction, adding, "But I have to say, I am glad it is no longer me bearing the brunt of that renowned obstinacy."

"I've never been obstinate a day in my life, Clinton Folville," Fiona said with an air of disdain. She pushed herself to her feet and moved away from the fire, adding under her breath, "I just speak my mind when faced with stone-headed men."

Braedan glowered at Clinton as he followed Fiona away from the fire, none too pleased at the turn this morn was taking. The sweet pleasure of the night had given way, first to the sorrow of the burial ceremony, then to this squabble with Fiona. But she was being difficult, he thought, stalking into their tree shelter behind her and letting the flap swing down to give them some privacy. If she actually believed he would let her come within a league of Draven again without—

"Why didn't you tell me last night of this—this . . . *need* you have to go off to search for Elizabeth in London on your own?" she muttered, turning to face him, her hands planted on her hips.

"Because I never thought you'd disagree with it, that's why. You were the one who insisted from the start that Will be kept in the dark about our plans to search the *stewes* together. Now there's no reason to hide it from him, because things have changed. It is too dangerous for you to come with me." He jabbed his hand through his hair, letting his breath out in an exasperated rush. "Christ, Fiona, I thought you'd agree it was best for you to remain here, away from Draven and his threats."

"Do you honestly think that it matters to Draven where I am?" she asked, raising her brow. "Yesterday made that more than apparent; if he wants to find me, he will. What's to stop him from coming here again, only this time with an entire regiment, and you hours away from me in London?"

"He won't come again so quickly," Braedan rejoined. "He'll be expecting us to retaliate in some way. You know Draven, Fiona . . . and he knows me. Elizabeth is still out there somewhere, as is my brother, rotting away slowly at Chepston under the weight of Draven's fist. He knows I will come after them. I want you nowhere near the bastard when I do—or at any other time, for that matter. I won't have you exposed to him like that again."

She paused for a moment, considering what he'd said. But he could see that she wasn't ready to give in just yet. Something more was at work in her and would need to come out before she'd agree to what he'd proposed, if she would consider it at all.

She fixed him with an even look. "And what of the agreement you coerced from me when you found me in Hampshire, Braedan, so that you could gain my help in navigating the *stewes*? Can you pretend now that you need me any less if you truly hope to find Elizabeth?"

"Damn it, Fiona, I was acting out of desperation then, as well you know. It was before I even knew about your connection to Draven or what he had done to you. I will not risk your being harmed again by him or anyone else."

"The worst harm would come in being separated from you." She twisted in his arms to look into his face, her gaze as troubled and as earnest as he'd ever seen it. "Don't you see, Braedan? If you are there and I am here, neither of us can help each other if the need arises."

"Nay, Fiona, you have to understand. Yesterday, when Draven's man held that blade to your throat . . .

when Draven himself had you in his grip, I—" Breaking
off into a curse at the bitter memory, he took her chin in
his palm, turning her all the way around in his arms to
face him completely. "I could have killed him for it,
Fiona. I almost did—and I almost lost you because of it.
I will not have you facing that kind of danger again for
my sake."

"And I won't have you facing it without me."

He gazed at her, frustration filling him. Part of him
could understand her need. It was the same as his, he
supposed; a desire to be near her combined with the
fierce need to protect. Yet another part of him felt
naught but ungovernable fear at the idea of Draven finding her again, of trying to bring her under his control . . .

"You will not be able to find Elizabeth on your own,
you know," she said, still clearly bent on convincing
him. "Any more than you could before you sought me
out weeks ago."

"I will make do. You can give me information that
will guide me through the *stewes* without having to be
there to do it."

"It is not so simple as that. You would need to talk
with bawds, procurers, and the sort in order to gain information on Elizabeth's whereabouts, and they are not
likely to tell you anything. Most will be suspicious of a
well-spoken man who comes round asking questions.
Usually, such men are attached to Church or civil authorities, who are trying to close down the houses whose
keepers fail to comply with all the laws regulating them.
Whoring may be legal in Southwark, but there are many
restrictions and rules to be followed nonetheless. The
questions you would be asking about Elizabeth would
be sure to make many of those in the life apprehensive,

since it is against the law to aid in the forced seduction of an innocent; they will fear to reveal anything that might bring them before the courts."

"Coin goes a long way to loosen tongues, Fiona, no matter what the level of fear involved."

She made a sound of exasperation. "It will take far more coin than what we've been able to gather these weeks, I think, to make them risk time on the pillory or worse. Most of the *stewe*-houses are in the Bishop of Winchester's liberty; any case involving a bawd from one of those brothels would be brought before his ecclesiastic court, with punishment to take place in the Clink. I know of no one willing to risk the hell of that fate, even for a short time."

"I'll just be sure to tell them I am *not* there on behalf of the authorities, then."

"You will still arouse suspicion, and if enough of them become wary about you, you'll risk having someone learn that you're an outlaw, wanted by Draven, which is exactly what we're trying to avoid." She shook her head, her mouth tight. "Besides, even if by some good fortune you were able to garner a clue or two about Elizabeth without being discovered for who you are, there is still the difficulty of finding specific houses without possessing a working knowledge of Southwark. You'd need to know the layout of the Borough, not to mention finding any of the houses that may have sprung up outside of the established areas."

"How many of them could be connected with Draven?" Braedan asked, just as determined to make her see that he could do this himself, without risking her. "He supplies women only to the authorized brothels, does he not?"

"He used to confine his interests to the sanctioned establishments, aye, but it is a large area nonetheless; some of those houses are in the bishop's liberty, but some are beyond that jurisdiction in the other wards. Draven had his fingers in many pots, even those years ago when he kept me. He has undoubtedly expanded his holdings since then, perhaps even into London proper. You will need specific information to find those places most likely to be housing Elizabeth, knowledge you cannot hope to obtain on your own."

"Damn it, Fiona, I will not let you go in there as we'd agreed when I sought you out," Braedan said more forcefully. "Some of those who knew of the Crimson Lady those years ago may be more likely to answer my questions for her than for me alone, but it would be deadly folly to attempt it. If Draven's holdings in the *stewes* are as pervasive as you claim, then news of your return would reach him in less than a day! He needs no more encouragement in his obsessive pursuit of you, by God."

She remained silent at that, and after a moment he took her hand, his touch playing over the elegant length of it before pressing his palm to hers and threading their fingers together in a warm clasp. Still she didn't speak, though her expression looked troubled.

He felt his heart thudding with slow, even beats, knowing that he would do anything he could to remove that look of worry . . . anything but bring her to Southwark and Draven's attention again. "You know, it will not be easy for me, either, being away from you," he added softly, hoping that she was coming to see his way of thinking on this. "But I could not live with myself if in trying to save Elizabeth I risked you. I could not do it,

Fiona, no matter how much more difficult it will make searching for her because of it."

She nodded, but after another moment's silence, she turned that studied gaze on him again. "What if I were able to go to London and help you *without* a great deal of risk, Braedan—with no more risk, in truth, than if I remained right here at the settlement?"

"How? We've already discussed it, and it isn't possible. Having the Crimson Lady make her appearance in the *stewes* would be the same as dangling a challenge before Draven's nose."

"But what if I didn't go there as the Crimson Lady, but rather as someone entirely different?" she said, sitting up, her body taut with enthusiasm as the idea appeared to take hold in her. She fixed her gaze on him where he'd sat up as well, her eyes alight with it. "Aye— what if I could go to Southwark with you, and meet with those who could most help our cause—only garbed in the padded costume of the embroidress I was in Hampshire? I could say I was come in search of my apprentice, Elizabeth, who shamefully left my service to pursue a livelihood in the *stewes*. That way none with whom we spoke would fear reprisal, since I would make it seem as if I was placing the blame on her, rather than seeking to accuse any of them of wrongdoing."

She looked at him hopefully. "It could work, Braedan! No one would recognize me as Giselle de Coeur in such a disguise and after all these years. I could still use my knowledge of the *stewes* to search for Elizabeth freely, but it would be as if I wasn't there, as far as Draven was concerned."

Braedan paused at her suggestion, his instincts telling him to deny it even as logic couldn't help but admit that it was an idea. What she was suggesting just might work. He leveled his gaze at her, his jaw tight. He wanted to believe that they could do it. In truth he would be secretly relieved not to be so far separated from her, but he hated the risk of it nonetheless. He exhaled in a sigh of defeat. "If I was to consider such a thing, would you agree to let me remain with you at all times while you questioned these . . . bawds and the like? You would never think to go alone?"

"We could go together, and if we dressed you in something more common, we could tell any who happened to question it that you're my servant, accompanying me in the rougher areas of Southwark for my own safety." She shrugged and gave him the hint of a smile. "It wouldn't be a complete lie, anyway."

"What, the part about my serving you, or my worry over your safety?" he asked, allowing himself a bit of a smile in return. "I think both are quite apt for how I feel, lady."

Acceptance of the plan began to seep into him, washing away any remaining arguments he might have posed against her going with him. With a sigh, he gathered her to him and held her close, breathing in the delicate scent of her hair and cradling her head in his palm as he pressed a kiss to the top of it. "Ah, Fiona, I do not know what enchantment you hold over me, but you have managed to talk me into something I swore I'd not entertain, not even for an instant."

"It will be for the best, Braedan," she murmured against his chest. "You'll see. We will find Elizabeth before the others are supposed to meet us a sennight from now; then your brother can be freed and Draven can be stopped for good. We'll have to set off soon, though, if

we're to reach the gates of London proper before nightfall. It would not serve to be locked outside once it is
dark, as much for your safety as for mine."

"Aye, I suppose you're right," he said, savoring the
feel of her in his arms for a long moment more. Releasing her at last, and with great reluctance, he turned to
begin packing up his portion of the belongings they'd
need to take on their journey. "Come, then," he murmured, glancing at her and trying to keep his still un-
shakable worry to himself. "If we're to do this, we'd
better get started."

The trip to London had been uneventful—far less tumultuous than Will's reaction when he'd learned that
she was accompanying Braedan there. He'd only re-
lented when she'd given him her word to keep to her
padded garments anytime she was visible in public,
whether they were searching the *stewes* or not. He
hadn't been happy about her decision to go, but he'd understood her need to stay with the man he believed to be
her husband, receiving ample assurance from Braedan
that he would watch over her with care. Finally, hugging
her tightly and gruffly mumbling good-bye, Will had
seen them off, with promises to meet them at the Bull in
Southwark a sennight hence.

The road into the city had gotten progressively more
congested as they neared the gates, and so it had been
near dusk when they'd finally entered London and made
their way to an inn, to purchase the use of a small but
clean room for the night. The first full day had been
spent getting their bearings and gathering what they
would need; the search would begin in earnest today.

Reaching behind her to fasten the topmost laces,

Fiona yawned and paused to stretch a bit. She felt well rested this morn and ready to begin their task, though she'd been experiencing a vague sense of unease ever since they'd entered the city gates. The true trial would come in a few hours, she knew, when they crossed the Thames to enter Southwark and the *stewes*. For now, simply accustoming herself again to the old embroidress's costume was keeping her busy enough not to dwell on how it might affect her.

"This feels strange after so many weeks without needing to wear it," Fiona commented over her shoulder to Braedan, as she adjusted the thick, black wimple over her hair and patted down the sides of her padded gown. "I'd almost forgotten how cumbersome all of this fabric is."

"And unattractive, too," Braedan mumbled with an exaggerated grimace, chuckling when she threw her boxwood comb at him in retaliation. "I cannot say that it is a welcome change, lady," he added, his eyes twinkling as he picked the comb up and walked over to hand it to her again, "though I will admit to being glad that it prevents anyone else from seeing you in your true and quite irresistible form."

With a scandalized laugh, she shook her head. "Braedan de Cantor, you are incorrigible."

"So I've been told," he answered, raising his brows and wiggling them, which drew another smile from her.

"Well, sir, since you're so free with your observations this morn, let me take a look at you and offer up some of my own," she clipped, stepping back to view him. He struck a less than modest pose, but she ignored his boldness, instead moving around him and examining the rolled-up *braies* and coarse-woven tunic, her finger to

her lips in mock concentration, and her gaze traveling up
and down his muscular and finely formed length.

"I trust I meet with your approval, milady," he murmured, still grinning wryly as he delivered an elaborate
bow with a flourish of his hand.

"Not quite."

"What do you mean *not quite*?" he echoed in feigned
dismay. "I am the perfect servant, clad in simple yet
durable cloth, sure to be convincing to even the most
suspicious of the bawds we will face this day."

She shook her head. "Nay. One detail is lacking." Going back to the sack of garments they'd purchased for
him in Threadneedle Lane for six pence, she rummaged
around in it for a moment, before reaching deep and
pulling out something soft and brown in color. It was a
hat. A felt toque with a chin strap, no less.

"Oh, no. I am not putting that on, Fiona. A soldier
has his limits, you know, even one as tolerant as I am. It
is the kind an old man would don!"

"It is the hat of a servant, and all the more useful for
being something you would never wear in your true
form as a knight," Fiona retorted, bringing it to him.
"Remember, the idea is to be unmemorable to those we
question. If anyone does decide to go to Draven with
news of two strangers sniffing about, they'll be hard-
pressed to describe us any differently from a hundred
other tradeswomen and servants. It will be useful for
gathering information about Elizabeth. Think on it that
way, instead of as a discomfort."

This time Braedan rolled his eyes, but he remained
still while she fastened the ridiculous hat on his head.
Once the chin strap was secure, he shook his head, test-

ing its hold, and Fiona laughed aloud, the sound tinkling merrily through the small chamber.

"Ach, Braedan, you look like one of the dancing monkeys the mummers lead through the market on Fair Day when you do that."

"Aye, well, if you were wearing this—" He stopped, realizing that she was wearing something that felt far more cumbersome than his hat, in the form of her voluminous wimple. Grumbling, he picked up their purse of coin and tied it at his waist, saying, "We might as well get on with it, then. I can see you're not going to bend in this, and we'll be here all day prating about it, if I allow it."

Making a *tsking* sound with her tongue, Fiona swept out the door he held for her, smiling all the way. Her good cheer lasted through the deliciously scented Baker Street, past Milk Street, with its plentiful, mooing cows and far riper aromas, all the way to the river's edge.

There she stopped with Braedan just behind, surveying the already-thick obstruction of people trying to make their way over London Bridge—the only means, other than crossing the Thames with a hired boatman, to reach Southwark from the city or to come back again. The whole place bustled with activity, the bridge itself clogged with masses of people, a multitude of smells, and noise. It was less than promising, and a fresh reminder of why she'd always found the city and life here to be difficult at best.

"What say you?" she asked Braedan, leaning in to him and speaking more loudly than usual to be heard over the noise of all the people. "Should we hire a boatman to take us across, or should we pay the bridge toll and brave the crowds? It may be past the noon hour before we reach bank side with that throng to contend with."

"It's an even dilemma, I'd say. With one we lose little more than time, but with the other we spend a greater amount of coin that we may need, eventually, in bribing those who can help us find Elizabeth."

As he'd spoken, Fiona was noting the flow of people, carts, and animals coming from Southwark as well as those crossing into the ward; more than a few of the women, some traveling singly, others in pairs or small groups, walked with their heads covered by the striped hoods required by law, to distinguish them as legal harlots.

A latent shudder swept through her, drawing Braedan's attention.

"What is it?" he asked, looking at her in concern.

"Nothing." She forced a smile. "Let's save the coin and walk the bridge. That's my choice, as long as you don't object."

He nodded, seeming content with the decision as they made their way toward the entrance to the heavily traveled bridge. Fiona tried to seem unconcerned as they made their way through the crowd, passing those who were moving more slowly, including a squabbling couple and a man with his cart tipped on a broken wheel, but she found it difficult to tear her gaze from those ray-patterned hoods bobbing through the crowd. Her mind burned with an image she had found fair success in suppressing these many years. She saw herself as a very young girl, standing just outside the mouth of the stone archway here on a clear summer morn, waiting for her mother to make her way home after a night spent working in the *stewes*.

She'd not known, then, what it was that took Mama away whenever it was dark; she'd only known how happy she felt when she came home, and so she'd chosen that morning to meet her at the bridge and share her walk back to the hovel they rented above a little shop at Cheapside on Ironmonger Lane, with its ever-present stench of hot metal and the clanging of hammers.

The crowd was less boisterous so early in the morning, and she'd been able to spot her mother in the throng, her russet hair with its straight part shining in the sun as she trudged, facedown, out of the opening at London end. She'd been ready to run to her, excited to tell her of the pence she'd found near the butchers' shops the evening before, which would mean fresh bread and perhaps a bit of cheese to break their fast instead of the dry crust that served as their usual fare. But before she could reach her, a man dressed in fine clothes had reached out and grabbed her mother by the arm, shouting angrily and pointing at her hair.

Fiona had stopped short before being forced to run after the man, who had begun to drag her mother down into the street. By the end of that terrible day Fiona had learned that the man was a London official; her mother had been brought before the Mayor's Court and condemned to pay a shilling eight pence or serve three days in the *thews* for failure to wear the hood that was required of her as a common woman and harlot of Southwark.

That sum of coin was unthinkable, considering their destitute situation, and so Fiona's mother had been forced to endure the punishment of the *thews*, led up and secured on that pillory with other women like her to be jeered at by all who passed by, her crimes read aloud for their entertainment. Fiona had stood in the shadows for each of the three days, watching her mother's ignominy with fists clenched and silent tears sliding down her cheeks.

And her life had never been the same again.

"Should we be making inquiries at any of the shops or houses on the bridge itself?" Braedan leaned in to ask her, pulling her from the painful memory with his question.

She looked around herself, feeling a little dazed to realize they'd traversed nearly half the span already. "Nay," she answered, trying to concentrate on the task before them. "We need not question anyone until we reach the Borough. That is where most of the inns and sanctioned brothels we're looking for are to be found."

Braedan slowed, studying her with that same, knowing gaze as before they'd entered the bridge. "Perhaps we should stop for a bit," he said, taking her elbow. "You're looking pale, of a sudden."

"I'm fine," she said, touching his hand and calling up a smile as she willed herself to shake off the difficult memories. "It is just warmer in these garments than I remembered, that is all."

"Then perhaps you should rest. The sun burns hot today."

"Nay. We should keep going so that we can reach the first of the alehouses we'll need to visit by the noon meal," she answered, sidestepping an overturned basket of cabbages and the red-faced woman who was angrily gathering them back up.

"Which will we seek out first?"

"The Unicorn, I think. It is a large establishment, and when I lived at Chepston, the brewster there also rented some rooms nightly to the women Draven supplied her. After that we can try the Maid's Head and the Lion."

"It sounds as if we'll be busy."

"Aye. It will be enough to keep us occupied for the day."

She glanced sideways at him as they continued on, reminded again of his strength in both body and heart; even in servant's garb he seemed a force to contend with, the whole of his attractiveness increased, for her, in knowing the tender care he offered as well. She tried to draw on that feeling to keep the rising panic that their imminent approach to the *stewes* was inspiring in her. On the day she'd fled this place for good more than four years ago, she'd vowed never to return. But her world had changed since then. Braedan had come into it, first as a thorn in her side and then, through the enigmatic workings of their hearts, as the man she loved enough to face the demons of her past. She would be strong through this. Aye, for Braedan's sake, and the sake of his foster sister.

And for myself.

The thought came unbidden, shoring up her resolve and helping her to keep placing her feet in front of each other though it brought her ever closer to the hellish memories of her past. Draven had stolen her innocence, but he hadn't been able to break her spirit. Not completely. She had lost herself for a while in the stifling prison of his possession, that much was true, but it had not been as hopeless as it had seemed. She'd found some of her strength again, in large part thanks to Braedan's acceptance of her. Thanks to his love. And with it came the fierce desire finally to thwart Draven and his evil . . . to face her fears in ways that had never seemed possible before.

All that she needed now was the strength of will to do it.

Chapter 16

❧◦◦◦❧

Braedan stood in the alley behind the Bell and Cock in the heat of late afternoon four days later, watching Fiona's animated discussion with the inn's alewife. Unsavory scents rose all around him both from refuse and the old thatching that was piled in heaps, as it was behind every building he'd seen in this liberty, but he tried to ignore the stench. The questioning going on right now was too important. If this was the woman Fiona had sought, then she might well hold some answers to Elizabeth's whereabouts.

At the moment their quarry looked supremely agitated, whether from her exertions within doors or from the conversation Fiona was trying to have with her, Braedan couldn't tell; the woman's face was ruddy, and some of her hair had escaped her tightly fitted cloth cap to hang in limp, damp strands down her cheeks. She kept gesturing as she spoke, her gaze darting suspiciously toward him.

He stepped back into the shadows a little more, trying to prevent her from gaining a clear view of him. He'd heard Fiona tell her that he was her servant, but there was no need to arouse further suspicion. The woman's wariness about him was surprising; they had visited upwards of a dozen alehouses and more than a few brothels since their arrival in London, and none of the others with whom they'd spoken had reacted so skittishly. They'd been alternately apathetic or curious, some of them even seeming eager to help her in finding a runaway apprentice—thinking, no doubt, that a payment of gratitude might be involved from a shopkeeper who was willing to search so diligently for her lost property. But by and large, they'd only garnered a few clues.

The best of those had landed them here.

He bowed his head deferentially and backed up a step to let Fiona pass by him when she finally finished the conversation and left the alehouse door. It was a show for the benefit of the alewife, who kept gazing after them for another long moment, her expression sharp and her posture rigid. Then, pursing her lips together, she grumbled under her breath and shook her head with a scowl before ducking back into the building and slamming the door shut behind her.

Braedan hurried to catch up to Fiona, pausing with her when they'd reached a safe distance to talk unobserved. "What did you learn, then?" he asked, trying to keep his sense of hopefulness contained; it was as likely as false a lead as the others had been.

Fiona remained silent, her brows knit together and her tawny eyes clouded with worry. When she still didn't answer after a moment more, he asked again, "Well, did she have information about Elizabeth or not? Tell me, Fiona."

"Aye, she knew something," Fiona answered softly, still staring with consternation at the ground before them. She finally turned her gaze upon Braedan. "She gave me the location of a brothel on Cokkeslane, claiming that a young woman matching Elizabeth's description and circumstances was known to work from some rooms there as recently as a fortnight past."

"Let's go, then," Braedan said, taking her arm and beginning to tug her the remainder of the way down the alley so that they could look for the house she'd mentioned. But she resisted, pulling back to keep them at a standstill.

"Nay, Braedan—wait—"

"What is it?" he asked impatiently.

"I just feel like something is not right about all of this."

Braedan frowned. He'd noticed an increasing sense of anxiety from her, more so since they'd decided two days ago to take rooms on this side of the Thames for the sake of ease in their search—but he also knew she'd never risk someone else's welfare without good cause. "Why should we hold back, lady? It is the first truly solid information about Elizabeth we've had so far."

"That is my concern. The alewife surrendered it too easily." Fiona was still frowning, and now she shook her head, making the folds of her wimple flap like crow's wings. "Afterward, when I tried to press a few of the coins we'd brought for the purpose into her palm, she would not take them."

"Perhaps she wanted to do a good deed without recompense."

"Not this woman. I knew of her during my years in the *stewes*, though I'd never spoken to her myself before; her name is Margery Kempe, and she was known for her talent in gathering profit. She would never turn down free coin." She gazed at Braedan again, her eyes intense upon him. "It was strange . . . almost as if she knew what I was going to ask before I asked it."

"You think it to be some kind of trap, then?"

"I cannot say. She's sending us to Cokkeslane, which is a difficult area, to be sure. The information could be honest, but then again, there could be another reason— or a specific person—behind her offering of it as well."

He cursed softly. "Draven . . ."

"I admit it doesn't seem likely that he could know we are here, and yet . . ." Her voice trailed off as she glanced back over her shoulder in the direction from which they'd come.

She'd been under a great deal of strain the past few days, Braedan knew, and he felt a renewed swell of concern. Staying in Southwark had been difficult for her, and searching the *stewes*, agonizing. He couldn't imagine what she must feel like to be here. He only knew how *he* would feel if he was being forced to confront his past at Saint-Jean-d'Acre all over again. To have to relive the hell of that time and place. And yet Fiona was doing that right now, revisiting circumstances that were likely more wrenching, even, than what he'd known on those battlefields.

She needed a rest from it, if only for a few hours. Some of what had to be done next could be done by him alone, and in light of what she suspected of the alewife, it was probably best for him to investigate it himself first anyway.

"Come," he said, gently, placing his hand on the small of her back. "What say you we go back to our rooms at the Tabard and sup? It's getting late, and it would be wise to rest for a while, I think."

"But what of Cokkeslane?" she asked in surprise.

"I don't think we should seek out the place right now; as you said, it might be a snare for us. If Draven is behind it, he would be expecting us to go there immediately. And if nothing is amiss with the information, then a few more hours won't matter."

"A few more hours?" She pulled away now with certainty to keep them standing in the alley and away from the main thoroughfare. "Are you intending to go back and search *tonight*? It would be madness, Braedan. Plumped-up widow's weeds or nay, if I am walking the streets of Southwark after dark, I will be construed as a harlot who may be purchased for the night."

"You won't be on the streets tonight; I'll be going back alone."

She made a sound of exasperation. "It is hardly less dangerous for you! You know it's against the law to be out past city curfew. You'll have to take up residence in the brothel for the night or risk arrest if you're caught out and about."

"I know how to keep to the shadows," he reassured her. "I didn't survive all those years in foreign lands with strange customs and unforgiving laws by dashing about blindly, you know." He touched her face and gave her a gentle smile. "I do cherish your worry for me, Fiona, but in truth I will be fine. It's better that I look into this myself anyway. If it is a trap, it will be easier for me to find my way out of it alone than for both of us to need escape it. My worry for you would prove most distracting, I fear."

She didn't look completely convinced, but she was wavering. Hoping to offer the final bit of argument that would bring her into agreement with him, he added, "You must admit, I will have a better chance of finding Elizabeth tonight than if we went right now; the women who work in the *stewes* are forbidden by law to live in the rooms they rent each night, are they not? If Elizabeth is indeed connected to that Cokkeslane house, as the alewife told you, then she or anyone who might know of her wouldn't likely be found there until after dark."

Fiona frowned, but after a pause was forced to nod reluctantly. "I suppose you're right about that part of it."

"It's settled, then; we'll go back to the Tabard to eat and rest," he said firmly, putting his hand to her back again and guiding her out toward the main road. As they came into sight of other people, he stepped back, maintaining a suitable yet protective distance between them, as befit a tradeswoman and her servingman.

Soon enough they neared the inn. But before reaching the entrance, Braedan pulled off his cap and stuffed it into his tunic, donning a short cape he pulled from the pack he'd been carrying with them, to initiate his second role as Fiona's husband, as needed whenever they were at the inn. When they entered the Tabard's main chamber, he paid no heed to her soft protests and used some of their coin to order a bath and some food sent up to them. But she seemed grateful to let him lead the way to their chamber after; it was a modest room, though clean and a welcome haven from the hubbub of the streets.

"Here. Let me help you with that," he said, as she twisted her arms behind herself trying to reach the laces of her widow's garments. His fingers worked with efficient speed to undo all of the ties and unfasten the bulky cushions she'd strapped to herself beneath the kirtle, as she unwound the fabric of the wimple from her chin and lifted the entire headdress from her hair. In a few moments she was clad in nothing more than her shift, and she made a groaning sound of relief as she stretched.

"It feels so good to be free of all that padding," she said, running her fingers through her plaits to loosen her hair as well. It spilled over her shoulders like a fall of dark fire, her sweet vanilla fragrance wafting from those luxurious tresses as she turned to face him. "Ah, Braedan, how did you know?" Her voice was soft and broken, and she gazed up at him with a look of such poignant vulnerability that it set something to twisting inside of him. "How do you always know just what I need and when I need it—even before I do?"

He couldn't answer her at first for the feelings unleashed in him then, and so he simply held out his arms to her. She curled into his embrace, and he stroked her hair, cradling her against his chest as he murmured endearments. His eyes stung as he held her close, feeling her hitched breathing and realizing, suddenly, just how much these days back in the *stewes* were wearing down that extraordinary resilience of hers. It had to end and soon, that much was clear; he didn't know how much more of it she would be able to stand. Pray God he would find an end to it tonight, by finding Elizabeth.

And if he didn't, he thought, leading Fiona to the bed to rest until her bath arrived, he would end it himself by arranging for one of Will's men to meet them outside the city when they convened to take action against Draven and bring her back to the settlement until the entire, ugly mess was finished. She would have to agree to go, for his sake if not for her own.

He would make her agree to it, he decided, stretching out behind her on the bed and pulling her into his arms to press a kiss to the back of her neck. Because he loved her too much not to.

Fiona watched the door latch shut behind Braedan some hours later, feeling the heaviness that had been lingering in her heart these past days swell anew. Being with him here tonight had helped for a while, the tender hours they'd spent since returning to this chamber like a balm to soothe her soul. They'd supped and then bathed together, his touch on her so gentle, so loving that she'd wanted to weep with the joy of it. But she hadn't; she'd simply soaked in the warmth of his body pressed close to hers in the little tub, stroking the cloth with its scented soap over him as he'd done to her until they were both beyond thinking anymore.

Then they had made love, more sweetly than ever before, until, exhausted and replete, they'd slept for a while. It had been a beautiful sharing of their bodies and their hearts, but even then, as she'd drifted off into restless slumber, she couldn't stop thinking that it had felt different, somehow. As if they'd been touched by sadness.

Like a farewell . . .

Then, with a murmured caution to keep the door bolted while he was away, he'd gone to investigate the alewife's story of the brothel on Cokkeslane.

He was right, she knew, about the wisdom in traveling alone to seek out Elizabeth, yet she worried about him nonetheless. If Draven was lying in wait, it would be disastrous, though Braedan had assured her that he would be prepared for that possibility. He'd go carefully and never leave himself without a route of escape, he'd said, kissing her face and giving her an encouraging smile just before he'd gotten up to dress.

She had to trust him to take care of himself as he'd promised, she decided, pushing herself up from the bed. She had to do something—anything—to pass the time until he returned. At the least she could tidy up and make herself presentable.

After washing up a bit with fresh water poured from the pitcher and basin, she eyed with a grimace the pads and heavy, black gown and wimple that comprised her embroidress's costume. She just didn't think she could bear putting them on again this night.

It had actually surprised her how much she'd come to despise that disguise, considering that she'd donned it every day for three years with hardly a thought. It had to be Braedan's involvement in her life, she decided; somehow the idea of pretending to be someone she wasn't was no longer as tolerable as it had been before. Braedan had seen her for who she truly was, and he had loved her anyway, with all of her failings and sins out in the open; after experiencing a remarkable gift of that kind, it was almost unbearable to go backward again. She wasn't sure, even, if she'd ever be able to go back to her old role as shopkeeper after all this was over. Every time she thought about it she felt nothing but sickness at knowing she would likely be without Braedan, then. Swallowing the pain, she set the clothes aside.

It wasn't necessary to wear the padded garments

again until the morn anyway, she reasoned. She chose instead one of the simple kirtles from the garments she'd brought with her from Will's settlement. Then she set about straightening the bedding and lugging the tub to the window to pour out the old bathwater into the gutter below. When that was finished, not much was left to be done but to clean up the scraps left from their evening repast. It was much too warm to need a fire, and so when all had finally been set to right, she sank down on the carved wooden chair near the hearth and stared into the empty grate, trying not to think of Braedan, Draven, or the darkness that seemed to be circling her heart, squeezing out the light a little more with each day she lingered in the *stewes*.

It was foolish to dwell so on any of it, she knew, and yet . . .

Making a sound of exasperation, she stood abruptly and paced to the window, pushing the shutter open a bit more to look out. It couldn't have been more than a half an hour since Braedan had left, but it already seemed like forever. She leaned her head on the casement and peered down into the alley below. There was naught to be seen but the red eyes of some hungry rodent, scavenging for its supper. Shivering, she pulled away from the window and closed the shutter, preferring the oppressive heat to that sight. Besides, though the night air that had swept through the open window had been cooler, it had been thick with the unpleasant scents of the city as well.

Pacing back to the hearth, she paused, readying to light a few more of the tapers the inn had provided with the cost of the room, when she heard a scratching at the door. She stiffened for an instant then rushed forward, buoyant with hope. Braedan, returned already? It seemed too quick, though. At the last moment she stopped, forcing herself not to open the door until she could be sure it was he.

"Yes?" she called, hoping that her voice sounded as strong and controlled as she intended it to.

"Pardon, mistress," a young female voice called back. " 'Tis Anna from the kitchens, come to get your tub back fer another customer's use tonight. Are ye done with it?"

Disappointment and relief warred in Fiona at once, though she stifled the first to answer, "Aye, Anna, just a moment." It wasn't the girl's fault that she wasn't Braedan, Fiona thought ruefully, as she reached to lift the latch on the door. She spoke as she pulled it open, "The tub is over near the window. I've emptied it already and—"

With a gasp, she stumbled backward and then froze, feeling as if her throat was closing altogether. The familiar scent of roses and spice swept over her at the same time that her gaze locked with the icy black eyes of the man who was leaning against the edge of the open portal, his arms crossed nonchalantly. From the corner of her vision she caught the frightened expression of the girl who'd called herself Anna as she darted away down the hall toward the stairs at the far end.

She'd be no help, then, Fiona's frantic mind managed to conjure. *No help at all . . . Oh, God . . .*

"Well, Giselle," Draven drawled softly, the faintest hint of a smile curving his sensual mouth, "I can see that you've lost whatever manners I'd managed to teach you in our years together. You've yet to invite me in." At that he pushed himself away from the doorway, as masterful and confident in himself as always, to take several steps into the chamber.

"So it seems I will just have to invite myself."

Chapter 17

Fiona stepped away from the door on legs gone numb, backing up until the foot of the bedstead stopped her from going farther. Draven had swung the door shut behind him; now he moved past her, shaking his head and making a clicking sound with his tongue as he quickly glanced around the room and out the shutter before closing it and moving by her again toward the empty hearth. Once there, he pulled off his leather gloves, setting them on the mantel before turning to face her with one arm resting next to them. He was a powerfully built man, and the position he took now forcefully reminded her of how he seemed to dominate whatever place he occupied, filling a chamber completely with his presence.

"You needn't behave as if I'm going to pounce on you at any moment, Giselle. It is rather offensive, you know."

"What do you want, then?" she asked, keeping her fingers clenched together in front of her.

"Nothing, right away," he answered, spotting the wooden chair and easing himself into it. He leaned back with a sigh, stretching his long legs out and lacing his hands together over his stomach. When he looked at her again, it was with that expression she remembered so well, his eyes both amused and intense upon her, an expression that sent shudders quaking through her, knowing as she did that he was merely playing for a while before he would impose his will on her in whatever way he chose.

"I will however, be requiring something of you in the very near future, when your paramour returns from his fruitless quest at Cokkeslane," he continued, watching for her reaction from beneath heavy lids.

"It *was* you, then."

He raised his brow. "You suspected my hand in it, did you? Very good. Perhaps you haven't lost all of the instincts I labored so arduously to instill in you . . . or *on* you, as the case may be," he added with another of his devilish, soft smiles. "Besides, you honestly didn't think your little disguises would prevent me from recognizing you, did you? My nephew's strength and military demeanor are difficult to miss." He gestured toward the heap of black clothing and padding that rested atop the trunk in the chamber. "And even that hideous gown and wimple could not mask the unusual beauty of your eyes."

She refused to say anything in return, fisting her hands at her sides and keeping her expression impassive in her determination not to feed his desire for an emotional response. She continued to stare at him from her position near the bed, trying to remember if there was anything in the room that she could use as a weapon against him. Her dagger was with her other clothing, set aside when she and Braedan had bathed and made love, and Draven was too near the tools for the fire for her to make use of them.

She moved not a muscle, hating him with every fiber of her being. The only thing that kept her from casting caution to the winds right now and attempting an escape was his earlier statement about Braedan's return. It meant that Braedan was still alive and that Draven's plan hadn't included ambushing and killing him at the brothel where he'd gone to investigate. It was enough to keep her passive for the time being, to hear what else her nemesis was brewing in his way of revenge on them.

"You're very patient," he commented, interrupting her thoughts. "Aren't you going to ask in what way your services will be required upon my dear nephew's return?"

"Nay. I know you'll tell me when you're ready."

He laughed aloud at that, the sound warm and rich. A startling contrast to the cold man she knew lurked beneath his handsome, polished surface. "Ah, Giselle, I confess I've missed that about you—your unadorned manner of speaking," he said, amusement still coloring his voice as he rose up out of the chair and approached her.

She stiffened, wary. He came to within a few inches of her before stopping, his expression an enigmatic combination of humor, longing, and vexation. At last reaching up one hand, he brushed a wisp of her hair back from her temple, saying quietly, "I did care for you, you know. More than for any other."

She paused, startled by his words and yet knowing in a way that went bone deep that they were as false as everything else that had ever happened between them. "You believed you *owned* me, Draven," she answered with finality. "There is a difference. I know that now."

He reacted as she suspected he would, his eyes darkening with anger and his jaw tightening as he pulled away. "You know nothing, Giselle. And I do own you. I always have. You just seem to have forgotten it. Though I can assure you, you'll be reminded of it quite thoroughly before we're finished."

He closed his eyes then and breathed in, raking his hand through his hair before staring at her again. "But first we must take care of the little problem of my nephew, who will undoubtedly come through that door in less than an hour, heart weary with disappointment and looking for his lover to ease his pain. You will have a task to complete then, and you will do it well, Giselle, or your precious Braedan will suffer more for it, I promise you."

The trembling had begun anew in her belly, and she struggled to ignore it. There still might be a way to get free of this nightmare for her and Braedan; she just couldn't see it yet. For now she'd have to pretend to go along with Draven and his twisted schemes.

"What is it you expect me to do?" she asked evenly.

"Nothing that you haven't done thousands of times before, sweet," he answered, the endearment profane to her ears. "You will enact a delicious pretense for my nephew, behaving, when he arrives, as if the two of you are completely alone. You will entice him into your bed, so that he will discard both his weapons and his caution—at which point I will reveal myself, call up my men, and commence the rest of what I have planned for the both of you."

"But why?" she couldn't stop herself from asking, disbelief shaking her. "Why go through all of that for the simple purpose of taking him into your custody?"

"There are two reasons, actually. For one, I do not wish to lose any more of my men beneath his blade. But more importantly because it will be supremely entertaining to watch the effect your betrayal will have on him. When all is said and done, he will not be able to deny that it was you who single-handedly lured him to his capture. His knowing, eventually, that you were coerced into the deed will lessen my satisfaction somewhat, of course, but that part cannot be helped."

Fiona thought she was going to be sick. It took all of her will to keep from sinking down to the edge of the bed with the horror sweeping through her. It was unbearable, knowing that she was to be the instrument of Braedan's pain. Numbly, she turned her gaze to Draven. "What then? What will you do with us after you've achieved your insidious plan?"

"I haven't decided yet," he said, shrugging. "Perhaps I'll bring you and my nephew back to Chepston for a while . . . or perhaps just order an immediate execution in the name of the crown. Either way I'll have to make it worth my while. You've both given me a great deal of trouble, and I'll need recompense for it."

Fiona stood there, stunned with the evil of what he was saying, her mind reverberating with the word he'd said near the last with such relish. *Recompense.* Aye, Draven always wanted payment of some kind. It was what had inspired him to conceive the sordid lie that was the Crimson Lady so long ago. *And therein lay the solu-*

tion, perhaps to this entire, foul situation, her mind asserted from somewhere in the depths of her misery. She could offer a solution that Draven would prefer in place of his own perverse plan. . . .

Her heart hammered as she turned the idea around in her mind, examining it from all sides. It might work, aye, but she feared it would be at a steep price; it would be a nightmare made flesh for her, though if it spared Braedan, then it would be worth the cost. . . .

"What if I agreed to go willingly back to Chepston with you and resume the life I left behind four years ago," she said before she could lose her will to see this through, "if I agreed to once again take up my role for you as the Crimson Lady?"

Draven stilled, his eyes narrowing on her as if he were trying to deduce her motives. "You think to save yourself by such an offer?"

"Nay, I seek to strike a bargain for my services to you."

"A bargain for what?"

"Braedan's freedom. He is an outlaw wanted by the crown thanks to you. That fate is a punishment in and of itself for a man such as he. He only came to London to seek out his foster sister and has no means of hurting you in your position of power," she lied, hoping that Draven knew nothing of the outlaws' plot against him. Her voice wavered. "You want me back; we both know that. Give over your pursuit of Braedan. Agree to let him go free tonight, and I will place myself under your control again for as long as you wish it, to do with me as you see fit, without fear of my leaving again."

Draven paused for a beat of silence, his expression even and his face as exquisitely handsome as always—all but for the shadows of stricken surprise that appeared, suddenly, in his eyes. "Good God," he murmured at last, almost as if to himself, though he kept his stare fixed firmly on her. "You've actually fallen in love with him, haven't you?"

Fiona wanted nothing less than to shout the truth of that, but she would never give Draven the satisfaction of making such an admission at his command. She lifted her chin a fraction and stared him down, knowing even as she did, that though she might not speak the words aloud, he would be able to read her true feelings anyway.

A little choked sound escaped him before he regained control of himself, the shadows in his eyes vanishing under a mantle of cool, hard mockery. "So be it, Giselle; it will only make what is to come that much more delicious." Shaking his head, he sat back in the chair near the hearth, and drawled, "But I'm afraid that, while your idea sounds tempting, sweet, truly, I cannot see how what you suggest would offer an improvement for me. I have you in my power *now*—unwilling, perhaps, but in my control nonetheless. If I did as you asked, I'd be giving up my chance to witness that delightful moment when Braedan realizes that you have betrayed him and I have bested him once and for all."

Nay! Her heart shouted, though she forced herself to remain still and silent. He couldn't reject her offer outright. She knew Draven, knew his obsession with her and how much he yearned to possess her again as before. It was the key to all of this, it had to be—

"And yet . . ." Draven spoke the words so softly that at first she wasn't sure he'd said them at all. But then he paused, looking off as if in thought, and her heart leapt with hope. "There might be one way that I would consider your offer—an addition to your suggestion that might provide what I require from this little adventure," he murmured, swinging his gaze to her again. The look in his eyes sent cold chills straight to her heart, and this time she did sit on the edge of the bed, unable to stand any longer for the weakness flooding her limbs.

Draven leaned back in his chair and smiled, the expression both perversely caressing and provoking at the same time. "It is clear, however, that any bargain struck between us simply wouldn't be the same unless the terms were initiated by you, my darling, and since your new-found heart is involved, I must have a care in the way it transpires. Therefore, I intend to make you a proposition. Discern what I am thinking about—come up with the adjustment to your bargain that has just now engaged my interest—and offer the terms to me as your own. Do so before your beloved returns from his visit to Cokkeslane, and I will agree to it. Fail to realize what the new proposal should be, and the plan will go ahead as I originally intended, with you serving as the lovely bait to ensnare him here at the Tabard."

He glanced to the door, his handsome head tilted as if he were listening for footsteps beyond the wooden panel. "But I would think quickly if I were you, Giselle. It won't be long now until one of my men will come up those stairs to let us know that your lover is on his way back to the inn, and then you'll be required to . . . get into position, shall we say, for the trap." He stretched his legs out again and crossed one ankle over the other, looking blissfully unconcerned that her heart was racing with fear or that desperate panic was spilling through her veins.

"You are truly diabolical, you know," she whispered,

her voice strained with emotions she refused to show him. "But even I didn't think you capable of sinking to the depths of such twisted evil as this."

"Ah, darling, I know," he added, his clear amusement scorning her pain, "It is one of my special charms. And you can revile me all you like for it, but just remember that in the meantime, your precious Braedan's life hangs in the balance . . . aye, his entire fate rests, in fact, on your very pretty head."

Braedan took the stairs to the second floor of the Tabard three at a time, heavy at heart but eager to see Fiona again. He didn't relish the news he would be sharing with her—that this latest promising information about Elizabeth had turned out to be nothing at all—but he longed to take her in his arms and hold her for the rest of the night, knowing as he did his plan to get her back to the more peaceful surroundings of the outlaw settlement come morn. He would miss her with an ache already begun at the mere thought of their imminent separation, and yet he knew getting her away from London and her painful memories of the *stewes* would be the best for her. It could be no other way.

Now he just had to find a way to make her understand that.

Reaching their door, he scratched softly, prepared to wait for a moment, since he knew she would be following his caution to keep it bolted tight until his return. "Fiona," he called out softly at the same time, "It is Braedan, love—you can unbar the door."

But the heavy wooden slab creaked open on its own weight with the slight pressure of his fingers against it, and he stood there, stunned, looking at it in disbelief.

That emotion gave way to consternation, then to fear. Shoving the door open the rest of the way, he threw himself into the chamber, his gaze searching frantically for Fiona. Instead, he saw standing near the hearth the young serving girl who had brought up their supper earlier in the evening; she'd jumped up at his entrance, her hand flying to her throat and a look of alarm freezing her already timid features.

"My wife," Braedan said hoarsely, from where he stood just inside the portal, "the lady who was sharing this chamber with me—where is she, and what are you doing here?"

The faint scent of spice and roses clung to the air in here, teasing Braedan's senses. It reminded him of something unpleasant, though he couldn't for the life of him place it at the moment for the turmoil that was winding inside of him. The serving girl's mouth gaped, her fear obviously stifling her ability to speak. But Braedan's fear for Fiona was greater; ignoring the fact that such an action would likely worsen the girl's condition rather than ease it, he stalked forward and grabbed her by the shoulders.

"Where has she gone? You must tell me now!"

"I—I—I, that is, she—oh, sir, she left the inn, she did. She—" The girl broke off into sobs, her eyes filling with tears as she cried softly, "Oh, please, sir, let me go. Yer hurtin' my arms, ye are . . ."

Shocked at his own lack of control, Braedan uttered a low-breathed curse and released her. "I didn't mean to grip you so hard. I am sorry." Clenching his jaw, he willed himself to keep calm, saying evenly, "I need to know what happened to the lady who was here. If you know anything, lass, you must tell me."

"My—my name is Anna, sir."

"Anna, I need to know when she left, and if she said anything about where she was going. Do you know?" He kept his panic subdued enough to maintain a reasonable tone with the girl, hoping to get better information out of her than he had thus far.

"I—I think so, sir," Anna answered, her voice wobbling with the effort. Swiping her fingers beneath her tear-streaked eyes, she added, "She left no more than a half hour since the last full strikin' of the bell, with the man that came to visit her. They left together, they did."

"*Man?*" Braedan echoed numbly. "What man? What did he look like?"

"He was tall and dark. Very dark, sir. Not his skin, but his clothes and such—and his eyes. Black as coal they were," she nodded, her wet lashes widening with the memory. "He were a lord o' some sort, and he spoke with a kind of commandin' tone that none who was in their wits would disobey."

Angels of grace . . .

Braedan's heart slowed to sluggish, painful beats as the full meaning of what Anna was saying sank in. The scent of roses . . . he remembered it now. It was Draven who favored that scent, mixed with spice. Oh God, Draven had Fiona . . . he'd come and taken Fiona . . .

Uttering a string of curses that made Anna shrink back against the mantel again, Braedan stalked to the trunk of his belongings and yanked it open. Pulling out a dagger, he shoved it in his boot to supplement the weapons he already carried with him, then wheeled around to the door, intending to hunt down the bastard all the way to the gilded halls of Chepston if need be.

"Wait—sir, you have to wait! The lord that was with

yer mistress, he said I was to give you a message from him. That's why I was set to waitin' here, for your return this night."

Braedan slid to a stop, the chill sense of dread that had been spilling through his veins congealing to ice. Without turning around, he managed to choke out, "What was the message?"

"That he has gone to an establishment on Stoney Street, the one with the red door across from the cobbler's shop, and that if you wish to talk with yer lady and gain news as well about another lady named Elizabeth, yer to meet him there."

Braedan's head throbbed. Christ, it ached, the pain seeming to stem from the very back of his skull and spreading forward in waves. He couldn't open his eyes yet—nay that would take too much effort—but his thoughts began to string together again, falling into place like the pieces of a riddle, until it all started to make sense.

Draven. He'd come after Draven, to the house in the midst of the *stewes* that Anna had described. He'd had to find Fiona, had to get to her and make sure that the bastard hadn't hurt her . . . how then had he come to be lying here in the dark of his thoughts, with his head pounding like a drum?

The last bit of memory slipped into place. In his mind's eye he saw himself approaching the red door, heard again the calls of the women from nearby buildings as they leaned out their windows, inviting him to sample their charms. He'd ignored them, ignored everything as he concentrated on finding a way to get to Fiona.

He'd known it was a trap that Draven was laying for him, and that his uncle was counting on his worry over Fiona to make him come anyway. And for once, Draven had been right; Braedan had known that he couldn't wait until help could be gathered before he went after Fiona. But he didn't plan to walk into the snare through the front door, either. He'd sidestepped that red-painted portal, slipping down the filthy alley along the side of the building to approach from the back.

But for all of his caution, just after he'd stepped into the unlit kitchen chamber with its thick smells of cooked cabbage and grease, three figures had shifted from the shadows, coming at him from behind. He'd barely had time to swing around with his already-drawn blade, slicing one of the men . . . hearing him cry out and watching him fall back, before his own head exploded with the pain of something hard slamming into the back of his skull.

Now he was someplace dark. At least he thought it was dark, for no light seeped through his closed lids. As he lay there, he heard voices as if from far away, beyond a door, perhaps, and weary from the effort it had taken to remember what had brought him here, he remained still, listening. It was a woman's voice, her words hushed, arguing with a man. "You weren't supposed to hurt him. You promised not to hurt him," she accused softly. The man's reply was too muffled to make out, though Braedan discerned his tone of irritation, and then something that sounded like a command.

Where was he, then—abovestairs at the red-doored building, or perhaps in a gutter somewhere, tossed aside by the men who had attacked him? *And Fiona.* Nearly overwhelming fear for her slid through him anew, making his arms and legs twitch as he struggled to bring himself the rest of the way out of the stupor . . . to open his eyes and get his bearings, so that he could take some sort of action.

With a groan that echoed through his skull, Braedan rolled up onto his side, and then sat as he cradled his head in his hands, still unable to open his eyes for the renewed throbbing his movement set off. He wasn't bound, at least; his weapons were gone, but his freedom of movement was a boon and likely meant that he wasn't being kept in Draven's chamber below ground at Chepston, where chains and all manner of painful confinements were the rule. The realization spurred him on to open his eyes at last.

Though his vision was blurry, he eventually could make out the pattern of the wooden slats on the floor, which was remarkably clean. And it wasn't completely dark, as he'd originally thought; light played over his boots, flickering as if from a torch somewhere across the chamber. Slowly, he lifted his head, bracing himself for the pain that would splinter through him with the motion and sucking in his breath when it came. But before he could lift his face all the way, he felt the touch of gentle fingers on his brow and cheeks, and breathed in the cool fragrance of vanilla. Hope flooded him; ignoring the lancing hurt that pierced his eyes, he jerked his head up the rest of the way, desperate to see who was soothing him so tenderly.

Fiona.

Saints be praised, it was Fiona kneeling before him, her face twisted with an expression of agony and relief that mirrored his own.

"Thank God—are you all right?" he asked her, his

throat aching as he gathered her to him in a fierce embrace. She held him just as tightly for one, brief moment before she pulled away and stood up without a word of response. When he looked up at her, bewildered at her withdrawal, her eyes were clear, her face seeming so cool and serene that he wondered if he'd imagined the anguish that had shadowed it before.

"What is wrong?" he asked.

"Nothing; I am fine."

Nodding, he pushed himself to stand as well from the low pallet he'd been on, though the action made the chamber dip with a sickening motion. When it righted again, he reached for her hand. "Come, then, we must go quickly before Draven realizes we've—"

"Nay, Braedan, there is no need to rush. All is well."

Her voice sounded so calm and controlled; she'd taken another few steps back as she'd spoken, her fingers linked together in front of her—and it was then that he saw it. The gown she was wearing. It was exquisite, of some silken fabric that draped and clung to her graceful body, accentuating her beauty in a way that made clear it had been crafted for her alone.

A gown of deep, crimson hue.

He frowned, not understanding why she would be wearing such a garment, but knowing also that there wasn't time to worry about it. They had to get out of here before Draven came back. "Of course there is a need to hurry," he said, stepping forward to bridge the distance she'd placed between them. "Come, Fiona. It is dangerous to remain here. I do not know how I came to be left unguarded with you, but I don't intend to lose the opportunity." He held out his hand to her once more, impatient to begin searching for a means of escape.

But she didn't take it. Instead, she moved farther away from him, and he froze with disbelief, that emotion blending with the nausea that was already pummeling his gut. He saw her look down at the floor for a moment; then she breathed in deeply before raising her gaze to his again, sadness full in her beautiful eyes, though her face remained as composed as before.

"We must talk, Braedan," she murmured at last. "Much has changed in the past few hours—much that affects what will happen between us from now on. It is why I have asked that you be brought to me, to hear the whole of it from my lips, so that you will know it is true."

"Hear *what* truth?" he asked, confused and more than a bit irritated at her strange behavior.

She paused again before saying, finally, "That I am going to remain in London. That I have chosen to take up my former life as the Crimson Lady again, here in the *stewes*." She looked him straight in the eye. "That I have decided to return to Draven."

Tense silence spread over them as Braedan tried to comprehend the meaning of what he'd just heard. It was impossible to reconcile the words with the woman who'd spoken them, and so in the end he simply blurted, "What by all the fires of hell are you talking about?" He stood unmoving, waiting for her answer, the thoughts that were rattling around in his brain so inconceivable that he couldn't help wondering if he was still sunk into his stupor and only believed himself to be awake.

"I'm telling you that I'm parting ways with you, here and now," she said, calm in a way that seemed almost preternatural. "I cannot continue to live as we have been, Braedan. Returning to the *stewes*, walking these streets, remembering my life here, I've come to realize that, whether or not I wish it were otherwise, I belong here, as the Crimson Lady. It is my destiny and the only future fit for me to embrace."

"That's ridiculous, Fiona. You sound like Draven for Christ's sake—" he began, only to break off when he saw her shaking her head sadly at him.

"Nay, Braedan, it is me, and I know exactly what I am saying. I confess that there was a time with you when I believed I could resist my nature and live a different kind of life, but I was wrong. It is too strong for me to deny any longer. It has been gaining power over me every day until tonight, when I came to my decision after you left. I am the Crimson Lady. I cannot escape that truth, any more than my mother before me could escape the reality of her life as a common woman."

He muttered a curse that made clear his feelings about that.

"Why do you doubt it, Braedan?" she asked, her voice revealing the first hint of intensity—of real emotion— that he'd been able to perceive since she'd begun spouting this gibberish. "I acknowledged my fears to you concerning this weeks ago," she continued heatedly. "Don't you remember?"

"Aye, I remember," he said, refusing to break his gaze with her, wounded to his soul as he felt by her insistence of such falsity. "But we dealt with it together—don't *you* remember, lady? Standing in the midst of a summer storm, we soothed it away with such sweetness that I know the moment will live on inside of me until my dying day. I remember it all too well, Fiona. Far better than you do, it seems."

He saw the delicate muscle above her jaw twitch, and her lips press tightly together for a moment before she added in a final, damning blow, "I am sorry, Braedan, but what happened between us . . . it was a mistake. I am choosing to remember it as a pleasant dream we once had, and I hope that, in time, you will be able to do the same," she continued, her voice wavering a little, "but like all dreams it had to end; we had to awaken to reality."

"A *dream*?" Braedan said incredulously. "Is that all you think we shared?"

With a growl of grief and pain, he strode forward and pulled her into his embrace, gripping her chin in one palm and forcing her to meet his gaze. "Damn it to everlasting hell, Fiona, but I want you to look into my eyes right now and tell me that what happened between us was a mistake—that it was naught but some *happy dream*." The words came out strained and broken as the agony of it all swept through him, threatening to drown him completely. Somehow he managed to hold back the pain long enough to add, huskily, "Look at me now and tell me that you don't love me as I love you."

Fiona stared up at him, her eyes bright with unshed tears and her expression no longer so composed. "Oh, God, Braedan, don't do this, please . . ." she whispered, the words full of such desolation that it raked his soul. "What is true cannot be helped. The demons are too strong to fight any longer . . . too strong to stop . . ."

"Say it, damn you," he commanded softly, his voice choked with emotion. "I will hear you say it, Fiona, or I will never believe it. Never . . ."

He heard her sharp intake of breath, saw her close her eyes and watched as a single tear spilled from beneath each of her eyelids to roll down her cheeks. After a moment she opened her eyes again to meet his gaze straight on. "If that is what you need, then so be it."

She blinked once, her lashes casting spiked, black shadows against the pallor of her skin before she murmured very deliberately and clearly, "I do not love you, Braedan. I never have. You were a pleasant diversion, but that is all. This life—my life as the Crimson Lady—that is reality for me." She swallowed, her expression so rigid and controlled that he wondered if it, too, would shatter soon, falling away like the splintering fragments of his heart. "I am sorry if hearing that hurts you, but you asked for me to say it, and now you must accept it as the truth."

Braedan's entire body had gone as rigid as if she had just buried a dagger in his chest. He couldn't move, couldn't breathe, couldn't do anything for the first few seconds after she spoke. When the shock began to ease, he was able to do little more than shake his head numbly before he finally let go of her and took a step back. Heat stung his eyes, but he refused to blink it away, keeping his gaze trained on Fiona. Only on her beautiful, angelic, treacherous face.

The agony of what she'd said was still reverberating through him when he sensed a movement from behind him, near the door.

"So sorry to see that this has worked out badly for you, de Cantor," a man's voice called in feigned sympathy. "My heart goes out, but I am sure you know as well as I, after your years of experience, that such things rarely run a smooth course—especially with women of our sweet Giselle's ilk."

Braedan's feet felt bogged in a swamp-mire as he

turned and stumbled back a few steps to face Draven. It was a movement of instinct more than anything else; his uncle's presence here was not unexpected. Nor did Braedan care, anymore, whether or not Draven intended to draw his blade and hack him down where he stood. Such would actually have been welcome as a way to end the misery that was rocking through him in ceaseless waves.

But Draven made no attempt of the sort, simply striding the rest of the way into the chamber, flanked by two guards who took up positions near Braedan while Draven himself ended at Fiona's side. Braedan stood looking at them, unmoving, the anger and outraged betrayal he should have been able to feel at the moment buried beneath the ashes of what used to be his heart.

"I've been watching the conclusion of your little conversation from behind that wall there—I hope you don't mind," Draven murmured, raising his hand to the side of the room toward Braedan's left, and smiling, as he added, "You see, we're in Giselle's old chamber for her work as the Crimson Lady, complete with the tiny viewing holes that always allowed me to ensure her safety during our years of commerce together. This room will be seeing much more frequent use in the years to come, I think."

He reached out and pulled Fiona against him; dimly, Braedan noted that she didn't resist, seeming pliant in Draven's arms, though her expression retained that blank cast he remembered so well from their first days together after leaving Hampshire.

Dragging his gaze from the pain of looking on her further, Braedan said hoarsely, "Before you set your men on me to finish this, Draven, just tell me one thing; have you any real news about Elizabeth, or was that just another of the perverse lies you seem to relish?"

"Finish this—you mean, order you *killed*?" Draven exclaimed, acting surprised. "Why wherever did you get that idea?" Then, with an exaggerated show of realization, he tapped his finger to his lips and murmured, "Ah, yes . . . that was my promise to you on several occasions, was it not?"

Lifting his hand away from his mouth with a shrug, he continued, "Well, no matter, the circumstances have changed, as I'm sure you've already deduced from Giselle's so very poignant confession to you. Since her willing return to me, I've been feeling magnanimous. In truth I intend to let you go, nephew. One good turn deserves another, after all, and you did allow me to leave after our confrontation on the road to London a week past."

"I should have killed you then, and I don't believe you now."

"Tsk, tsk, such pessimism. You're a rather doubting man, aren't you? First you question Giselle's sincerity, and now you suspect me . . . but view it this way, Braedan, my boy. If you ever needed additional proof that Giselle's change of heart was *her* idea and not mine, then in this you would have it: I have you both here at my mercy, right now, just as planned. I'd intended, in fact, to make you pay dearly for your actions against me. But she surprised me in such a pleasant way that it caused me to reconsider. Her willing return to the fold, her sudden realization of her true nature and her rightful place with me, has satisfied me like nothing else could have."

Smiling then, he used his fingertip beneath Fiona's

chin, turning her face toward his and taking her mouth
with a kiss of possession that sent waves of sickness
flooding through Braedan. He turned away in disgust,
hardly caring when Draven pulled back, and said,
"Needless to say, I am overjoyed with her decision, and
as a gentleman, I will require nothing further from you.
You may go and continue to live your outlaw life as you
see fit, provided you do not cross paths with me again. I
am still the sheriff near Alton, and I will uphold the law
there. So have a care in your existence on the fringes of
society, de Cantor."

As if from somewhere far away and outside himself,
Braedan saw Draven make a gesture to his guards; they
stepped forward, and he felt them take him by the arms
and begin leading him from the chamber. He didn't trust
himself to look again at Fiona as he left, didn't attempt
to halt the guards' progress in any way, too bone weary
and sickened by all that had transpired that he knew he
could have sunk down to the floor right there and never
risen again.

But then his uncle called out to him, almost as an
afterthought, "Oh, and by the by, de Cantor—about
Elizabeth—it grieves me to tell you my inquiries revealed
that she passed from this bitter world some three months
ago. It seems she expired while giving birth to a brat
with no sire to claim it. A pity, truly . . ."

The awful words seeped into Braedan's numbed consciousness, igniting him from his stupor. With a bellowing growl of rage and grief, he thrashed into motion,
yanking out of his guards' grip to throw himself back
into the room intending to strangle the life from Draven
with his bare hands if no other weapon could be found.
But before he covered half the distance, the guards

caught up to him again, fighting to subdue him until one of them finally pulled back and slammed a fist into his temple . . .

And then the world shattered into a painful, blinding flash of light before he sank into blackness, the last sight seared into his mind that of Draven's superior, mocking smile, and the wounded look in Fiona's golden eyes.

Chapter 18

❧

Fiona stood rigidly as she watched Draven's men dragging Braedan from the chamber, certain that if she moved, the grief that was pounding through her would unleash itself in a torrent and swallow her whole. Her senses felt raw, her mind unwilling to grasp the enormity of what she'd just done. It was too painful to bear, and so she simply kept breathing in and out, praying that the numbness would last until Draven had finished gloating and would leave her alone.

He stood next to her, tall and oppressively powerful. Her mouth still burned with revulsion from the effects of his kiss; it had taken every ounce of her will not to yank herself out of his arms when he had done that in front of Braedan. Inside she had been crying out, wanting to beat him away and sob her agony aloud, but she'd remained quiet and impassive under his possessive assault, just as he'd expected of her.

But she hadn't done it for him. Nay, just the opposite. She'd let Draven kiss her that way because she knew it would be the final affront to Braedan—the final betrayal she could offer to ensure that he would believe the impossible. And so she had staged the most difficult and wrenching pretense of her life, knowing that no matter what it cost her, for Braedan's sake she couldn't allow herself to fail in it.

And it had worked. The look of disgust in Braedan's eyes, then, was something she'd never forget. It had sealed their fates and seared her soul in a way that she knew would never heal, no matter how long she had remaining to her between that moment and the hour of her death. Without Braedan she was already dead anyway, in every way that truly mattered.

"Well done, Giselle," Draven said quietly next to her, still smiling, his gaze fixed to the closed door through which Braedan had been taken. When he turned his head to look down at her, she couldn't help thinking that his striking masculine beauty was all the more perverse for the evil it hid beneath. "How does it feel, sweet, to have been the instrument of your lover's demise?" he added, clearly relishing her pain. "I must congratulate you on your finesse, you know. You've managed to accomplish in one fell swoop what I never could have hoped to attain through endless planning and effort—nay, not even if I had subjected my dear nephew to months of agonizing torture in the trying."

Draven's statement settled home, and Fiona choked back her rising nausea. The anguish she'd been feeling from the moment Braedan had let her go swelled to greater power, burning her eyes and closing her throat, but she refused to look away, not wanting to give

Draven the satisfaction of seeing her crumble before him. She hadn't thought she could endure anything worse than the pain of losing the man she loved, but this taunting set off a renewed flood of sickness and impotent rage.

Draven met her gaze with the fierceness of his own, her suffering clearly gratifying to him as he beat her down further with the hammer of his words.

"It is a delicious irony, is it not, Giselle?" he continued. "In choosing this path, you have finally become what you've always said you despised—someone just like me. You lured in the man you claim to love and then methodically set about destroying him in the most painful way possible. As surely as if you'd taken that dagger of yours and slowly carved out his heart. It was beautiful to behold, sweet. Utter perfection."

"My God, I hate you, Draven," she breathed, staring straight into his dark, empty eyes. "From the depths of my soul, I do."

"That is good, Giselle," he answered just as softly, never breaking his gaze from hers as he reached up to stroke his hand from her cheek and down the side of her throat to the curve of her breast, cupping her there with a touch that was feather light and yet filled with the dark possession she knew so well. "That is very good," he continued in his quiet, cultured voice, "because I want to see the hate burning in your eyes when I have you writhing beneath me once more. I want to drive out all of the gentleness that *he* put there—the tenderness you refused to give to anyone but him . . ."

He leaned in then as she stood frozen, his mouth brushing in a profane caress over hers before he shifted to whisper in her ear, "You see, I long ago relinquished my need for your love, Giselle. You forced me to give it up with your stubborn resistance to me. But your hate . . ." He laughed softly, his breath riffling the hair at her temple. ". . . ah well, that is mine to savor and enjoy. And enjoy it I will, sweet, until you're begging me to give you release from it."

Abruptly he pulled away from her, leaving her no time, even to gasp in response. Emptiness beat through her, dulling her ability to react to anything anymore. She was so tired, so tired of all the pain and the struggle. She watched as Draven walked over to the shutter, pushed it open, and peered out; her mind felt wrapped in wool from all that had happened in the past hours. The sky was hidden by the many half-timbered houses and buildings all around them, but thick darkness outside the window showed it to be the middle of the night.

"It will be dawn in a few hours," he murmured, leaning against the casement for a moment before he shifted his gaze to her again. "You should rest while you can, Giselle. For though you are indeed very tempting, I've decided to wait until we're back at Chepston to undertake the completion of our . . . reacquaintance shall we say. It will be in my chamber, I think—the place where I had you for the very first time those many years ago . . ."

Pushing himself away from the window, he walked deliberately to the door, pausing when he reached it only long enough to look over his shoulder and murmur, "Aye, rest now, Giselle, for soon it will be light. And when darkness falls again, it will be time for you to begin making payment on your end of our little bargain."

* * *

Braedan was in the grip of a nightmare, a sleeping vision worse than any he'd ever experienced before. It had to be that, for how else could he explain the sense of complete desolation, and the relentless, unbearable thoughts that kept hammering his brain?

Fiona doesn't love me. Elizabeth is dead.

But he, unfortunately, was still painfully alive . . .

Grimacing, he rolled to his side, only to feel agony tearing through every joint and muscle he possessed. It was real, then, and not just some horrible dream. The metallic taste of blood in his mouth was no figment of his imagination; he'd wager his sword on that—except he had no sword. Nay, or any daggers either, the lot of his weapons having been confiscated by Draven's guards when he was first taken.

It was a night he would have liked to forget, if only his aching body would let him; he'd been pummeled not once, but twice in the course of a few hours, and then left in this pile of refuse in the alley, to go on his merry way, when he awoke—a shell of a man with no future other than to live out his life as an outlaw to the crown. Considering the fact that he had faced Draven's wrath unarmed and still made it out alive, he supposed he should have been thankful. Most men in his position would have been glad, perhaps, even eager to embrace the freedom of the existence that loomed before him.

But Braedan wasn't most men. And Draven was sorely mistaken if he thought that there would be no retribution for what had happened last night—for what he'd done to Elizabeth and for the twisted mess he'd made of Fiona's life. Sorely mistaken indeed.

He rolled to sitting with a groan, brushing something

wilted and green from his leg and cracking his eyes open just enough to see the first light of dawn filtering through the shadows around him. It was nearly morning, then. He tipped his head up a little, wincing when the swollen lump there connected with the wattle-and-daub wall of the building at his back. Squinting, he looked around, trying to gain his bearings. Surprise cut through some of his fogginess. It seemed that Draven's guards hadn't cared to move him very far before they'd discarded him like the kitchen scraps. He was sitting in the alleyway of the *stewe*-house with the red door. The same house that he'd come to last night in search of Fiona.

Before he could prepare himself for it, another wave of hurt and grief engulfed him. It didn't seem possible that it had been hours since Fiona had stood in this place and denied ever loving him. It felt like only an instant ago, the pain was so fresh. Of a sudden his mind was assaulted with memories from other, happier times . . . of Fiona smiling at him as she leaned over to pick another clump of flowers from the forest floor, of her nestled in his arms before the fire as they kept watch over Nate—of her beautiful face and the passion quickening in her eyes as they made love . . . all of it dissolving into the agony of the previous night.

Her rejection had hurt him, more deeply than he'd thought possible. Part of him still didn't believe it to be true. He would have wagered his life on the honesty of her love. How in God's name could he have been so wrong?

He pushed those self-defeating thoughts back as well as he could, knowing he needed to pull himself together. There was much to be done. Elizabeth's soul and his own honor demanded it, even if his heart felt like it had

been shredded from his chest, leaving naught but an
empty, bloody hole in its place.

He was just about to attempt to ready himself to
stand, when a flurry of movement at the front of the
stewe-house made him go still once more. Keeping to the
shadows behind an old crate, he tried to position himself
to see what was happening. The door had opened and
several people spilled out into the gray and misty light.
Soldiers. They were all wearing Draven's colors, though,
so they had to be his men. Braedan had never seen the
faces of the three who attacked him in the kitchen to
know whether or not they were among this group. There
looked to be a half dozen or so, not seeming in any
hurry, though it was early for any but merchants and
farmers to be about.

Braedan moved closer to the front corner of the building, still keeping hidden but wanting to have a better
view of the street. The guards were talking, most of them
looking none too pleased. When they all went silent,
Braedan strained his neck to see why. It seemed that
someone was standing in the open doorway of the
dwelling, the figure of the person casting a long, dark
shadow onto the street in front. The shadow abruptly
moved and widened, as if a second person had joined the
first, then it immediately began to shift and contort,
along with the sounds of scuffling that could be heard
clearly from the spot where Braedan was hiding.

"You will come with me calmly, Giselle, or I shall be
forced to drag you through Southwark to the river, and
that choice will not be such a pleasant one, I can assure
you."

"Nay! I will not go until you answer me."

Draven. *And Fiona.* Shock tingled up Braedan's spine.

Instinctively, he tensed in preparation to leap from the shadows and grip his wretched uncle by the throat. He wanted to squeeze the life from him breath by breath until nothing was left. But common sense won over. Draven had too many of his men with him; any attempt at aggression against him would surely be doomed before it began. Braedan would have to wait—and plan—for a more opportune time to seek revenge.

Pressing himself against the shadowy wall, Braedan eased closer to the street. Part of him yearned with a kind of quiet desperation to catch just one glimpse of Fiona again—to see her beautiful face one last time—while the more brutalized part of him wanted no more than to pretend indifference to her plight. This was the life she'd embraced, he reasoned, and Draven was the man to whom she'd chosen to return. It was no longer his concern, he told himself. And yet . . .

In the end his battered heart held sway, and he craned his neck to see her. The scuffling had ceased, though no one was moving from their positions on the street. The guards were off to the side, looking uncomfortable as they tried not to stare at Draven and Fiona, who stood in front of the door.

"I am growing impatient," Draven said, his voice sharp, but not so quiet that Braedan couldn't hear what he'd said. "Make your choice, Giselle. Walk civilly with me to the dock or be dragged there. It is of no matter to me, other than the embarrassment you will cause yourself by creating such a spectacle in the street. But you will choose now."

Fiona was facing in Braedan's direction, and almost against his will he searched her with his gaze, his heart twisting at her pallor, her stricken expression and those haunted eyes, looking up at Draven. She seemed to be pleading for something, and Braedan wanted to curse with the pain it caused him, seeing her brought to this low state before his uncle. But it couldn't be helped. She had made her decision last night.

"You swore to me that you wouldn't hurt him," she murmured finally, her voice sounding so wounded and strained that Braedan might not have recognized it as hers if he'd not seen her standing before him. An uncomfortable inkling began to gnaw inside him then, a feeling that swelled into pure horror with what she said next.

"It was our agreement," Fiona continued, "Braedan's freedom—his life—for my willing return to you. I did what you wanted. I cast him off—" Her voice broke, and she looked away for an instant before fixing her gaze back on Draven. "I want to know what you ordered done to him after he was taken from here. Tell me, Draven, or I will not move from this place freely."

"Very well, then. We will go the more difficult way," Draven snapped, grabbing her by the arm and yanking her forward to begin pulling her down the street with him.

She continued to resist, though her struggles were ineffective against a man of Draven's size and strength. Braedan clenched his fists, rage pumping through him, but there was nothing he could do for her. Not with so many of Draven's men standing guard. It was not that he worried for his own skin, but it would do Fiona no good if he were dead—and the seven against one odds he would be facing, unarmed, would likely ensure that outcome.

His mind was ablaze with self-recrimination and

shame as he watched them move down the street. God help him, but he had been so blind. He should have known better, should have trusted his instincts where Fiona was concerned. *Should have believed in her love for him, no matter what she'd said to him last night.* It was one of the lessons she'd been trying to teach him all along, with herself as the best example—that the world he'd spent his life judging as only bad or good was rarely either one alone, but rather somewhere in between. . . .

Throwing his head back, he squeezed his eyes shut as tightly as his fists, using all of his will to stay where he was until the whole group of them had gone from his sight and hearing.

They were heading for the river and on to Chepston; that seemed fairly certain, as his uncle's estate stood across the Thames. Later Braedan was to meet Will's band of men and any other outlaw gangs who'd decided to join him at the alehouse called the Bull, and the attack on Draven was to be planned then. Suddenly, though, time had become of the essence. They could no longer afford to take a few days in plotting it all out, not with Fiona's safety hanging in the balance. There had to be a way to make it happen more quickly. Perhaps if he caught Will and the others at the city gates, instead of waiting to meet them at the Bull . . .

With that hopeful thought in mind, Braedan stumbled out of the alley and into the street, shaking the remaining fogginess from his brain before setting off at a run for the south end of London Bridge. He prayed that the drawbridge was already down to permit the crossing of travelers from Southwark to the city proper, hoping against hope that the other outlaws would agree to join him and Will's men in launching their attack on Draven later today. If not, he and Will would go anyway, their goal to save Fiona; and, if need be, leaving Draven's reckoning for another time. . . .

For Braedan feared that her life would depend on it.

Chapter 19

The afternoon was fast waning, Fiona realized, shivering as she gazed through the tiny cracks of a shutter in Draven's bedchamber. The breeze from outside was seeping through to brush her face, easing, a little, the cloying and unbearable scent of roses that hung in the air. The chamber had always seemed soaked in the fragrance, and the memories that the smell brought back made her stomach twist with nausea.

She stood at the casement feeling strangely empty, the despondency that had settled over her since yestereve grown as heavy as a blanket to smother her. Though it was probably sinful to think it, she would have welcomed such an end right now; aye, anything to stop the painful thoughts that kept battering at her soul.

It was almost certain that Braedan was dead.

The awful probability of it couldn't be denied, for Draven had continued to refuse her questions about what had happened to him once the guards had dragged him away. It would have been easy enough for Draven to say anything he wanted to appease her—to fabricate a lie if he'd chosen to do so. But he hadn't. Yet he hadn't confirmed Braedan's death, either . . . and therein was the catch. As satisfying as it might have been for Draven to share that devastating tidbit with her, she knew he was wise enough to realize it would be a mistake to make her feel too desperate. Leaving her in such a state would only serve to mute the pleasures he intended to take with her in his bed that night.

So he had withheld all information, taking the chance that the lack of it would torment her nearly as much as hearing the truth. And though she hadn't wanted to admit it, even to herself, he had been right. The uncertainty over what had happened to Braedan was driving her mad, and there was nothing she could do about it. Nothing, except to prepare for the inevitable consummation of the day in the only way left open to her.

She was going to kill Draven.

She'd decided as much on the short journey to Chepston, even knowing that by committing his murder she would be adding a mortal sin to those already aligned against her tattered soul. But there was no choice left, unless she was instead to turn the instrument of death on herself. That, too, was a possibility, she'd resolved, if her attempt to kill him failed.

Either way, she would be dead when all was said and done, whether by her own hand, or at the Standard in Cheape, where the city officials would hang her for the crime of murder. It didn't really matter anymore. She only knew that she'd never allow Draven to touch her in an intimate way again . . . never permit him to sully what she'd shared with Braedan, the one man she'd truly loved, and who had loved her so completely in return.

But coming up with a method for killing Draven was proving far more difficult than she'd imagined. She'd been over it in her mind again and again, and nothing seemed possible. He'd taken her dagger back at the Tabard, and once at Chepston, he'd secured her in his chamber, which had been carefully emptied of anything that might be used as a weapon.

She'd not been allowed to leave the room for anything, not even to take a meal in the main hall. The fact that she might have come into contact with Braedan's younger brother Richard might have had something to do with that, she'd decided. Not that Richard would have known her from any of the other doxies that Draven occasionally brought to Chepston before setting them up in the *stewes*, but it was clear that Draven was taking no chances. No one had ever been able to accuse him of not staying one step ahead of those who might wish him harm; it was how he'd remained alive for so long, even with the prodigious number of enemies he'd earned along the way.

Yet there had to be something he'd overlooked— something he'd forgotten in his arrogant sense of superiority. Looking around the chamber from her position near the window, she searched for the room again. The wide, high-posted bed with its red damask hangings held no hope. It was naught but the instrument of her fear and shame, being the most likely place that he would choose, tonight, to take full possession of her again. Pushing aside that disturbing thought, she continued her study of the room.

The hearth was of stone, but none were loose enough

to pry free, and the wooden logs for burning had all been taken away with her arrival. There was a chair and the desk at which Draven often perused his reeve's accountings; but both pieces of furniture were too massive for her to consider moving, much less lifting and using as a weapon. There was nothing else, all other implements, including the washbowl and pitcher, having been moved to the smaller locked chamber adjacent to this one.

Panic began to rise in her throat, the despair of knowing that her time was running short spurring her to step away from the window and look from a different position. Her trunk was the only remaining object in the chamber, and she knew well that there were no weapons, or anything that could be made into one, inside of it. Draven had made sure of that, examining the contents of it and rifling through her possessions, removing all but those things he deemed innocuous.

He'd replaced her clothing with a selection of crimson kirtles as before, leaving little else in the trunk but her soaps and her herb box, and that only after he'd looked to be sure she'd not gathered any that had the potential for fatal effects. He'd been as thorough as always, blowing her a mocking kiss just before leaving her alone for a few hours, to contemplate her misery until his return at dusk.

But perhaps he'd not been thorough enough.

Walking quickly to her trunk, she fell to her knees beside it and flipped it open to pull the herb box from beneath the layers of hated gowns. Sitting back on her heels with it in her hands, she examined its size and construction. It was of good, solid wood, banded with steel, in length as great as her arm from shoulder to wrist, in breadth, half that span. Aye, it just might work, she thought, turning it over to look at its base. She might not have her dagger any longer, but perhaps she could acquire the next best thing: a large and sharp splinter of wood.

She clicked the latch of the herb box and opened it. Taking each small vial and nestling it carefully beneath the crimson gowns, Fiona worked to empty it, planning, once all the contents were removed, to smash the box against the stone hearth and scavenge a splinter of suitable size and sharpness from the remains. It would be risky, that much was certain. She already knew how difficult it was going to be to fortify herself to murder, regardless; adding an improvised weapon to the mix might make it near impossible.

But night was coming soon, and with it, Draven. A wooden dagger would have to do.

A sudden grating sound outside in the hallway made her jump. Startled, she tossed the nearly empty herb box back into her trunk, slammed the lid shut, and scrambled to her feet, just in time to see the massive wooden door of the chamber swing open. Draven walked in. He entered without a word, drawing the door closed behind him and throwing the inside bolt. It clanked home with a finality that resonated in Fiona's bones, echoing through the lushly appointed chamber like a bell of doom.

"What are you doing here?" she asked uneasily. "It is at least another hour until dark."

Draven raised his brow at her and walked forward with slow, measured steps, removing his tunic and unlacing his shirt as he came, making her feel like a doe trapped in the lair of a wolf. "I've decided to get started a bit early, sweet," he murmured, the corner of his lips quirking up. "The thought of enjoying your delectable body once more has had me distracted all afternoon. I did not wish to wait longer."

"Nay!"

He stiffened at her outburst of denial, fixing his gaze on her, and so she deliberately softened her tone in a bid for more time, adding, "I—I am not ready yet."

"But I am."

Icy fear swept over her, raising gooseflesh on her arms. He would not be dissuaded. *But it is too soon!* her mind cried. *There hasn't been enough time to prepare.* Her entire body tensed, the urge to flee rising up, as powerful as it had been when she'd first been brought to this chamber to face him eleven years ago.

Her breath came shallow, and she backed up a step, then another and another until the stone wall was at her back, desperately trying to think of what to do. Without the improvised weapon she'd planned, her choices were few: She could fight against the inevitable joining he intended with her or attempt to flee him. Fighting him would be useless. He'd shown her, on the night he'd carved that horrible mark into her chest, that he was no longer opposed to tying her down, if need be. If she made clear that she wouldn't participate in his carnal games willingly, he'd simply lash her to the bed and take his pleasure with her that way.

And as for fleeing . . .

That wasn't likely unless she could disable him, somehow. It was possible, she supposed. She, as well as any, knew how sensitive men were in certain areas of their anatomy. And though she'd never herself committed such an act, she'd heard the discussions of other women of the *stewes* who had been forced to take action against abusive men with a well-placed kick to the spot. Somehow, she imagined that it would be wonderfully satisfying to drive her knee into that part of Draven. He'd be left crouched over and gasping, at least for a few moments, which would give her time to lift the bolt and escape the chamber. Where she would go after that would be a problem she'd have to face then, if she was able to get that far.

Aye, he wouldn't suspect such an act of rebellion from her.

But it meant that she had to let him get close enough—and comfortable enough—so that she could do it.

"You haven't begun to disrobe yet, Giselle," Draven said in a low tone, still looking only at her and coming ever closer to where she was pressed against the wall. "I trust you have not forgotten the way of it between us."

"Nay, Draven," she whispered hoarsely, never taking her eyes from him, "I haven't forgotten."

"Good. Turn around, then."

Silently, she did as she was bid, facing the wall, though she closed her eyes, fortifying herself to remain still through just a few more of the steps she knew he'd always favored in his seductions of her.

For one long, breathless moment nothing happened, not even a movement of air, the painfully taut seconds stringing on and on . . . until he finally touched her. She shivered when his hands slipped beneath the silky mass of her hair, moving it to one side to expose the delicate lacings at the back of her crimson gown. He began to untie them, then, his long and elegant fingers moving slowly in their work, and she couldn't suppress a little shudder, knowing that he intended to take his time with her.

Soon her kirtle loosened under his efforts, gaping

enough that she could feel the brush of cooler air on her skin. As always before in her years as his possession, he'd forbidden her the wearing of a chemise beneath her gown, preferring, as he'd said, the softness of her skin brushing directly against the silk of her clothing. It was an almost-forgotten sensation, this feeling of near nakedness, but all the more unwelcome in that she was being made to endure it once again with Draven.

He eased the unlaced edges of her gown farther apart, forcing her to clutch the falling bodice of her kirtle to her breasts or risk being exposed even more to his gaze. Gritting her teeth, she squeezed her eyes shut more tightly to keep from crying out. *Just a little more*, she repeated to herself over and over. He ran his fingertips lightly up the length of her spine, following that action with the press of gentle kisses along the sensitive skin at the back of her neck. Just a little more and he would turn her to face him again—and then she could make her move on him.

She held herself rigid under his sensual assault, focusing on thoughts of Braedan to keep her strong. It was only because of him that she could do this at all, she realized, her eyes stinging with bittersweet tears. He had ended Draven's power over her forever, and she would never need fear succumbing to his control over her again.

Calm filled her, suddenly, easing the frantic thoughts that had been thrashing through her mind. Aye, she could do this. She was stronger than she'd ever been before, thanks to Braedan's love. She only needed to wait until the moment was right, then she would strike.

"Ah, Giselle, you're as delicious as I remembered," Draven murmured, still pressed against her body from behind, his lips playing with exquisite skill across the shell of her ear before dipping to suckle on the lobe. "Succulent. I shall enjoy tasting your—"

"My lord Draven—pardon, my lord, but you must come quickly!"

The shout was accompanied by a fervent pounding on the door that made Draven jerk away from her, cursing. She turned, adjusting her gown to keep herself covered as she watched him stalk to the portal, lift the bolt, and yank the door open.

A terse conversation followed, but it took place in the hall; from where she was standing, she couldn't hear its content. Whatever it was, it was serious, she decided, for Draven soon leaned back into the room, his expression as black as the one he'd worn after Braedan bested him during the roadside ambush, muttering that he would return shortly, after he'd resolved a problem that was brewing in the courtyard. Then he left, pulling the door shut behind him; she heard the bar dropped into place from the outside, sealing her in the chamber again.

Quickly reaching back and grasping her laces, Fiona did the best she could at tightening them again, hoping that they weren't so crooked that she'd be left indecent. Then she rushed to the only window in the chamber that looked over a portion of Chepston's walled-in courtyard. Pushing open the wooden shutter, she peered out, trying to see. Faintly, she heard a commotion going on somewhere beyond the thick stone walls of the crenellated tower that blocked most of her view; the noise of men's shouts and a few clanging sounds rose up. Had some of Draven's men come to blows with each other, then? It was impossible to tell without seeing anything.

But whether or not it was a scuffle between some of his own soldiers or an attack from the outside, Fiona knew it presented her an opportunity. Draven and the men who had been guarding her would be distracted in quelling the insurgence—and that meant she might find a way to escape, if she could see herself clear of this chamber.

Pulling the shutter closed, she headed back toward the door, pausing to test its strength. It was solid wood, hard and unyielding; it wouldn't break, even if she was able to drive something sturdy into it. Nay, she would have to think of another way, a means of knocking off the thick bar that confined her inside its cradle.

Her heart pounded with nervous excitement. She set about the task, resolving to gain her freedom from this room while Draven was occupied elsewhere—knowing that if she was successful, she might well be able to escape Chepston Hall altogether.

Braedan kept his sword at the ready as he made his way along the main floor of Draven's home. The blade bore signs of gore already, having been used in battle against three of Draven's men as he'd entered the estate; chances were it would be used again, several times, before the day was done. To his misfortune, he'd yet to cross paths with Draven himself, though he'd made sure that the outlaws who'd joined him from both the Coterel and Folville gangs, as well as Will and his men, knew he wanted to be the one to make the final confrontation with him if it was possible.

The attack had gone as planned thus far, but much more needed to be accomplished before Braedan would breathe easier. It was why he was there, prowling through the keep instead of outside where he could be lending his arm to the outlaw effort.

He had to find Fiona and his brother Richard.

Both of them needed protection from Draven for different reasons, it was true—and though Braedan's heart burned to see Fiona again, to hold her close and tell her how sorry he was for not believing, he knew that Richard had to be found first. Without him this insurgence might well fail, and then Fiona would be in greater danger than ever. For though Braedan felt confident that he and the other outlaws could take Chepston into their control, in order to finish the deed and see Draven brought to justice for his crimes, he knew he needed to either kill him, or bring the law to Chepston. And while killing him would have been preferable for the satisfaction it would offer, it would be a mistake, he knew, at least if he ever hoped to prove his innocence and get back the life Draven had stolen from him by branding him outlaw.

But bringing the law to Chepston for a hearing on Draven would be no easy task either. The word of a score of outlaws would hold little weight with the authorities. They needed an emissary who was above reproach—someone who would be convincing enough to make the sheriff and his men come and investigate. Richard was the perfect choice. Although he was young, the fact that he was an unsullied member of the de Cantor family went far in his favor, as did his status as Draven's own ward.

All Braedan had to do was to find him.

He paused at the second to last door in the corridor, examining it. Aye, it looked to be the one he remembered from the brief visit he'd had with Richard before his own arrest and confinement below. The bar was off the cradle, though, leaving the room's occupant, if there was one, free to come and go as he pleased. Braedan frowned. Sword hilt gripped firmly in his right hand, Braedan used his left to test the door. It was unlatched, even from the inside, swinging open with a loud creaking sound. Braedan maintained a wary stance and ducked inside.

It was a good thing he'd tread carefully, he realized in the next moment. An arrow whizzed by his head to embed itself in the wall with a *thunk*. Cursing, Braedan dropped to his knees and rolled behind a large piece of furniture that looked like a wardrobe of some kind, wondering what the devil he was going to be able to do with only a sword to keep his bow-wielding assailant from piercing him through.

"Braedan?"

The sound of that voice sent relief spilling through him, but that softer emotion was followed quickly by a burst of irritation. "Damn it, Richard—you nearly killed me with that thing!"

He heard a swishing sound, then a *thump*, and, peering around the corner of the wardrobe, he saw that his lanky younger brother had jumped down from his hiding place inside the drawn curtains of the bed. Richard stood there, looking a little sheepish, though his eyes held the same shadows that Braedan remembered from his brief visit with him right after returning home from Saint-Jean-d'Acre. It made Braedan's gut clench to see it, the realization that his fifteen-year-old brother seemed more like an angry old man than a carefree youth hitting home with a vengeance.

"Where in hell did you get that crossbow?" Braedan

asked, scowling as he stood from behind the wardrobe and sheathed his sword.

"From him," Richard answered, jerking his thumb toward a guard who was lying, apparently senseless, on the floor next to the tapestry-covered wall. "He came in a few moments ago. It seems that Draven sent him to fetch me to the main hall for safekeeping." Shrugging, Richard took a few steps forward, flicking his gaze to the arrow sticking from the wall near the door. "Sorry about the bolt, Braedan; I thought you were another guard. I'm a much better shot with a regular bow, but I'm not allowed to have one inside the keep."

"How fortunate for me," Braedan said dryly.

Richard crossed the remaining distance between them, coming to a stop in front of him, and Braedan felt a little shock. His brother was nearly of a height with him now; he must have shot up five inches since their last meeting a few months ago. And his features . . . by the Rood but he was looking more and more like their sire every day, Braedan thought with a flush of pride.

"Braedan, I . . . it's just good to know that you're still alive," Richard said quietly, his voice cracking in the way of most lads his age. "I wondered whether or not Draven had really gotten to you. He claimed he had, you know."

Braedan's gut twisted, angered at the suffering his brother had already been made to endure at Draven's hands, and sick about the pain he himself was going to be inflicting when he added to it with the sad news about Elizabeth. It could wait for a bit, though, Braedan decided. It would be better to let him handle the changes a little at a time.

"Our dear uncle has a habit of saying many things that aren't true," he answered finally, giving Richard's shoulder a squeeze. "But you already know that, better than most, I'd warrant."

Richard nodded, frowning as he stared at Braedan, as if trying to convince himself he was really there. Braedan held out his arms, then, and Richard fell against him, gripping him tightly as he returned the hug. Any remaining awkwardness between them dissipated, easing to a sense of quiet understanding, and Braedan's throat closed, aching.

The fact that any strangeness existed between them to begin with was not so much because of their years apart, Braedan knew, as from the unnatural life his brother was leading under Draven's corrupt control. It was well past time that Richard should have been fostering with a suitable family, and yet Draven had kept him secluded here, learning little other than the debilitating skill of hate. His brother's treatment was just another example of the cruel injustice Draven had inflicted on their family—and another reason, if any more were needed, of why he had to be stopped for good.

Pulling out of their embrace after a moment, Richard cleared his throat to ask gruffly, "So, is the uproar going on around here your doing, then?" He jerked his head toward the casement and the few shouts and clangs still coming from outside somewhere.

Braedan nodded. "It's an uprising against Draven. But before we speak of it further, I have to ask you something important. Did Draven bring a woman here earlier today? A beautiful woman, with auburn hair."

Richard made a scoffing sound. "Draven always brings women here. Scores of them. He's a lecherous swine."

"Nay, you must think, Richard. This woman would

have come just today—this morning, wearing a crimson gown. Have you seen anything of her?"

Richard frowned. "He came in with a group of his men while I was breaking my fast in the hall this morning. I only saw them from a distance, but I think he had a woman with him, aye, though I didn't notice her dress, for the cloak she wore. Why? Is she important to the revolt?"

"She is important to *me*," Braedan murmured, clenching his hands into fists. "I have to find her and quickly, but I cannot until I have done what I came here to do. I need to ask for your help against Draven, Richard."

"*My* help?" Richard's expression showed his surprise. Then he seemed to stand a little straighter, and his jaw took on a resolute line. "Aye, Braedan, you've my arm if you need it. Just tell me where you need me in the fray, and I will go, right now."

"It's not your arm we'll be needing, brother, but rather your wits and your speed," Braedan answered. "In fact, you're the only man who can complete the task."

"What is it?"

"I need you to go to London proper and bring back either William de Lier or Thomas Romain. If neither can be found, go to Guildhall itself and use the de Cantor name to gain an audience with Sir John Briton."

"*What*? Fetch one of the sheriffs or the mayor himself and bring him *here*?" Richard's mouth fairly gaped. "God almighty, Braedan, you must be daft to want that. If we bring the law into this, you'll go to Newgate, then on to the scaffold for sure!"

"I don't think so. Not once they hear what you're going to tell them about what Draven has been doing and demand a trial for it. We'll be waiting here for you, holding him for ransom until you get back with someone with the authority to hear the case and pass judgment. Either that, or he'll be dead, in which case we'll need the law anyway, to investigate the events that led us to that end."

"I suppose it's a bit late to be asking, but who exactly is the *us* you're talking about?"

"The other outlaws I brought with me. Men from the Singleton, Folville, and Coterel gangs, all of whom share a common interest in stopping Draven for good."

Richard let loose a string of low-breathed curses, earning him a sharp look from Braedan. "I can't believe it," Richard said, shaking his head in amazement. "An outlaw uprising. All right, then. You've convinced me. Tell me how you got into Chepston, and I'll leave for London the same way."

"Through the western gate. We secured that first, and it should still be under our control. Just go carefully, and all should be well."

Richard nodded, but Braedan gripped his arm, stopping him for just a moment more. It was time, unfortunately. It could be put off no longer. "I need to tell you one more thing, Richard. I wish I could spare you it, but it's something you deserve to know and should use in convincing the law that justice is on our side in this. It concerns Elizabeth—"

"You have news of Elizabeth?" Richard snapped to attention, worry stiffening his entire body as he searched Braedan's somber gaze. "What's happened—is something the matter? Has she been struck with the same illness that took her parents?"

"Nay, it's not that," Braedan answered, interrupting

the flood of questions he knew was Richard's way of denying what he could already read in Braedan's face. "I'm sorry, lad, but the truth of it is that Elizabeth is dead. It happened in the *stewes*. When, I haven't been able to learn yet, but it seems that it was the result of a difficult childbirth."

"*Childbirth?*" Richard choked, jerking away from Braedan's grip, his eyes filling with tears of anger and grief. He remained frozen, pain evident in every tense line of his body. "Ah, damn him to everlasting hell!" he cried out at last, burying his head in his hands to add brokenly, "He killed her, Braedan! Sure as you're standing there, he did. He forced her into that shameful life, that bastard . . ."

Braedan rested a hand on his brother's shoulder, his own heart heavy at the pain of Elizabeth's loss; she'd come to his family's seat at Dandridge House to foster with them before he'd left to fight with the king, and she'd been a sweet child even then. But Richard had known her better, having been raised with her in the same household for years. Braedan had long suspected that his brother cherished a budding tenderness for her; Richard's stricken reaction now made clear that he'd been right.

"It was a foul and sinful thing Draven did," Braedan murmured, trying to offer Richard the only comfort he knew of at that moment. "But we have a chance to stop him. Can you rule your grief—will you channel it into a force of resolve and take that chance with me?"

Richard looked up then, the pain in his gaze tearing through Braedan like a knife, and making him grit his teeth. "Draven is responsible for buying and selling countless women like Elizabeth," Braedan continued, holding his brother's gaze, "including the woman he brought here this morn—the woman that I love. And that is all the more reason why we must succeed in this today. Will you do as I bid you, Richard? Will you bring back the law so that we can crush him into oblivion with it?"

Silence hung over the room for several full and aching seconds before Richard seemed able to master his feelings enough to answer hoarsely, "Aye, Braedan, I'll go." His jaw clenched, the wounded look in his eyes draining and shifting to cold determination. "I promise you, an entire army of the law will follow me here, once I've done telling them my story. Just have the bastard shackled and ready for me when I return with them."

Chapter 20

Fiona dragged the trunk over to the only window she'd yet to try in her attempts to get free of Draven's room during the past quarter hour—an ornate half arch, higher than the others. Panic and frustration hummed through her, and her rasping breaths edged on hysteria as she scrambled atop the wooden chest, praying that there would be even a small ledge onto which she could climb out. And if there was, that she could find a way to squeeze through the narrow window opening to get to it.

Slipping, she banged her knees on the metal reinforcements at the corner of the trunk, but she swallowed her yelp of pain, concentrating on standing and curling her fingers over the flat edge at the bottom of the window. She went up on her toes, pulling herself up at the same time with her hands, almost enough to peer over the edge to what was below. Just a little more and she'd—

The grating of the bolt was followed quickly by the sound of the door itself being slammed open against the corridor wall. Fiona had twisted around in her precarious position atop the trunk, and now she slipped off, still landing on her feet, but with a force that jarred her teeth. The faint sounds of shouting and clanging weapons filtered into the chamber even as Draven came stalking through the open door, looking disheveled and sweaty, his torn shirt still partly unlaced, and a bloodied sword in his grip.

"Come on," he muttered at her, grabbing her with his free hand and yanking her against him. He kept her pinned there with his arm clenched tight around her throat as he began pulling her toward the hall. "Since these damned bandits seem so interested in your whereabouts, what do you say we let them have a look at you on our way out, eh?"

Fiona could barely choke out a response, not only because his arm was pressed against her throat, but because the sight that greeted her as they made their way down the corridor and into the main hall shocked her into silence. They burst through the archway and into chaos. It was a war—or at least what she imagined it must feel like to be in the midst of one. Men were fighting all around, swords clashing, grunts and screams echoing through the cavernous chamber, all lit by the golden light of the sun as it began to set, its rays shining through the costly glazed windows that Draven had insisted on putting in two years after she'd first come to Chepston.

Draven dragged her along the outer perimeter of the chamber, keeping their backs to the wall to prevent anyone attacking from behind. His sword was at the ready in his free hand, should anyone come at him face on, as he pulled her slowly closer to the main door leading to the only stairway that led out of the keep and to the ground one story below. But everyone seemed too occupied with the fighting they were already embroiled in to notice them.

Eyes wide and arms curled up to pull on Draven's arm so that a little more air could get into her lungs, Fiona stared wildly around, trying to get some sense of what was happening here. Draven's guards she recognized by their colors, but except for realizing by their motley garments and lack of a standard that the men they fought weren't a cohesive army of uniformed soldiers, she couldn't tell who the intruders were.

Until she caught a glimpse of fiery red hair nearer to the door. The man faced away from her as he fought, but in the struggle he shifted positions with his adversary, and her heart leapt with joyful recognition. *Will!* Almost in the same instant her searching gaze lighted on several other familiar faces clustered at this end of the chamber . . . Clinton, then Rufus and Grady, and two others she knew to be Folvilles. *Good God*, she thought, stunned. *This is the uprising that the outlaws had been planning against Draven back at the settlement.*

Suddenly, Draven yanked her harder and growled a command, wanting her to come more quickly, but she resisted; instead, she pulled back against his motion just as hard in her own direction, not caring that it sent waves of pain radiating down her neck and into her spine. She was looking desperately for the one other familiar face she sought among all the combatants . . . the one man she ached to find there—fighting, it was true, but living and breathing nonetheless—among the others.

But she couldn't find Braedan. He wasn't among the outlaw rebels.

And if he wasn't here, fighting with Will and the others to take Draven for the ransom of a hearing to restore his own good name, it meant that he was unable to fight. That he was dead, killed outside the *stewe*-house at Draven's command, as she'd suspected all along.

Only then did her resolve desert her, swept away by the waves of grief that had been swelling within her since last night. She slumped in Draven's grip, not caring anymore what happened to her. Let him lop off her head or trample over her, or toss her into the middle of the fray, for all she cared . . . none of it mattered anymore. But he didn't do any of those things. He stopped with a surprised grunt at her sudden heaviness sagging against his arm, pausing long enough to shift his hold on her away from her throat, where the prolonged weight of her body pressing down into his arm would have choked the life from her.

They'd come to a stop when she went limp against Draven, and now she noticed dimly that her action had had another effect as well. The fighting seemed to be lessening, though it continued in front of her as if she was watching it in the midst of a terrifying yet disconnected dream . . . but some of the men, the outlaws and a few guards who were still standing, began to see them. It helped, of course, that the battle was nearly over from the looks of things. The struggling and clanging of weapons had lessened. From somewhere deep inside she felt a kind of surprised joy; it seemed that the insurgents had claimed the victory.

Suddenly a hue and cry arose, the outlaws taking up the call from one another to warn of Draven's imminent

escape. The ranks seemed to shift and for an instant confusion reigned as some of the outlaws stayed in the main
fighting area to subdue and secure the remaining guards,
while the others all converged on her and Draven, where
they'd stopped at the front of the great hall, beneath the
narrow, railed dais that jutted from the wall just above
their heads—the place Draven had always favored during feasting for his table of honor, thanks to the eleva-
tion it gave him over his guests.

How ironic for him, Fiona thought darkly, that instead of being safely up there as was his custom, he was
today being forced to mingle with his hot-eyed and
bloody guests, who were even now approaching him
with their gory blades upraised.

Suddenly, she stiffened, instinct drawing the reaction
from her as he yanked her back squarely against him to
lift the edge of his sword with a quick, smooth motion to
her throat.

"You will all back away from us and let us pass from
this chamber, or the woman will die," Draven called,
forcing her to lift her chin to avoid being cut by the blade
he jerked harder into her to emphasize the statement.

Will stood, chest heaving, near the front of the pack
that was clustering before them, and she saw fear flare in
his eyes. But in the next instant his expression went utterly calm, his gaze flicking for an instant above her.

"Nay, Draven," he called out, stepping forward,
switching his sword to his other hand in order to pull a
dagger from his boot. He straightened again. "It is *you*
who will be the one doin' somethin' for *us*. Let her go
now before you end up havin' another crime to answer
to us for. You've enough on your head already."

Draven laughed, the sound echoing through Fiona's

ears with the same tenor of utter control he'd seemed to wield over her for most of her life. "Do you honestly think that I would obey the commands of a ruffian like you, Singleton? I've been lenient with you thus far in pursuing and punishing you for your roadside crimes. It is something I'll be remedying in future if you don't order your men to step down now."

"That I cannot do, Draven, even if I was fool enough to want to. You see, they're not all my men," Will answered, his eyes glittering with malice.

"Aye, some of them are mine," Clinton Folville growled, stepping from the crowd to stand next to Will.

"And the rest are mine," rasped a pock-faced and angry-looking bear of a man, who elbowed his way forward to stand with Clint and Will. Fiona felt Draven's arm spasm against her belly, his other hand twitching just enough to shift the edge of the blade against her throat. It was all that prevented her from gasping as she recognized the third man to be Eustace Coterel, the leader of a gang of outlaws more feared than any others in these parts for their vicious barbarity, especially when dealing with noblemen they held for ransom.

Will shook his head, making a clicking sound with his tongue. "I don't claim to be a font o' learnin', Draven, but I'd say it looks like you've managed to make enemies of one too many outlaws in your day." He nodded to Fiona, adding, "Now why don't you let her go, and we can discuss our terms like reasonable men."

"Our terms?" Draven echoed, his voice dripping with sarcasm. "You must be jesting. The only terms I'll be making are my own—which is for you to back away or witness your sister being slaughtered in front of your eyes."

As he was talking, Fiona kept watching Will, noticing how his gaze lifted to just above her several times, the last time, just then, accompanied by a slight nod of his head. Draven continued, seemingly oblivious to it, looking around the group of outlaws to prevent anyone from getting a jump on him. "Giselle is a delectable bit of skirt, I'll admit, and I've enjoyed her fully on many occasions, but there are many others like her who are less trouble with whom I can sate myself."

"Like Elizabeth, you bastard?" a voice above them called flatly. It sent a jolt of disbelieving joy through Fiona almost at the same instant that she saw Will fling his dagger at Draven's foot. Then a crashing weight fell into them from above. Draven's grip had loosened on her when Will's blade bit deep, his shout of pain rocking through her; but with the impact she suddenly felt herself being yanked away from his grasp by a pair of strong hands. There was a confusion of shouts and scuffling for an instant until she regained her balance and found herself supported in Will's embrace, but she twisted her head frantically to see who had knocked Draven to the floor.

The man rolled to standing at the same time that Draven managed to get up on one knee, both of them reaching to scoop up their swords from a half crouch before coming at each other with growls of rage. *Braedan!* her heart cried out, her hand flying to her mouth. Oh, God it was Braedan—he was alive! She watched him, fear threading through her joy as he and Draven clashed again and again, their swords locked against one another.

But before long Draven stumbled on his injured foot; he fell hard into Braedan, making them both tumble to the floor again, though it was Braedan who managed to roll to the top; Draven's blade went spinning from his grip, and Fiona saw Braedan pull his fist back to land two punishing blows to his uncle's jaw before lifting his sword and raising it, point down, above Draven's throat. "This is for Elizabeth," she heard him rasp, "and for Fiona and all the women you've tainted with your filthy touch!"

"Go ahead, de Cantor," Draven gasped in reply, sneering. "It won't change the fact that one of your beloved whores is dead while the other cast you off to return to me. Just remember that when you're about to hang from the gibbet for murdering a peer of the realm!"

"Your lies have no more power here, Draven. Fiona did what she thought she had to in order to spare me," Braedan grated, his chest heaving and the point of his blade still digging into Draven's throat. "I know that now, though I was too blind to see it before." He paused, clearly waging some kind of battle within himself before he shook his head, easing back the pressure on his weapon against Draven's neck. "And though I'd relish nothing as much at this moment as sending you straight to the hell you've earned, I love her too much to throw away whatever chance we may have together by killing you now. The law can be brought in full against you with the same result in the end. You're not worth more."

As he spoke the last part, he lifted his sword from Draven's throat, keeping it at the ready as he grabbed a fistful of his shirt and hauled him to his feet. "Here," he said to Will, shoving Draven in his direction. "Bind him and secure him somewhere until the authorities arrive. I've sent a messenger to get them, and they should be here soon."

"The authorities?" Draven echoed, before letting go a rusty laugh. "How delicious. Aye, I'm sure they'll race right over at your bidding. Outlaws command such influence over government officials these days."

Braedan refused to answer, so Draven continued taunting him, looking utterly undefeated, Fiona noticed with a shudder, even standing bruised and bloodied as he was in front of them all.

"You're a fool, de Cantor," he mocked. Will yanked Draven's arms behind his back to begin tying his wrists with a piece of rope, but it hardly slowed him down. "The only thing your fugitive messenger will get for his pains is a pair of irons clapped on his legs and a lengthy stay in Newgate."

The other outlaws had begun to mill around restlessly at Draven's threats, but Braedan simply sheathed his sword, continuing to ignore him in favor of turning to Fiona at long last. She met his gaze, her tawny eyes moist with happiness, and he smiled back at her, the world seeming to narrow down only to her as he walked closer. With a little cry, she ran the rest of the way to him, throwing herself into his embrace, and he held her close, more thankful to have her safe in his arms again than he'd ever been about anything in his life.

"How did you learn the truth about what had happened?" she asked softly, pulling away enough to look up into his face.

"It doesn't matter." He shook his head, pressing a gentle kiss to her brow before pulling her close again. "I never should have doubted you at all."

Will muttered something to Draven, and he and Rufus began to pull the bound man from the chamber, but before they'd gone five paces, Draven twisted in their grip, calling out to the room at large, "You should know that I dispatched several of my own men to the authorities when this all began. One of London's sheriffs will most assuredly be arriving soon, as de Cantor promised, but with far different results than he claimed. All of you will be facing charges, not me. His messenger is already warming a prison cell, you can warrant—which is where each of you will end as well if you don't give over this ridiculous plot of yours and release me immediately!"

Will scowled, and Braedan heard the mumblings among the outlaws increase as they exchanged looks with one another. Irritation filled him. *Damn the wretch for trying to stir the pot like this.* He'd wanted to avoid addressing Draven directly again, but it seemed he'd have no choice, unless he wanted an open rebellion of outlaws on his hands.

"You're wrong, you know," he called over the hum of dissent his uncle's claim had provoked. Giving Fiona's hand a squeeze, he stepped away from her and walked to where Will and Rufus held Draven, pausing when he stood right in front of his uncle. The room fell mostly silent again, everyone waiting to hear what the man who'd led them in plotting the attack would say.

"I can assure you that my messenger is not in prison. He never has been, nor is he likely ever to be. In fact, the authorities will be more likely to come at *his* call than they would at yours, Draven, considering some of the trouble you've caused around the city with your bribes and corruption." Braedan stared at his uncle, meeting his icy gaze with the stoniness of his own. "You see the man I sent to London comes from a long line of king's justices, well respected for their honor and integrity. No alderman, sheriff, or mayor in England would think to turn him away unheard—because he is a de Cantor. I sent my brother Richard. So let me hear no more of your idle threats, Draven. It is clear that you try only to save your own skin, and such behavior is unbecoming in a man of your position."

Draven kept silent, though his mouth looked as tight and his face was sharp with resentment, as if he had tasted something bitter. But some of the outlaws who'd been disgruntled at Draven's original warnings remained unconvinced by Braedan's explanation, and the rumblings of discontent increased.

"Why in hell are we waitin' for the law to show here anyway?" someone bellowed from the crowd. "Truth be known, we've no assurance they won't try to take us in along with Draven, when all's said and done!"

"Aye!" another called. "They've no reason to show restraint with us."

"I say we get on with it and hold a trial of our own, lads," Eustace Coterel shouted above the rest, and at the sound of his commanding, raspy voice, the room quieted again. Braedan felt Fiona slip into place beside him, tucking herself against him, as the Coterels' leader stepped into a more open area near the front, where he could be seen better. "The law ain't to be trusted, I say. The likes o' him," he added, jerking his thumb in Draven's direction, "will make sure that any panel set up to judge him will be thick with boughten men. 'Tis high time we had a turn ourselves! I say we form a jury of our own, with either de Cantor or else Folville—who was a peer o' the realm before he were an outlaw—servin' as chief justice to pass judgment on the mighty Lord Draven here and now!"

A resounding swell of cheers echoed through the hall.

Draven paled, but Braedan waited until the men had quieted a bit, his heart torn between a desire to see Draven pay for his crimes and his knowing that staging a mock trial would bode ill for them all.

Finally, he spoke, commanding their attention with his voice. "By now you all know well that I cherish no affection for the man we hold here today. That he deserves to be tried and prosecuted for his crimes is unquestionable, and yet I also know that taking the law into our own hands would be unwise, unless we want our actions viewed as little more than the wild deeds of men who hold no respect for true and timely justice. I cannot support such a trial for that reason."

"The rest o' the world thinks nothin' of takin' the law into its own hands when it comes to our kind, de Cantor," Coterel spat, glowering. "Any citizen apprehendin' an outlaw can execute him without trial and receive no punishment for it under the *law*, by God! I say to hell with it. Let's do it our way."

"Wait, Eustace," Will called through the rising clamor for justice. "I've no love for the bastard either, but Braedan's right—we planned all along to hold Draven for the ransom of a fair hearin' and trial in the king's court for his crimes, nothin' less. The sheriff will be here soon, and—"

"The sheriff's comin' is all the more reason to get on wi' it now," Coterel growled. "Since de Cantor's taken himself out, I put forth the name of Clinton Folville for chief justice of this trial—and ask among you men, who will serve on the jury to be hearin' it?"

From the cheers, shouting and scuffling that broke out at that, it was clear that there would be no preventing this, Braedan realized grimly. He held Fiona against him, protecting her from the shoving and jostling of the crowd as someone reached out and grabbed Draven from Will's grip, hauling him, gape-mouthed, to stand behind a table at the makeshift court that was being hastily constructed underneath one of the hall's great stone arches. Twelve men were soon lined up to the side of him, with Clinton stepping forward to direct the proceedings.

"This is a travesty," Draven said incredulously, looking around him. "None of you have the authority to—"

"Is the jury prepared to hear the list of crimes leveled against this man?" Clinton intoned loudly, cutting off Draven's complaint.

"Aye," the motley group answered, more or less in unison.

"Very well," Clinton continued, pacing in front of Draven's table, his hands behind his back, to stand opposite the jury of outlaws. "For the crime of persecution of those in his shire, leading to seizure of lands and fortune, along with branding as fugitives to the crown, are there any present who wish to speak of Kendrick de Lacy, Lord Draven's guilt?"

"Aye!" a man in a tattered coat cried out from the back of the crowd. " 'Twas Draven 'imself took possession of half me livestock and so much of me grain that I couldn't feed what was left. When I couldn't pay me taxes because of it, he took the rest, then had me named an outlaw!"

"He did the same to me, as well," said an older man, holding a crumpled toque in his hands and looking a bit anxious.

"And me!" came another shout, followed by a half dozen others who called out similar tales of Draven's corruption and greed.

When the furor had ebbed, Clinton rocked back on his heels, his expression solemn. "I, myself, have cause against Lord Draven as well," he said loudly. "It was at his bidding that I lost my family's lands and estate, taken by the crown when Draven falsified a report he gave during an inquest into a deadly brawl with which I was involved." Looking around the chamber when he was done speaking, Clinton said, "Now, then, are there any others here wishing to speak in Lord Draven's defense?"

The room nearly echoed with silence.

"Very well. Men of the jury, how say you to these charges?"

The outlaw jury clustered together for a moment, the rumbling of their voices evident until they finally stepped away from each other to line up again. The man at the end nearest Draven called out, "Guilty!"

Clinton nodded. "On to the next charge. For the excessive and brutal punishments of those sentenced under his jurisdiction, including the maiming and death of children, does anyone wish to speak?"

"Aye, I'll speak," called old Grady, stepping from the cluster of men around Will. "I know 'twas at Draven's orders that me adopted lad, Nate, were shot in the leg with a crossbow bolt for poachin' some three week past. He woulda died, too, were it not fer this fair lady here," he said gruffly, nodding toward Fiona.

"Nate only took a bit o' venison every now and again to help stave off the Reaper. He be no more'n twelve years, but he knows the ways of Draven's cruelty. When he saw Draven's foresters after him, he ran. 'Twas either that or risk havin' his hand cut off, like he knew Draven did to Thomas Flinder last month, fer no more than takin' a bit o' bread from Digby's bakeshop."

Several others from the crowd added their stories to Grady's, many of the outlaws showing the jury their own scars and mutilations, some given by Draven's own hand.

When they were all finished, and no one spoke in Draven's defense for the charge, Clinton stepped up and spoke again. "Men of the jury, what say you to this charge against Lord Draven?"

The consultation took even less time before they reached a conclusion. "Guilty!" they echoed again.

"For the next charge, then," Clinton intoned, walking slowly in front of the "courtroom" with his hands clasped at the small of his back, "the abuse of rank and station in the capture, forced seduction, and sale of innocent women into the brothels of the Southwark *stewes* . . ." Clinton's gaze flicked to Fiona. ". . . and for the continued use of said women in repeated and unwilling acts of carnal sin, are there any to speak out to these charges?"

"I'll speak to it," one of the Folville men called out hoarsely. "Draven stole my daughter away and ruined her, makin' her think she'd have a future with him. She died in the *stewes* of Southwark near five year ago, now."

"Aye, my sister was seduced into shame by him last year," said another.

"My sister died o' the pox after he lured her to work in one of his brothels eight years ago," a red-nosed man—one of Clinton's men—added, his haunted gaze fixed on Draven. "Then he had me branded an outlaw when I tried to bring 'im up on charges for it. He's got the juries in these parts all bought out in 'is favor, he does."

Braedan called out, his voice hard and implacable, "I will add that Lord Draven is responsible for the forced seduction and death of my foster sister, Elizabeth Haversom. She died bearing a child whose conception was forced on her through the shameful existence into which she was sold."

After a moment's silence, Clinton looked to Fiona. "And you, lady?" he asked. "Have you anything further to add to the charges against Lord Draven?"

Fiona paused, and Braedan could feel her trembling; he gave her hand an encouraging squeeze, which she returned before stepping forward to address the chamber, "Only that the charges stated against him in regards to his use of women are true in my experience. I was just fifteen when Draven purchased me and made me into the Crimson Lady. By my accounts, at least fourscore women were bought by him during the years I spent under his control, with at least a score of them perishing, including Mary Gilbert, Janet de Barkin, and Margaret Wylughby, as a direct result of the childbearing or disease brought upon them through the work they were forced by Draven to undertake in the *stewes*."

A sober quiet settled over the chamber; even Draven had remained uncharacteristically silent through the entire proceedings, though his expression was black and his demeanor haughtily dismissive of the entire process against him. When no one else stepped forward to speak for or against Draven, Clinton looked to the jury again, asking, "All right then, men, what say you to these charges?"

"Guilty!" came the answer a third time, after almost no deliberation.

"Christ Almighty, man, 'tis enough to condemn the

bastard a dozen times over already!" Eustace Coterel called from the edge of the crowd of outlaws observing the court. "There's no need to call out any more of 'is crimes. Let's just hang 'im from 'is own battlements and be done with it!"

A clamor of support arose at that, louder than any of the rest that had come before, and the crowd surged forward, nearly knocking over Braedan, Fiona, Will, and the others from the Singleton gang who'd hung back with them.

"What do we do now?" Fiona called to Braedan over the noise, still clinging to him as the mass of outlaws shoved and shifted forward in their quest to hang Draven.

"There's not much we can do. They seem bent on having their justice," he yelled back, holding her tightly as he balanced them against the push of the crowd, trying at the same time to see what was happening at the front of the mob where Draven had been. The tide of men had surrounded him and swept him up, it seemed, carrying him bodily toward the spiral stone staircase Braedan knew led to the crenellated walls above the keep.

Looking back to Will and his men, he shouted, "We may not be able to stop them, but let's see if we can at least try to slow them down."

Will nodded, and they pushed into the throng, Braedan leading the way, holding tightly to Fiona, and followed by Rufus, Grady, and the others a little behind. Soon they burst into the cooler air of the outdoors, the battlements lit with the fiery hues of the setting sun. The crowd of men surged and parted as Eustace and several of his gang dragged Draven toward the nearest wall, jumping up onto the small ledge just below the top edge of the wall, hauling a struggling Draven up onto it as well, before forcing him farther up onto the narrow space between the jutting, squared crenellations.

Braedan saw him sway a little as he caught a glimpse of the dizzying distance between himself and the ground, his eyes widening, until one of the Coterels yanked him back to a more stable footing.

"You can't do this!" Draven yelled, beginning to struggle again as another man emerged from the keep's stairwell with a thick rope in his grip, brandishing it like a flag as he stalked toward the self-appointed execution- ers. "The king will have your heads on stakes for this!" Draven continued to shriek, his voice cracking with fear as he nearly tipped again, trying to elude the noose they looped over his head before tying the other end firmly over one of the foot-high chunks of stonework that pro- jected up from the top edge of the wall.

"Braedan, we have to do something!" Fiona cried softly, gripping his hand, her gaze fixed with horror on the dark proceedings taking place in front of them. "If we let them hang him like this, any chance you may have for gaining the king's official pardon—for getting your life back—will be lost!"

"Aye," he admitted, the grim truth of it resounding through him more loudly than the shouting mob. "You're likely right. Yet other than trying to take on all of these outlaws together myself, I do not know what I can do to stop them. They will not hear reason."

Fiona was quiet for a long moment before she said resolutely, "Then perhaps they will hear me."

Before he knew what she was about, Fiona pulled away from him, ignoring his shouted caution against it, delving into the crowd and pushing her way to the front. He lurched into motion behind her, her smaller form slipping with greater ease through the throng, so that he reached her only as she burst into the empty semicircle just in front of the impromptu place of execution. She turned to stand almost directly below Draven's boots and the men who held him in preparation to throw him from the walls to hang.

"Stop!" she called out, holding up her hands in a plea for silence as she paced in front of them. "You must hear me in this, I beg of you!"

To Braedan's surprise, most of the outlaws, blood-thirsty as they were, began to quiet, shocked into it perhaps, by the strangeness of seeing a woman speaking out so. The fact that the woman was Fiona, who was not only beautiful but also probably recognizable to some as the Crimson Lady in her scarlet-hued gown, didn't hurt the cause, either. Braedan kept close enough to offer her aid if she needed it, while still keeping far enough to the side to give her the freedom to say what she wished.

"I have as much of a claim against Kendrick de Lacy, Lord Draven as any of you here," she said, her voice wavering at first, before becoming stronger as she met Braedan's gaze, seeming to draw strength from his presence. "And while I, too, wish to see him pay for the crimes he has committed, I do not think he should die this way. It would be too easy. If you continue now, he will perish, but to what end, other than to say it is done? There will be no investigation, no trial before the public, no sentencing or disgrace to be endured. Nay, all that will come of it will be renewed persecution of us as outlaws, for his unsanctioned murder."

"She's right. Listen to her," Draven said hoarsely

from his precarious perch above her, only to be jerked to silence again by one of his captors.

"It is not for your sake that I am saying this, Draven," Fiona answered, skewering him with her gaze, "but for the sake of everyone here." She looked back to the gathering of outlaws. "I say it for all of you—for my brother and his people, as well as for myself and the man I love," she continued, letting her stare shift to Braedan with her feelings for him shining full in her gaze.

Eustace Coterel had stood quietly near the front of the crowd while Fiona had spoken, his arms folded over his barrel chest, but now he broke his silence. "Aye, Giselle, 'tis true that you more than most should have a say in what happens next. And yet if we do not take action against Draven now, none may ever come. He could go free, as he has so oft before when he's run afoul of the very law he is supposed to uphold, relyin' on his slippery tongue and padded purse to get him off. Justice will not be served."

"But an even greater injustice will come to pass when some of you are hunted down and killed for taking part in the deed of killing him. And it would be an injustice of the worst sort indeed, if a man like Braedan de Cantor is condemned to spend the rest of his life in hiding, trapped as an outlaw—first by the despicable actions of this man," she said, her expression intense as she jerked her head toward Draven, "and then by the lot of you, thanks to what you're planning to do here. You cannot go through with it; you cannot hang Draven this day."

"That is a statement with which I'll have to agree!" a man's voice called from the very back of the crowd, near the door from the stone stairway. The sun was finally beginning to dip behind the horizon, setting in a brilliant blaze of color so that at first Braedan couldn't make out the identity of the man who'd spoken. But then he stepped forward and Braedan breathed an inner sigh of relief at the sight of the distinctive blue robes and chains of office that he wore. It was Thomas Romain, one of the two sheriffs of London.

The sheriff moved forward under an aura of command, backed by several score of his soldiers, who spilled from the stairway and around from the other corners of the rectangular battlements, having attained the wall through other doors positioned around the keep. The outlaws backed up, swords raised, though none of them were foolhardy enough, Braedan realized, to attempt an engagement with such a show of force; that action would have been disastrous, it was clear, thanks to the sheriff's superior numbers.

"No one is going to hang this day," the sheriff called out, "though whether or not a hanging—or several," he said, letting his pointed stare shift round the outlaws, "will be needed eventually, remains to be seen."

"Hang the whole lot of them," Draven snarled, glowering at the men who still held him, as well as the outlaws clustered below him. "I confess I am glad to see you arrived, Tom. Send your men forward and place all these ruffians under arrest. Especially these two." He nodded at Fiona and Braedan where they stood together again, Fiona having returned to Braedan's side upon the sheriff's entrance. "They led this despicable hunt of me, and I'll see them rot for it."

"No one said the investigation would be focused on the outlaws alone, Draven. You have some answering to do yourself based upon what I heard from young de Cantor."

Draven gave a snort. "All lies. The young one is no different than his brother; they're both hypocrites and thieves. But we'll sort through all of that in due time, Tom. Just hurry your men along and we'll get about it as soon as I'm down from here."

The outlaws milled about uneasily, not able to leave, thanks to the unexpectedly numerous ranks of the sheriff's men, yet unable to fight them for the same reason. They weren't fool enough to resist this show of power, but they weren't going to make it easier for the law to take their prize captive, either; clustering together, they formed a kind of barrier around Draven's position so that it took the soldiers time and effort to penetrate the masses to get to their goal.

The sheriff made a call for torches, to combat the increasing dark from the setting of the sun, as Draven waited for the guards to reach him, needing them to untie his hands so that he could get down from the shadowy ledge without killing himself. In the meantime, he took the opportunity to sneer down at Braedan and Fiona, until it was all Braedan could do not to yank him from the stone outcrop and throttle the expression from his face. If not for Fiona, he might have done just that, but he didn't want to risk upsetting her more than she already had been that day. Nay, not even for the pleasure of making Draven choke on his own teeth.

But then Draven was reckless enough to start talking, and Braedan found himself clenching his jaw until it ached in order to remain still.

"How does it feel, knowing you've been bested yet again, de Cantor?" his uncle mocked softly. "Your precious men of justice have arrived, and with them my return to power. Coterel was right when he said I'd never be prosecuted if I left this place alive. I won't. Because most people aren't as stupidly honorable as you. Money can buy anything, man . . . aye, even a favorable verdict in the king's own court."

"It can't buy everything, Draven!"

The quavering voice had rung out from somewhere above the battlements—even above Draven himself, poised as he still was on the ledge near the crenellations. Fivescore outlaws, soldiers, and lawmen turned to see who had spoken, including Braedan and Fiona, who gasped with worry at the sight of Richard, perched atop the roof of the main keep across from them. The massive stone structure towered above the open span of the battlements where everyone was standing, the top of the roof reaching at least twenty feet over Draven's head.

"It cannot buy a life back," Richard shouted out tremulously. "Nay, not Elizabeth's, though you stole it from her as surely as if you sliced her through with that dagger you're so fond of wielding."

"Stupid boy," Draven muttered. "What do you think you're—"

"Come down from there, Richard," Braedan called out, cutting Draven's insult short. His uncle wisely chose to remain silent. "You cannot change anything by joining her in death, lad. It is a long drop from there and is sure to be unpleasant if you slip. Come down now."

Faintly, Braedan could see Richard shake his head, and he tensed, desperate over his brother's safety. It was becoming difficult to see his face clearly in the dark, but Braedan knew it would only take one false step for

Richard to go tumbling down to his death on the battlements.

"I'm not planning to meet Elizabeth just yet Braedan," Richard answered, his voice strained with emotion as he suddenly shifted to stand at the very edge of the roof, drawing exclamations of shock and surprise from the onlookers. "Nor will anyone else meet with her this night; sweet soul that she was, she is in a better place—a paradise the likes of which I can only aspire in my dreams. But I might achieve it yet, brother. For though I am not the honorable and good man that you are, I am still a de Cantor, and like all de Cantors, I live only to see justice done."

He moved again, this time to lift something, and in that instant, Braedan felt the sickening jolt of realization. But he was too late to stop what was about to happen. Oh, God, too late . . .

"And my justice demands that I tell you, Kendrick de Lacy, Lord Draven, that you have been judged and found guilty of grievous crimes, for which you must now face a reckoning," Richard called out, his voice cracking and ragged with restrained sobs that seemed to shake him, as he notched an arrow into his bow, pulled back, and took aim.

After a beat of heavy silence, he growled hoarsely, "Now go to hell, where you belong."

With that, he let fly his arrow, swift and true. The deadly whisper of its passing filled the air above the battlements for a moment, followed by the dull, thudding sound of its entry. Draven gasped, jerking to utter stillness midbreath, his eyes widening in disbelief as he stared down at the quivering bolt embedded in his chest. It all lasted but an instant, yet it seemed forever before soundlessly he began to tip, the force of the arrow shot taking him over the crenellation and out of sight. . . .

Toppling him into the eternity of oblivion.

Chapter 21

❦

Chepston Hall
One week later

 It was to be the day of reckoning for them all.

Fiona stood in the cavernous main chamber of Chepston Hall, where she, Braedan, and the other outlaws had been kept under heavily guarded house arrest for the past week, listening to the rain pattering on the costly, glazed windows and awaiting the sheriff's return to pronounce his decision in the inquiry over Draven's death. Richard was the only one of all who had been present that fateful night not allowed free run of Draven's walled-in estate; he'd been kept under separate guard in a locked chamber on the upper floor thanks to the seriousness of the charges brought against him.

Of course Braedan had been sick with worry, and much of his time these seven days had been passed behind closed doors with the sheriff or others involved in the inquest, using his knowledge of law and his birthright in the judiciary system to help provide the officials with information on where to seek the evidence that would prove the outlaws'—and Richard's—case against Draven. She knew he understood better than any, that if it was decided that the attack on Draven's estate wasn't warranted, many of the outlaws would face actual trials, with time spent in the hellish bowels of Newgate, the Clink, or Marshalsea, awaiting their turn in court. And if Richard was charged as guilty in the unjustifiable murder of Draven, a nobleman with whom he'd shared a family connection . . .

Fiona shuddered to think what kind of death the lad would endure for it.

"De Cantor had better come through for us, or there may be another murder done before we're finished," she heard one of the Coterels mutter from within the cluster of them standing behind the stone arch a few paces from her. "Aye. If we're goin' to be hanged in the end, we might as well have our own bit o' justice first," another who was standing there added.

They couldn't see her, she knew; but she'd been aware of the steadily rising tensions among all of the outlaws being held there while the inquest dragged on, realizing that it was a minor miracle none of them had yet come to blows with each other. The sheriff had seemed cognizant of that as well, hurrying the investigation so that it might be completed that day, with the results meaning either a mass transport of them all to prisons, or their release and exodus back to their own homes and communities. Either way it would get them separated from one another and out of Chepston.

"How goes it, sister?" Will murmured, coming to stand with her as she waited for Braedan to emerge from his final meeting with the sheriff and the lesser officials.

"As well as can be expected." She clenched her hands together, her entire body tight with worry. "I want this over with now, Will, and yet I am afraid of what may happen. It is both a longing and a dread, and I cannot seem to reconcile it in myself."

"I understand," he answered sympathetically. "I, for one, will be glad never to set eyes on this cursed house or its lands again, I can tell you. I didn't think I'd ever feel as heartily tired of a place as grand as this one, but every corner of it seems tainted with Draven's presence, so that I cannot draw in a free breath of air. 'Tis a worse prison, perhaps, than one of those to which we may be sent come nightfall."

"Pray God it does not come to that," Fiona murmured, staring with trepidation at the door closeting those who would be making that decision for them. As if on the wings of her thoughts, it opened, and Braedan strode through. The mass of outlaws, all of whom had been gathered in the main chamber again for the reading of the charges and verdicts by the inquest officials, quieted at his entrance, and it seemed as though every gaze was trained on him as he approached her.

"What is it, Braedan?" she asked him, searching his face. He looked somber—more so than he'd seemed since the moment Richard had fired his fatal shot at Draven—and it sent a ripple of fear through her.

"Nothing," he answered, taking the hand she offered him and squeezing it tight. "I've done all I can, Fiona. It is up to Providence now. The sheriff will be entering this chamber in a moment to read out his findings, but as one of the accused I was not given privilege of hearing the inquest officials' final decision. I do know that a parchment arrived this morning from King Edward himself, though again, I know not what it contained."

Before she could question him further, the soldier near the door from which Braedan had come straightened at a signal from someone within that secluded chamber. Calling out loudly for order, he pounded the base of his spear on the wooden floor of the great hall, an action that was repeated by every guard positioned at intervals around the spacious chamber.

"All will rise and assemble for the conclusion of the official inquest into the detainment and death of Kendrick de Lacy, Lord Draven!"

At that proclamation, a fresh stream of heavily armed soldiers came through all of the doors to take up post standing guard with those already in place at every portal; Fiona felt a sinking sensation, knowing they had been sent to keep order and subdue any potential uprising by the outlaws should the verdict read prove unpopular. Braedan kept her hand clasped warmly in his own as he led her and Will toward the front of the assembly of outlaws. They were all gathered, she noted ironically, in almost the very same spot that they had chosen as the stage for Draven's impromptu trial on the night of his death. And though she felt no remorse over his loss, she couldn't help but shudder to think that they all might end this day with naught but the prospect of facing the same end that he had come to, only without a crossbow bolt to speed their way.

The large door at the front of the chamber opened again and the sheriff came through, followed by the London coroner, and half a dozen violet-robed aldermen, all of whom had participated in the investigation and deliberation of findings. The men took their positions just behind the sheriff and coroner, who took places standing behind the large table that had been placed there for the purposes of the day's proceedings.

The sheriff unrolled a parchment he carried, spreading it on the table before him and weighting the corners with fist-sized stones. Then he glanced over what was written there one last time before straightening and calling out in an official tone, "Let this conclusion of inquest begin. The city council has examined the evidence presented concerning the detainment and subsequent death of Kendrick de Lacy, Viscount Draven, a peer of King Edward's realm and sheriff of Alton in the neighboring shire, and has reached a decision in the culpability of the outlaws and one woman involved in the uprising, as well as the responsibility of Lord Draven's ward, one Richard de Cantor, in Lord Draven's death. This reading will address the council's findings for each."

Fiona looked at Braedan, wondering if he was feeling the same sense of foreboding that was gnawing at her. But he looked calm, his back straight as he faced the panel, and his gaze resolute. "Where is Richard?" she whispered to him, as the sheriff paused before reading out the findings.

"He'll be brought down just before the findings in Draven's death are read," he told her quietly, leaning in to speak, but keeping his gaze focused on the sheriff and the council.

Nodding, she took a deep breath and steeled herself to listen to the sheriff as he read the charges, then called off the names of each of the nearly twoscore outlaws involved in the uprising against Draven, noting those who were deceased as a result of the action. As the only female participant, her own name was read last. And then he announced the council's findings and verdict.

"As concerns the charges against the aforementioned defendants, of organized revolt and kidnapping of said deceased within the estate of Chepston Hall, with the intent to commit murder, this inquest has found that sufficient evidence exists concerning the guilt of the deceased to warrant the action undertaken in attempt to gain relief from said deceased's corruption of office, use of bribery, forced seduction, and other false practices."

A hum of surprise swept through the chamber, and Fiona sagged with relief against Braedan. He pressed a kiss to her brow, closing his eyes for a moment as he breathed in deeply and murmured a prayer of thanks.

The sheriff continued, "In light of said findings, His Royal Highness, King Edward, has, for the price of a reasonable fee, payable to the crown by each defendant involved in the revolt, offered a writ of full pardon, extending his thanks, as sovereign, for the furtherance of justice in His kingdom. Also upon conclusion of these proceedings, the two defendants of former rank, Clinton Folville, Baron of Herrick, and Sir Braedan de Cantor shall have restored to them all rights of status, titles, and holdings, while all other defendants in this case shall be free to return to their homes and previous trades, with the admonition that any further unlawful activity undertaken will render said writs of pardon worthless."

"What in hell are we supposed to do, then, man?" one of the Coterels yelled from the back of the chamber. "Many of us have been outlawed for a decade or more and have no trade and no homes to return to, even if we wanted to pay for the right to go back to 'em!"

The sheriff paused, looking out toward the part of the crowd with a nod. "A useful question to be sure. However, King Edward has shown his further mercy and wisdom by extending the following offer: Any of you wishing to serve Him in His army and travel to warlike climes abroad may do so and thereby obtain a writ of pardon without further fee required."

More grumblings continued at that, but the tenor was more accepting than it had been upon the first part of the proclamation of pardon. However, everyone fell silent again upon the coroner's call to bring forth the final prisoner in the inquest. Fiona felt Braedan tense beside her, his gaze fixed on the door through which two armed guards led the shackled Richard. Fiona felt a little flare of relief on sight of him; he didn't seem to have been treated badly in the week since they'd seen him last.

He was led to a position in front of the chamber, nearer to the table at which the inquest panel was seated. As he was led past them, he caught Braedan's gaze, his own showing his anxiety, but it was laced with joy at seeing his brother again. In the next moment, however, all of them were forced to direct their attention back to the sheriff, as he had begun to read the charges and verdict of the council in this final aspect of the case.

"The council finds that Richard de Cantor did knowingly and willfully take the life of his relation by marriage, Kendrick de Lacy, Viscount Draven, an action that is against the just precepts of this kingdom, and as such is punishable under law."

Fiona's heart plummeted with grief, aching for Braedan and for Richard, until the Sheriff continued with his statement, sending her emotions in an entirely different direction.

"However, upon examination of the facts in this case—particularly the grievous injustice done to one Elizabeth Haversom, foster sister to the accused—we, the council, find Richard de Cantor to be justified in the vengeful action taken against Lord Draven, and hereby remand him to the care and custody of his brother, Sir Braedan de Cantor, with all rights and privileges restored."

A shout went up then, and Braedan gave a whoop of his own, turning to Fiona and picking her up to swing her around, both of them laughing aloud, before he set her down and strode to meet his brother in a fierce embrace. Tears glistened in Fiona's eyes as she watched them, her heart filled with so much gladness she thought it might burst. Will came up next to her, smiling and hugging her close with an arm round her waist, as the other outlaws began to ready themselves to depart Chepston Hall as free men.

"This official inquest is ended," called the coroner, shouting above the swelling noise of the crowd. "Your writs of pardon may be obtained at Guildhall, London, for payment of said fee or agreement to join the king's army. And now you are free to—"

"Wait!"

The room went quiet at the powerful voice echoing through it, and Fiona went rigid with surprise. It was Braedan who had shouted the command. He had released his brother to stride forward toward the sheriff, calling out, "We cannot leave. There is yet one more proclamation to be read!"

The sheriff, coroner, and aldermen looked as bewildered as Fiona felt at Braedan's strange announcement; that feeling only increased when he leapt onto the table, standing tall so that he towered over the chamber, to be easily seen and heard by all.

"I beg this assembly's indulgence for one moment more," he said, looking over the crowd, "for though I share your eagerness to leave this place and begin life anew, I cannot do so without answering one last charge, this one made to me several months ago."

He paused for a moment, his gaze seeking Fiona's; when they met, it was as if she were melting under the force of the love she saw there. Love for her so strong that the rest of the world around them seemed to fade, leaving only her and Braedan, enclosed in a sphere of warmth and light.

"You see those months ago, on one bitter, rain-soaked night," he continued, "I pushed my way into a shop in Hampshire and received a charge the likes of which I had never known before. It was a call to see things differently, to open my eyes to the beauty and truth that are oft hidden beneath other guises—to stop judging the world and those in it as simply dark or light. A very special woman offered me this challenge—"

Braedan stopped to hold out his hand to her, and she moved toward him, feeling as if she were floating, his handsome face wavering for the happy tears stinging her eyes. He helped her up on the table to stand beside him, taking both of her hands in his. His love for her was clear in his expression, so that even if he'd not spoken another word, she'd have known the feelings in his heart. But he did speak more, sending joy spilling through her and making her want to laugh and cry at the same time for the beauty of it.

"It was this woman who gave me that gift," he murmured, "a gift of herself, most precious and pure. And now that I have answered her charge, I wish to offer her one of my own, one that will allow us to throw aside the pretenses under which we have had to labor for so long."

Taking her hand and raising it to his lips, Braedan pressed a kiss there before saying in a husky voice that resounded through her soul, "I would consider myself the most fortunate of men if you would let me stay by your side, Fiona Byrne, to laugh with you, mourn with you, learn from you and cherish you for the rest of our lives together—no more the Crimson Lady, but instead the one, true lady of my heart. Ah, my love, will you do me the honor of becoming my wife?"

Fiona wasn't sure that she could speak at first, so full was she with love for this man. But she wanted the world to hear what she was feeling as well, and so, laying her palm gently against his cheek, she looked up into his eyes, smiling through the tears in her own as she whispered, "Aye, Braedan de Cantor. I do accept your charge. I will marry you and spend the rest of my days finding ways to make you see the truth—that you are as much a gift to me, and that I do not want to spend another moment without you."

The cheers rose up around them as, with a murmured, "God, I love you," he pulled her to him, their lips meeting in a kiss of passion and promise that washed away all the remaining hurts of the past. . . .

Cleansing them of all but the power of their love, as surely as if they stood together, embracing beneath the falling rain of a sweet summer shower.

Epilogue

Dandridge House
April 1293

Braedan crossed the grounds to the main keep of
his family home with long strides, hoping to find
Fiona inside; the first of the violets they'd taken from the
forest to plant in the old walled garden had come into
bloom at last, their purple blossoms unfurled atop delicate stems. Smiling, he imagined how she would look
when she saw how well they'd taken hold, clumped in
patches within the fragrant herb garden they'd wrested
from the barren bit of earth that they'd found when
they'd come there a year earlier.

The entire estate had fallen into disrepair in the nearly
two years that it had been empty before he'd regained it
with the pardon granted him at Chepston Hall, and he'd
felt discouraged at the extensive labor he knew it would

take to make it feel like a home again. But all through last autumn and winter they'd worked slowly at rebuilding the place, first with Richard, who'd lived with them before going off to squire for a year with Clinton Folville, then just he and Fiona, cleaning and repairing, bringing in new tenants to work the lands surrounding the estate, and filling the house with laughter and light.

It was coming to fruition, he thought, happiness swelling in him as he took the steps up to the main floor of the house three at a time. Dandridge had become a home again, thanks to Fiona and—

The sound of giggling burst through the open doors of the solar at the top of the staircase, and Braedan stopped just outside, wanting to catch a glimpse of what was happening inside before going in himself. He peered around the door, a flood of tenderness washing through him at the sight of Fiona, crouching on the floor, playing with Elizabeth's plump and rosy-cheeked son, who was now just more than a year old.

It had been an unexpected boon, finding the babe as they did nearly three months after their release from Chepston—the result of a persistent search, aided by some of the new information that had been uncovered during the sheriff's investigation into Draven's corruption. Now neither they nor Richard could imagine what life would be like without the happiness brought by this child, who already showed signs of his mother's gentle disposition and sunny smile.

Our lives are truly full of blessings, he thought, taking the last few steps into the room and going over to sit on the floor near Fiona and little Adam. She smiled up at him when he came in, and he told her about the violets; accepting with a kiss the tiny bunch he offered her, she promised to go and look with him as soon as Adam went down for his nap. Then she took the tiny wooden cart she'd been pushing with the child and sent it scooting a bit away so that he would crawl after it.

"Look at that," she said, smiling. "I don't think it will be too long before he'll be walking."

"Aye, he's growing bigger and stronger every day," Braedan murmured, sliding behind her on the floor, letting her lean back against him as he cupped his hands around the lush, curving fullness of her belly. "As is this little one," he added, another swell of fierce joy stabbing through him. Their child moved under his touch, the sweetness of that life yet another miracle that neither of them had expected after all of those years Fiona had believed herself barren.

A cozy fire crackled behind the grate, warming them as they watched Adam play, and Fiona sighed with contentment. "I love you, you know," she murmured, sliding her palms over his hands.

"And I you, Fiona—with my whole heart and soul," Braedan replied, after a moment moving to stroke his fingers up her back to her neck, kneading the tight area along her spine.

"You should rest more, love," he murmured, kissing a trail up the delectable skin behind her ear and eliciting a happy groan for his efforts. "You seem tired. Have you been doing too much again?"

"Perhaps just a little," she admitted, "although it is natural, I think, to feel tired this close to the babe's arrival." Closing her eyes, she nestled back into his embrace. "Sitting like this with you makes me feel much better, I confess."

He held her close, letting the sweet vanilla scent of her

that had so captivated him from the very beginning fill his senses; Adam chortled again, knocking the wooden cart toward them, and Braedan grinned and rolled it back, enjoying the boy's squeal of delight before looking down at Fiona to watch the light flicker over her beautiful features. After a moment she smiled, too, her mouth curving in that way that never failed to make him want to kiss the corners of it before plundering the sweetness of its depths. In a voice gone husky she said, "Now that I'm thinking of it, however, there is one other thing you could do that would make me feel even better than I do right now."

"What is that?"

"Tell me again how much you love me."

Smiling, Braedan shifted her in his arms so that he could kiss her, before brushing his palms over the swell of their child again. "More than the heavens could encompass and with everything that I am," he murmured, relishing the rightness of that feeling in his heart, as well as the sound of her soft, answering sigh. "And I'll tell you again and again, Fiona, as often as you like . . . because from now until forever, my darling, I love you."

Author's Note

Prostitution in the Middle Ages was a fact of life, legalized in many places, and accepted if not always condoned by the Church. According to the practical mentality of the time, male carnal urges could not be denied: Without release, it was believed that many unmarried men would resort to forcing themselves on the wives, sisters, and daughters of their communities. A different outlet needed to be found for them, hence the sanctioning of the *stewes*.

Most cities had their own ordinances and laws governing the practice of prostitution, and London was no exception. Whenever possible, I tried to remain true to what my research revealed about the *stewes* of Southwark, with the exception of the law forbidding common women from going about in public without striped hoods; that law did exist in certain of England's coastal cities, but not in London itself. The London street names

used are, however, authentic, as is the mention of the
Tabard Inn, which was an actual place in medieval
Southwark; some of you may recall that inn as the spot
from which the travelers set out in Chaucer's *Canterbury
Tales*.

In addition to using factual place names, I attempted
to replicate as closely as possible thirteenth-century atti-
tudes toward criminal activities and prostitution, incor-
porating details from actual court cases. For example,
the element concerning the outlaws' choice of either paying an exorbitant fine or signing themselves over to the
crown as mercenary warriors is based in truth; the granting of pardons in exchange for military service seems to
have been a fairly common practice throughout the
Middle Ages, with some career criminals committing
heinous acts and receiving full pardons for subsequent
service several times over.

In fact, the actual man upon whom I loosely based
several of my outlaw characters—one Eustace Folville—
was, with several of his brothers, the leader of a notorious and violent gang that committed many horrible
crimes, including kidnapping and murder. He received
death sentences and then was later pardoned based on
service to the crown some six different times over the
course of his life. The Coterels were also an actual outlaw gang from the Midlands, and reading about them
and the Folvilles served as part of the inspiration for the
imaginary bandits I created in my story.

For those interested in reading about the real outlaws,
as well as about the laws of the Middle Ages regarding
criminal activity and prostitution, I can recommend
three texts: *Common Women: Prostitution and Sexual-
ity in Medieval England,* by Ruth Mazo Karas, *The Me-*

dieval Underworld, by Andrew McCall, and *Pleasures & Pastimes in Medieval England* by Compton Reeves. All provided a good overview of their topics and were quite accessible in terms of style and format.

Finally, I'd like to offer a few words about the strange concoction of herbs that Fiona mentions in connection with the elaborate ruse Draven dreamed up for use by the Crimson Lady and her customers. That mixture, too, is based upon research indicating that in centuries past, certain combinations of ingredients were discovered and used by those dabbling in the black arts. It was applied topically as a paste or swallowed in a liquid, with hallucinations resulting soon after. It was in this way, apparently, that some of those accused of and tried for witchcraft confessed to flying over barns and visiting other members of their community in their bedchambers late at night: The drugs made them believe that that was exactly what had happened. At some point within the last couple of decades, a professor and his assistant at a university in Massachusetts apparently stumbled upon one of those old recipes; they were able to re-create the mixture and document its effects—results which support the hypothesis stated above.

However, while all of the research was admittedly fascinating, the writing of Fiona and Braedan's story engrossed me far more. If any two characters deserved a happy ending, they did, and I truly enjoyed every moment of time I spent as I followed them to that well-earned conclusion. I hope that you did too. As always, thanks for coming along on the journey.

—MRM

COMING IN JULY—
SUMMER'S HOTTEST HEROES!

STEALING THE BRIDE by Elizabeth Boyle
An Avon Romantic Treasure

The Marquis of Templeton has faced every sort of danger in his work for the King, but chasing after a wayward spinster who's run off with the wrong man hardly seems worthy of his considerable talents. But the tempestuous Lady Diana Fordham is about to turn Temple's life upside down . . .

WITH HER LAST BREATH by Cait London
An Avon Contemporary Romance

Nick Alessandro didn't think he would ever recover from a shattering tragedy, until he meets Maggie Chantel. But just when they are starting to find love together, someone waiting in the shadows is determined that Maggie love *no one* ever again. Now Nick has to find the killer—before the killer gets to Maggie.

SOARING EAGLE'S EMBRACE by Karen Kay
An Avon Romance

The Blackfeet brave trusts no white man—or woman—but the spirits have spoken, wedding him in a powerful night vision to a golden-red haired enchantress. Kali Wallace is spellbound by the proud warrior but will their fiery love be a dream come true . . . or doomed for heartbreak?

THE PRINCESS AND HER PIRATE
by Lois Greiman
An Avon Romance

Not since his adventurous days on the high seas has Cairn MacTavish, the Pirate Lord, felt the sort of excitement gorgeous hellion Megs inspires. Though she claims not to be the notorious thief, he knows she is hiding something—and each claim of innocence that comes from her lush, inviting lips only inflames his desires.

REL 0603

Have you ever dreamed of writing a romance?

*And have you ever wanted
to get a romance published?*

Perhaps you have always wondered how to
become an Avon romance writer?
We are now seeking the best and brightest undiscovered
voices. We invite you to send us your query letter to
avonromance@harpercollins.com

What do you need to do?

Please send no more than two pages telling us
about your book. We'd like to know its setting—is it
contemporary or historical—and a bit about the hero,
heroine, and what happens to them.

Then, if it is right for Avon we'll ask to see part of the
manuscript. Remember, it's important that you have
material to send, in case we want to see your story quickly.

Of course, there are no guarantees of publication,
but you never know unless you try!

*We know there is new talent just waiting
to be found! Don't hesitate . . . send us
your query letter today.*

*The Editors
Avon Romance*

MSR 0302